Praise for Jonathan Coe's

MIDDLE ENGLAND

"*Middle England* contains great charms." —John Williams,
The New York Times Book Review

"Brilliantly funny. . . . A compelling state-of-the-nation novel, full of
light and shade, which vividly charts modern Britain's tragicomic
slide." —*The Economist*

"[Coe's] affectionately witty attitude to our human foibles is always
uplifting." —*The Times* (London)

"Timely and timeless. . . . This plaintive clarion call is an acerbic,
keenly observed satire peppered with the penetrating wit for which
Coe is so justly admired." —*Booklist* (starred review)

"A sweeping and very funny state-of-the-nation novel. . . . Coe—a
writer of uncommon decency—reminds us that the way out of this
mess is through moderation, through compromise."
—*The Observer* (London)

"[A] witty and knowing satire." —*People*

"Brilliant. Read it too fast, finished it too soon." —Nigella Lawson

"Coe astutely blends political insight with assured storytelling."
—*Library Journal*

"Coe's writing is as smoothly accomplished as ever. His comic set
pieces—funerals, dinners, clown fights . . . are very funny."
—*The Guardian*

· JONATHAN COE

MIDDLE ENGLAND

Jonathan Coe's awards include the John Llewellyn Rhys Prize, the Prix Médicis Étranger, the Bollinger Everyman Wodehouse Prize, and, for *Middle England*, the Costa Novel Award and the Prix du Livre Européen. He lives in London.

www.jonathancoewriter.com

Also by Jonathan Coe

FICTION

The Broken Mirror
Number 11
Expo 58
The Terrible Privacy of Maxwell Sim
The Rain Before It Falls
The Closed Circle
The Rotters' Club
The House of Sleep
The Winshaw Legacy
The Dwarves of Death
A Touch of Love
The Accidental Woman

NONFICTION

Like a Fiery Elephant: The Story of B. S. Johnson
Jimmy Stewart: A Wonderful Life

MIDDLE ENGLAND

MIDDLE ENGLAND

JONATHAN COE

Vintage Contemporaries
Vintage Books
A Division of Penguin Random House LLC
New York

The Library of Congress has cataloged the Knopf edition as follows:
Names: Coe, Jonathan, author.
Title: Middle England / Jonathan Coe.
Description: First American edition. | New York : Alfred A. Knopf, 2019.
Identifiers: LCCN 2019010993 (print) | LCCN 2019012982 (ebook)
Subjects: LCSH: BISAC: FICTION / Satire. | FICTION / Literary. |
GSAFD: Political fiction. | Satire. | Black humor (Literature).
Classification: LCC PR6053.O26 (ebook) | LCC PR6053.O26 M56 2019 (print) |
DDC 823/.914—dc23
LC record available at https://lccn.loc.gov/2019010993

Vintage Contemporaries Trade Paperback ISBN: 978-0-525-56684-7
eBook ISBN: 978-0-525-65648-7

Book design by Maria Carella

www.vintagebooks.com

Printed in the United States of America
10 9 8 7 6 5 4 3 2 1

For Janine, Matilda and Madeline

MERRIE ENGLAND

1

DEEP ENGLAND

145

OLD ENGLAND

317

Author's Note

431

MERRIE ENGLAND

✦

In the century's last decades, "British" as a self-description
began to offer something else . . . It had room for newcomers
from abroad and for people like me who found its capacious-
ness and slackness attractive. Here was a civic nationalism
that meandered pleasantly like an old river, its dangerous force
spent far upstream.

Ian Jack, *Guardian*, 22 October 2016

1.

The funeral was over. The reception was starting to fizzle out. Benjamin decided it was time to go.

"Dad?" he said. "I think I'm going to make a move."

"Good," said Colin. "I'll come with you."

They headed for the door and managed to escape without saying any goodbyes. The village street was deserted, silent in the late sunshine.

"We shouldn't really just leave like this," said Benjamin, glancing back towards the pub doubtfully.

"Why not? I've spoken to everyone I want to. Come on, take me to the car."

Benjamin allowed his father to hold him by the arm in a faltering grip. He was steadier on his feet that way. With indescribable slowness, they began to shuffle along the street towards the pub car park.

"I don't want to go home," said Colin. "I can't face it, without her. Take me to your place."

"Sure," said Benjamin, even as his heart plummeted. The vision he had been promising himself—solitude, meditation, a cold glass of cider at the old wrought-iron table, the murmur of the river as it rippled by on its timeless course—disappeared, spiralled away into the afternoon sky. Never mind. His duty today was to his father. "Would you like to stay the night?"

"Yes, I would," said Colin, but he didn't say thank you. He rarely did, these days.

*

The traffic was heavy, and the drive to Benjamin's house took almost an hour and a half. They drove through the heart of Middle England, more or less following the course of the River Severn, through the towns of Bridgnorth, Alveley, Quatt, Much Wenlock and Cressage, a placid, unmemorable journey where the only punctuation marks were petrol stations, pubs and garden centres, while brown heritage signs dangled the more distant temptations of wildlife centres, National Trust houses and arboretums in front of the bored traveller. The entrance to each village was marked not only by the sign announcing its name, but by a flashing reminder of the speed at which Benjamin was driving, and a warning notice telling him to slow down.

"They're a nightmare, aren't they, these speed traps?" Colin said. "The buggers are out to get money from you every step of the way."

"Prevents accidents, I suppose," said Benjamin.

His father grunted sceptically.

Benjamin turned on the radio, tuned as usual to Radio Three. He was in luck: the slow movement of Fauré's Piano Trio. The melancholy, unassuming contours of the melody not only seemed a fitting accompaniment to the memories of his mother that were filling his mind today (and, presumably, Colin's), but also seemed to mirror, in sound, the gentle curves of the road, and even the muted greens of the landscape through which it carried them. The fact that the music was recognizably French made no difference: there was a commonality here, a shared spirit. Benjamin felt utterly at home in this music.

"Turn that racket off, can't you?" Colin said. "Can't we listen to the news?"

Benjamin let the last thirty or forty seconds of the movement play out, then switched to Radio Four. It was the *PM* programme and immediately they were plunged into a familiar world of gladiatorial combat between interviewer and politician. In one week's time there would be a general election. Colin would vote Conservative, as he had done in every British election since 1950, and Benjamin, as usual, was undecided, except in the sense that he had decided not to vote. Nothing they were likely to hear on the radio in the next seven days would make any difference. Today's big story seemed to be that the prime minister, Gordon Brown, fighting for re-election, had been caught on microphone describing a potential supporter as "a sort of bigoted woman," and the media were making the most of it.

"The prime minister has shown his true colours," a Conservative MP was saying, gleefully. "Anyone who expresses these legitimate concerns is simply a bigot, in his view. And that's why we can never have a serious debate about immigration in this country."

"But isn't it true that Mr. Cameron, your own leader, is every bit as reluctant—"

Benjamin turned the radio off without explanation. For a while they drove in silence.

"She couldn't stand politicians," Colin said, bringing some subterranean train of thought to the surface, and not needing to specify who he meant by "she." He spoke in a low voice, thick with regret and repressed emotion. "Thought they were all as bad as each other. All on the fiddle, every one of them. Fiddling their expenses, not declaring their interests, holding down half a dozen jobs on the side . . ."

Benjamin nodded, while remembering that in fact it was Colin himself, not his late wife, who was obsessed with the venality of politicians. It was one of the few subjects on which this habitually taciturn man could become talkative, and perhaps it would be better to let this happen now, to stop him from being distressed by more painful thoughts. But Benjamin rebelled against the idea. Today they had bid farewell to his mother, and he wasn't going to let the sanctity of that occasion be tarnished by one of his father's rants.

"What I always liked about Mum, though," he said, by way of diversion, "was that she never sounded bitter about stuff like that. You know, if she disapproved of something, it didn't make her angry, it just made her sort of . . . sad."

"Yes, she was a gentle soul," Colin agreed. "One of the best." He said no more than that, but after a few seconds took a grimy-looking handkerchief out of his trouser pocket and wiped both eyes with it, slowly and carefully.

"It's going to be weird for you," said Benjamin, "being by your-self. But I know you'll manage. I'm sure of it."

Colin stared into space. "Fifty-five years, we were together . . ."

"I know, Dad. It's going to be tough. But Lois will be close by, a lot of the time. And I'm not far away either. Not really."

They drove on.

*

Benjamin lived in a converted mill house on the banks of the River Severn, on the outskirts of a village just north-east of Shrews-bury. The house was approached down a single-track road, overhung with trees, its hedgerows densely overgrown on either side. He had moved to this absurdly remote and secluded spot at the beginning of the year, the sale of his two-bedroom flat in Belsize Park hav-ing funded the purchase, with enough capital left over to support his modest lifestyle for a few years to come. The house was far too big for a single man, but then he had not been single when he had bought it. There were four bedrooms, two sitting rooms, a dining room, a large open-plan kitchen complete with Aga and a study with generous leaded windows overlooking the river. So far Benjamin had been extremely happy there, dispelling his friends' and family's early suspicions that he had made a terrible mistake.

The house was full of treacherous corners and steep, nar-row flights of stairs. It was entirely unsuitable as a place to bring his eighty-two-year-old father. None the less, with some difficulty Benjamin managed to get him out of the car, up the stairs into the sitting room, up the next flight of stairs—shorter, but with a tricky right-angled turn—into the kitchen, through the back door, and then down the flight of metal steps on to the terrace. He found him a cushion, poured him a can of lager and was about to settle down with him for some stilted waterside conversation when he heard a car pull up outside the front door.

"Who the hell's that?"

Colin, who had not heard anything, merely looked at him in bewilderment.

Benjamin sprang up and hurried back into the sitting room. He opened the window and looked down at the forecourt to see Lois and her daughter Sophie standing at his front door, on the point of knocking.

"What are you doing here?" he asked.

"I've been trying to call you for an hour," said his sister. "What did you turn your bloody phone off for?"

"I turned it off because I didn't want it to start ringing in the middle of a funeral," said Benjamin.

"We were worried sick about you."

"You needn't have been. I'm fine."

"Why did you run off like that?"

"I wanted to get away."

"Where's Dad?"

"He's here with me."

"You could have told us."

"I didn't think."

"Didn't you say goodbye to anyone?"

"No."

"Not even Doug?"

"No."

"He'd come all the way from London."

"I'll send him a text."

Lois sighed. Her brother infuriated her sometimes.

"Well, are you going to let us in and give us a cup of tea at least?"

"OK."

He led them through the house, and they joined Colin on the terrace while Benjamin stayed in the kitchen to make a pot of tea and pour some white wine for Sophie. He carried the drinks out on a tray, taking the steps carefully, blinking as the evening sunlight hit him.

"It's lovely out here, Ben," Lois said.

"Must be great for your writing," said Sophie. "I could sit out here and listen to the river and work for hours."

"I've told you," said Benjamin, "you can come here any time you want. You'd get that thesis finished in no time."

Sophie smiled. "It's done. I finished it last week."

"Wow. Congratulations."

"She never understood what you saw in this place," said Colin. "Neither can I. Middle of nowhere."

Benjamin absorbed this comment and couldn't see that it merited a reply, even if he'd been able to think of one.

"Ah well," he said, and sat down, at last, with a weary little sigh of satisfaction. He was just about to take his first sip of tea when he heard another car pull up outside the front of the house.

"What the hell . . .?"

Once again from the sitting-room window he looked down on to the forecourt, and this time saw that the car belonged to Doug, who was bent over with his bottom sticking out of the door, retrieving a laptop case from the back seat. Then he straightened up and Benjamin found that from this angle he was allowed a view of something he'd never noticed before: Doug's bald patch. He was developing a pronounced bald patch. Briefly this gave Benjamin a twinge of mean, rivalrous satisfaction. Then Doug saw him and shouted:

"Why's your mobile turned off?"

Without answering, Benjamin came downstairs to open the front door.

"Hello," he said. "Lois and Sophie have just arrived."

"Why did you leave without saying goodbye?"

"It's like the beginning of *The Hobbit*. An unexpected party."

Doug pushed him gently to one side. "All right, Bilbo," he said. "Are you going to let me in?"

He ran up the stairs, leaving Benjamin standing in surprise, and headed straight for the kitchen. Doug had only been to the house once before but seemed to remember his way around. By the time Benjamin caught up with him, he had already taken his laptop out of its case, installed himself at the kitchen table and was tapping at the keyboard.

"What's your Wi-Fi password?" he asked.

"I don't know. I'll have to look at the router."

"Hurry up, then, will you?" As Benjamin disappeared into the sitting room on this errand, Doug called after him: "Nice speech today, by the way."

"Thank you."

"Well, not speech—eulogy—whatever you call it. Brought tears to a lot of people's eyes, that did."

"Well, I suppose that was the idea."

"Even Paul seemed moved by it."

In the act of scribbling down the password, Benjamin froze at the mention of his brother's name. After a moment he walked slowly back into the kitchen and placed the scrap of paper next to Doug's computer.

"He had some nerve, showing up today."

"His mother's funeral, Ben. He's got a right to turn up for that."

Benjamin said nothing, just picked up a dishcloth and began wiping some mugs.

"Did you speak to him?" Doug asked.

"I haven't spoken to him for six years. Why would I speak to him now?"

"He's gone now, anyway. Back to Tokyo. Flight was leaving Heathrow at—"

Benjamin wheeled around. His face had gone pink. "Doug, I don't give a shit. I don't want to hear about him, all right?"

"Fine. No problem." Doug resumed his tapping, chastened.

"Thanks for coming up today, by the way," Benjamin said, in an effort at conciliation. "I really appreciate it. Dad was very touched."

"You chose a lousy day for it," Doug grumbled, not looking up from the screen. "Four weeks I've been following Gordon around on the campaign trail. What's happened in that time? Fuck-all. Today all hell breaks loose and I'm not even there. Stuck in some crematorium in Redditch . . ." His fingers clacking away, he seemed oblivious to the brusqueness of these words. "Now I've got to give them a thousand words by seven o'clock and all I know is what I heard on the car radio."

Benjamin hovered at his shoulder ineffectually for a moment or two, then said: "Well, look, I'll leave you to it." There was no reply, so he drifted away, and was half out of the kitchen door on his way to the terrace when Doug said, without looking up: "All right if I stay the night?"

Taken aback by the question, Benjamin hesitated for a moment, then nodded.

"Sure."

*

None of the guests sitting out on the terrace that evening would ever know it, because he would never share the truth with any of them, but Benjamin had bought this house in order to fulfil a fantasy. Many years earlier, in the month of May, 1979—when Britain was on the brink, as it was now, of a momentous general election—he had sat in a pub called The Grapevine, in Birmingham's Paradise Place, and he had fantasized about the future. He had imagined that the girl he was in love with, Cicely Boyd, would still be his lover decades later, and once they were married, and approaching sixty, and their children had left home, they would be living together in a converted watermill in Shropshire, where Benjamin would write music and Cicely would write poetry and in the evening they would hold splendid dinner parties for all their friends. *We shall give the kind of dinners that people never forget*, he had told himself. *People will spend evenings at our house that will become treasured memories.* Of course, it had not happened quite that way. He had not seen Cicely for years after that day. But eventually they did find each other again, and they lived together in London for a few years which were . . . well, miserable, if truth were told, because Cicely had been so ill, and such a pain to live with, and then, in a last-ditch attempt to live out that fantasy, a perverse effort to recapture the past by realizing his past's vision of the future, Benjamin had suggested selling their flat, and using some of the money to buy this house, and using some of the rest of the money to send Cicely to Western Australia for six months, where a doctor was rumoured to have developed an expensive but miraculous cure for MS. And three months later, when the house was bought and he was starting to furnish and decorate it, Cicely had sent him an email from Australia with good news and bad news: the good news being that her condition had, indeed, improved almost beyond measure, and the bad news being that she had fallen in love with the doctor and wouldn't be coming back to England after all. And Benjamin, very much to his own surprise, had poured himself a large tumbler of whisky, drunk it, laughed like a suicidal lunatic for about twenty minutes and then carried on painting the dado rail, and he had not really thought about Cicely since. And that was how he now came to be living in an enormous converted watermill in Shropshire all by himself, at the age of fifty, and finding to his quiet amazement that he had never been happier.

He was glad that Lois and Sophie were there, that evening, even though his sister had come looking for him in anger. He knew that his father's petulance was simply a mask for the melancholia into which he would sink more and more deeply as the hours went by. He could rely on Lois and Sophie to strike the right balance, a balance between mourning Sheila's passing (only six weeks after a diagnosis of liver cancer) and trying to share more cheerful stories of family life: stories of rare but memorable dinner parties thrown on an audacious whim back in the 1970s, with food, drink and fashion that now beggared belief; ill-fated holidays in North Wales, the sound of sheep bleating mournfully in the fields and rain drumming without relief on the caravan roof; more adventurous holidays in the 1980s, a trip made by Colin and Sheila to Denmark to visit old friends, taking the infant Sophie with them this time, doting on their only grand-child. Sophie spoke of her grandmother's kindness, the way she had always remembered what your favourite meals were, always took an interest in you and remembered your friends' names and asked the right questions about them, she had been like that right up until the end, but then Colin was starting to look lost and miserable again so Benjamin clapped his hands and said, "Right, who's for a bit of pasta?," and went into the kitchen to boil up some *penne* (it had to be *penne* because his father couldn't cope with anything that needed to be wrapped around a fork) and heated up some of his home-made *arrabbiata* sauce (he had a lot of time to practise his cooking these days) and when he brought the food out on to the terrace, just as the evening was turning chilly and the sun was starting to set, he tried to persuade his father to have a decent amount, more than half a bowlful at least, and he took some of the pasta out of the bowl when

Colin said there was too much, and put some back in when it looked like there was too little, and then he said, "Is that the right amount now?," and tried to lighten the mood by adding. "Not a *penne* more, not a *penne* less," which he thought was a particularly appropriate joke, since Jeffrey Archer was one of his father's favourite authors, but Colin didn't seem to get it, and then Doug pointed out that the singular of *penne* was actually something else, wasn't it?, *penna* or something, and that kind of killed the moment, so they all ate their dinner in silence, listening to the river as it drifted by, and the whistle of the wind in the trees, and the slurping of Colin as he struggled with his pasta.

"I'll put him to bed," Lois whispered at about nine o'clock, after her father had had two whiskies and was starting to nod in his chair. It took her about half an hour, while Doug went back into the kitchen to check on the subs' changes to his article and Benjamin talked to Sophie about her thesis, which was on pictorial representations of nineteenth-century European writers of black ancestry, a subject on which he was not well informed. When Lois rejoined them, she looked grave.

"He's in a right old state," she said. "He's not going to be easy from now on."

"What did you expect him to be doing today?" said Benjamin. "Turning cartwheels?"

"I know. But they were together fifty-five years, Ben. He did nothing for himself in that time. He hasn't cooked himself a meal for half a century."

Benjamin knew what she was thinking. That, as a man, he was bound to find some way of ducking the task of caring for their father. "I'll come and see him," he insisted, "twice a week, maybe more. Cook for him. Take him out shopping."

"That's good to know. Thank you. And I'll do what I can too."

"So there you are. We'll manage somehow. Of course—" and in making the next observation, he was fully aware of treading on thin ice "—it would be easier if you spent a bit more time in Birmingham."

Lois said nothing.

"With your husband," he added, for clarity.

Lois took an irritable sip of cold coffee. "My job's in York, remember?"

"Sure. So you could come down every weekend. Instead of . . . what, every three or four?"

"Chris and I have been living like that for years, and it suits us very well. Doesn't it, Soph?"

Her daughter, rather than rallying to Lois's cause, said merely: "I think it's weird."

"Nice. Thank you. Not all couples like to live in each other's pockets. I haven't noticed you and your current boyfriend racing to move in with each other."

"That's because we split up."

"What? When?"

"Three days ago." Sophie rose to her feet. "Come on, Mum, it's time we drove back. I'd like to have a chat with Dad before bedtime, even if you wouldn't. I'll tell you all about it in the car."

Benjamin came out with them to the forecourt, kissed his sister and gave his niece a long hug.

"Great news about the thesis," he said. "Not so good about the boyfriend."

"I'll survive," said Sophie, with a wan smile.

"Give me the keys," said Lois. "You've had three glasses of wine."

"No, I haven't," said Sophie, handing them over all the same.

"You drive too fast anyway," said Lois. "I'm sure that was a speed camera flashing at us on the way over."

"I don't think so, Mum—it was just the sunlight on somebody's windscreen."

"Whatever." Lois turned to her brother. "I think we did her proud today. That was a beautiful speech. You've got a lovely way with words."

"I should have. I've written enough."

She kissed him again. "Well, I think you're the best unpublished writer in the country. No contest."

One more hug, and then they slammed their doors and Benjamin waved after their headlights as the car reversed cautiously down the driveway.

*

It was still warm enough, just about, to leave the sitting-room window open. Benjamin loved to do this, when the weather allowed it, to sit there alone, sometimes in the dark, listening to the sounds of the night, the call of a screech owl, the ululation of a predatory fox, and above all the murmur, ageless, immutable, of the River Severn (which was a new incomer to England at this point, having crossed the border with Wales only a few miles upstream). Tonight was different, though: he had Doug for company, even though neither of them saw any hurry to get into conversation. They had been friends for almost forty years, and there wasn't much they didn't know about each other. For Benjamin, at least, it was enough for them to sit there, on opposite sides of the fireplace, glasses of Laphroaig in hand, and let the emotions stirred up by the day gradually settle and subside into quietude.

Eventually, however, he was the one who broke the silence.

"Happy with your piece?" he asked.

Doug's response was unexpectedly dismissive.

"I suppose it'll do," he said. "I feel a bit of a fraud these days, to be honest." When Benjamin looked surprised, Doug sat upright and launched into an explanation. "I honestly think we're at a crossroads, you see. Labour's finished. I really think so. People are so angry right now, and nobody knows what to do about it. I've heard it on Gordon's campaign trail the last few days. People see these guys in the City who practically crashed the economy two years ago and never felt any consequences—none of them went to jail, and now they're taking their bonuses again while the rest of us are supposed to be tightening our belts. Wages are frozen. People have got no job security, no pension plans, they can't afford to take a family holiday or do repairs to the car. A few years ago they felt wealthy. Now they feel poor."

Doug was becoming animated. Benjamin knew how much he liked to talk like this, how even now, after twenty-five years as a journalist, nothing excited him as much as the cut-and-thrust of British politics. He didn't understand his friend's enthusiasm, but he knew how to play along with it.

"But I thought it was the Tories everyone hated," he said, dutifully, "because of the expenses scandal. Claiming for mortgages on their second home, and all that stuff . . ."

"People blame both parties for that. And that's the worst of it. Everyone's become so *cynical*. 'Oh, they're all as bad as each other . . .' That's why it was always going to be close—until today."

"You think it'll make that much difference? It was just a mistake. An unguarded moment."

"That's all it takes, these days. That's how volatile things have become."

"Then surely this is a good time for someone like you. Lots to write about."

"Yes, but I'm . . . out of touch with all that, you see? That resentment, that sense of hardship. I don't *feel* it. I'm just a spectator. I live in this bloody . . . cocoon. I live in a house in Chelsea worth millions. My wife's family own half of the Home Counties. I don't know what I'm talking about. And it shows up in my writing. Of course it does."

"How are things with you and Francesca, anyway?" said Benjamin, who used to envy Doug his rich and beautiful wife but no longer envied anybody anything.

"Pretty rubbish, as a matter of fact," said Doug, staring moodily into space. "We're in separate bedrooms these days. Good job we've got so many of them."

"What do the kids think about that? Have they said anything?"

"Hard to tell what Ranulph thinks. He's too busy obsessing over Minecraft ever to talk to his dad. As for Corrie . . ."

Benjamin had noticed, for some time, that Doug never referred to his daughter by her full name, Coriander. He hated the name (which had been his wife's choice) even more than its unfortunate twelve-year-old bearer did. And she herself never, ever answered to anything other than "Corrie." Use of her full name would usually be met with glassy-eyed silence, as if some invisible stranger were being addressed.

"Well," Doug continued, "there might be some hope there still. I've got a feeling she's starting to hate me and Fran and everything we stand for, which would be excellent. I do my best to encourage it." Helping himself to a refill of whisky, he added: "I took her to the old Longbridge factory a couple of weeks ago. Told her about her grandad and what he used to do there. Tried to explain what a shop steward was. Pretty tough, trying to get a private-school girl from Chelsea to understand 1970s union politics, I must say. And, Christ, there isn't much of the old place left."

"I know," said Benjamin. "Dad and I go and take a look occasionally."

The thought that, many years ago, their fathers used to be on opposite sides of Britain's great industrial divide made them both smile, and set off parallel trains of reminiscence which ended, in Doug's case, with the question: "What about you? You're looking well, I must say. Living inside a John Constable painting obviously suits you."

"Well, we'll see about that. It's early days yet."

"But the whole Cicely thing . . . you're really OK with that?"

"Of course I am. More than OK." He leaned forward. "Doug, for more than thirty years I've been stuck in a romantic obsession. And now it's gone. I'm free. Can you imagine how good that feels?"

"Sure, but what are you going to do with this freedom? You can't just sit here all day making pasta sauce and writing poems about cows."

"I don't know . . . Dad's going to need a lot of looking after. I suppose I'll be doing a fair bit of that."

"You'll soon get bored of that drive to Rednal and back."

"Well . . . maybe he could move in here."

"Would you really want that?" Doug asked, and when Benjamin didn't answer, and he noticed that his whisky glass was empty again, he rose effortfully to his feet and said: "I think I'm going to turn in. Early start tomorrow if I'm going to be back in London by nine."

"OK, Doug. You know your way, don't you? I think I'll stay here for a bit. Let it all . . . sink in, you know."

"I know. It's rough when one of your parents dies. Actually it doesn't get much rougher than that." He put a hand on Benjamin's shoulder and said, with feeling: "Goodnight, mate. You did well today."

"Thanks," said Benjamin. He clasped Doug's hand briefly, although he couldn't bring himself to add "mate." He never could.

Alone in the sitting room, he poured himself another drink and went to sit on the broad wooden sill that ran around the bay of the window. He opened the window a little further and let the cool air flow over him. The wheel of the mill had been out of use for many decades now and the river, undiverted, unharnessed, flowed past steadily, without agitation or fuss, in a perpetual rippling stream of good humour. The moon was up and Benjamin could see bats darting to and fro across the backdrop of the luminous grey sky. Suddenly a powerful sadness stole over him. The reflections he had been trying to ward off all day—on the reality of his mother's death, the agony of her last few weeks—could no longer be kept at bay.

A piece of music came back to him and he knew that he had to listen to it. A song. He crossed over to the shelf where his iPod rested in its speaker dock, took out the device and started to scroll through the list of artists. It seemed the last one he had been listening to was XTC. He scrolled back past Wilson Pickett, Vaughan Williams, Van der Graaf Generator, Stravinsky, Steve Swallow, Steely Dan, Stackridge and Soft Machine before reaching the name he was looking for: Shirley Collins, the Sussex folk singer whose records he had started collecting in the 1980s. He loved all of her music but there was one song in particular which, during the last few weeks, had come to take on a special significance. Benjamin selected the song, pressed Play, and just as he reached the bay window again to sit down and gaze out at the moonlit river, Collins's strong, austere, unaccompanied voice, heavy with reverb, streamed out of the speaker and filled the room with one of the most eerie and melancholy English folk tunes ever written.

Adieu to old England, adieu
And adieu to some hundreds of pounds
If the world had been ended when I had been young
My sorrows I'd never have known

Benjamin closed his eyes and took another sip from his glass. What a day it had been, for memories, for reunions, for difficult conversations. His ex-wife Emily had been at the funeral, with her two young children and her husband Andrew. From Japan there had been his brother Paul, with whom he was no longer on speaking terms: he couldn't even bring himself to make eye contact with him, either during his eulogy or at the reception afterwards. There had been uncles and aunts, forgotten friends and distant cousins. There had been Philip Chase, most loyal of his friends from King William's School, and there had been Doug's unexpected appearance, and there had even been an e-card from Cicely in Australia, which was much more than he'd been expecting, from her. And above all there had been Lois to stand beside him, Lois whose loyalty to her brother was absolute, whose eyes dimmed with sadness whenever she thought no one was watching her: Lois whose twenty-eight-year marriage remained a mystery to him and whose husband, who stayed dotingly close to her all day, was lucky to be rewarded with so much as the occasional glance in his direction . . .

Once I could drink of the best
The very best brandy and rum
Now I am glad of a cup of spring water
That flows from town to town

The melody carried Benjamin back, back to the last two weeks of his mother's life, when she had been unable to speak, when she had been sitting propped up in bed in the old bedroom, and he had sat in the room with her, for hours at a time, talking at first, trying to sustain a monologue, but finally realizing that the task was beyond him, and deciding instead to create a music playlist to fill the silence between them. So he made the playlist, and put it on shuffle, and for the rest of their time together—the rest of her life—Benjamin spoke to her only rarely, but sat on the edge of the bed and clasped her hand as they listened to Ravel and Vaughan Williams, Finzi and Bach, the most calming music he could think of, wanting things to end for her on a note of beauty, and there were more than five hundred songs on the playlist, and this one didn't come up for a long time, almost until the final day . . .

Once I could eat of good bread
Good bread that was made of good wheat
Now I am glad with a hard mouldy crust
And glad that I've got it to eat

. . . Lois and his father were in the house too, but they didn't have his staying power, they drifted in and out of the bedroom, they had to keep themselves busy downstairs, making tea, cooking lunch, but Benjamin had never had any problem with inactivity, it suited him fine just to sit there, it suited his mother as well, it suited both of them just to gaze out of the window at the sky, which that day, he remembered, had been the deepest, heaviest grey, a lowering sky, an oppressive sky, perhaps merely typical of that dreary April, or perhaps, it had occurred to him, something to do with the cloud of volcanic ash which had drifted across Europe from Iceland and was making newspaper headlines and wreaking havoc with airline schedules across the continent, and it was while he was contemplating this sky, its preternatural mid-morning darkness, that Shirley Collins's song had been plucked out at random by the iPod's algorithm and began to tell its mournful story of ancient misfortune . . .

Once I could lie on a good bed
A good bed that was made of soft down
Now I am glad of a clot of clean straw
To keep meself from the cold ground

Paying attention to the words now, Benjamin guessed that this was a song from the eighteenth or early nineteenth century, and gave voice to the misery of a prisoner awaiting transportation, but the associations that it set off in his mind, tonight, had nothing to do with crumbling cell walls or rat-infested mattresses: he thought, instead, of what Doug had told him about the anger he had encountered in the last few weeks on Gordon Brown's campaign trail, the sense of simmering injustice, the resentment towards a financial and political establishment which had ripped people off and got away with it, the quiet rage of a middle class which had grown used to comfort and prosperity and now saw those things slipping out of their reach: "A few years ago they felt wealthy. Now they feel poor . . ."

Once I could ride in me carriage
With servants to drive me along
Now I'm in prison, in prison so strong
Not knowing which way I can turn

. . . Yes, it was possible to extract this meaning from the words, to infer a story of loss, of loss of privilege, that resonated across the centuries, but in reality everything that was beautiful about the song, everything that reached inside Benjamin now and clawed at his heart, came from the melody, from this arrangement of notes which seemed so truthful and stately and somehow . . . *inevitable*, the kind of melody that, once you heard it, you felt as though you'd known all your life, and that must have been the reason, he supposed, that just as the song was coming to a close that morning, just as Shirley Collins was repeating the first verse in her richly accented, mysteriously English voice, a voice that cut through the words like a shaft of sunlight cutting through the waters of a wine-dark river, just as the first verse was being repeated, something bizarre happened: Benjamin's mother made a sound, the first sound she had made for days, everyone had been assuming that her vocal cords were useless now but no, she was trying to say something, at least that was what Benjamin imagined she was doing, for a moment or two, but then he realized, these were not words, this was not speech, the voice was too high, the pitch was too varied, even though it was hopelessly unmatched to the pitch on the recording, nevertheless his mother was *trying to sing*, something in the tune had touched upon a distant memory for her, it was coaxing out, or trying to coax out, some primal, instinctive response from the depths of her dying frame, and as the final verse came to an end, Benjamin's spine tingled at the sound of this other voice, this impossibly thin, impossibly weak voice which must have belonged to his mother (although he could not recall having heard her sing before, not once, in all the time they had spent together), but which seemed, at that moment, to be coming from some disembodied presence in the room, some angel or ghost which was foreshadowing the immaterial essence his mother was about to become . . .

> *Adieu to old England, adieu*
> *And adieu to some hundreds of pounds*
> *If the world had been ended when I had been young*
> *My sorrows I'd never have known*

*

The song was over. Quietness fell over the sitting room, and darkness hung over the river outside.

Benjamin wept, silently at first, then with short, heaving, convulsive sobs which shook his body, making his ribs ache and the little-used muscles in his fleshy stomach twitch in agonizing spasms.

When the fit was over, he continued to sit on the window seat, and tried to will himself to get ready for bed. Should he look in on his father? Surely the whisky and the emotional upheaval of the day would have sent him into a deep sleep. Yet Benjamin knew that his father slept poorly these days: that had been the case for months if not years, long before his wife's illness. He seemed to live in a perpetual state of low-level anger, which disturbed his nights as well as his days. What he had said to Benjamin about speed cameras today— "The buggers are out to get money from you every step of the way"— was typical. Colin could probably not have specified who "they" were, but he sensed their arrogant, manipulative presence, and resented it keenly. Just as Doug had told him, "People are getting angry, really angry," even if they could not have explained why, or with whom.

Reaching up to close the window at last, Benjamin took one final look at the river. Was he imagining it, or did it seem slightly higher than usual tonight, and slightly faster? When he had bought this house, many people had asked him whether he had considered the risk of flooding, and Benjamin had dismissed the matter loftily, but these questions had sown a seed of doubt. He liked to consider the river his friend: a good-natured companion whose behaviour he understood, and in whose company he felt at ease. Was he deluding himself? Supposing the river were to abandon its quiescent and reasonable habits: supposing it, too, were to become angry for no simple or predictable reason. What form might that anger take?

2.

Sophie had suffered a number of romantic disappointments over the years. Her first serious relationship, with Philip Chase's son Patrick, had not survived university. During her MA year at Bristol she had met Sohan, the man she considered her soulmate, a handsome English Literature student of Sri Lankan parentage. But he was gay. Then there had been Jason, who, like her, had been studying for a PhD at the Courtauld. But he had cheated on her with his supervisor, and his successor, Bernard, had been so immersed in his doctoral thesis on Sisley's notebooks that she had quietly terminated that relationship without his even noticing. So much for intellectual boyfriends, Sophie had now decided: if she was going to find someone else (and there was no particular hurry) she would try casting her net beyond the world of academia.

In the meantime, a stroke of good fortune had come her way: at the end of the summer term, a colleague from Birmingham University had emailed, inviting her to apply for a two-year teaching fellowship there. She applied; she got it; and in August 2010 she packed up her room in Muswell Hill and drove herself and her possessions up the M40, back to the city where she had been born. And having no better alternative, for the time being, she moved in with her father.

Christopher Potter was living, at this time, on a leafy street in Hall Green, a street that branched diagonally off from the Stratford Road but seemed far removed from its constant processions of north- and southbound traffic. It was a semi-detached house and he was supposed to be sharing it with his wife, but in effect he lived alone.

For many years the family home had been in York, where Lois was a librarian at the university, and Christopher practised as a personal injury lawyer. In the spring of 2008, with their only daughter then living in London, and with the health of Christopher's mother and both of Lois's parents in decline, he had suggested they moved back to Birmingham. Lois had agreed—gratefully, it seemed. Christopher had sought, and obtained, a transfer to his firm's Midlands office. They had sold their house and bought this new one. And then, at the last minute, Lois had made an amazing announcement: she did not want to leave her job, she was not convinced that her parents needed her to be close by, and she could not bear the idea of returning to the city where, more than thirty years earlier, her life had been derailed by a personal tragedy that still haunted her. She was going to stay in York, and from now on they would just have to see each other at weekends.

Christopher had accepted this with as good grace as he could muster, on the basis (never made explicit) that it was only a temporary state of affairs. But he wasn't happy, he did not like living alone, and he was delighted when Sophie told him about her new job, and asked if she could move in for a while.

Sophie herself found it strange and unsettling to be back home with her father. She was twenty-seven and it was no part of her life plan that she should still be living with one of her parents. She had quickly grown to like the overcrowded, improvised, somewhat self-satisfied cosmopolitanism of London, and wasn't yet convinced that she could find its equivalent in Birmingham. Christopher was affable and easy to talk to, but the atmosphere in the house was oppressively quiet. She quickly started to welcome any opportunity to get away, even it was just for a day or two; and if a trip down to London was involved, she would be doubly grateful.

On Thursday 21 October, then, she left the university campus promptly at 3 p.m. She was in good spirits: her seminar on the Russian romantics had been a success. She was already popular with her students. As usual, she had driven on to campus. Her grandfather Colin, his eyesight now being too weak for driving, had recently made her a gift of his ailing Toyota Yaris. (The days when he bought British out of patriotic duty were long gone.) She was booked on a late-afternoon train to London and, in order to save money, was using the slower, cheaper route that went through the Chilterns and ended up at Marylebone station. First of all, she had to drive to Solihull station and park the car. She had envisaged a quiet and leisurely progress along the arterial roads, taking pleasure in driving through a city which—unlike the capital—was as easy to navigate by private as by public transport. But she had not allowed for some heavy traffic, and after half an hour or so began to worry that she would miss her train. As she drove up Streetsbrook Road she put her foot down hard on the accelerator and the car reached thirty-seven miles per hour. It was a thirty-mile limit, and a speed camera flashed as she drove by.

*

Leaving the train at Marylebone, she found that she had time to walk to her rendezvous with Sohan. She cut across the Marylebone Road into Gloucester Place and then wandered through the half-empty back streets, with their tall, creamy Georgian houses, until she reached Marylebone High Street. Here it was livelier and she had to shuffle and swerve through the crowds of early-evening pedestrians. Listening to the different languages on the street, she was reminded of a time a few years earlier when Benjamin, too, was still living in London. Colin and Sheila had come down to see him and she had gone for dinner with her uncle and grandparents to an Italian place in Piccadilly. "I don't think I heard a word of English spoken on the way here," Colin had said, and she had realized that the thing he was complaining about was the very thing she most liked about this city. Tonight she had already overheard French, Italian, German, Polish, Urdu, Bengali and a few others she couldn't identify. It didn't bother her that she didn't understand half of what people were saying; the Babel of voices added to the sense of benign confusion she loved so much: it was all of a piece with the general noise of the city, the kaleidoscope of colour from traffic lights, headlights, brakelights, streetlamps and shop windows; the awareness that millions of separate, unknowable lives were temporarily intersecting as people crisscrossed through the streets. She savoured these reflections even as she quickened her pace, glancing at the time on her phone screen and worrying that she was going to be a few minutes late reaching the university building.

Sohan was already waiting for her at a table in the Robson Fisher bar, a dimly lit enclave frequented mainly by postgrads and teaching staff. In front of him were two glasses of Prosecco. He pushed one towards Sophie.

"Goodness," he said. "You're looking pale and sickly. Must be that terrible Northern climate."

"Birmingham is not the North," she said, kissing him on the cheek.

"Drink up, anyway," he said. "How long since you've had one of those?"

Sophie took a long sip. "We can get it where I live, you know. It arrived in about . . . 2006, I think. Are the celebrities here yet?"

"I don't know. If they are, they'll be in the Green Room."

"Shouldn't you join them?"

"In a while. There's no hurry."

Sohan had invited Sophie along—for moral support, as much as anything else—to watch him chair a public discussion between two eminent novelists, one English, the other French. The Englishman, Lionel Hampshire, was famous after a fashion—at least in literary circles. Twenty years earlier he had published the novel which had won the Booker Prize and made his reputation: *The Twilight of Otters*, a slender volume made up partly of memoir, partly of fiction, which had somehow caught the spirit of its time. If nothing he had written since then had measured up to its success (his latest, a bizarre excursion into feminist sci-fi called *Fallopia*, had just received a panning in the literary press), he did not seem unduly concerned: the prestige surrounding that early prizewinner had been enough to keep a lucrative career afloat ever since, and he still carried himself with the air of one whose laurels provided a solid resting place.

The French writer, on the other hand—Philippe Aldebert by name—was an unknown quantity.

"Who is he?" Sophie asked.

"Oh, don't worry, I've been reading up," said Sohan. "Big star over there, apparently. Prix Goncourt, Prix Femina. He's written twelve novels but only a couple of them are published here—you know what the Brits are like: they don't appreciate Johnny Foreigner coming over to the land of Dickens and Shakespeare and telling them how it should be done."

"Are you nervous about chairing?" Sophie asked.

The event had been organized jointly by the French and English departments. Sohan was now one of the youngest members of the latter, still a mere lecturer, but the fact that he already wrote for the *New Statesman* and the *TLS* made him the natural choice for an occasion like this, which was intended for the general public as well as for the staff and students.

"A little," he admitted, and held up his glass. "This is my third."

"I don't really understand your title," Sophie said, looking at the flier which was lying between them on the table. It announced that the theme under discussion tonight was to be "Fictionalizing Life; Living in Fiction". "What does it mean?"

"How should I know? You've got two writers here who have nothing in common except their colossal opinion of themselves. I had to call it *something*. They both write fiction. They both write about 'life'—or their version of it, anyway. I don't really see how I can go wrong with a title like that."

"I suppose not . . ."

"Well, look, it will all be over by nine, so I've booked a table for nine thirty. Just the two of us."

"Aren't you expected to go to dinner with everybody else?"

"I'll make some excuse. It's you I want to see. It's been ages. And you're looking so pale!"

*

The lecture theatre was almost full: there must have been an audience of almost two hundred. A few students seemed to have come along, but most of the patient, anticipatory faces Sophie saw around her seemed to belong to people in their fifties or over. From her position in one of the top rows, she found herself looking out towards the stage across a sea of white hair and bald patches.

Ranged on the stage were four speakers: Sohan, the two distinguished novelists and a lecturer from the French department, who was there to translate M. Aldebert's answers into English for the audience, and to whisper a French translation of Sohan's questions into his ear. The chair and the translator looked anxious: the two writers beamed at the audience expectantly. After some interminable opening remarks from the vice-chancellor, battle commenced.

Whether it was the disjointedness imposed by the translator's presence, or Sohan's obvious nervous tension, the discussion didn't get off to a smooth start. The questions posed to each writer were long and rambling, while the answers came in the form of speeches rather than the intimate and free-flowing conversation Sohan had been hoping for. After about fifteen minutes, during the latest monologue from Lionel Hampshire, which found him making confident generalizations about the difference between French and British attitudes towards literature, Sohan could be seen to retreat behind his page of notes, which he seemed to be scanning frantically. A few seconds later Sophie felt her phone vibrate and realized that he was in fact sending her a text message.

Help I've already run out of questions what next?

She glanced to the left and right of her, but neither of the people in the adjacent seats seemed to have noticed who the message had come from, or even that it had come at all. After thinking for a moment, she wrote back:

Ask PA if he agrees that the French take books more seriously.

Sohan's reply—a thumbs-up emoji—came very quickly, and a few seconds later, after Lionel Hampshire's latest address finally slowed to a halt, he could be heard saying to M. Aldebert:

"I wonder how you would respond to that? Is that just another typical British stereotype about the French—that we think you're more respectful towards writers than we are?"

After a translation of the question had been whispered into his ear, M. Aldebert paused, pursed his lips and seemed to cogitate deeply. "*Les stéréotypes peuvent nous apprendre beaucoup de choses,*" he answered at last.

"Stereotypes can be very meaningful," the translator translated.

"*Qu'est-ce qu'un stéréotype, après tout, si ce n'est une remarque profonde dont la vérité essentielle s'est émoussée à force de répétition ?*"

"What is a stereotype, after all, except a profound observation whose essential truth has been dulled by repetition?"

"*Si les Français vénèrent la littérature davantage que les Britanniques, c'est peut-être seulement le reflet de leur snobisme viscéral qui place l'art élitiste au-dessus de formes plus populaires.*"

"If the French revere literature more than the British do, perhaps this is merely a reflection of their essential snobbery, which prioritizes elitist art over forms which are more popular."

"*Les Français sont des gens intolérants, toujours prêts à critiquer les autres. Contrairement aux Britanniques, me semble-t-il.*"

"The French are an intolerant, judgemental people. Not like the British, I think."

"What makes you say that?" Sohan asked.

"*Qu'est-ce qui vous fait dire ça?*" whispered the translator.

"*Eh bien, observons le monde politique. Chez nous, le Front National est soutenu par environ 25 pour cent des Français.*"

"Well, let's look at the political world. Our National Front commands the support of about twenty-five per cent of the French people."

"*En France, quand on regarde les Britanniques, on est frappé de constater que contrairement à d'autres pays européens, vous êtes épargnés par ce phénomène, le phénomène du parti populaire d'extrême droite.*"

"In France, we look at the British and we are impressed that, unlike most other European countries, you don't have this phenomenon—a popular party of the far right."

"*Vous avez le UKIP, bien sûr, mais d'après ce que je comprends, c'est un parti qui cible un seul problème et qui n'est pas pris au sérieux en tant que force politique.*"

"You have UKIP, of course, but my understanding is that they are a single-issue party, who are not taken seriously as a political force."

Sohan waited for him to elaborate further, and when he didn't, turned to Lionel Hampshire and asked him rather desperately:

"Would you care to comment on that?"

"Well," said the eminent novelist, "as a rule I'm wary of these broad generalizations about national character. But I think Philippe has probably put his finger on something here. I'm not an uncritically patriotic person. Far from it. But there is something in the English character that I admire, and Philippe is right about it—I mean our love of moderation. Our *immoderate* love of moderation, if you like." (This choice phrase plopped into the reverent silence of the room and set off a ripple of laughter.) "We're a pragmatic nation, politically. Extremes of left and right don't appeal to us. And we're also essentially tolerant. That's why the multicultural experiment in Britain has by and large been successful, with one or two minor blips. I wouldn't presume to compare us to the French, in this regard, of course, but certainly, speaking personally, these are the things I most admire about the British: our moderation, and our tolerance."

"What a load of self-satisfied bullshit," said Sohan. But, regrettably, he did not say it on stage.

*

"Do you think so?" Sophie asked.

They were sitting in the Gilbert Scott restaurant at St. Pancras station, conducting a post-mortem on the event. It was an expensive choice of restaurant, but they had decided that, since their meetings were going to be so few and far between from now on, each one should be treated as a special occasion. Sophie had ordered a green pea risotto, while Sohan was experimenting with prawn and rabbit pie, which turned out to be delicious.

"These people don't know what they're talking about," he continued. "This so-called 'tolerance' . . . Every day you come face to face with people who are not tolerant at all, whether it's someone serving you in a shop, or just someone you pass in the street. They may not say anything aggressive but you can see it in their eyes and their whole way of behaving towards you. And they *want* to say something. Oh yes, they want to use one of those forbidden words on you, or just tell you to fuck off back to your own country—wherever they think that is—but they know they can't. They know it's not allowed. So as well as hating you, they also hate *them*—whoever they are—these faceless people who are sitting in judgement over them somewhere, legislating on what they can and can't say out loud."

Sophie didn't know what to say. She had never heard Sohan speak so candidly or bitterly on this subject before.

"In Birmingham," she faltered, "people seem to get on . . . I don't know, there are a lot of people from different cultures, and . . ."

"You would see it that way," Sohan said, simply. But he had been looking forward to this dinner, and wanted to keep the mood light, so he switched topic by picking up his iPhone, finding an image on Facebook and thrusting it towards her. "By the way—what do you think?"

Sophie found herself looking at the face of a waxy young man as he gazed stonily at the camera from behind his untidy desk.

"Who is it?"

"One of my postgrad students."

"What about him?"

"He's single." Sophie stared back at him, stupefied. "Well, you're looking for someone, aren't you?"

"Not really," she said. "Anyway, give me a break. He looks like an anorexic Harry Potter."

"Charming," said Sohan, and summoned up a different picture from Google Images. "OK, what about him?"

Sophie took the phone again and squinted at the middle-aged, disappointed face on display.

"Who's this?"

"One of my colleagues."

She looked closer. "Getting on a bit, isn't he?"

"I don't know how old he is. I know he's been writing the same thesis for nineteen years and hasn't finished it yet."

Sophie looked closer still. "Is that dandruff?"

"Probably just dust on the screen. Come on, I shared an office with this guy last year. He's fine. Yes, there were a few . . . personal hygiene issues, but—"

Sophie passed the phone back. "Thanks, but no thanks. No more academics. I'm through with pebble glasses and stoop shoulders. My next boyfriend's going to be a *hunk*."

Sohan gave an incredulous laugh. "A hunk?"

"Tall, dark and handsome. With a proper job."

"Where are you going to find one of those, up there?"

"'Up there'?" repeated Sophie, her eyes dancing with amusement. "It is up, isn't it?"

"Everything's 'up', to you. Everything north of Clapham."

"So my view of the world is London-centric. I can't help it. I was born here, this is my city and it's the only place I'll ever live. Bristol was a passing aberration."

"Come and visit me in Birmingham. It'll open your eyes."

"All right, I will. But tell me what the men are like."

"They're the same as anywhere else, of course."

"Really? I thought men from the Midlands were shorter."

"Shorter? What gave you that idea?"

"I thought that was why Tolkien invented hobbits." When Sophie broke out into affectionate but mocking laughter, he dug himself deeper into the hole. "No, seriously—don't most people these days think *Lord of the Rings* is really about Birmingham?"

"There's a connection, obviously. There's a museum now, at the place which is meant to have inspired him, just down the road from where I live."

"Arsehole Mill," said Sohan, deadpan.

"Sarehole," Sophie corrected. "Look, come and see for yourself. It's a lovely city, really."

"Of course it is. A land of boundless romantic and sexual opportunity. Next time you come down here, I'll be taking you *both* out to dinner. You and your hobbit boyfriend."

With which words, he poured them both a final glass of wine, and they drank a toast: to Middle Earth, and Middle England.

3.

When Doug received an email from the Downing Street press office announcing a raft of new appointments, he did some googling. The name of the new coalition government's deputy assistant director of communications had caught his eye: Nigel Ives. There had been a boy called Ives at school. Timothy Ives. And while it wasn't such an unusual surname, it had set off a distant memory. Benjamin had once told him that in a moment of weakness, some years earlier, he had accepted Timothy Ives's friend request on Facebook, and had discovered, among other things, that he had a son . . . Wasn't the name Nigel? That, too, could be a coincidence. But in any case, Doug emailed Nigel, and Nigel emailed back, and when they met for an off-the-record chat at the café next to Temple tube station, the first thing Nigel said to him was:

"I think you were at school with my father."

"Timothy? At King William's in Birmingham, back in the seventies?"

"That's right. He was terrified of you."

"Really?" said Doug.

"But he also worshipped you."

"Really?" said Doug.

"He was convinced you despised him."

"Really?" said Doug, remembering that this was definitely true. Timothy Ives had been a short, runtish boy, and the older boys in the school—especially Harding—had been ruthless in exploiting him, constantly requiring him to run errands and do favours. "How is he, anyway? What's he up to?"

"He's become rather a successful proctologist."

"You don't say."

"I'm sure you don't suffer from haemorrhoids, Douglas, but if you did, my father could ease your pain."

"I shall certainly bear that in mind."

"But I dare say you didn't come here to talk about your piles."

"I don't have piles, and I wasn't talking about them."

"Quite."

"No, I came here because I wanted to raise the possibility that you and I might begin a . . . warm and mutually beneficial relationship. If the Tories and the Lib Dems can form a coalition and find ways to work together, then . . . who knows? Maybe so can we."

"Indeed. You're talking about the spirit of the age, Douglas. A complete break with the old two-party system. No more petty antagonism. Just common ground and cooperation. It's a *very* exciting time to be entering politics."

Doug looked at Nigel and wondered how old he might be. Straight out of university, by the looks of it. His cheeks were pale, rosy and looked like they never needed to be shaved. His dark suit and tie were smart but characterless, like his side-parted hair. His expression was bland, his tone of voice permanently enthusiastic but otherwise inscrutable. He could only be in his early twenties.

"But how are things really shaping up at Number Ten?" Doug asked. "You've got two very different parties, here, with very different agendas. It can't last for long, can it?"

Nigel smiled. "Dave and Nick and the team respect you as a commentator, Douglas, but we know it's your job to look for trouble. You're not going to find it here. Dave and Nick have their differences, of course. But at the end of the day they're just two regular guys who want to get on with the job."

"Regular guys?"

"Exactly."

"Regular guys who just happened to go to unbelievably expensive private schools before shimmying up the political greasy pole."

"*Exactly.* You see how much they have in common? Wasn't it

brilliant, watching them that first day together in the Rose Garden? Larking about for the cameras, having a laugh . . ."

"So there's no ideological divide?"

Nigel frowned for a moment. "Well, Dave went to Eton, and Nick went to Westminster. That's a pretty big difference, I can see that." He soon brightened, however. "But honestly, Douglas—or can I call you Doug, now?"

"Sure, why not?"

"Honestly, Doug, you should hear the bantz between them at the cabinet table."

"Hear the what, sorry?"

"The banter. Bantz."

"Banter?"

"The jokes, the laughs, the mickey-taking. Believe me, I've heard a lot of this kind of stuff, especially at uni, and we're talking top banter here."

"Let me get this straight—you're referring to . . . cabinet discussions?"

"Absolutely."

"So a few days ago there were thousands of young people out on the streets of London, protesting about huge rises in tuition fees, which Nick Clegg promised not to support and is now supporting, and in the meantime the new chancellor is announcing massive cuts to public spending, and you tell me that basically this is all being driven by . . . banter?"

Nigel hesitated. He seemed nervous about how his next remark would be received. "Doug, don't take this the wrong way, but I think this is a generational thing. We're talking about a generational divide. You and your friends and my dad were brought up in a certain way. You're used to an antagonistic form of party politics. But Britain's moved on. The old system's broken now. May 6th showed us that. On May 6th Britain was asked to choose a new direction and the people spoke with a loud, unanimous, decisive voice and what they said could hardly have been clearer. They said, 'We don't know.'" He smiled pleasantly in response to Doug's bewildered silence. "'We don't know,'" he repeated, shrugging and spreading his hands. "Two years ago the world experienced a terrible financial crisis and nobody knows how to deal with it. Nobody knows the way forward. I call it radical indecision—the new spirit of our times. And Nick and Dave embody it perfectly."

In a mechanical response, Doug nodded his agreement, but deep down he couldn't tell whether Nigel was joking or not. It was to become an increasingly familiar feeling over the next few years.

4.

DECEMBER 2010

The letter from West Mercia police dropped on to Sophie's mat one late-October morning. Cameras had caught her vehicle on Streetsbrook Road, doing thirty-seven miles per hour in a thirty-mile limit. She was offered a choice between putting three points on her licence or paying £100 to attend a Speed Awareness Course. Naturally, she chose the latter.

Her appointment was for two o'clock in a faceless office block on Colmore Row, early in December. She arrived and was shown to a reception area on the ninth floor, equipped with two machines selling fizzy drinks and chocolate bars, and two dozen chairs arranged against the walls in a square. Most of these chairs were occupied when she entered the room. There were men and women of all ages, and all skin colours. A few wry, muttered, half-humorous conversations were taking place. The atmosphere in the room reminded her of school: boys and girls who had been caught out in minor misdemeanours and were now waiting outside the headmaster's study to receive their punishment. Sophie chose not to sit down, but wandered over to one of the grime-covered windows and looked out over the city, the shopping malls and high-rises, the old rows of terraced houses in the distance and, further still, the concrete tangle of Spaghetti Junction, all looking grey and blurry in the weak afternoon light.

"Right, everybody," said a young, energetic male voice, behind her. "Could you all follow me, please, and we'll take our seats and get started."

Sophie had not seen who the speaker was. She followed the

shuffling line of people into the next room, which was set up like a classroom, with bench seating, desks and a screen at the front for PowerPoint presentations. The overhead strip lighting was fierce and joyless. At the front of the class a tall, well-built man was standing with his back to them, arranging some papers on a table. Then he turned round.

"Good afternoon, everyone," he said. "My name is Ian and I'm going to be your facilitator for this afternoon's session. And this is my colleague Naheed."

The door at the back had opened and a very striking woman— almost as tall as Ian, probably only in her thirties but with frizzy, shoulder-length hair already streaked with grey—advanced up the aisle between the two rows of desks. She leaned back very slightly as she walked, carrying herself with confidence, smiling hellos to the people sitting on either side of her. The smiles were challenging and combative. Sophie liked the look of her at once, and thought that it must take balls for a woman like that to stand up in a room full mostly of men, mostly of white men, and take them to task for their driving errors.

Neither of these instructors, in fact, fitted her expectations at all. Ian, far from being the elderly, finger-wagging pedagogue she had rather unkindly been picturing in her mind, seemed to be in his mid- to late-thirties, with the build of a rugby player, a welcoming, open face with a fine bone structure and distractingly long eyelashes. This feature, in particular, drew most of her attention while he was making his preliminary remarks, although she managed to focus again when he started asking everyone in the room to describe their speeding offences, and to say something in their own defence if they could. He listened to each answer with perfect gravity and attentiveness; whereas with Naheed, the smile never quite left her lips, and the amused glint never quite left her eyes.

The answers themselves were interesting. As Sophie listened to the speakers, so different in age, class, gender and ethnicity, all with such different stories to tell, she realized that they were in fact united by one common factor: a profound and abiding sense of injustice. Whether they had been exceeding the speed limit in order to keep an urgent appointment, or (in one case) to take a sick relative to hospital, or (in another) because they'd bought a Chinese takeaway and wanted to get home before it went cold, or perhaps had simply arrived at their own, personal judgement that the speed limit was unreasonable and they were going to ignore it, they all burned with a righteous sense of indignation, a feeling that they had been singled out, picked on, by malign, unseen forces: forces drunk on their own power, and determined to bolster that power by making life difficult for ordinary citizens who had been caught doing nothing worse than pursuing the blameless objects of their daily lives. The whole room was heavy with this feeling. It smelled of victimhood.

Sophie was determined to have no part of it. As chance would have it, she was the last person to be asked to give an account of herself, and she decided she was going to buck that trend, come what may.

A few seconds later Ian was turning his attention to her, and Naheed too, from the front of the room, was asking her, with those mischievous, questioning eyes, to share her story with the instructors and with her fellow miscreants.

"Well, there's not much to tell," she said. "I was driving in a thirty-mile-an-hour limit. According to the letter I got, I was doing thirty-seven miles an hour. So that's that."

"So why were you speeding, do you think?" Ian asked. "Any particular reason?"

Sophie hesitated for a short moment. It would be so easy to trot out the obvious explanation: she had thought she might miss her train. How boring was that? She was not prepared to play the innocent. And besides, she had decided that she wanted to make an impression on Ian, somehow.

"I suppose Huxley expressed it better than anyone," she said, taking the plunge.

Ian was puzzled. "Who?"

"Aldous Huxley," Sophie explained. "The novelist and philosopher. He wrote *Brave New World*."

He still gave no indication of recognizing the name. "OK. And what did he have to say?"

"He said that the nearest thing we have to a new drug is the drug of speed. 'Speed, it seems to me, provides the one genuinely modern pleasure.'"

Naheed and Ian, who until now had given the impression of having heard pretty much everything during their time teaching these courses, exchanged a brief glance. Implicit in the glance was a question about which of them was going to deal with this unexpected contribution. Sophie was impressed by the quickness of understanding between them, the wordless ease with which an agreement was reached.

Ian approached her, and sat on the edge of her desk.

"So, speed for you is like a drug, yeah?" he said, smiling.

She nodded, and smiled back. They both seemed to know perfectly well that she wasn't being serious.

"And you were doing thirty-seven miles an hour?"

She nodded again. His smile was very disarming.

"Well, you weren't exactly mainlining heroin, were you? That would be doing . . . about eighty, I'd say."

Sophie remained silent, while continuing to hold his gaze.

"Or snorting crack cocaine. What would that be—sixty miles an hour, fifty?" When she still didn't answer, he went on: "Whereas, thirty-seven in a thirty limit? In drug-taking terms, that's a bit like . . . oh, I don't know, putting two teaspoons of coffee in your cup instead of one."

There was a chorus of chuckles from around the room.

"I think the point my colleague is trying to make," said Naheed, "is that it's a nice quote, but perhaps you were just trying to impress us. More likely that you were in a bit of a hurry to catch your train, or something like that."

Sophie was still enjoying the last few moments of amused, appraising eye contact with Ian, and only really caught the end of this comment. She did notice, however, that there was a quiet authority in Naheed's voice as she said it, as there was in everything that she said throughout the session. Her knowledge and experience commanded respect, even though the resentment felt by some of the men at being lectured on this subject by a woman—by an Asian woman—was palpable. Sitting next to Sophie was a ruddy-faced, middle-aged man in a business suit with tousled white hair and a permanent air of barely suppressed contempt. His name was Derek, he had been clocked doing fifty-three miles an hour in a forty limit because "I know that bit of road like the back of my hand," and the hostility he felt towards Naheed already seemed to extend to Sophie as well, after she had rebuffed some of his early, heavy-handed attempts at conspiratorial humour.

Halfway through the afternoon the class broke for refreshments— Ian and Naheed did not join them, but withdrew to some private space of their own—after which they were divided into two groups in order to watch videos illustrating a number of different driving scenarios and the dangers inherent in them. Sophie and Derek were in the same group, with Naheed as their leader.

"Now, take a good look at this stretch of suburban street," she said, freeze-framing the screen and emphasizing details with her pointer. "Look at the signage, look at the possible obstructions and hazards. Tell me what the speed limit is, and tell me what speed you would consider it safe to drive at in these circumstances."

After some discussion Sophie's group correctly identified the speed limit as thirty miles an hour (although many of them guessed wildly, and wrongly), but when she went on to suggest that it would be prudent to drive at twenty on this occasion, Derek was adamant that thirty miles an hour was perfectly appropriate.

"No, I don't think so," Naheed answered. "Your friend is right, in this case."

"That's your opinion," said Derek.

"Yes, it is, and everybody is entitled to their opinion, which is not the same as saying that everybody's opinion is as valuable as everybody else's. What did you say you did for a living, sir?"

"I'm a retail manager. Sports equipment, mainly."

"Good. Then, when it comes to sports equipment, your opinion is more valuable than mine. But perhaps, when it comes to road safety—"

"I've been driving for forty years," he interrupted. "And I've never had an accident. Why should I take lessons from someone like you?"

There was a beat, a flicker, while Naheed registered the impact of those last three words, but it was so fast you could hardly notice it, and she answered, with perfect composure:

"You see that sign? Of course you do, and you know that it means there is a school in this street. Can you see the entrance to the school? No, because this van, parked on the right-hand side, will be obstructing your view until you are right alongside it. So there is a good chance a little girl might come out from behind this van without you seeing her. At twenty miles an hour you will hurt her badly. At thirty miles an hour you will probably kill her. But if you drive along this part of the street at thirty miles an hour, it's true that you will probably shorten your journey by five seconds or so. So that's the equation. Those are the two things you have to weigh up against each other. Five seconds of your life, versus the whole of somebody else's. Five seconds, versus a whole lifetime." She paused, her eyes still gleaming, the rumour of a smile still spreading from the edges of her mouth. "Is it a difficult decision? I don't think so. Perhaps you do."

Her smile was a challenge, now, a weapon, aimed directly at Derek. He glared back at her, but said nothing.

When the class was over, Sophie found herself sharing a lift with him. He nodded in curt recognition, then looked away, and for a moment she thought they were going to ride down to street level in silence. But then he said:

"Well, there's four hours of my bloody life I'm never going to get back."

Sophie weighed her response carefully: "Better than getting those points on your licence, though, isn't it?"

"I don't know," said Derek. "I think that's what I'd go for, next time, instead of having to sit there being lectured by that sanctimonious b—"

Sophie didn't answer at first. She was simply relieved that he had tailed off without actually saying the word. It wasn't until they stepped out into the wintry air of Colmore Row, the huddles of office workers making for the stations and the bus stops, the endless ebb and flow of traffic, the late-afternoon sky as black as midnight, that she said: "I'm sure the other guy would have said exactly the same things." Then she added his name, "Ian," without knowing why. It was unnecessary, really.

Derek's route home, whatever it was, lay in the opposite direction to hers. But he had a parting shot for her.

"Do you know what that was?" he said. "What we saw, this afternoon?" And before she had time to speak, he answered his own question: "The new fascism." He raised his arm in a gesture of farewell and said: "Welcome to Britain, 2010. Cheerio!"

"Drive safely," Sophie answered, and they turned away from each other, taking their different paths.

*

Sophie had only walked a few yards before she ducked into the nearest Starbucks, deciding that a bucket of milky coffee was what she needed before facing the quiet rigours of another evening in her father's company.

Mocha in hand, she looked around for a seat, and saw that Naheed was sitting, alone, at a table by the window. She gravitated towards her but then, not wanting to appear presumptuous, took a seat at an empty table nearby. But Naheed had seen her, and gave her a little wave and a nod of the head, which Sophie chose to interpret as an invitation.

"Hello," Naheed said, as Sophie sat down opposite her. "I thought you'd be on the motorway by now, doing ninety-five miles an hour in the outside lane for kicks."

Sophie laughed and said: "And I'd have thought you needed something stronger than a coffee after an afternoon like that."

"Hardly," said Naheed. "I'll be driving home, and we all have to stay squeaky clean."

"Of course," said Sophie, feeling silly for having suggested it.

"Besides, that session wasn't bad, not bad at all. You were a polite and well-behaved lot, on the whole."

"I'm full of admiration," said Sophie. "I mean, I do a bit of teaching myself, but it's different . . . My students have chosen to be there, and they're keen to learn, most of them."

"I like my job," said Naheed. "It's worthwhile, and I'm not bad at it these days, even if I say so myself."

"Absolutely," Sophie agreed. "I learned a lot today, although it wasn't what I was expecting. For some reason I thought you'd all be policemen."

Naheed smiled. "No. These courses aren't run by the police. Most of us used to be driving instructors. And you," she said, "where do you teach?"

"At the university. Art history. Not so worthwhile, maybe. At least, I don't suppose what I teach saves many lives."

"No need to apologize for what you do," said Naheed.

Her phone buzzed on the table and she glanced down at it, wondering whether to take the message. The great dilemma of modern social etiquette.

"Go ahead," said Sophie. "We all would."

Naheed glanced at the screen. "Well, it's only Ian." She peered at the message. "Saying that I did a good job today."

"That's nice of him."

"He's a nice guy." Impulsively, she picked up the phone and tapped a reply, then looked across at Sophie, that now familiar gleam in her eye. "Want to know what I said?"

"Not if it's private."

"I told him I was having coffee with the speed junkie."

Now Sophie laughed. "That's my nickname, already?"

"During the tea break, we always sit around thinking up names for you all. We're supposed to be planning the second half of the session, but . . . well, we've got that down pat now, more or less."

"Tell me some of the others," said Sophie.

"I don't think I should."

"What about Derek? The sports equipment guy."

"Mr. Angry. Not very original, I know, but it fitted the bill. We always get one or two like that, by the way. One thing you learn in this job—there's a lot of anger out there."

"It's brave of you to put yourself in the firing line."

"Not really. And it's not always to do with race anyway. People like to get angry about anything. A lot of the time they're just looking for an excuse. I feel sorry for them. I think for a lot of people . . . there's nothing much going on in their lives. Emotionally. I mean, maybe their marriages have dried up, or everything they do has become a kind of habit, I don't know. But they don't *feel* much. No emotional stimulation. We all need to feel things, don't we? So, when something makes you angry, at least you're feeling something. You get that emotional kick."

Sophie nodded. This seemed to make perfect sense. "And you? You don't need to get angry to feel that you're alive?"

"I'm lucky," said Naheed. "I have a nice husband, and two beautiful children. They do the job. What about you?"

"Oh, I'm kind of . . . between relationships at the moment . . ." Sophie faltered, but while she was saying it, Naheed's phone buzzed again.

She glanced at the screen and said, coolly: "Well, then, this is a very timely message." She looked up. "It's Ian again. He's asking me to get your phone number."

In all her life, Sophie had never met anyone with such a piercing gaze, or such an eloquent, ambushing smile. She felt as though she might wither beneath it.

"Shall I give it to him?"

5.

Benjamin was driving from Shrewsbury to Rednal again, following the course of the River Severn, through the towns of Cressage, Much Wenlock, Bridgnorth, Enville, Stourbridge and Hagley. He had been driving this way, there and back, at least twice a week for the last year now. Two hundred journeys or more. No wonder that he now felt he knew every bend in the road, every landmark, every traffic roundabout, every pub, every petrol station, every Tesco Express, every garden centre, every old church that had now been converted into flats. He knew where the worst queues were likely to be, and where you could find a rat-run to bypass a particularly troublesome set of traffic lights. Not that he needed to do that today. The roads were quiet. The cold snap which had brought snow to these parts at the beginning of the month had receded, giving way to cloudy skies and mild temperatures: dull, nondescript weather, which suited the journey and suited the occasion. It was a Saturday morning like any other. It was Christmas Day, a day that Benjamin had come to loathe with a passion.

He pulled up outside his father's house just after eleven o'clock. The house where he had grown up. The house his parents had bought in 1955. A redbrick detached house, with an extension added over the garage in the early 1970s. He knew the house so well now that he no longer saw it, no longer noticed it, and as such he no longer knew it at all, and would probably have found it difficult to describe in any detail to a stranger. The only thing he noticed this morning was that the plants in the window box outside the living room were all dead, and looked as though they had been that way for months.

Inside he could see that all was reasonably clean and ship-shape as usual. He was paying for a cleaner to come in once a week, on Thursdays, as he didn't trust his father to look after the place. On the draining board in the kitchen were a single plate, a single knife and fork, a beer glass and a frying pan. Since the death of his wife, Colin had not cooked himself a meal that required anything more complicated than a frying pan. He would fry some tomatoes and have them on toast with a fried egg; perhaps some mushrooms if he was feeling adventurous. The only time this diet would vary was when Benjamin cooked for him, or took him out for dinner somewhere. Today at least he would be getting a decent roast lunch.

Colin was wearing a patterned jumper of the sort favoured by golfing celebrities and daytime TV presenters of the 1980s. When he came downstairs from his latest visit to the bathroom he was carrying a plastic bag containing a number of inexpertly wrapped presents, the only concession to Christmas anywhere in the house as far as Benjamin could see.

"I thought you were going to buy a Christmas tree," he said.

"I did. It's out the back."

Benjamin looked out of the kitchen window and saw the tree leaning up against a wall of the garden shed, still enclosed in its plastic netting.

"Well, that was a waste of money, wasn't it?"

"I'll put it up tomorrow."

"Tomorrow will be too late. What about decorations? Mum always put up some decorations."

"Oh, I couldn't be bothered to get them down from the attic. Maybe next year, when I'm feeling a bit more chipper. Are you just going to stand around criticizing, or can we go now?"

Benjamin looked at his watch. It was only ten past eleven. They had masses of time to get to Lois's.

"Where's your overnight bag?"

"I've changed my mind. You can bring me back here after dinner. I don't want to stay with your sister, it's too much trouble all round."

Benjamin sighed. The change of plans annoyed him for selfish reasons.

"Now I'll have to stay here with you."

"Why?"

"You can't be alone on Christmas night."

"Why not? I'm alone every other night. You do what you like, don't worry about me. The last thing I want to be is a burden."

Having to calm his father's repeatedly expressed fear of becoming a "burden" was one of the few truly burdensome things about being in his company. But Benjamin had learned that there was nothing to be gained by arguing. He picked up the bag of presents and escorted Colin to the car.

*

Lois and Christopher, Sophie, Benjamin and Colin sat around the lunch table, teetering, gravy-soaked towers of turkey and vegetables rising up on the plates in front of them, paper crowns on their heads. The atmosphere was bordering on funereal.

"We're doing this for Dad," Lois had insisted to her brother in the kitchen.

"He doesn't want us to. The whole thing's a complete waste of time."

"Well, thanks a lot. That's really helpful. I could have stayed at home, then."

"Isn't this your home? Nobody seems to know nowadays."

They ate in near-silence. Benjamin tried reading out some of the jokes from the crackers, but they felt lumpen, with all the sparkle of random quotations from one of the gloomier Ingmar Bergman films. The only person to smile was Sophie, and that turned out to be not in response to the joke, but a text message.

"Who was that from?" Lois asked, as only a mother could.

"Ian," Sophie answered. "Just wishing me a Happy Christmas."

"Where's he spending it, then?"

"With his mother."

"New boyfriend," Christopher explained to his father-in-law, pronouncing the phrase loudly and slowly in the mistaken belief that Colin was going deaf.

"Good-oh," said Colin. "Not before time. You could do with some grandkids, you two."

Sophie took a sip of wine and said: "Jumping the gun a bit, aren't you, Grandad? He's not even my boyfriend. We've only been on two dates."

"Well, somebody's got to continue the family line," Colin blundered on. "The rest of you haven't exactly excelled in that department."

"Give it a rest, Dad . . ." said Benjamin.

"There are five of us around this table. Is that it? Is that the best you lot can manage? Your mother and I had three kids. I thought there'd be a few more little Trotters in the world by now."

The silence that followed this outburst was more awkward and profound than ever. Everyone else around the table knew something that Colin didn't: Benjamin already had a daughter, who lived in California, from whom he was estranged.

"I'm sure Paul will soon find someone in Tokyo," said Lois. "He'll probably come and visit you in a few years with a whole army of pretty little half-Japanese children."

Colin scowled and attacked his sprouts.

After lunch, they went for a walk—all except Colin, who crashed out on the sofa with the *Radio Times* and complained that there was nothing on television.

"What do you think I bought you this for?" Benjamin asked, waving Colin's present at him. It was a DVD of Morecambe and Wise Christmas specials.

"I don't want to watch old stuff."

"Yeah, but you don't like any of the new stuff." Benjamin crouched down by the television and inserted the DVD. As he did so, a vivid memory recurred: Christmas Day 1977, thirty-three years earlier, when he and his family had sat down to watch these two comedians' final show for the BBC. His grandparents had been there too, and in laughing along with them Benjamin could remember feeling this incredible sense of oneness, a sense that the entire nation was being briefly, fugitively drawn together in the divine act of laughter. "Twenty-seven million people used to watch this, you know," he reminded his father.

"Because we only had three channels." Lois had entered the room, and was standing behind him. "And there was nothing else to do. Are you ready? It'll be dark before we set out at this rate."

The four of them set off together, strolling through the quiescent back streets which only the occasional muted display of Christmas decorations or fairy lights made less ordinary today. Soon Benjamin was lagging behind, lost in his private thoughts as usual. Sophie noticed and lingered, waiting for him to catch up.

"Everything OK?" she asked.

"I'm fine." He smiled and put his arm around her briefly, rubbing her back in a clumsy gesture. "Thanks for my present, by the way. So thoughtful."

"You don't really like him, do you?"

Sophie had given Benjamin a copy of *Fallopia* that she had bought on the night of Sohan's interview with the two famous writers. It was inscribed, "To Benjamin—All the best, Lionel Hampshire."

"Well, the reviews for this one have been a bit . . . mixed," Benjamin said. "But I'm looking forward to it. What was he like, in person?"

"Just what you'd expect."

"Oh dear."

They had arrived at the Tolkien museum, and behind it the little stretch of grassland that had recently been designated "The Shire Country Park," both of which set off a train of thought in Sophie's mind. "That was the night," she said, "that Sohan pointed out how 'Sarehole' was an anagram of 'arsehole'. How could we all have missed that for so long?"

Benjamin didn't answer. He was looking ahead at Lois and Christopher, walking arm in arm in a way which almost gave them the air of a happily married couple. He was annoyed with his sister for making that sarcastic comment about the dearth of TV channels in the 1970s, which undermined (without her realizing it, probably) one of his most cherished early memories. It was still a cornerstone of his belief system that Britain had been a more cohesive, united, consensual place during his childhood (all that had started to unravel with the election result of 1979), and the fuzzy glow he still got from watching seventies comedy shows was proof of that, somehow. But of course, for

Lois, none of that could be expected to register: for her, that decade had been a time of tragedy, of horror. He told himself that he must never forget that, and never stop making allowances for it.

A sharp reminder awaited him when they returned home, in any case. Colin had given up on Morecambe and Wise and was watching the BBC news. He looked stricken. Lois sat down beside him, while Benjamin went into the kitchen to put the kettle on.

"You all right, Dad?" she asked.

"It's that woman," he said, tonelessly, eyes not leaving the screen. "That girl in Bristol. The one who went missing last week. They've found a body now. They haven't said it's her, yet, but . . . Well, who else can it be?"

Lois said nothing, but her whole body tautened. Christopher sat down on the arm of the sofa and put his hand on her clenched, twisted shoulder. This was the tableau Benjamin saw when he re-entered the room: his sister frozen, with a man on either side of her.

"What her parents must be going through," Colin said, looking up at Christopher now, his eyes pale and liquid. "I know exactly how they feel." Now he clutched his daughter's arm with a quick, violent passion. "Years ago, we almost lost her, you know."

Benjamin watched, hesitated, realized that he had no role, and withdrew. As he made silently for the kitchen, he could hear his father repeating: "We almost lost her."

6.

After the sex, Sophie fell into a deep sleep, and when she awoke she did so very slowly, late in the morning, becoming aware first of the grey light filtering through the curtains, and then the satisfying ache in her tired limbs and then the rough, sandpaper-like texture of Ian's unshaven face as he brushed against her cheek and kissed her.

"Morning, sweetie," he said. "I'm just popping out to get some stuff."

"Mm-hm."

"Sleep well?"

"Very well."

"I was going to get bacon, eggs . . ."

"Sounds lovely."

". . . mushrooms, tomatoes, fresh orange juice . . ."

"Do you spoil all your girlfriends like this?"

"Want a Sunday paper?"

"Why not?"

"*Sunday Times* OK?"

"I'd prefer the *Observer*."

"I'll get them both."

He drew away and sleepily she reached up, placed her arms behind his neck and pulled him back towards her for another kiss. In the process, the duvet slipped away from her body, a reminder that Sophie was naked, while Ian was fully clothed. The situation excited them both. As a consequence, it was another twenty minutes before Ian went out on his shopping expedition.

When he was gone, Sophie waited a few more happy, post-coital minutes before getting out of bed. She noticed there was a white bathrobe hanging on the back of the bedroom door, and, slipping into it, she pulled open the curtains. She had walked home with Ian the night before—or rather, early in the morning—but, being somewhat the worse for drink, and pulsing with anticipation after taking the decision to sleep with him for the first time, she had not taken much notice of where he lived. This morning's view was unfamiliar, and it took her a few moments to orientate herself. She appeared to be in one of the newish developments of flats behind Centenary Square. She could see the rear of Baskerville House, and the massive construction site where the new Library of Birmingham was beginning to take shape. (The noise from that must be pretty deafening during the week, she thought.) There were few signs of human life out there this morning, apart from a man walking his dog across a stretch of grass and two teenage boys sitting at opposite ends of a see-saw in a children's playground, looking bored. Traffic hummed past unceasingly somewhere in the near-distance. It was a typical Birmingham Sunday, it seemed: for everyone but her.

She had not slept with many men in her life; for Sophie it was a commitment as well as an adventure. Last night, and this morning, felt like a delicious tiptoe into the unknown. Being left alone for a few minutes in Ian's empty flat was an unexpected bonus. So far, in the course of three longish but rather one-sided conversations, he had managed not to give too much away about himself. Here, perhaps, was an opportunity to get to know him better.

Her first instinct when visiting someone else's home was always to look at the books. The academic reflex, deeply ingrained and quite irresistible. It didn't get Sophie very far today, however. She already knew that Ian was, by his own admission, "not a great reader." She also knew that she herself probably read more than was healthy for her, set too much store by reading, had a kind of neurotic obsession with literature and its supposed moral benefits. All the same, what she found on his shelves was disappointing. A handful of sporting autobiographies, some reference books (also mainly to do with sport), some bestselling novels from a few years back, two or three road-safety manuals. She counted them: fourteen books in all. There were about the same number of DVDs, mainly James Bond and Jason Bourne films. The DVD player was on the floor next to a widescreen TV, and a weird-looking electronic device with handles that was either some sort of elaborate sex toy or (more likely, Sophie realized, with some relief) a games console. She picked it up and turned it around in her hands, briefly curious about this bizarre object whose functions were so mysterious to her. None of her previous boyfriends, it occurred to her, had ever owned anything like it.

There was a square coffee table in the centre of the living space, with a fair number of watermarks and coffee stains on the surface, and one copy of a magazine—called *Stuff*—on its lower shelf. The sofa and the chairs were probably from IKEA: at least, they bore a marked resemblance to the sofa and chairs in every flat she had ever rented herself, all of which had come from IKEA. There were no plants anywhere to be seen, although there was a large framed reproduction of Van Gogh's sunflowers on the wall.

The far end of the living space consisted of an open-plan kitchen. There was nothing much in the fridge, apart from beer, butter, cheese, milk and a pack of sausages that were eight days past their "best before" date. The freezer was empty apart from ice cubes and a box of Magnums, of which only two remained.

This was disappointing: Sophie was learning almost nothing here about the man she was in the process of choosing as her new partner. When a quick tour of his bathroom yielded even more meagre information, she gave up and put the kettle on to make coffee. While waiting for it to boil, she retrieved the copy of *Stuff* and sat down at the kitchen table to read it.

The front cover showed a young, attractive brunette clutching an iPad to her hip while pouting and staring into the middle distance. Despite the presence of the tablet in her hand, it looked as though she was planning to spend the night clubbing rather than working, since she was wearing a white mini-dress which barely covered her crotch, with sheer panels exposing large portions of her cleavage and midriff. Flicking through the magazine, Sophie could see that this was a recurring pictorial theme, and that she was being invited into a strange parallel universe in which cutting-edge technology was used exclusively by beautiful young women who only liked to work, take photos or play games while wearing lingerie and swimwear. The cover promised a preview of the iPhone 5 ("How Apple will reinvent the smartphone wheel . . . again"), a round-up of "Killer Tech that will change the future," a nostalgic survey of "39 Gadgets that Changed the World—Starring Sky+, Wii and 10 years of iPod" and a feature on "How to build your own FPS." Sophie, needless to say, had no idea what an FPS was or why anyone would want to build it: floral-patterned sofa? Freshly painted shed? Turning to the relevant article, she discovered that in fact it was an acronym for First Person Shooter, and this referred to a sub-genre of games based around someone firing a gun (obviously) seen from the perspective of the person doing the firing. Once again she felt the mild, transgressive frisson of stepping outside her own comfort zone, and she read on with increasing fascination, stumbling over terminology she had never encountered before—megatextures, game engine, radiosity, latency—and becoming so absorbed in the article that she found it quite frustrating, for a moment at least, to be interrupted by the opening of the front door. But she was glad to see Ian again, especially when, as soon as he set eyes on her, he stopped in his tracks, laden with shopping bags, and said:

"Wow."

"Wow?"

"I can't believe it's you. I can't believe it's you, here, in my flat. You look . . . incredible."

He was not paying her an idle compliment. With her hair still tousled and her body still glowing from their last bout of lovemaking, and the white bathrobe hanging so loose that it was almost falling off her, Sophie looked like every *Stuff* reader's masturbation fantasy made flesh. She only needed to be fondling an Olympus PEN EP-3 ("sleek metal casing and what is apparently the world's fastest autofocus"), or drooling over her BlackBerry Bold 9900 ("packs in a touchscreen and QWERTY keyboard, and runs the zippy new BlackBerry 7 OS") for the vision to be complete. No wonder Ian looked happy. He kissed her again, a long and tender kiss on the mouth, to which she responded with lingering eagerness, before he pulled away reluctantly and said, in the voice of a man who could not quite believe the turn reality had taken, lost in a waking dream:

"Come on. We should eat."

During breakfast Sophie confessed to the disappointment she had felt while attempting to probe the mysteries of his flat.

"I mean, you couldn't make it any more anonymous if you were some kind of government agent trying to keep his identity secret. Don't you ever feel the need to personalize it at all? A few pot plants, a bit of colour here and there, some more pictures on the walls?"

"I know what I'd like to put on the bedroom wall," said Ian. He arranged his fingers into a rectangle and squinted through them, as if framing a photograph. "A picture of you looking like that. Only then I'd never get up in the mornings."

Sophie smiled, drawing away slightly and pulling the robe more closely around herself.

Later, back in bed, they made love again and then, after a long while resting in each other's arms, they stirred themselves and started reading the newspapers together and now their mutual nakedness became comfortable rather than erotic. They sat side by side and Sophie relished the feeling of their points of unimpeded contact: their upper arms pressed against each other, her gently curving hip nestled against Ian's straighter, more muscular one, the embrace of their feet as she felt her ankle being gently caressed by his toe. It all felt subtly right and inevitable, and the ease with which their bodies dovetailed was mirrored by the relaxed frivolity of their conversation. It was the first Sunday of the year and there wasn't much serious news in the papers. A giant urban fox had been captured and killed in Maidstone and there was a photograph of a seven-year-old boy holding it aloft—or at least trying to, since the boy and the animal were roughly the same size. A study in the Netherlands had shown that women eating a diet high in fruit and vegetables were more likely to have baby girls. Three pigs were believed to be on the loose on the streets of Southampton, the police mysteriously linking their escape from a local farm with a "breakdown in the relationship" of the couple who owned it. If she'd been alone Sophie would not even have bothered to read most of these stories but it was fun sharing them with Ian, laughing at the oddness and silliness of the world, getting to know his sense of humour. The mood only changed (and even then it was a fleeting change) when he turned to a story about Joanna Yeates, the young woman from Bristol whose body had been found on Christmas Day.

"I see they've released that guy," he said, scanning the first couple of paragraphs. "Her landlord. The one they took in for questioning."

"Good," said Sophie.

"Good? Why's it good?"

"Because they didn't have any reason for holding him in the first place."

"Yeah—but look at him."

He showed her the picture of Christopher Jefferies, the sixty-five-year-old suspect who had been taken in for three days' questioning by the Bristol police and then released without charge. Unconventional in appearance, "eccentric" even, an English teacher with a fondness for romantic poetry, known occasionally to dye his hair a subtle shade of blue, he was perfect fodder for the English newspapers, who had been persuaded of his guilt from the moment they set eyes on him and had spent the last few days saying as much while keeping within the bounds of the law.

"Look at him?" said Sophie, leaning over. "What about him?"

"I mean, what a weirdo!"

Sophie was taken aback. "Well, for a start," she said, "I can't see anything especially weird about him from that picture. And apart from that, it's quite a leap from being a 'weirdo' to being a murderer, isn't it?"

Ian glanced at her and saw that her cheeks were flushed and at the base of her neck a little patch of skin had darkened to red. Without further comment, he quickly turned to another story on the same page. "Look at this: 'A clothes shop in Lisbon has promised free clothes for the first hundred people who turn up on the first day of their sale wearing nothing but underwear.'"

Sophie relented and smiled. This time she took the paper from his hands and studied the photo of shivering customers as they stood in a crowd outside the shop, waiting for it to open.

"Nice bum," she said, pointing to one of the men. "Not as nice as yours, though."

At which point she put the newspaper aside, and they moved on to other things.

7.

Midway between Shrewsbury and Birmingham, not far from the M54 and considered such a geographical fixture that it had its own official sign on the motorway, there stood one of the district's main attractions and, indeed, one of its principal glories. Woodlands Garden Centre. It had begun life, back in 1973, as a mere shop: a compact, humble emporium selling plants and earthenware pots and bags of compost. Today, almost forty years later, it had blossomed and expanded into a kingdom, a mighty empire, whose subjects could roam for hours—for an entire day if they wanted to—through a succession of different purlieus and provinces in which every aspect of human life was represented, catered for and commodified. Outside, it is true, stretched a vista of plants, shrubs, ferns, flowers, vines, cacti and all other manner of vegetable life which, though amazing in its extent and variety, was exactly what you would expect to encounter in such an establishment. It was only when the customers entered the covered area of Woodlands that the true scale and inclusivity of the place became apparent. You were confronted, first of all, by acres—limitless pastures—of garden furniture, stretching as far as the eye could see. Not just chairs and tables but entire four-piece suites that would not disgrace the sitting room of a country mansion, to say nothing of benches, divans, rocking chairs, loveseats, ottomans, Chesterfields, dining tables, drinks tables, coffee tables, occasional tables and everything else that might conceivably be required to turn a back garden into an outdoor living space. And even then, even taking into account the dozens of enormous barbecues, far more elaborate and sophisticated than anything most people would have in their kitchens, and the astonishing array of garden lighting—floodlights, spotlights, fairy lights, solar-powered lights, flashing lights, glowing lights, twinkling lights—even then, you would barely have begun to scratch the surface of Woodlands' possibilities. There was a kitchen furniture department; a pet shop selling everything from goldfish to rabbits; a clothes shop dominated by Barbours, wellington boots and racks of polyester shirts and trousers; a huge section devoted to crafts and hobbies—painting, embroidery, needlework, crochet, miniature railways, model aircraft, anything the human mind could conceive to fill the empty hours of childhood or retirement; an extensive grocery shop selling everything from Cheddar cheese to English wine; a section devoted to CDs (with an emphasis on Frank Sinatra, Vera Lynn, Johnny Cash and other stars of yesteryear) and DVDs (with an emphasis on British war films, Ealing comedies, John Wayne movies and other nostalgic items); a toyshop with a particularly impressive array of jigsaw puzzles depicting farmyard scenes from pre-industrial days, Spitfire and Hurricane aircraft in mid-flight, scenes of traditional English village life, vintage cars and the like; and even a bookshop, again with a backward-looking slant, since besides the inevitable thousands of titles devoted to gardening there was also a thriving market in books of local history. Many of these were collections of old black-and-white photographs or sepia-tinted postcards and boasted titles such as *Images of Bygone Dudley*, *Chaddesley Corbett in Pictures* or *Bridgnorth as It Used to Be*. A good number of them, if you checked their spines carefully, were published by an imprint called Chase Historical.

The founder, publisher, editorial director, marketing manager, publicity officer and art director of Chase Historical, in the person of Philip Chase himself, was currently sipping a cappuccino in the throbbing heart (or perhaps the well-filled stomach) of Woodlands, its restaurant. Here, where steak-and-ale pie and beer-battered fish and chips remained the most popular items on the menu despite the chef's repeated attempts to give it a more international flavour, queues of white- and grey-haired customers built up all day, clutching their wooden trays, eyes feasting eagerly on the lemon drizzle cake, the scones and jam, the pots of thick brown Yorkshire tea. On this weekday morning—the first day of the spring half-term—the restaurant was doing brisk business, and Philip was pleased, because these people were his customers too, and soon many of them would be browsing in the bookshop, and sales today would be healthy. He continued to sip his cappuccino and check the time on his phone. He had arranged meetings with two people in this restaurant today, and the first one was already late.

This first person was Benjamin, as it happened, who—having misremembered the time of the meeting—believed that he was running early, and was killing time at the entrance to Woodlands' children's theatre. Yes, this Xanadu among garden centres even boasted a theatre—a performance space, at any rate—which came into its own at times like this, when the schools were on holiday and parents would go to any lengths to absolve themselves from the responsibility of keeping their offspring amused for half an hour. It provided gainful employment for several of the local children's entertainers, whose trade was otherwise largely confined to weekend birthday parties. This morning, from eleven o'clock to eleven thirty, a small but excited audience was being treated to the antics of Baron Brainbox, a portly figure dressed in gentleman's tweeds of the 1930s, with a gold fob watch in his pocket, a red ping-pong ball on his nose and a garish multicoloured mortar board set precariously atop his head. Benjamin had been watching his act for about ten minutes and had to admit that he was thoroughly enjoying it. The children were basically being given a maths lesson, seasoned with terrible puns, conjuring tricks and slapstick, all of it executed with enthusiasm rather than accuracy. It was a fairly shambolic show, but the Baron himself seemed to be enjoying himself, to judge from his frequent corpsing, and this was communicating itself to the young audience. He cut such a lovable and engaging figure, in fact, that Benjamin could not see how anyone could fail to warm to him, and was therefore surprised to hear a voice beside him in the doorway growling:

"I hate that cunt."

Benjamin turned. The figure standing next to him was wearing a white medical coat, wellington boots, a false moustache and a World War Two pilot's leather helmet.

"He always goes on too long. Always overruns. Deliberately cuts into my slot, the scheming bastard."

There was a blackboard next to the door, with the schedule of today's entertainment chalked up on it. The act due to take the stage at eleven thirty was billed as "Doctor Daredevil." It was now eleven thirty-three.

"Let me take a wild guess," said Benjamin, pointing at the name. "This is you?"

"Too bloody right," said the Doctor. "And that bastard was supposed to be off stage five minutes ago."

Hearing their voices, Baron Brainbox now glanced over in their direction and, glimpsing his rival, his face darkened into a scowl. Benjamin sensed that the situation was about to turn nasty, and decided that he didn't want to get involved. On the point of leaving, he was taking one final look at the charismatic entertainer and his spellbound circle of children, when something strange happened. This time, when he noticed Benjamin looking at him, something dawned on the Baron's face: something akin to recognition. It was almost as if he were about to step forward, out of the circle, out of character, and greet Benjamin in the manner of an old friend. But before anything like this could happen, the Doctor intervened—rushing towards the performance space and berating his rival, at the top of his voice, for not finishing his show at the agreed time. A bitter dispute broke out between the two clowns—the children looking on with a mixture of amusement and confusion, none of them sure whether this was still part of the entertainment or not. Benjamin decided this was definitely the time to withdraw, and, without giving more than a passing moment's thought to that odd change of expression on the Baron's part, he strolled across to the restaurant.

"Where've you been?" Philip asked.

"I'm not late, am I?"

"Eleven o'clock, we said."

"Really?"

They had been meeting here every month for the last year or so, ever since Benjamin had moved to the mill house. They'd chosen it simply as a midway point between their homes, but there was also the pleasing coincidence (which Philip had been the one to notice) that Woodlands itself was almost exactly as old as their friendship. They had met at King William's School, the elite academy that stood near the centre of Birmingham and had a tradition of producing alumni who, in the words of the school song, "made her great and famous through the globe." Neither Benjamin nor Philip, it must be said, had quite fulfilled that promise yet. Where some of their contemporaries had gone on to become captains of industry (such as the loathed sports champion Ronald Culpepper, now apparently the owner of diamond mines in South Africa and rumoured to be worth more than 100 million pounds) or—in the case of Doug—prominent members of the London commentariat, both Benjamin and Philip appeared to have settled for the quiet satisfactions of under-achievement. When Philip's long-running newspaper column "About Town with Philip Chase" had been axed in the mid-2000s, he had been disappointed but hardly surprised; and having already spotted a gap in the market for better-than-average local history books, he set about establishing his own imprint, wrote the first three titles himself and was now, five years later, making a decent living at it. He was comfortably settled with his second wife Carol, after a first marriage which had ended in amicable divorce. As for Benjamin, having done very well out of the London property market, at the age of fifty he was probably best described as retired. If he had plans for the future, he was keeping them to himself, and nothing much seemed to disturb his peace of mind: not even the knowledge that he had wasted the last thirty years of his life in a futile romantic obsession, or consumed some tens of thousands of hours working on a gigantic literary and musical project so overreaching, unwieldy and misconceived that even he now realized it would never reach a conclusion, let alone a public. The burden of all that wasted emotional investment and intellectual energy might well have crushed some people; but not Benjamin. He had been through the tunnel of trauma and emerged, blinking, into the benign flatlands of equanimity, through which he was now content to wander with no particular object in mind; very much like one of Woodlands' typical customers, with half an hour to spare in the garden furniture department and no intention of buying anything.

"Well, we've only got a few minutes," said Philip, looking at his phone again. "I've got a meeting with a potential author at a quarter to."

"Anyone interesting?"

Philip had a letter on the table beside him. He unfolded it and passed it to Benjamin. "Postcards of old Droitwich and Feckenham, apparently. 'An unmatched collection,' it says."

"You can hardly turn that down." He skimmed the contents of the letter, and drew breath sharply at one or two phrases. "Ooh— sounds a bit cranky."

"They're all a bit cranky. Cranky is fine. In moderation, like everything else. Some people would say we're a nation of harmless cranks."

"I suppose," said Benjamin, and thought back to the scene he had just witnessed in the children's theatre. What motivated someone, after all, to dress up as Baron Brainbox and earn a living by making a fool of himself in front of crowds of children? Wouldn't they all be living in a duller country without people like that?

There seemed nothing particularly eccentric about Philip's potential author, in any case, when he arrived and introduced himself a few minutes later. The worst that could be said about him was that he appeared rather distracted and ill at ease. He was a dishevelled figure, with unkempt grey hair, a padded winter anorak covered with stains, and watery blue eyes that looked warily out through a large pair of old-fashioned wire-rimmed spectacles. He shook Philip's hand, introduced himself as Peter Stopes and gave a questioning glance in Benjamin's direction.

"This is my friend Benjamin Trotter," Philip explained. "Anything you say in front of me can be said in front of him." He realized that he sounded like Sherlock Holmes introducing Dr. Watson to a new client in the consulting rooms of 221B.

"I was a tad surprised when you suggested meeting here," said Peter, sitting down opposite him. "I had assumed that conversations like this usually took place in the privacy of your office."

Philip's office was in fact the front bedroom of his house in King's Heath, but he wasn't going to admit that.

"Well, Peter," he said, "let's see what you've got for me. Postcards of Old Droitwich, wasn't it? Did you bring some along?"

"Postcards, yes, *and* accompanying text," said Peter, with great emphasis. "And yes, I have them with me, somewhere . . ."

He began searching the pockets of his anorak, of which there seemed to be a surprising number. Finally, after three or four attempts, he found what he was looking for, and drew out a scuffed Manila envelope, folded in two, from which he extracted half a dozen ancient, creased and folded postcards. He laid them out carefully on the table in front of Philip, in two rows of three.

"Ah yes, the Droitwich Lido," said Philip, picking up the first. "Very nice. This looks like the 1940s, I'd say."

"1947, yes," Peter confirmed.

"And this is a good one of the Chateau Impney. Strange building to find in that part of the world. Built by John Corbett, the industrialist, for his wife in the 1870s. She was half-French."

"Indeed."

"Well, these look very nice, I must say, Peter. How many more do you have?"

"More? No, this is it. This is everything."

Philip was shocked into temporary silence.

"But . . . we would normally need at least a hundred, for this kind of book."

"Normally, yes. But this is not intended to be a normal kind of book. The *text*, Philip. In this case it's the text that is everything."

Philip said, reluctantly: "Then perhaps you'd better tell me a bit more about it."

Peter glanced nervously from left to right.

"I think we should go somewhere less public."

"Not easy," Philip pointed out, "in a garden centre."

"Necessity is the mother of invention," said Peter. "I think I have a solution. Follow me."

He rose to his feet and walked out of the restaurant, easing his way past the growing queues of lunchtime diners. (It was never too early, it seemed, for sausage and mash or a ploughman's lunch.) Philip followed him, throwing a baffled glance back at Benjamin and saying: "You don't have to come too."

"I wouldn't miss this for the world," said Benjamin. "This is even better than the children's theatre."

They soon realized where Peter Stopes was leading them. At the rear of the Woodlands building, hidden from the car park, hidden from the main road, lay its most secret—but for many its most precious—enclave. For here were the sheds. Modest garden sheds, at first, just big enough to house a lawn mower, a leaf blower and a handful of tools, but soon there were also summer-houses, gazebos, pavilions and ornate labyrinthine structures which combined elements of all of these; structures designed to furnish the married Englishman with perhaps the thing he craved most of all: a place where he could escape his family without actually leaving home.

There were twenty-five or thirty such sheds, arranged to form a sort of village, with streets, lanes and by-ways criss-crossing each other in between the buildings. It was the least-frequented part of the Woodlands empire, and today, it seemed, Benjamin, Philip and the mysterious author had it to themselves. Peter knew what he was doing.

After glancing back and forth to make sure that they weren't being followed, he led them into the second of the sheds. It was towards the lower end of the Woodlands range: a basic cuboid structure, with one small window and a roof rising to an apex which was not high enough to allow any of them to stand upright. In fact even to get the three of them in there together at once was a tight squeeze. They stood, crouched and squashed together for a few uncomfortable seconds before Benjamin said:

"I think we should find a bigger shed."

"Agreed," said Peter.

It was too small for them all to turn around, but with some difficulty they managed to reverse out into the open air, one after the other. Then they walked on. The next shed Peter found was only marginally bigger.

"I'm sure we can find something better than this," said Philip, when they were all squashed in together again.

"Of course," said Peter. "But I am actually looking to buy a shed in the near future. And this one looks about right. I need somewhere to work on my books, you see."

Philip and Benjamin eyed up the shed as best they could in the confined space, trying to gauge its suitability as a home office.

"It's a bit small," said Philip.

"We only have a small garden."

"I think you could get a desk in here," said Benjamin. "A little one. I reckon this could work."

"I also need somewhere to house my instruments. My wife doesn't like them cluttering up the house."

"Instruments?"

"Musical instruments. I run a small local music group. We play traditional English tunes on the original instruments."

"What do you play?" asked Benjamin, almost afraid to learn the answer.

"The crumhorn, and the sackbut."

"Let's find a bigger shed," said Philip.

Finally they chose the biggest shed of all. It had three rooms, central heating, hot and cold running water, and a large table in the central room, surrounded by bench seating with tastefully embroidered cushions. They sank down into this with some relief.

Then there was a long silence. When Peter at last seemed to be about to speak, the others drew in closer, anticipating—correctly—that he would do so in a low voice.

"Now, Philip . . . As I said, in the case of this book, it's the text that is the important thing. And I don't use the word 'important' lightly. It tells a story which I have personally uncovered, and which, when it is widely known, will change the way that people think about one of the most significant issues of our time."

He allowed a few moments for this impressive claim to sink in, and was about to continue when Philip said:

"Well, in that case, why do you want me to publish it? I'm only a small publisher."

"True. But from little acorns, oak trees can grow. And besides," he admitted, "I must confess you're not the first publisher I've approached. My proposal has already been considered by some of the larger London houses. I hope you're not offended."

"Not at all. How many other publishers did you send it to?"

"Seventy-six."

Philip thought about this and said: "Well, photographs of old Droitwich might seem a bit niche to some people, I suppose . . ."

"Even throwing Feckenham in as well," Benjamin added helpfully.

"The photographs are just a pretext," said Peter. "As I've told you before, the text is the important thing. The story. Now, what I have to tell you—" his voice sank even lower "—must never leave the walls of this shed."

Benjamin and Philip nodded their solemn assent.

"I'm assuming that you noticed something those photographs have in common? Something about all the *people* in them?"

Suddenly Philip knew just where this was going. "Go on, I'll buy it," he said, in a weary voice.

"What they have in common, is that they are all indigenous English folk. Now, the title of my book is *The Kalergi Plan*, and it starts from the premise that if you were to take such photographs now . . ."

And after that, it did not take long for Peter Stopes's demented farrago of an idea to come tumbling out. Besides, Philip, who had made a study of these kinds of belief some years earlier, was familiar with it already. The white races of Europe, apparently, were being subjected to a gradual genocide. They were being slowly bred out of existence, and the whole process was the devilish invention of an Austrian aristocrat from the beginning of the twentieth century called Richard von Coudenhove-Kalergi. "The Kalergi Plan," as some liked to call it, was a plan to create a pan-European state in which, in the words of his book *Praktischer Idealismus*, "the man of the future will be of mixed race. The Eurasian-Negroid race of the future, similar in its appearance to the Ancient Egyptians, will replace the diversity of peoples with a diversity of individuals." And this genocidal pan-European state, of course, was already well established, and doing its fiendish work, in the form of the European Union, of which Kalergi was nothing less than the spiritual founder.

A few minutes later, Benjamin and Philip were walking back to their cars through the February drizzle, Peter Stopes and his six old postcards having been sent packing by the Chase Historical editorial director in no uncertain terms.

"So, was he just making all of that up?" Benjamin asked.

"Oh no—Kalergi existed, and he probably is the founder of the EU, if you want to trace it right back," said Philip. "But the way these people twist his ideas is incredible. Maybe what I said about cranks being harmless was a bit naive."

"No, I don't think so." Benjamin reached his car first, and fumbled for his keys. "We just got unlucky today. There aren't many like him."

"I bloody hope not. Shall we meet somewhere else next time?"

"No, I like it here." Benjamin fastened his seat belt, shut the car door and opened the driver's window. "It's always an adventure. You never know what you're going to find. Sometimes it's good, sometimes it's nasty, a lot of the time it's as weird as hell. But that's England for you. We're stuck with it."

He waved out of the window as he drove off, leaving Philip to wave after him, and then to shake his head ruefully, wondering whether Benjamin was starting to carry this whole equanimity thing a bit too far.

8.

Ian talked a lot about his mother. He rarely spoke of his father, who had died when he was still a teenager, or his older sister Lucy, who was married and lived in Scotland and didn't seem to have much to do with the rest of the family, but his mother was clearly an important presence in his life. She lived alone, in a small village somewhere near Stratford-upon-Avon, and every Sunday he went to visit her. Sophie (who was inclined towards over-analysis of her relationships anyway, but especially so in this case, as she was determined—*determined*—that this one should not fail) vacillated in her mind between finding their closeness touching and finding it alarming. It seemed of a piece with Ian's thoughtful and generous nature, certainly; at the same time, was it really healthy for a thirty-seven-year-old man to see his mother so regularly, to speak to her on the telephone so often?

Of course, he was anxious that Sophie should meet her as soon as possible, but for many weeks she resisted the suggestion. It was not until they had passed numerous other landmarks—his first dinner with Lois and Christopher (which had been a great success), the first time they had spoken the words "I love you" to each other (during a quiet moment in a particularly boring film she had taken him to see at the Electric), the day Sophie finally moved into his flat (bringing with her boxes and boxes of books to fill up those empty shelves)—that at last she relented. And so, one bright Sunday morning in April found them driving out of Birmingham along the A3400 and into the unimposing Warwickshire countryside; their destination being the village of Kernel Magna, where Ian had been born and had spent the greater part of his life.

Sophie enjoyed the journey, not least because she liked the way that Ian drove. There was something sexy about watching a man do something he was so good at: his constant relaxed alertness, his courtesy to other drivers, the sense of his being in easy command of a complex, responsive machine. For some reason it made her want to put a hand on the inside of his thigh and try distracting him. After she had teased him sufficiently in this way, and once conversation between them had started to run dry, they played a word game. It was Ian's idea: you took the last three letters from the number plate of a nearby car and made a phrase out of it.

"Come on, I'll start," he said, and read out the initials from a Vauxhall Astra waiting ahead of them at a junction. "TLX—Tony's Lovely Xylophone."

Sophie laughed. It was a stupid way of passing the time—the kind of game she had always imagined she might play with her children, if she ever had any—but it gave her a gleeful sense of being on holiday from the deadly earnestness of academic smalltalk (socializing within the department could be quite an ordeal). And Ian's sense of fun, as so often, was catching.

"All right," she said. "ZCH—Zoo Captivates Harpists."

"WPL," said Ian, glimpsing a VW Golf as it sped past. "Wankers Prefer Lesbians."

"YMG—Your Magnificent Gallstone."

Finally, they both spotted a big black Range Rover as it reversed out of a driveway.

"DPP—Derrida Purposely Prevaricates," said Sophie, at the exact moment that Ian came up with: "Dead Panda Pongs."

They burst out laughing and then, before Sophie had had time to reflect on the difference between their suggestions, they passed the sign that welcomed them—and other careful drivers—to Kernel Magna itself.

It was not quite the picture-postcard village that Sophie had been anticipating. It would probably not have passed muster as the model for one of those jigsaws that enjoyed such healthy sales in the toyshop at Woodlands Garden Centre. For one thing, as you approached it from the north, estates of brand-new, characterless houses, built of the same pale red brick and all standing slightly too close to one another, sprang up on either side of the road. They looked nice enough, but Sophie could not imagine herself living in one of them.

"That used to be mine," said Ian, pointing towards one house in particular, although she had no idea which one it was. "Lived there for nearly two years," he added, half to himself.

The speed limit was thirty, but he slowed down conscientiously to twenty-five miles an hour as they drove past a convenience store, an Indian restaurant, an estate agent and a hairdresser's, all grouped within a few yards of each other.

"That's it," Ian said. "That's all that's left of the village, now. This—" he indicated a large abandoned building on the left "—used to be the local pub, but then one of the big chains bought it up, and it wasn't making them any money, so they closed it after a couple of years. Not much life here these days."

"Any of your friends still live here?"

"Nope. They've all moved out. Simon was the last one to go— he's in Wolverhampton, now."

Sophie was still trying to remember the names of all Ian's friends. "Which one's Simon, again?"

Ian gave her what was almost—but not quite—a reproving glance. "My best friend. We were at primary school together."

"He's the one who joined the police?"

"That's right. OK, this is Mum's house, here."

He pulled into a driveway and parked in front of a tall, three-storey house, dating from the 1930s or so. A white-haired figure was already sitting in the front bay window, looking out for them. She was up and on the doorstep before Ian and Sophie had even had time to get out of the car. She was a tall woman—five foot eight or nine, Sophie would have said—and despite her age her posture was still good; she stood strong and upright, with a straight back. Her eyes were blue, her teeth well preserved, her gaze searching; only the slight hint of a tremor as she held out her hand to Sophie gave any hint of her seventy-one years. She was, it was immediately clear, a formidable woman.

"Mmm," she breathed, as she looked Sophie up and down intently while clasping her hand in both of hers. "Even prettier than he said you were. My name is Helena, dear. Do come in."

She led them into the sitting room and poured them glasses of sweet sherry, a drink Sophie realized she had never tasted before.

"Really," Helena said, when smalltalk about the journey had been exhausted, "I think my son might have brought his new lady friend to see me before today. I gather you've already moved in to his flat, dear, is that correct? So this . . . relationship, must be very advanced already. It seems rather a topsy-turvy way of doing things."

"Well . . . that's completely my fault," said Sophie, with a nervous glance at Ian. "He's invited me lots of times before now, but it's never quite worked out. Sundays are . . . always a bit busy," she improvised desperately.

"Do you go to church?" Helena asked, with a kind of lethal innocence.

"No, but . . ."

Ian came to her rescue. "I think I terrified her, Mum, by talking about you too much."

"How silly," said Helena, rising to her feet. "I wouldn't say boo to a goose. Now, let me get lunch ready."

"I'll come and help," said Ian.

Left alone in the sitting room, Sophie looked around her at the pictures on the mantelpiece and the walls. Family photos, mainly: one of Ian as a schoolboy, aged about thirteen, in a double frame with a girl some three or four years older: Lucy, obviously. There were several pictures of Helena's late husband: a black-and-white one, in which he was wearing army uniform (National Service?); a nice one of the two of them, she wearing a swimsuit, he an open-necked shirt and shorts, taken on some distant family holiday (the south of France, maybe? The 1960s?); and a much later one, given pride of place on the mantelpiece, in which he was wearing a suit and looked to be about fifty: not long before he died, perhaps. Then there was a picture of Lucy graduating (a small one, tucked away on a shelf next to the television), but only Helena and a young Ian were with her. All the pictures needed dusting, Sophie noticed.

For lunch, Helena had prepared ham on the bone, with a warm potato salad. They ate not in the dining room, which Helena said was too dark at this time of year, but in the kitchen; which Sophie thought was rather dark as well.

"Ian was telling me," she ventured at one point, "that you've lived here for more than forty years."

"That's right. We moved here the year that Lucy was born. I don't suppose I shall ever move now, even though the village is not what it was, not by any means. My son can probably tell you: there used to be a butcher's, an antiques shop, an ironmonger's. All family businesses, of course. It was very different back then. The post office closed down about five years ago. That was a great blow. Now I have to drive into Stratford if I want to send a parcel. And the parking there is so very difficult. And of course there was Thomas's!"

"What was Thomas's?"

"The village shop. A *proper* village shop. Not just selling food but toys and stationery, books—all sorts of things."

"That's going back a bit, Mum."

"Some of us have long memories."

"Anyway, there's a shop now."

"That place?" Helena shuddered. "Hardly the same thing. One can hardly go in there and expect to have a conversation with the person behind the till. You never know what language they're going to be speaking, for one thing. Which reminds me, did I tell you about my new cleaning woman?"

Ian shook his head.

"My lovely cleaner," Helena said to Sophie, "who has been coming here since goodness knows when, has finally retired and moved to the coast. Devon, I believe. So now the agency has sent this new girl. Grete is her name. She comes from Vilnius. Lithuania, of all places! Can you imagine?"

"Doesn't really matter, does it," Ian said, "so long as she can clean? What's her English like?"

"Excellent, I must say. Although her accent is very strong, and I do wish she would speak a little louder."

"Perhaps she's scared of you. A lot of people are, you know."

Understanding that this remark—in part at least—referred to Sophie, Helena turned to her guest, and her tone softened. "Anyway, my dear," she said. "Do tell me all about your work at the university. My son says that you know absolutely everything there is to know about old paintings."

"Not exactly," Sophie answered, wincing inside. "Like all academics, I work in a very specialized field. My thesis was about contemporary portraits of black European writers in the nineteenth century."

"*Black* Europeans? Who on earth could you mean?"

"Well, Alexander Pushkin, for instance, whose great-grandfather was African. Or Alexandre Dumas—the man who wrote *The Three Musketeers*?—whose grandmother was a slave from Haiti."

"Goodness, I had no idea. The things one learns!" Helena exclaimed, in a way which suggested there were some things she would rather not learn at all.

"So I examined portraits of these figures, to look at the different ways each artist had acknowledged—or failed to acknowledge—their black ancestry."

"How utterly fascinating. Would anybody care for some rhubarb crumble?"

Having closed off the subject effectively in this manner, Helena busied herself fetching the pudding from the oven, and making custard. Afterwards Ian (whose visits to his mother nearly always involved carrying out some odd jobs on her behalf) went upstairs to fix a toilet seat that had come loose. Helena, meanwhile, took Sophie outside.

"Do you know," she said, "I think that for the first time this year, it's *just* warm enough to take tea in the garden."

They sat on a wrought-iron bench, painted white and overlooking a flower bed which would, no doubt, offer a fine display of colour in a few months' time. Helena put her arm through Sophie's and held her in a grip which was terrifying in its steadiness and ferocity.

"I'm so glad that my son has found you," she said. "His last two girlfriends were not at all suitable—although a mother is bound to say that, of course. I would so love for him to have a steady companion; a life companion. Speaking for myself, I feel the lack of that very keenly, even though it's—goodness!—more than twenty years since my lovely Graham passed away."

"It must have been . . . very sudden, unexpected?"

"Completely. A heart attack, at the age of fifty-two. He was in the prime of life. He loved his family, loved his work . . ."

"Which was?"

"He worked at the old Pebble Mill studios in Birmingham. He was a studio manager. A *senior* studio manager, I should say. It was a long drive to work every day, but he didn't mind. He loved every minute of it. He was a BBC man through and through. I don't know what he would think of them today . . . Lucy was away at university when it happened. She kept her distance, which I'm sure was her way of dealing with it. I can't blame her for that. But it was Ian and I who had to live with the worst of it, here in this house. That was when we became so close, I suppose . . ."

"You didn't . . . You never found anyone else?"

Helena drew back and looked at her, a smile of faux-astonishment on her face. "It would never have occurred to me. Not once."

They fell silent. It was very quiet here. The occasional passing car, the occasional snippet of birdsong. Quiet, Sophie thought, but somehow not restful.

"It was Graham who planted this garden," Helena continued at last. "This bed here, the closest one, is the rose bed. You must come here in a few months, in July. There will be such a display! We have many varieties, but my favourite, the loveliest of all, is a Damask rose, called York and Lancaster. It is a white rose, with the most delicate hint of pink in some of the petals. *Just* the colour of your skin." She looked directly, now, into Sophie's eyes, and in the old woman's unwavering gaze, Sophie could read many things: among them a plea, so eloquent she might have been expressing it in words, that Sophie should not hurt her son in any way; and behind it, far behind it, but just as real, a threat: a threat that if she did hurt him, there would be consequences. All of this remained unspoken. The only words she spoke were: "That's what you seem to me, my dear. A lovely rose. An English rose."

And Sophie, profoundly disconcerted, could only look down into her cup, and take a careful sip of tea.

9.

As soon as the taxi had deposited them all back at the house, Coriander ran upstairs to her room. She made straight for the record player on her dressing table, forcing herself not to look either to the left or right of her, not to see the collage of pictures plastered all over the walls, and put on side two of her vinyl copy of *Back to Black*. Only then, as the defiant, heartbreaking chorus of "Tears Dry on Their Own" filled the room, did she dare to look around her, at the gallery of images which, before they went on holiday, had been a celebration of the living, but in their absence, impossibly, had become a shrine to the dead.

There were photos of her in every conceivable pose and context: sitting on a washing machine in a laundromat, strumming a Les Paul guitar; on stage in tight red shorts and black leather jacket, her heavy black eyeliner teased into that distinctive flick; standing with her husband Blake as they gazed raptly into each other's eyes, he in pork-pie hat, she in check sunfrock and red bra; a posed photo of her seated, wearing angel wings, a strand of black hair covering one eye, a beauty spot visible above her bored, pouting mouth; another photo of her on stage, wearing a cropped vest top from which her breasts spilled sexlessly, ballet pumps and big hoop earrings, her wild hair pulled into a beehive by a chiffon scarf with Blake's name embroidered on it; a terrible picture of her towards the end, anorexic, desperate, her cheekbones jutting, her eyes haunted. There was also a huge, blown-up photo of her record collection, or parts of it: LP covers scattered across the frame; albums by Count Basie and Sarah Vaughan, Dinah

Washington, Aretha Franklin, Diana Ross, Louis Armstrong, Sidney Bechet, Sammy Davis Jr. Coriander's eyes roamed hungrily over the pictures as the album played. When she heard the thin rawness of Amy's voice on "Some Unholy War" she had to bite back the tears. There were lines in that song—"just me, my dignity, and this guitar case"—which always caught her in the gut and twisted her inside out but now, in the knowledge that the singer was dead, that there would be no more songs, no more music, made the listening experience almost unbearable.

When it was over, Coriander felt that she had made the first steps in the process of regaining her own identity, after three nightmare weeks trapped in a Tuscan villa with her family. It was good to be back in her bedroom again, back in her own house. There was nothing else about this house that she liked, but she did feel at home in this room.

Coriander was fourteen years old. She lived in a house currently valued by local estate agents at a little over six million pounds, spreading over five floors, tucked away in a hard-to-find backwater between the King's Road and Chelsea Embankment. Her father, Doug Anderton, was a prominent left-leaning commentator in the national media. Her mother, the Hon. Francesca Gifford, was a former catwalk model who had found religion and become a leading light on London's charity circuit, the doyenne of fundraising auctions where the cheapest seat at a dinner table cost ten thousand pounds. Coriander hated her mother and felt alienated from her father. She felt no connection with her younger brother, Ranulph, or her older half-brother and -sister, Hugo and Siena, all of whom had been in Italy with her. She hated her private day school in Hammersmith, and hated the fact that she was being privately educated in the first place. She hated Chelsea and she hated south-west London. There were times when she felt that the only thing she loved—loved with a fierce, corrosive passion—was the voice of Amy Winehouse. And now Amy was dead. She had died just a few days into their holiday, and Coriander, until now, had been given no opportunity to mourn.

What next? She did not want to stay here, stuck inside all afternoon. She wanted to get out and see her friends and find out what she had been missing during those three monotonous weeks under the Tuscan sun. There was no need to tell her parents what she was doing. Her father had already gone to his study and was working on a piece about the riots, and her mother was in the downstairs sitting room, looking through the mail. Marisol, their Filipina housekeeper, was upstairs doing the unpacking and sorting the washing, and none of them would be looking at any of the video monitors on the security system. Within a few minutes Coriander was outside, through the garden gateway and walking down Flood Street towards the shops and the crowds. She took out her BlackBerry and, without slowing down, without looking around to see where she was going, she tapped out a quick message to her friend Grace: "See you at Starbucks in 5?" But Grace came straight back with "Soz am in Turkey"—which was news to Coriander, as she had been messaging with her only the day before (but then Grace's family often took foreign trips on a sudden whim). So she went to the coffee shop by herself and ordered a frappuccino and sat at a table for a while, messaging some of her other friends. Two of them were just up the road, shopping in Brandy Melville, and they suggested meeting for frozen yoghurt in the new place up by Sloane Square, but Coriander was bored by the idea. For some time, in fact, she had been bored to death with this part of London and the crappy social possibilities it offered. Sometimes—not so often these days, it was true—her father tried to persuade her that she was lucky to be living next to the King's Road. He would tell her stories of the bands who used to hang out here in the 1960s, the writers, beatniks and hippies who used to drink in the Chelsea Potter, the coming of punk and the opening of Malcolm McLaren and Vivienne Westwood's shop SEX at number 430. Coriander had heard these stories from Doug a hundred times and she had come to the conclusion that they meant as little to him as they did to her. He hated Chelsea too, was angry with himself for ending up living there, and repeated these consoling fables simply to rationalize his own bad choices and compromises. For his daughter, they made no difference to the fact that nowadays this was a terminally uncool place to live, a hangout for spoiled little rich girls, and hideously monocultural to boot: you might hear a few different languages being spoken, as the billionaire

Eurotrash swanned about from designer outlet to designer outlet, but there was no real diversity here, no variation in skin colour. Not like Hackney, not like Islington, not like North London. (Because that was one of the things that had made Coriander love Amy Winehouse so much. She *was* the voice of North London. Rowdy, seedy, cheap, cool, multicultural North London, home of Camden Market and Air Studios and Dingwalls Dancehall and the Hackney Empire and every other worthwhile thing that had ever come out of this over-rated, self-satisfied city.)

Sucking on her frappuccino, she flicked through a few dozen earlier messages until she found the one that had come through yesterday afternoon. Shit, if only they had been home by then, instead of dozing around the swimming pool like a bunch of zombies. It sounded like it would have been amazing. The message was from AJ, a young and handsome black boy she'd met at a club in Hackney a few weeks earlier. Not that he'd written it himself. He was forwarding it from somewhere. It said:

Everyone from all sides of London meet up at the heart of London (central) OXFORD CIRCUS!!, Bare SHOPS are gonna get smashed up so come get some (free stuff!!!) fuck the feds we will send them back with OUR riot! >:O

Dead the ends and colour war for now so if you see a brother . . . SALUT! if you see a fed . . . SHOOT!

We need more MAN than feds so Everyone run wild, all of london and others are invited! Pure terror and havoc & Free stuff . . . just smash shop windows and cart out da stuff u want! Oxford Circus!!!!! 9pm, we don't need pussyhole feds to run the streets and put our brothers in jail so tool up, its a free world so have fun running wild shopping ;)

Oxford Circus 9pm if u see a fed stopping a brother JUMP IN!!! EVERYONE JUMP IN niggers will be lurking about, all blacked out we strike at 9:15pm-9:30pm, make sure ur there see you there. REMEMBA DA LOCATION!!! OXFORD CIRCUS!!!

MUST REBROADCAST TO ALL CONTACTS!!!

"Pure terror and havoc." Coriander liked the sound of that, very much indeed.

*

She may have missed out on the Oxford Circus experience, but all was not lost. "Things are starting to kick off on Mare Street," AJ now told her via BBM. She jumped on the tube and by the time she reached Hackney and hooked up with him, about forty-five minutes later, she could see what he meant. There was a big white lorry stuck at the junction of Mare Street and another road, blocking traffic. A crowd, mainly young people, mainly black, was beginning to gather but it was a shapeless, disorganized mass of people compared to the row of police that was ranged up against it, riot shields at the ready. At the periphery of the crowd there were passers-by and spectators, circling around the edges, some of them trying to get to the shops or to get home, many of them using their phones and cameras to take videos of the building confrontation. Nothing much was happening yet, apart from isolated scuffles between the front-line policemen and a handful of guys who were stepping forward to argue with them, but the air was buzzing with the possibility of violence. To Coriander it was thrilling but at the same time she was scared and she kept close to AJ, clinging on to him and taking comfort in the muscular tautness of his upper arm through the soft texture of his hoodie.

Soon things began to get more lively. Someone forced open the doors of the lorry and discovered that it was carrying a load of wood. People started to grab the wood—planks, broomsticks, old window-frames, all sorts of stuff—and then they were passing it out through the crowd. Coriander took one and realized that what she had been handed was a makeshift weapon. Seconds later, she heard the sound of breaking glass behind her and looked round to see that a couple of men were smashing up the windows of the bus which had been parked and abandoned when the traffic came to a halt. The sound sent a rush of adrenalin through her and the next thing she knew— without stopping to think about it—she was running over to the bus as well, and starting to hammer on the bodywork with her little stick, which was about the size of a child's cricket bat. She was mortified when it barely dented the bodywork and she could hear people laughing at her.

"What the fuck do you think you're doing?" AJ said, catching up with her and grabbing her by the arm. "Do you want to get arrested or something?" When she didn't answer, he said, "Come on, let's back off. If we're going to watch this we need to find somewhere a bit safer."

They withdrew to a side street and stood on the corner with the main road, watching the scuffles and taking videos. Coriander had discreetly dropped her stick, but she noticed that someone else walking past her had strapped the blade of a Stanley knife to his.

"Fuck," she said, "look at that."

AJ said, "There's some dangerous people here."

Coriander said: "Do you know him?"

AJ said, "No. I thought some of my friends were coming but I can't see them yet. We'll be fine. Just watch yourself."

Behind them in the street, an argument was breaking out. Two Rastas were trying to get down the street back to their flat but the police weren't letting them through. The police had Alsatians on chains and the dogs were lunging at the two men. There was a chaos of noises: the shouts of the policemen telling the guys to back off, the shouts of the Rastas in protest, the incessant, deafening barking of the dogs, the scream of sirens going past in the background and the confused sounds of struggle from Mare Street, where the bulk of the crowd was now being pushed back down the road by the rows of riot police. AJ and Coriander joined the group of people watching the stand-off between the police and the Rastas. A white journalist was filming the argument on his video camera. One of the men was shouting that a dog had been set on him and had bitten him while his hands were in the air, another was shouting at a police officer that "We are all equal—tell me to move, then tell the white man to move." The dog was straining and yapping at him while he shouted, "You hit my friend with a truncheon, man, you hit him with a fucking truncheon." Finally the policemen let them through but the one who'd been bitten kept saying to anyone who would listen: "I'm not violent, right? But that's how they're dealing with us down here. They come out on our streets and tell us what to do. What do they fucking expect? Half the people round here have got a story to tell about the fucking police . . ."

And so it went on. They ducked back on to Mare Street and found that as well as the wood from the lorry, protestors had now armed themselves with bottles looted from the local Tesco. "Grab some missiles, bro, just grab some missiles!" a man shouted at them. A white guy pushed his way to the front of the crowd, stood in front of the line of police, then turned his back, bent over and mooned at them. Coriander could see the cleft of his white buttocks reflected in one of the riot shields. The crowd laughed and cheered and applauded, and the gesture seemed to embolden them to start throwing their missiles. In return, the police surged forward, pushing them further back down the street. As they began to retreat, they started to pick up rubbish bins from the pavement and either hurl them back at the police or set them on fire. Coriander found herself being pushed and jostled, squashed between strangers, staggering, almost tripping and falling. Soon they were in another street and this one contained a designer outlet called Carhartt and its alarm system was blaring madly and people seemed to be running into it and running out again with whatever they could grab—Battle Parkas and bomber jackets and pullovers and trench coats. Coriander ran in with the others and in a frenzy, without thinking about it, she grabbed two Newton vest liners in rover green, but when she got out into the street again AJ was waiting for her and he just said, "Put those back," so she went back inside and chucked them on the floor and then ran back out to follow him.

They ran past a Mazda MX5 which had been set on fire. There was an amazing energy in the air and what Coriander could taste at the back of her throat was not the smoke from the burning car but the sharp, invigorating taste of anger. The rioters were angry at the killing of Mark Duggan four days before and the years of unfair treatment from the police, and the police were angry at the lawlessness of the protest and the violence they were being threatened with. Years of anger, years of bitter, rancorous, resentful co-existence were rising up and coming to the boil. It was fantastic. "It's not about the protesting side of it," AJ's friend Jackson would tell her later as they recovered in London Fields, drinking Strongbow and smoking weed. "It's about showing the five O that they can't run around taking the piss out of the young man and get away with it. So we're going to smash up the area and let them know the next time they do that kind of shit this is what's going to happen. Fuck 2012 and the Olympic Games. If this is what it boils down to then we'll fuck that up too. You can't go around hunting the young man like that. I walk down the street, all the police tell them how they've got drugs on them, this that and the other. We are going to search you. If we don't search you now we're going to take you down to the station and strip-search you. They take the piss. So this is what's going to happen and I'm glad it's happened. I'm not glad for the youth that got killed. But the police have to get what is coming to them because they take the piss. Liberties."

*

It was after ten o'clock that night when Coriander came home. Her mother was already in bed and her brother was playing some game on his Xbox but she felt like talking to someone so she went to find her dad. Doug was at his desk, still working on his article.

"Hey, Dad," she said.

"Hey there," he said, leaning back in his swivel chair, putting his hands behind his head and stretching.

"What are you writing about?"

"I'm trying to do a think piece about the riots. It's not really working."

"Why not?"

"I suppose I don't really know what I think."

"Can I have a read?"

"Sure."

He went to make himself a coffee while Coriander sat at his desk and scrolled through the piece. When he came back, mug in hand, he asked:

"So, what do you think?"

"It's fine," she said.

"Fine?"

"It's just . . ." She tossed out the words with the carelessness that only a fourteen-year-old girl could muster. "Well, I suppose it's just the sort of piece you'd expect, from someone who lives the life you do."

"What do you mean?" he said, horrified.

Coriander was already on her way out of the room. She paused in the doorway just long enough to say: "You need to get out more."

Shit, he thought: even my daughter can see it. He stood there for a few seconds, absorbing the hammer blow, while Coriander started climbing the two flights of stairs up to her bedroom. Then he called after her, "Where have you been all day, anyway?" but there was no answer. Soon "Some Unholy War" was pounding out of her speakers again, at top volume.

10.

The riots continued for several more days, and spread to other cities, including Birmingham.

On Wednesday afternoon, with reports of a massive police presence on the streets, crowds of rioters in the city centre and random, more isolated groups of looters at loose on the outskirts, Ian was advised to cut short his afternoon class and send everyone home.

Leaving the building on Colmore Row a few minutes later, he could immediately see that something unusual was happening. Hundreds of youths were out on the streets, many of them wearing hoodies and with their faces covered. They were matched by an equal or even greater number of police, wearing high-vis jackets and carrying riot shields. Although there were some white rioters and some black policemen, the impression of a racial confrontation was overwhelming. Ian's route back to the flat lay a few minutes to the west but, drawn by a natural curiosity, he decided to stay there for a while, to wander among the crowd in an atmosphere which at the moment seemed to be more bored and aimless than incendiary.

It was a hot August afternoon and, in the midst of all the unrest, many people were still trying to shop or simply get from one part of the city to another. Again, they were mainly young people, but there were also some elderly shoppers and some children out for the afternoon with their parents. Police with megaphones were shouting at everyone to clear the area, to make way, to get home for their own safety. Ian pushed through the static, meandering crowd and made his way down Cherry Street towards Corporation Street. Most of the policemen, he thought, looked young and nervous. He wondered whether his friend Simon Bishop was there somewhere. He and Simon had grown up together in Kernel Magna, and Simon was now a Level Two officer in the West Mercia police force's Territorial Support Group. He was based in Wolverhampton and spent a lot of his time these days working behind a desk, but Ian knew that he had volunteered for enhanced riot training a couple of years earlier and there was a good chance that he would be deployed on the street on a day like this. Every copper in the West Midlands must have been brought into central Birmingham today, if the numbers were anything to go by.

He stopped outside McDonald's and spoke briefly to a young woman who was lingering uncertainly there with her teenage daughter.

"I want to get down to New Street Station," she was saying, "but they've blocked it off."

"Come on," he said. "Let's have a word with them. They've got to let us through."

He set off downhill, down Corporation Street towards New Street, easing his way through the crowds and stopping every so often to make sure that the woman and her daughter were able to keep up with him. Most people parted to let them through but there were some groups of young men (kids, really) who were uncompromisingly hostile, refusing to budge or even closing ranks to block their way. But the closest of the closed ranks, Ian found, was the line of policemen blocking their access to New Street.

"Sorry, nobody gets past this point," said a constable, holding his riot shield up in a threatening way to stop them from passing. "You want to get to the station, you walk the long way round. It's for your own safety."

"What do you mean?" said Ian. "There's nothing happening."

"There will be soon, mate."

"Look—thank you," said the woman, taking her daughter's hand and starting to lead her in the other direction, up towards the Town Hall, where the crowds were much thinner. "We'll take our chances up this way, I think. Stay safe!"

"You too," Ian called after them.

As he raised his hand in a small gesture of farewell, a tall, muscular guy in grey hoodie and baggy trousers crashed into him, and when Ian shouted out "Oy!" in protest, he turned and seemed to be on the point of saying something in reply, but then took stock of Ian's height and build and thought better of it. As they sized each other up momentarily, Ian noticed that something was sticking out of the man's pocket. It looked to him like the handle of an oversized hammer. The guy turned and started walking back up Corporation Street and instinctively Ian followed him. He kept him in his sights as they pushed through the increasingly restive crowds. Halfway up the street, the man stopped and joined up with a group of his friends. There were five or six of them. Ian stopped about ten yards away, keeping an eye on them but trying not to make it too obvious that he was watching. They didn't seem to be up to much, just standing there chatting and laughing. From the bottom end of the street, down by the lines of policemen, he could hear chanting: some kind of anti-police slogan—he couldn't make out the words—and then there was shouting, it sounded like a scuffle was breaking out. He craned his neck in that direction to see what was going on. The atmosphere on the streets was definitely changing now, he didn't like the feel of it. The buried threat of violence was rising to the surface, and for the first time he was aware of the sound of a police helicopter circling overhead. Maybe the sensible thing to do would be to head home as quickly as possible. But just as he was thinking this, there was the sound of a loud, deadening thud and the smashing of glass. He turned back towards the sound and saw that the man he'd been following had taken out his hammer and was using it to smash the window of a sweet shop. The other men with him also had hammers or big pieces of wood, apart from one of them who had wrenched a rubbish bin away from its fixture on the pavement and was repeatedly hurling it at the window. The glass was strong and they hadn't managed to smash through it yet. Afterwards, Ian would think, Why a sweet shop? Why a sweet shop of all things?—but for now, he didn't stop to reflect. Something kicked in—not unrelated to some slow-burning anger at the way the guy had pushed passed him a few minutes earlier, maybe—and he forced his way through the circle of people who were standing and watching the mayhem—either enjoying it and cheering it on or rooted to the spot in silent horror—and he seized the guy by the arm and said something to him—something stupid like, "What the hell are you doing? This is just a sweet shop, for fuck's sake"—and that was the last thing he remembered for about two days.

*

Sophie had been in London, doing some research at the British Library, on the day Ian received his injury. He was taken to the Queen Elizabeth Hospital, where the doctors carried out rigorous tests until they were satisfied there was no cerebral damage; but he continued to suffer from concussion and was still in hospital on Saturday morning. Sophie offered to collect his mother from Kernel Magna and bring her over for an afternoon visit. She had already spoken to Helena on the phone and knew that she was very distressed by the whole episode.

She knocked on Helena's door at around two o'clock, and was surprised to find it opened by a young woman she did not recognize. She was petite and had short blonde hair and pale blue eyes.

"Sophie?" the woman said.

"Yes?"

"I'm Grete. I do the cleaning for Mrs. Coleman. Come in, she's almost ready for you."

"You work on Saturdays?" said Sophie, following her inside.

"No, not at all. But Mrs. Coleman has been very upset by what happened to her son. I was a little worried about her so I came to check on her and also to bring something to eat. I was worried that she might not be eating."

"Sophie?" a voice now called from upstairs. "Is that you?"

Sophie hurried up the stairs and found Helena, already wearing a lightweight coat, searching her own bedroom with an air of distraction.

"My glasses," she said. "I put them down here somewhere. Can you see them?"

They were on the bed, almost invisible against the dark green coverlet.

"Thank you. Is that girl still here?"

"Grete? Yes, she just let me in." Sophie helped Helena fasten the buttons of her coat. "I'm not sure you'll need this in the car, you know. It's quite warm today."

"What's she *doing* here, though?" Helena asked.

"I got the impression she just wanted to see that you were OK."

"Well, that's rather odd, don't you think?"

"Not really."

"She brought me some soup. Mushroom soup."

"I know. I can smell it. Smells lovely."

"It was full of garlic, or sauerkraut, or some such. I'm afraid I couldn't finish it. Do you think she wants . . . I mean, do you think she's expecting anything in return?"

"I wouldn't have thought so. Come on, you're good to go."

Sophie took her arm and escorted her down the stairs, then thanked Grete and watched her drive off down the village high street. After that, there was all the business of getting Helena into the car and fastening her seat belt. Sophie guessed that the drive to the hospital would take just under an hour. Could they hope to sustain a conversation for all that time? Could they avoid contentious subjects? Having discussed, again, the circumstance of Grete's visit—which Helena seemed to regard almost as an impertinence—they fell into a silence which Sophie struggled to break by chatting randomly about the weather, the traffic, holiday plans, anything that was safe and neutral. But it now appeared that Helena's mind had started to dwell, inexorably, on images she had seen on the television and in the newspapers over the last week, and on the injuries sustained by her son.

"Where will it *end*, Sophie? Where will all this dreadful business end?"

Of course, Sophie knew what she meant by "this dreadful business." But it was the middle of a quiet Saturday afternoon in August. They were driving along the A435, not far from the Wythall roundabout, and the sun shone placidly on the roofs of cars, the traffic signs, the petrol stations, the hedgerows, the pubs, the garden centres, the convenience stores, all the familiar landmarks of modern England. It was hard, at that moment, to see the world as a dreadful place. (Or a very inspiring one, for that matter.) She was about to formulate some bland response—"Oh, you know, life goes on," "These things blow over after a while"—when Helena added:

"He was quite right, you know. 'Rivers of blood'. He was the only one brave enough to say it."

Sophie froze when she heard these words, and the platitudes died on her lips. The silence that opened up between her and Helena was fathomless now. Here it was, after all. The subject that wouldn't, couldn't, be discussed. The subject that divided people more than any other, mortified people more than any other, because to bring it up was to strip off your own clothes and to tear off the other person's clothes and to be forced to stare at each other naked, unprotected, with no way of averting your eyes. Any reply she made to Helena at this moment—any reply that tried to give an honest sense of her own, differing views—would immediately mean confronting the unspeakable truth: that Sophie (and everyone like her) and Helena (and everyone like her) might be living cheek-by-jowl in the same country, but they also lived in different universes, and these universes were separated by a wall, infinitely high, impermeable, a wall built out of fear and suspicion and even—perhaps—a little bit of those most English of all qualities, shame and embarrassment. Impossible to deal with any of this. The only practical thing was to ignore it (but for how long *was* that practical, in fact?) and to double down, for now, on the desperate, unconsoling fiction that all of this was just a minor difference of opinion, like not quite seeing eye-to-eye over a neighbour's choice of colour scheme or the merits of a particular TV show.

And so they drove on without speaking, for ten minutes or more, until they reached King's Heath and were driving alongside Highbury Park and Sophie said, "The leaves are turning already," and Helena answered, "I know. So pretty, but it seems to happen earlier every year, doesn't it?"

*

The new Queen Elizabeth Hospital, one of Birmingham's proudest and most recent glories, had been open for little more than a year at this time. Its three nine-storey towers, glitteringly modern in white aluminium and glass, dominated the skyline as you drove out of Selly Oak towards Edgbaston. Inside, the enormous atrium with its glass ceiling induced a sense of calm and admiration and even gentle optimism, so that for once the experience of entering a hospital did not result in an immediate lowering of the spirits. It was such a pleasant space that Sophie could imagine coming here just to visit the café, maybe to read a book and do some work. In fact, even today several people seemed to be doing just that. She recognized one of her colleagues from the humanities department, deep in some volume by Marina Warner.

She and Helena took the lift up to a ward on the fourth floor, where they found Ian sitting up in bed in his pyjamas. His head was still bandaged but he seemed cheerful enough, drinking a cup of tea and talking to his friend Simon Bishop. Simon rose to his feet when he saw them, and kissed them both on the cheek. He had already met Sophie twice over dinner, and made no secret of the fact that he thought Ian had made a spectacular catch.

"I was just going, Mrs. C," he now said, to Helena. "I don't want to be in your way."

"Don't be silly, Simon. It's always lovely to see you. What a week you must have had!"

"It's been tough, I wouldn't argue with that. And the worst thing is that we failed."

"Failed? How did you fail?"

"Three deaths. Three members of the public. We failed to protect them."

Simon was referring to the three young men—Abdul Musavir, Shahzad Ali and Haroon Jahan—who had been mown down by a car while trying to protect a row of shops on the Dudley Road in Winson Green on Wednesday night. It had been the single most deadly incident anywhere in the country, during the whole six days' rioting.

"That was very sad, especially for their families," said Helena. "But they put themselves in harm's way, after all . . ."

"Not really, with respect," said Simon. "No one could have anticipated an attack like that, out of the blue. To be honest, what your idiot son here did was far more reckless."

Ian smiled weakly. He reached his hand out to Sophie and she enfolded it in a tight clasp with both her own.

"Yes, I plan to have a word with him about that," said Helena, "when he's feeling better." It was an ominous statement, like so many of hers.

Towards the end of the visit, Simon said: "Tell you what, Helena: let's leave the lovebirds together for a while. Come on, I'll buy you a cup of tea."

Taking her by the arm, he led her out of the ward and towards the lifts. She turned and blew her son a reproachful kiss before passing through the doorway.

"So," said Sophie, turning to Ian and feeling the immediate sense of relaxation that always (she had already noticed) came over her when she was no longer in Helena's presence, "how's the local hero really feeling today?"

"Great," he answered. "And how are *you* feeling? How was the drive over?"

"Oh, we got through it," Sophie answered. "It was fine, actually. I mean, she started quoting Enoch Powell at one point, but we . . . got past that. So you'll be coming home soon? In a day or two?"

"Sounds like it."

"Do you feel ready?"

"Sure. They just say not to do anything too exciting for a while, or anything that involves physical exertion."

"Oh," said Sophie, smiling and looking crestfallen at the same time. "That's a shame. I was hoping we could do something that was exciting *and* involved physical exertion."

Stealthily she moved her hand across the blanket towards Ian's crotch area. She gave a squeeze and felt a stirring underneath. Ian squirmed beneath the bedclothes, in a kind of blissful frustration.

"You behaved like a total prat on Wednesday," she now told him. "And I've never fancied you as much as I have since then."

It was true. She knew for a fact that not one of her other friends, academic colleagues or former boyfriends would have acted as Ian had done in those circumstances. It had been an entirely foolish, dangerous, counter-productive thing to do, and she had never felt more proud, or more strongly attracted to him.

"Listen, when you've finished tormenting me," he said, blushing and glancing quickly around at the other occupants of the ward, "there were a couple of things I wanted to ask you."

"Yes?" said Sophie, not moving her hand an inch.

"When you . . . when you take Mum back tonight, do you think you could take the bins out for her? They're not collected till Monday but she can't really do it herself."

"OK."

"And can you check the cables at the back of her TV? Something's up with the sound, apparently."

"She mentioned that, yes. Sure. Anything else?"

"Erm . . . yeah." He took her hand, moved it away from the affected area, and gave it a fervent squeeze. "There was one other thing." He looked directly into her eyes. "Will you marry me, please?"

Everything seemed to go silent. The world seemed to stop turning. And this delusion—if that's what it was—seemed to go on for ever.

Finally Sophie laughed and said: "You're joking, right?"

At which Ian laughed and said: "Yes."

She was not relieved, exactly: but at least she could breathe normally again. Or could at first, until he added: "Of course I'm joking. The bins aren't collected till Tuesday."

The silence returned; longer and more profound than ever. Until he repeated the question:

"Well? Will you?"

And the thing that most surprised her, when she looked back, was how easily the answer had come to her.

11.

When Doug met Nigel Ives at the café next to Temple tube station on 19 August, one week after the riots had ended, Nigel was looking his usual cheerful self.

"Good morning, Douglas," he said. "I took the liberty of ordering a cappuccino for you."

"Thanks," said Doug, stirring in some extra sugar. "Now let's cut to the chase. What exactly is going on in this country?"

Nigel's eyes were wide with innocent confusion. "To be honest with you, Douglas, if these little conversations are going to be productive, your questions are going to have to be a bit clearer than that. You see, that could really mean anything. If you're talking about the slowdown in high-street sales, then, yes, the chancellor will admit that's slightly disappointing—"

"I'm not talking about the slowdown in high-street sales."

"OK—well, if you're talking about the phone-hacking scandal, then the home secretary would be the first to admit that the revelations so far have been disturbing, and that's why there's a robust ongoing investigation—"

"I'm not talking about the phone-hacking scandal."

Nigel shrugged his shoulders. "Well, in that case I've no idea what you could be referring to." He sipped his coffee and then, with foam still clinging to his upper lip, said: "Unless you mean the riots, of course."

Doug smiled. "There we are. You got there in the end. Of course I mean the riots."

Nigel seemed puzzled. "Well, we can talk about those, if you like, but you do realize that they finished more than a week ago? I thought you'd want to talk about slightly more topical things than that."

"I think this will be the most important story for quite some time to come," said Doug.

"Really?" Nigel seemed astonished. "You really think it's that important?"

"Let me spell it out for you," Doug said. "Civil unrest on an unprecedented scale. Not just in London but all over the country—Manchester, Birmingham, Leicester. Incredible damage to property. A situation which looked, for a while, as though it was going to get completely out of control. Hundreds of people injured and already five fatalities. Could it *be* any worse?"

"I know you media people always like to paint a gloomy picture. Always talking Britain down."

"For God's sake, even your boss decided to cut his holiday short and fly home to address parliament."

Nigel pursed his lips solemnly. It seemed to be this final argument that weighed most heavily with him.

"All right, Douglas. You're right. It was a pretty desperate situation. But it was precisely Dave's decisive action that means the whole thing can be put behind us now."

"Put behind us? What happened last week revealed an incredible fault line running right through British society. How can we just put it behind us?"

"Let's get one thing straight, Douglas. These events had nothing to do with political protest. They were criminal, not political. In the Commons, Dave was quite clear on that point."

"He may have been clear, but that doesn't make it true."

"That may be an important distinction to you, Douglas. But you're a writer. You put more value on words than most people do. Dave spoke to parliament in plain, simple language, and what he said struck a chord with people up and down the country. That's what real leadership looks like."

"So the coalition is not going to take any political lessons from these events at all?"

"Of course they are. We need more police on the streets."

"That can't be the whole solution, surely?"

"And they need better equipment. Helmets, riot shields . . ."

"What about some more long-term thinking?"

"Water cannons, perhaps. Pepper spray."

"I was thinking of a more radical approach."

"Tear gas, tasers . . ."

"But what about tackling things at the root?"

"Are you suggesting we give the police guns, Douglas? Armed police, on the streets of our cities? Really, I'm surprised at you. I didn't know you had such an authoritarian streak. But all options have to be kept on the table. We'll bear it in mind."

Doug sat back in his chair and regarded Nigel thoughtfully. He had many years' experience of dealing with politicians and their spokespeople, but he'd never encountered anyone quite like this.

"But Nigel, these weren't just people randomly and spontaneously running into shops and stealing stuff. Yes, there was a bit of that, especially towards the end. But look how it started. The police shot a black man dead and then refused to communicate with his family about it. A crowd gathered outside the station to protest and the mood turned angry. This was about race, and about power relationships within the community. It was about people feeling victimized. Not listened to."

"Those are all very good points, Douglas. Excellent points."

"What's more, there's a pattern behind the shops that people targeted. Most of them weren't local businesses. In fact, sometimes, when people tried attacking the smaller shops, they were stopped by the other rioters. Of course, this was criminal behaviour and nobody's condoning that, but it also tells us something about ourselves, as a society. People went for these big, powerful businesses, the chain stores, the global brands, because they see them as being part of the same power structures which hold them back and keep them in place."

Nigel shook his head in admiration. "This is deep thinking, Doug. Important thinking. Of course, Dave is going to commission a major report. I think you should help with the writing of it."

"Hey, I'm not a sociologist. I don't have any answers. I don't have a clue where the solution lies, really."

"Well, that puts you on exactly the same page as Dave and Nick, because they don't have a clue either."

Doug smiled. "Banter not helping out, this time, then?"

"*Banter?*" The word seemed to flummox Nigel completely. "Banter? What on earth are you talking about?"

"I thought that was the glue holding the coalition together. The thing that helped Dave and Nick to get along, despite their differences."

Nigel's tone was grave and recriminatory as he said, "I hope I'm not speaking out of turn, Douglas, but really, I think you should get serious about this. We've been discussing a situation that could have very profound implications and consequences. Don't forget that London has to host the Olympic Games next year, for one thing. Nothing like this can be allowed to happen in 2012. The best minds in the country have got to come together and make sure these terrible events never repeat themselves. I don't think this is the time to start talking about banter. To be honest, I'm surprised at you. I thought you were a more serious person than that."

Duly chastened, Doug finished the last of his coffee and both men rose to their feet. Outside the café, at the entrance to the tube station, they shook hands.

"Well, thank you, Nigel," Doug said. "It's been an education, as always."

"No problem. My father sends his regards, by the way. He hopes that your piles have cleared up. A problem like that can turn very nasty if it isn't treated properly."

12.

Eight months later, on 7 April 2012, at the approach to Chiswick Pier on the River Thames, the Oxford–Cambridge boat race had to be temporarily halted when a man was spotted in the water swimming ahead of the boats. He was later identified as Trenton Oldfield, an Australian national and graduate of the London School of Economics who claimed that he had disrupted the race as "a protest against inequalities in British society, government cuts, reductions in civil liberties and a culture of elitism." The race was restarted half an hour later, and the Cambridge crew won by four and a quarter lengths.

On the same afternoon, some one hundred miles away in the unremarkable village church of Kernel Magna, the wedding of Sophie Potter and Ian Coleman took place in a simple traditional ceremony.

The bride wore a stunning A-line dress in white organza, with a Queen Anne neckline and a chapel-length train. The groom looked handsome and imposing in full morning suit. Sitting on the left-hand side of the aisle, among the bride's friends and family, Sohan could not help thinking that they made an impressive couple, but at the same time he was surprised and unsettled. Sophie had always said that she would never wear white at her wedding. For that matter, she had always said that she would never get married in church. For that matter, she had always said that she would never get married at all.

Something to ask her about at the reception, perhaps.

"I give you this ring, as a sign of our marriage," said the groom, in a measured, confident tone. "With my body I honour you, all that I am I give to you."

"All that I have I share with you," said the bride, in a solemn, fragile voice, "within the love of God, Father, Son and Holy Spirit."

You bloody hypocrite, Potter, Sohan thought. You don't believe in God any more than I do.

Something else to say to her at the reception. But he knew what she would say back: "You're just jealous because you can't get married." Which at the moment was true, although David Cameron was rumoured to be doing something about it. New legislation was on the cards, apparently. Which couldn't come soon enough, as far as Sohan was concerned. He wanted the right to be a hypocrite in front of all his family and friends as well.

*

After the service, the guests were driven in convoy to a country house hotel about twenty minutes away; a picturesque, expansive mansion built of yellow Cotswold stone, with gardens that stretched down to the banks of the River Avon. A marquee had been set up in the grounds and it was here, Sohan realized, that they were expected to spend the next five or six hours. He was at table number three; not quite the top table, obviously, but at least he wasn't banished to the furthest reaches. His closest neighbour had already taken her seat: a striking-looking Asian woman with grey streaks in her long black hair, and a permanent air of suppressed amusement in her mouth and her eyes.

"Hello," she said, as he sat down. "Naheed. Friend of the groom."

"Sohan," he answered. "Friend of the bride." He looked around at the other guests who were starting to drift into the marquee. "Considerate of them," he said.

"Sitting the only two brown people next to each other?" she guessed, correctly.

"Yep. Are you drinking?"

"For once, yes."

"Me too. Here, let me fill you up."

They clinked glasses and sipped the indifferent Sauvignon gratefully.

"Known Sophie long?" she asked.

"About five years. You and Ian?"

"About the same."

"We met at university. Bristol."

"Ian's a work colleague. But also a friend."

"He seems . . . nice."

"He is nice. And even nicer, in the last year. She appears to have made him very happy."

"You think they're a good match?"

"Pretty good. Don't you?"

Sohan took another sip, by way of reserving judgement. He watched as Benjamin came into the marquee, with the shuffling Colin on his arm, and made his way to the top table.

"Do you know those two?" he asked Naheed. She shook her head. "I'm wondering if that's Sophie's uncle, the one she's always talking about."

"I've no idea. But the elderly lady they're sitting next to is Mrs. Coleman, Ian's mother."

"She looks quite the matriarch."

"A force to be reckoned with, definitely. And next to them is the maid of honour. Joanna, I think she's called. Do you know her?"

"Barely. I don't even think Sophie knows her that well. She doesn't have many close women friends. It should have been me, really."

Naheed laughed. "You?"

"Sure, why not? I'm her best friend."

"You could hardly be the maid of honour."

"Well, whatever the male equivalent is. Butler of honour, or something. I don't understand these stupid traditions."

"Me neither. Here, have another drink. I've got a feeling it's going to be a long evening."

*

It was two hours later, when the food had been eaten and the speeches were over, that Sophie had the chance to talk to them. She was on her way back from the toilet when they caught her attention and, pulling up a chair, she sat down between them and put her arms around Sohan and kissed him tipsily on the cheek.

"Hello, gorgeous," she said. "Are you having a nice time?"

"Very nice, thank you, darling," he said. "The food was wonderful and so were the speeches. Especially the best man's."

"That's Simon. He's Ian's oldest friend."

"Well, I loved his joke about the Chinese waiter who couldn't pronounce the letter 'r' and kept saying 'l' instead. I always find a little light racism spices up the palate after a heavy meal."

"Now now . . ." Sophie admonished.

"Better still—" he clasped Naheed's hand and gave it a squeeze "—I've made a new best friend. Now I know everything there is to know about the Highway Code, which is very useful, and she knows everything there is to know about the use of the stream of consciousness in the works of Dorothy Richardson, which is perhaps less useful but just as interesting."

"Hello," said Sophie, turning to Naheed. She hadn't seen her for a few months: not since she and her husband had come round to their flat for dinner, some time before Christmas. "I can't believe I haven't spoken to you yet. I mean, you're the one person here who . . . none of this would be happening without." Her grammar was shot to pieces this evening, she realized, either because of alcohol or emotion or both.

Naheed smiled. "Come on, don't exaggerate. Your parents might take issue with that, for one thing."

"True."

"And besides, I think Baron Brainbox should take some credit." Her eyes shone with amusement as she explained: "Never heard of him? Well, you should, because he changed the course of your life. He's a children's entertainer—very much in demand in our part of the world, for children's parties especially. But he always performs for much longer than he's supposed to. And I don't normally go to Starbucks after work, but my daughter was at a party in town that afternoon, and I was supposed to be picking her up, but then I got a phone call from the girl's mother saying that the party was still going on. So I had a bit of time to kill. And if I hadn't, then . . . well, history would have been different. So—here's to Baron Brainbox."

She and Sohan raised their glasses and drank the toast, laughing. But Sophie looked more serious.

"Shit. That's a disturbing thought. And you can go further back than that. What if that speed camera hadn't caught me on the road to Solihull?"

"Ah yes," said Sohan, *The Road to Solihull*. One of the less successful road movies."

"No, you're quite right," said Naheed. "Or what if you'd taken a different route altogether? You know, this is what fascinates me about driving. Every few minutes you come to a different junction, and you have to make a choice. And every choice you make has the potential to alter your life. Sometimes radically." Looking directly at Sohan, she continued: "I know you professors think that you have all the answers and understand the mysteries of life better than the rest of us. But if you want to study the human race in all its diversity and complexity, study the way it drives. We driving instructors are the real experts in human nature. We're the true philosophers." To Sophie, she added: "That applies to Ian as well. Remember that. And now, if I may, I'm going to give you a little kiss." She leaned forward and planted her mouth tenderly, feelingly, on Sophie's cheek. "You deserve all the happiness in the world, both of you. I hope you find it."

Sophie was lost in her reflections on this exchange, and this gesture, as she made her way back to the top table. When she got there, she found that her grandfather and Ian's mother were becoming quite intimate. He was plying her with dessert wine while she was showing him photographs of her late husband, although it was true that he didn't seem to be paying much attention to these. She was telling him of Graham's twenty-five years' loyal service to the BBC, of his reverence for the Corporation and all it stood for.

"*Used* to stand for, I should say . . ."

That was not the first time, Sophie thought, that she'd heard her mother-in-law (Jesus Christ, that's what she was now!) talking in this way about the BBC. What on earth was she on about?

Colin, at least, seemed to understand.

"I know, it's all been taken over by the political correctness brigade now, hasn't it?"

She decided this would be a good moment to step in.

"Grandad, can I have a word with you a minute?"

"Not now, love. Helena and I are just in the middle of something."

"I'm sure she doesn't want to hear—"

"More wine, Helena?" he said, filling her glass to the brim and beyond, so that some of it spilled over on to the tablecloth.

Sophie hurried to where Lois was sitting.

"Can you please do something about your father?" she said. "He's pissed and he's coming on to Ian's mother."

"Right." Lois rose to her feet and walked quickly around the table towards Colin's seat, her expression sharp and resolute.

"Does your room have a view of the river?" she could hear him saying. "Mine has a lovely view of the river. I was just thinking that if you wanted to see it, you could pop in for five minutes, we could open a bottle of wine from the minibar . . ."

"Dad!" said Lois.

"What?" He turned round. "Not you as well."

"What the hell do you think you're doing?" she whispered.

"Leave me alone. I know perfectly well what I'm doing."

"I think we all do."

"Leave me alone, I said. Where's the harm in it? Your mother's been dead two years now. I've got needs, like everyone else."

"Tonight," hissed Lois, "is not about you and your needs."

"Leave me alone," he repeated. "I reckon I'm on to a sure thing here."

He turned his back on her and resumed his conversation with Helena, who seemed far more anxious to show him more pictures of Graham than to discuss her room and whether it had a river view or not. Thwarted, Lois looked around for her brother; but, as usual, he was nowhere to be seen. Why was Benjamin *never* there when you needed him?

*

Benjamin wondered whether he was developing an addiction to staring at rivers. There was an almost full moon tonight and the patterns of light it set dancing across the surface of the Avon were captivating. The sun had set half an hour earlier, and although it was chilly out here by the water, with a breeze that sent ripples across the river and a rustle through the branches of the willow trees, he felt no inclination to move from the bench which someone had thoughtfully placed on the riverbank. He was a shy person and smalltalk exhausted him. It was one thing chatting to members of his own family, but spending three or four hours making polite conversation with strangers . . . And besides, there was something about this whole occasion that made him uneasy. It was only the second time that he'd met Ian, and while he seemed pleasant enough, Benjamin was not convinced he was the right person for his niece to be marrying. What did they have in common, really?

As these troubled thoughts ebbed and flowed in his head, and the river stirred restlessly beneath the strengthening breeze, Benjamin became aware that he was not alone. Ian's older sister, Lucy, was standing next to the bench, arms folded, shivering slightly.

"Mind if I join you?"

"No, not at all."

He moved over. She sat beside him, and took out an electronic cigarette.

"All right if I . . .?"

"Of course."

"Horrible things. But at least they don't give you cancer."

For a while she puffed away on the cigarette and neither of them spoke. Music started up from the marquee: some maudlin power ballad from the 1980s, drifting over through the night air and suggesting that the dancing had begun.

Finally Lucy said: "You're close to Sophie, aren't you? She talks about you. Tells everyone you're the intellectual of the family."

Benjamin smiled. "The one who's never amounted to anything, you mean."

"That's not how she puts it." Now Lucy chose her words carefully, one at a time. "My brother," she said, "doesn't really understand the life of the mind."

"Then perhaps he and Sophie will complement each other," said Benjamin.

"Opposites attract, you mean?"

"Something like that."

"Let's hope so." Then she added, in an apologetic way: "Weddings freak me out, I'm afraid. Bring out the old cynic in me. Probably because I've had three of my own already." She inhaled and blew out a line of steam. "All those hopes. All those promises. Love, honour, comfort, protect, forsaking all others—that's some pretty heavy shit right there." The song playing in the marquee was instantly recognizable now (to her, at any rate): "'The Power of Love,'" she said, smiling coldly. "Do you believe in it?"

Benjamin, for whom this conversation was getting more and more uncomfortable, found this an impossible question to answer. "It's powerful all right," he managed at last. "But not always in a good way." Then he stood up. "I think I'd better get back inside. Are you coming?"

"Not just yet."

"OK," he said, and left her sitting alone on the bench while he retraced his steps slowly, pensively, back to the marquee and the lights and the music.

For a while he stood on the edge of the dance floor and watched. There were about twelve couples dancing, or at least leaning up against each other for support while they shuffled around in circles. Sophie and Ian were not currently among them. Then Sophie came up behind him and tapped him on the shoulder.

"Come on, Uncle, give me a dance!"

It was the moment he'd been dreading. He had no sense of rhythm—not one that he knew how to express physically, at any rate—and he had a principled objection to dancing to music that he didn't like, which was most music. (The music that he did like, nobody could possibly dance to.) But he couldn't deny his niece anything tonight. And he reckoned that even he would not be noticeably outclassed in the present company. So he took Sophie's hand, and allowed himself to be led to the centre of the dance floor, and then he put his arm around her, a bit tentatively, a bit stiffly at first, but then she relaxed, and he relaxed, and she smiled up at him, and she looked so dreamy, and so blissful, that he smiled just as warmly back at her, and after that it was the easiest thing in the world to move around between the other dancing couples, finding the rhythm of the music, leaning into it; and then it dawned on Benjamin that these present moments with Sophie, who he'd known since she was a baby, who had been (in many ways) like a daughter to him, were also their final moments together, that after tonight everything would be different—maybe better, maybe worse, but irrevocably different—and he knew that he wanted to savour them for as long as possible, so even when the first record ended, they didn't leave the dance floor, and soon they were dancing to a second record, and then a third. And it was halfway through the third song that Ian approached them, and taking Benjamin gently by the arm, he separated him from Sophie, and said, "Excuse me, do you mind if I have my wife back?" And Benjamin said, "Of course," and backed away, and then he went to find the bar, knowing only one thing for certain now: that he needed another drink.

13.

Benjamin was amazed to realize that he had been living at the mill house for two and a half years. Where had the time gone? Apart from driving over to visit his father in Rednal two or three times a week, he could not see that he'd done anything very constructive in those thirty months. Carrying out odd pieces of repair work on the house, driving into Shrewsbury to buy food, cooking himself ever more elaborate delicacies . . . None of it added up to a life well spent, he was forced to admit. Perhaps the loss of Cicely had been a harder blow than he'd thought, and he'd been living in a state of emotional shock since then. Or perhaps, at the age of fifty-two, he was getting prematurely complacent and lazy.

In all that time, he had not even thought much about his novel. Or his novel sequence, his *roman fleuve*, whatever the damn thing was supposed to be called. *Unrest*, the project on which he'd been working ever since he was a student at Oxford University in the late 1970s, now extended to some one and a half million words, or somewhat longer than the complete works of Jane Austen and E. M. Forster put together. Supposedly combining a vast narrative of European history since Britain's accession to the Common Market in 1973 with a scrupulous account of his own interior life during that period, it was further complicated by the fact that it also had a musical "soundtrack," composed by Benjamin himself, whose precise relationship to the text he had never quite been able to decide. Shapeless, sprawling, prolix, over-ambitious, misconceived, unpublishable, in parts unreadable and by and large unlistenable, the whole thing had started to lower over Benjamin like an oppressive cloud. He couldn't bring himself to abandon it, but he had lost all sense of whether it possessed the slightest merit. What he needed was some objective advice.

He turned to Philip first of all, as so often. He was a reliable friend in any kind of crisis, and these days, better still, he made his living by editing difficult manuscripts and knocking them into shape. But when Philip received the files by email, and realized the scale of the job he was being asked to undertake, panic took hold of him, and he phoned Benjamin with a different suggestion:

"Come to The Victoria in John Bright Street on Monday night," he said. "We'll have a proper committee meeting about it."

"Wait—there's a committee?" Benjamin asked.

"Don't worry. I'm putting one together."

The Victoria, which Benjamin had never visited before, turned out to be a sepulchral Victorian pub tucked away in a hard-to-find corner beside the Suffolk Street Queensway in central Birmingham. It was Monday, 4 June, and in honour of the Queen's diamond jubilee, which the nation had been celebrating over a long weekend, there had been four days of torrential rain up and down the country. When Benjamin arrived, lugging a print-out of his *chef-d'œuvre* in two substantial hold-alls, the downpour had finally stopped but the streets still glistened with fresh rainwater and reflected lamplight. Inside the pub he found himself confronted not just by Philip but by two other faces from the past.

First of all there was Steve Richards, another of his old friends from King William's School. Steve had been the only black boy in their year, and had suffered the ensuing barrage of racial taunts and jokes with unflagging dignity and resignation. These days he was doing well: his daughters had grown up and left home, and after many years in the industrial sector he was now pursuing his lifelong research interests as director of something called the Centre for Sustainable Polymers at one of the Midlands' leading universities. He carried an air of quiet contentment, besides looking younger than Benjamin and considerably healthier.

Sitting next to Steve was a figure Benjamin couldn't identify at first. In his mid-sixties, perhaps, with a goatee beard and shoulder-length grey hair, he did look vaguely familiar, but after a few moments' uncertainty it became clear that he would have to introduce himself by name:

"Benjamin? It's Tom. Tom Serkis. Don't tell me you don't remember."

Mr. Serkis . . . Yes! Their English teacher in the sixth form. The man whose great contribution to King William's history was the setting up of a school magazine called *The Bill Board*, where Benjamin, Philip, Doug and others had all cut their journalistic teeth. Benjamin hadn't clapped eyes on him for thirty years or more. And now that he looked closely, apart from general symptoms of the ageing process, nothing about him had changed, nothing at all: same haircut, same ragged tweed jacket; even his jeans were flared, 1970s-style.

"Well," Mr. Serkis said, "I guess it's not so surprising that you didn't recognize me. Had a bit of an image makeover since then. See?"

He indicated his left earlobe, which was pierced and sported a small golden earring.

"Ah—yes," Benjamin nodded, rather bewildered. "That must be it. Makes all the difference. Well, what are you up to these days?"

"Still teaching. A nice comp in Lichfield. Bit different to King William's, but just as much fun, in a way. Different challenges. Still, I shall be retiring at the end of this term. That's it—hanging up my mortar board. Oh, but they were great days, weren't they, the 1970s? When Steve here played Othello and you wrote that shocking review. The fuss that caused! And Doug, of course, with all his political stuff. He's done well for himself, hasn't he? Are you still in touch?"

"On and off," said Benjamin. "He married one of the wealthiest, poshest women in London and they live in a mansion in Chelsea."

"Ha! I wonder what his father would have thought of that. Shop steward at Longbridge, wasn't he?"

"He was—but I can assure you Doug's fully conscious of the irony. Tortured by it, you might even say."

"But then he always had a thing for posh women," Steve reminded them. "Ever since he bunked off to London one weekend when we were still at school and lost his virginity to some Sloane on the Fulham Road."

"True," said Benjamin; and took a moment to reflect that perhaps he was not the only person, after all, to have had the course of his adult life determined by a teenage romance.

After more pleasant reminiscences along these lines, Philip called everyone to order and reminded them that they had business to conduct tonight. Meanwhile the widescreen TV at the back of the pub showed images from outside Buckingham Palace, where a concert was bringing the Queen's jubilee celebrations to an end. Shirley Bassey was singing "Diamonds are Forever" while Her Majesty looked on with good-humoured bemusement.

"Look at that bloody parasite," said Mr. Serkis, scowling up at the screen.

The three friends were shocked.

"Oh, I don't know. I think she does a good job," said Philip.

"Very good for tourism," said Benjamin.

"She came to visit the university once," said Steve. "Nice lady."

There was a brief silence as they all suddenly realized, under Mr. Serkis's disappointed gaze, how conservative and middle-aged they sounded. Embarrassed for them all, Philip quickly moved on.

"Now, Benjamin, did you bring the book?"

"I did."

Taking it out of the two hold-alls, sorting the different sections into the right order, removing all the rubber bands and so on, took some considerable time, not least because the table they were sitting at turned out not to be big enough for the mountains of paper, not to mention the stack of CDs on which the music files were stored. They moved to the next table—the biggest one in the pub, capable of seating a party of ten—where Phil, Steve and Mr. Serkis stared at the manuscript for some moments in stupefied silence.

"Shit," said Steve, "I mean, I knew it was long, but . . ."

"How did you manage it, Ben?" Mr. Serkis said. "Did you never think about just . . . stopping?"

"I can't stop," said Benjamin, simply, "until I've reached the end."

"Fair enough," said Steve.

Shirley Bassey left the stage to prolonged applause, and was replaced by Kylie Minogue.

"Now, what I did," Philip explained, "was that I asked Steve to read the personal material, and got Tom to read the political bits, and I listened to the music and tried to work out how it would all fit together."

"Sounds like a plan."

"Yes, well . . . Let's see how everyone got on. Steve, what was your first impression?"

"It's too long," said Steve, without hesitation.

"OK. Tom, what did you make of the—?"

"It's way too long," said Mr. Serkis, without even waiting for the question to be finished.

"Good," said Philip. "I can see a pattern emerging here. So that's helpful. Now, when it comes to the musical side of things, that's a bit more complicated. You see, I'm not quite sure . . ." He paused and looked at Benjamin in an apologetic way. ". . . I'm not quite sure what *function* the music performs, in the overall scheme of things. Some of it felt a little bit . . . well, redundant."

The author/composer bristled, and said: "When you say some of it . . .?"

"Well, I suppose what I really mean is . . . all of it."

"*All* the music?"

"Yes."

"Redundant?"

"Redundant is a bit harsh, I know," said Philip, "but . . . but accurate in this context, I feel."

An uneasy hush fell over the table. On the television, Kylie Minogue was belting out "Can't Get You Out of My Head" with an energy that belied her forty-four years.

Benjamin was silent for a long time, and then he blurted out:

"Yes, you're right. I know you're right! The whole idea of combining music with printed words was ridiculous from the very start. I never thought it through, I never really asked myself what I was doing, I . . ."

Without saying any more, he took the pile of CDs from the table and crammed them back into one of the hold-alls.

"There. I feel better. We've got something simpler now. It's just a book. It's just a very, very long book."

"Too long," said Steve.

"Too long," Benjamin agreed.

"One way of making it shorter," Mr. Serkis suggested, "would be to get rid of some of the political, historical stuff."

Benjamin considered this. He felt that his former teacher was not being entirely honest with him.

"When you say *some* . . ." he prompted.

"I mean all of it. I mean, it's interesting, and what have you, but . . . I didn't feel it had that essential quality, that special something . . ."

"You're talking about half the book," Philip reminded him.

"Yes. Well, we all agree that it's too long."

"OK," said Benjamin grimly, and removed sections II, IV, VI, VIII, X, XII, XIV, XVI and XVIII from the table, stuffing the reams of paper back into the bags in which he'd brought them. The table was now only half-covered with printed pages, and the book suddenly looked much more manageable.

"Right, Steve. Your thoughts."

"My thoughts. OK. Well, first off, I only had a week to do the reading, so I didn't manage to read everything. But what I read I enjoyed. There were some great descriptive passages, and . . . well, Benjamin, you're a very talented writer. But you don't need me to tell you that."

"Thanks, Steve."

"What was weird about it, though, given what a talented writer you are, and how great some of the descriptive passages were, and all that . . . What was weird, I suppose, was how . . . well, how boring it was."

The longest and most shocked silence of all succeeded this remark. Nobody knew what to say, but they were all very aware of the sound of Elton John singing "I'm Still Standing" outside Buckingham Palace.

"Boring?" said Benjamin at last, in a trembling voice. "OK. I wasn't expecting that, but if that's what you thought . . ."

"Don't get me wrong," said Steve. "I mean, there was one section I really enjoyed. The one about you and Cicely."

"Ah! Yes," said Philip. "I read that too. Now I really like that section. That was really written from the heart, I thought."

"You mean it wasn't boring?"

"The point is—well, this is the great story of your life, isn't it, Ben? The great romance. How you met her at school, how you found her, how you lost her again, how she came looking for you years later . . . And the way you tell it—it's in a different league to the rest of the book. The writing's on another level altogether."

"But that's only about two hundred pages out of the whole thing."

"True, but—you know, two hundred pages is a good length for a novel. Much better than five thousand."

The section in question was in a little pile of its own, at the corner of the table closest to Benjamin. He picked it up and flicked through the pages.

"You're saying that I should just keep this, and . . . junk the rest?"

"I reckon you could get it published. I'm sure you could."

"But it's not meant to be separate from the rest of the book. It doesn't have its own title, or anything."

"I bet we could think of a title."

"That scene," said Steve, "when she's been gone about three or four years and you buy that jazz record and you put it on and there's a tune that makes you think of her. What's it called? 'A Rose Without a Thorn'. Now that's beautiful."

"Steve's right. There's your title," said Philip.

"Yes, that's not bad . . ." The more Benjamin thought about the idea—although he was too proud to admit this—the more he liked it. Maybe it had been the effort of carrying those two big bags full of paper from the car park to the pub, but he had a strong sense, right now, of this book as a physical burden, one which had been weighing him down for thirty years but which had tonight been miraculously lifted from his shoulders. It was almost too good to be true; which was perhaps why he kept thinking of objections. "But still, no one will ever want to publish it."

"I'll publish it," said Philip.

"You?"

"Yes, me. I'm a publisher."

"I think I'd rather try a proper—I mean, a bigger publisher, first."

"Of course," said Philip. "Send it to Faber. Send it to Jonathan Cape. You'd be crazy not to. But then, if they don't want it, I'll publish it. It's about time I published something decent."

Benjamin was moved by the generosity of this offer. "Would you do that?" he said.

"Of course."

"Still, I'd rather it was a serious—I mean, one of the more established publishers."

"Sure. That goes without saying."

With the matter settled, they turned their attention to Paul McCartney, who was currently struggling his way through a rather approximate version of "Let It Be" outside the palace gates. It was only a few minutes later that Philip realized Mr. Serkis had taken little part in the final stages of the conversation.

"So, do you agree with us, Tom? Do you think Benjamin should have a crack at getting just one part of it published?"

"Well, I didn't read that bit," he reminded them.

"No, but you read a lot of the other sections."

"True," he said, ruefully.

"So on the basis of that, do you have any advice?"

"Do I have any advice for Ben, on the basis of what I read?"

"Yes."

The song came to an end, the audience applauded, Mr. Serkis furrowed his brow, chose his words with care, and turning to Benjamin said:

"Have you ever thought of taking up teaching? It's not too late, you know."

14.

Sophie was sitting outside a bar in the Vieux Port, sipping her second glass of rosé—rendered rather anaemic by the ice cubes that had quickly melted in it—when her phone rang. It was Ian. For a moment she considered not answering. Then she remembered that she'd promised to call him as soon as she arrived and she'd forgotten and now she felt guilty. So she took the call.

"Hi there," she said.

"Where are you?"

"I'm at the Vieux Port, having a glass of wine."

"You got there OK, then? You said you were going to call."

"Yeah, I'm sorry, I forgot."

"I was worried."

"Well, if there had been a bomb on the plane it would have been on the news by now."

"I know. I was tracking your flight anyway, on FlightRadar."

"Aren't you sweet to be so concerned."

"What's your room like?"

"It's your typical student room."

"What's Marseille like?"

"I don't know. All I've seen so far are the halls of residence and this bar. Which is very nice, I must say."

"I can hear music."

"Yeah, there are some guys with a beatbox rapping in the square about twenty yards away. I think it's that sort of town."

"Have you eaten yet?"

"Dinner's at nine. There didn't seem to be much going on so I thought I'd come here by myself for a drink first."

"Where are you eating?"

"Some restaurant."

A beat.

"I miss you."

"Me too," said Sophie. Because that, after all, was what you were supposed to say when your husband told you that he missed you.

*

The Quatorzième Colloque Annuel Alexandre Dumas was taking place in the third week of July at the university of Aix-Marseille. A call for papers had gone out twelve months earlier, and Sophie had submitted the chapter from her thesis about contemporary portraits of Dumas, without any expectation of it being accepted. But the organizer of the conference, François, had written back in his charmingly almost perfect English to say that "the objective of the conference this year is to be multidisciplinary as well as multi-locational," a statement which still puzzled her, in some respects. Anyway, her paper had been accepted, that was the important thing, and here she was, at her first international academic conference. What's more, it was taking place on the Mediterranean coast, where the sun never stopped shining and the average daily temperature was 33 degrees Celsius, while England, even in July, continued to suffer from downpours so torrential that the Olympic torch relay had had to be halted during the final stages of its progress from Beijing to London.

Dinner that Sunday evening was an al fresco affair at a restaurant on a steep, busy street leading up to the Cours Julien. They were a multinational and multilingual party, with French, German, Italian, Turkish, Iranian and Portuguese guests, and one American: a thoughtful, quietly spoken man from Chicago of around Sophie's age. His name was Adam, his presence there was funded by a special fellowship for African-Americans and he turned out to be a musicologist working in the field of film music.

"That's interesting," she said, happy to find herself sitting next to him towards the end of the evening, when things were getting more informal and people had started to swap places. "So what's the Dumas connection?"

"It's pretty tenuous," he admitted, "but I'm giving a paper on the different *Three Musketeers* scores. Hopefully these guys will see it as a bit of light relief."

"Sounds great. I hope there'll be plenty of clips. Which one's your favourite, by the way?"

"No spoilers," he said. "If I told you that, you'd have no reason to turn up and listen."

"Oh, I'll be there," said Sophie. "It's obviously going to be the highlight of the week."

Afterwards, she reflected that this was a vacuous thing to say, not least because it sounded sarcastic when it wasn't meant to be. But Adam didn't seem to mind, or even notice, so she didn't let it trouble her for long. Already she was high on the warm air, the good food and, most of all, the sheer relief at having left the leaden skies of England behind for a few days.

*

Sophie's paper was only the second to be delivered, late on Monday morning. The venue was the Espace Fernand Pouillon on the main university campus, right next to the railway station. She could see at once that this was going to be a tight, well-run conference. She spoke in English, with a scrolling French translation of her paper projected on to the screen behind her. She spoke for an hour on William Henry Powell's portrait of Dumas. The audience's questions afterwards were thoughtful, engaged and numerous: they spilled over into lunch, and for a while Sophie was buoyed up by a feeling of success, and by the enthusiasm of her fellow scholars.

By the middle of the next afternoon, however, she realized that she had already started to feel out of place among this gathering of Dumas experts, not to say fanatics. She remembered that there was, after all, a reason she had decided to have no more academic boyfriends: that habit of focusing obsessively on one subject and letting the rest of the world go unremarked and unnoticed. And Dumas, it turned out, gave plenty of scope for obsession: Sophie had not quite appreciated the energy and productivity of the man, the hundreds of novels, the millions of words, the "assistant authors" hired to help with the writing of books, the altogether industrial scale of production. All she had read, herself, was *The Count of Monte Cristo* and (many years ago) about half of *The Three Musketeers*. Most of the papers, naturally enough, were focused on the writing, and concerned texts that she was not familiar with, and over breakfast, lunch and dinner, the conversation tended to be Dumas, Dumas and Dumas. On Tuesday, halfway through a desperately dry presentation on the plays (which nobody seemed to read these days anyway) she decided that she would skip the rest of the afternoon and explore the city by herself.

She understood, now, what François had meant when he described it as a "multi-locational" conference. The intention, as he had explained to everyone over dinner on Sunday, was not to be confined by the Marseille campus but to make the impact of the conference felt throughout the city and indeed throughout the region. Adam's talk on film music, for instance, would take place in the Conservatoire at Aix-en-Provence, half an hour away. Thursday's keynote lecture, which was about Dumas's concept of imprisonment, would be given at the Château d'If, in the very cell where the writer had imagined the confinement of Edmond Dantès. And Tuesday's sessions were taking place at an arts centre called La Friche La Belle de Mai, housed in a former tobacco factory in the third arrondissement. Slipping out of the lecture theatre in the midst of an interminable summary of the plot of *Charles VII chez ses grands vassaux*, Sophie stood for a moment blinking in the fierce sunlight of the courtyard. Her first impulse was to phone Ian. She thought of him as her antidote to this pinched, airless academic universe, and suddenly craved even a few minutes of normal conversation with him: but there was no answer from his phone. No matter—she was on her own for the rest of afternoon, and that was fine in itself. She browsed in the bookshop for a while, went outside to watch half a dozen guys going through their paces in the skateboard park, and then visited one of the exhibition rooms, to lose herself in a series of panoramic, sharp-focus, black-and-white photos of Beirut cityscapes.

After passing a couple of hours at La Friche in this way, she took a bus back downtown, along La Canebière, and then, getting out at the Noailles Metro stop, she wandered uphill through the Marché des Capucins, strolling at random through these narrow, intersecting streets, each one filled with shops selling every kind of French and African food, the air filled with the tantalizing aroma of familiar and unfamiliar spices. The streets were crowded with shoppers, and Sophie could see that the heady mixture of cultures that gave London its modern character was to be found here in even denser, more concentrated form. She loved it. She felt that she could lose herself in this city.

*

The next morning, she had promised Adam that she would be there for his talk on film music. The organizers had chartered a coach which drove them along the motorway to Aix, and then to the Conservatoire Darius Milhaud, a handsome, restful building named after the region's most famous composer, which stood in the Rue Joseph Cabassol. Adam's paper, illustrated with music and film clips, was clever and engaging, although she heard mutterings from some of the more hardcore Dumas scholars that it wasn't sufficiently on-topic for their taste. During some of the more analytical passages, it's true, he lost her, but there was something soothing and attractive about his accent, so from time to time she drifted off and just focused on that. And she enjoyed the big, semi-serious reveal at the end, in which Adam argued that the most sophisticated and experimental music composed for any of the Dumas screen adaptations, in his opinion, was Scott Bradley's score for *The Two Mouseketeers*, a Tom and Jerry short from the 1950s.

Afterwards, bent on an early lunch, most of the delegates hurried off up the road in search of the restaurant François had booked. But

Sophie needed the toilet, and when she came out everyone had gone: everyone except Adam, who was standing in the hallway talking to one of the young teachers at the Conservatoire.

"That was great," Sophie said, breaking in on a pause in their conversation. "I really learned a lot. Thank you."

But Adam was interested in something else altogether.

"This piano," he said, indicating a rosewood grand standing in a corner of the hallway, "is actually Milhaud's piano, can you believe that?"

Sophie had at least heard of Darius Milhaud, since he was the kind of composer her uncle Benjamin was always enthusing about, but she didn't know anything about him and couldn't quite match Adam's excitement.

"Can I really play it?" he said to the teacher.

"Yes, of course. Be our guest."

He sat down on the stool and raised the lid and said: "Is it specially tuned to play in two keys at once?" The teacher laughed; Sophie didn't. "Sorry," he said. "Musicologist's joke." And then he started to play. He was improvising, it seemed: plangent, bitter-sweet chords which made Sophie think of Ravel and Debussy and late-night cocktail bars. She drifted over to the doorway while he played, looking out at the street, the yellow-stone buildings in the morning sunlight. Aix was very different to Marseille: quiet, prosperous, calming; perhaps a little complacent. Opposite the Conservatoire was a shop selling English-language books: its sign was a teapot painted like a Union Jack. Sophie wandered over and looked in the window. Adam's music still floated out from the open doorway into the street. She could hear it quite clearly. Then it stopped and she heard him thanking the teacher and saying goodbye and then he was beside her.

"Beautiful," she said, turning to him. "I was listening to it out here. You play so nicely."

"Thank you," he said, but with the shyness—or modesty—that she was beginning to realize was typical of him, he didn't know what to do with the compliment. "Nice bookshop—shall we go inside?"

Afterwards, Sophie could never quite decide what it was that gave the next few minutes such a special quality in her memory. Perhaps it was the atmosphere in the bookshop, which was so serene and other-worldly, and where they were the only customers. Perhaps it was because there were few things so intimate, to her mind, as two people browsing among books together. Perhaps it was the watchful, smiling attention of the woman behind the counter, who greeted them so politely, in such good English, and seemed to assume that they were a couple. Perhaps it was because, when she picked up a copy of *The Twilight of Otters*, by Lionel Hampshire, and said to Adam, "My God, he gets everywhere," it didn't matter that he didn't see the joke, and he laughed anyway. Perhaps it was because, when he picked up a book by an American writer whose name she'd never heard and said, "My father wrote this," it made perfect sense that he should be a writer's son. Whatever the reason, once Sophie had bought the book, and they had said goodbye to the bookshop owner, whose eyes shone knowingly at them from behind strands of chestnut hair, and they were back in the street and walking towards the restaurant, something had changed between them; some almost imperceptible shift in their centre of gravity.

*

Sophie avoided Adam for the next day and a half, and spent that time alone, discovering more of Marseille, venturing into the coastal enclaves of Malmousque and the Vallon des Auffes, and spending three or four hours in the rough-cast concrete sanctuary of La Cité Radieuse, the most famous of Le Corbusier's apartment buildings. (She had a soft spot for Brutalist architecture, and while she was excited—like everyone else—to see the new Library of Birmingham taking shape, she hoped that John Madin's Central Library, a 1970s masterpiece, would be spared the wrecker's ball.) She did not rejoin the conference again until Thursday afternoon, which was the time for their journey to the Château d'If. It was hotter than ever—thirty-six degrees—and the reflections from the sun on the waters of the Vieux Port were dazzling. The sea trip took little more than twenty minutes: they chugged slowly out of the Vieux Port at first, past the Fort Saint-Jean and the huge waterside building site where the new, ultra-modernist Museum of European and Mediterranean Civilizations was nearing completion, and then picked up speed as they made for the island of If itself, passing massive cruise ships from all over the world moored in the harbour for the day, and pleasure-seekers crossing their path in speed boats and on jet skis: for this was the height of the tourist season, and Sophie had the strange, disorientating sense of being at work (of sorts) among holidaymakers. The crossing was calm, and as the chateau came into closer view, she found that it was hard to imagine it as a strategic fortress, or—as it had been later in its life—a brutal and inescapable site of incarceration. Today, its turrets and battlements baked creamy white by the Mediterranean sun, it looked wholly benign and welcoming. A tourist attraction, and an impossibly beautiful one.

The view of the chateau as they approached it, however, had not prepared her for the views that the chateau, in turn, would offer of the city and the coastline once you had climbed the steep spiral stairs to the rooftop terrace. Sophie saw the whole of Marseille spread out before her, the jumble of ancient and modern buildings, the sprawl of apartment blocks to the west, the verdant wilderness and vertiginous cliffs of the Calanques to the east, and, watching over it all, the commanding tower of the Basilique Notre-Dame. Between the chateau and this vista stretched the ocean, rolling gently, sparkling beneath the sun, a rich, flawless ultramarine to its very depths. And all of this was bathed in *light*: yes—that, she realized, was what they were missing in England, that was the factor that made everything here seem so vivid, so sensual, so full of energy, so ineluctably *alive*. What a pinched, miserable existence they all seemed to live by comparison, back in the country she was obliged to call home. From Marseille to Birmingham, Marseille to Kernel Magna: these places didn't seem to belong to different countries, or even different planets, they seemed to belong to different orders of existence altogether. This light was making her feel alive in a way that she hadn't felt for years: perhaps since she was a child. Her colleagues on the terrace were all busy taking photographs from every different angle and every different vantage point, but Sophie knew there was nothing to be gained from this, and she kept her phone in her bag. No arrangement of pixels was going to capture the emotion of this moment, this utterly new, intense sensation of livingness.

The chateau closed to the public at five thirty: they had been granted unique and, she imagined, unprecedented access for two further hours. At six o'clock, while the tourists were gathering on the jetty for the last return boat to Marseille, they made their way to the cell on the ground floor which had been named after Edmond Dantès, Dumas's unfortunate hero. It was a deep but oddly spacious stone-flagged room, with a fine ray of sunlight streaming in from a window high up in the wall. Here the keynote speaker, Guillaume, had set up his PowerPoint presentation, and he spoke for rather more than an hour on *L'Incarcération comme métaphore de la paralysie psychologique*. Sophie enjoyed his talk and was impressed by it, but she was impatient to leave the cell and get out again: out into the evening light.

At seven thirty they were offered a choice. The boat would take them back to Marseille and to the restaurant which had been booked for them that evening; but it could also detour to the other islands in the Frioul archipelago, just a few hundred yards away across the water. If anybody wanted to disembark at the port on Ratonneau, they were free to do so, and could then take one of the public boats back to the city later in the evening.

Most people chose to return to Marseille at once; they were fired up by Guillaume's paper and couldn't wait to discuss it over dinner. Sophie, Adam and three of the others, however, were curious to visit these other islands, and so they were deposited there a few minutes later.

The islands of Ratonneau and Pomègues were linked by a long stone causeway, adjacent to the little port where they disembarked, on a quayside which was lined with shops and bars. It was for one of these bars that the others made at once, wanting nothing more than to enjoy a drink outside as the evening air finally started to cool.

"What do you think?" said Sophie. "Shall we join them?"

"I don't know . . ." said Adam. "I feel like a walk. Isn't there meant to be a beach near here somewhere?"

They consulted a map on the harbourside wall and then set off along a flat, dusty road that led away from the port and towards the

Calanque de Morgiret. Clearly they were going against the tide of visitors, because a continual stream of people—couples, family groups, noisy parties of young men—walked past them in the opposite direction, carrying towels and beach bags. Ratonneau was a rocky island, the landscape so starved of vegetation that it appeared almost lunar. Before long the dust made Sophie's throat feel dry and ticklish, and the heat was intense even this late in the day. But it only took a few minutes to walk to the little pebbly beach, where a few people were still swimming or snorkelling in the warm, turquoise water.

"Shame we didn't bring bathers," said Adam, looking out at the sea from the escarpment above the beach, and shielding his eyes against the low beams of the setting sun.

"I was just thinking that," said Sophie, although part of her was relieved: she was acutely conscious of the paleness of her own body beneath her lightweight summer dress.

They walked a little further, up a steep, winding path which led them to a stony ridge high above the beach. Even this walk was tiring, so they found a flat rock by the side of the path and sat down eagerly, thankful that, up here at least, the hint of a sea breeze made the heat more tolerable.

After a long, companionable silence, Sophie said: "I started to read your dad's book."

"Yeah?"

"Very nice. It has a bit of an Updike feel to it."

"A few people have said that. He doesn't like Updike." He smiled. "But at least he'd be pleased you weren't comparing him to James Baldwin. The truth is, my father's the kind of guy who can take any compliment and turn it into an insult. I wouldn't describe him as an easy person to be around."

"Are you close to him?"

"Haven't seen him," said Adam, "for about two or three years. He and Mom split up a while ago. Much to the relief of me and my sister. They fought all the time. It was . . . intense." Taking care not to look at Sophie directly, he said: "I'm guessing you come from a different kind of family. You seem . . . Well, you seem pretty calm about things."

"Yes, my parents don't fight, exactly. They just seem to live in a permanent state of . . . I don't know how you'd describe it. Semi-hostile indifference."

Adam laughed. "Sounds very British."

"Yes, that's exactly what it is. They keep calm and carry on, even though my mother . . ." She tailed off, not wanting to pursue this any further.

"And you?"

"Me?"

"Married life." He glanced down at her wedding ring. "How does it suit you?"

"Oh. Well, it's a bit early to say. It's only been three months . . ."

"Ah—so recently? Congratulations."

". . . But so far, it's been good. Very good. I feel very . . . grounded."

"Excellent. I'm happy for you. And him."

"Ian. His name's Ian."

"And what does he do?"

"He's a teacher."

"Of course. Art history?"

"No. He teaches people how to drive more safely. That was how I met him. In one of his classes."

"Really? I don't see you as a dangerous driver. Do you have a wild streak that you haven't been sharing with any of us?"

"No," said Sophie, more thoughtfully than the question perhaps warranted. "I don't believe that I do."

They must have sat there for half an hour or more; long enough to watch the sunset in all its leisurely glory. Behind them, on the other side of the island, the moon was rising, throwing enough light for them to follow the path easily when they began to feel hungry and set off in search of the port and its restaurants. They couldn't find the other conference guests: a *navette* had just left for Marseille, according to the timetable, and perhaps they had decided to take it. The next boat wasn't for an hour, but there was no urgency in any case: the last one left at midnight.

They found a quiet waterside bar and ordered *moules marinière* with *panisses* and *salade Niçoise* and a carafe of rosé with plenty of ice. By the time they had finished eating, it was half past ten and two more boats had left and it was beginning to feel as though they had the island almost to themselves.

"It's so peaceful here," said Sophie. "I can't believe we're only twenty minutes from the city. It's like another world."

"Do you want another drink?" Adam asked.

"No. Let's go back to the beach."

The water was calmer, now, and lay dark and welcoming, illuminated only by a path of moonlight that stretched towards the horizon. There was no one else on the beach. Neither Adam nor Sophie spoke, or suggested what they do next; it was an entirely mutual and spontaneous decision to slip out of their clothes, pick their way painfully across the stones to the water's edge and launch themselves into the sea. Spontaneous and chaste: neither of them looked at the other until they were fully submerged, although Sophie still managed to feel, somehow, a vivid sense of the contrast between their skin colours. She had never skinny-dipped before, and had no idea how delicious the still-warm water would feel against her bare skin. She was a strong swimmer—unlike Adam, it seemed, who remained crouched in the shallows, half-swimming, half-walking—so she struck out towards the mouth of the cove, into the furthest, deepest part of the inlet, thinking it wise to get as far away from him as possible. There she swam backwards and forwards, crossing from one rocky side to the other ten times or more, until, when her arms and legs began to ache, she flipped over and floated on her back for a few minutes, watching the moon and the stars, and thinking that she had never felt so happy, so at peace with herself, so at one with the elements of water and air. She closed her eyes, felt the gentle stirrings of the Mistral caressing her face, and surrendered to the embrace of the ocean; passive, trustful, unresisting.

She and Adam spoke little to each other after that, not even on the midnight *navette* back to Marseille. Their evening together lay under a spell, and they both knew that to talk would be to break it.

It was almost one o'clock when they reached the halls of residence where the conference delegates had been accommodated. Their rooms were at opposite ends of the same corridor.

Outside her door, Sophie reached up to kiss Adam on the cheek. "Well, goodnight," she said. "That was beautiful."

"It really was," he murmured, and as he said it, his mouth seemed to brush across her face until it was in contact with hers. Which was fine, Sophie thought, because after all, what was this, but a friendly goodnight kiss? His mouth was open, and hers was open, which was fine. She felt a little jolt through her body as their tongues met. But that was fine. This was just a friendly goodnight kiss. Although it did seem to be going on for a long time. And now his hand was moving, moving slowly but purposefully across her body, no longer touching her back in the lightest of hugs but now travelling up across her stomach towards her breast, her left breast, where it lingered, where she allowed it to linger, pressing herself more firmly against him so that his hand, without wanting to, was pressing more firmly against her breast, and the sensation was exquisite, it was sending waves of pleasure through her body and she wanted nothing more, at this moment, than to yield to those waves, to give in . . .

. . . but no. No no no no no. This was not all right. This was not fine. This was not a goodnight kiss any more. Abruptly she pushed him away and leaned back against the door, panting and reddening. She looked down at the floor, and he looked away down the corridor, also breathing heavily, and Sophie ran her hands through her hair and said:

"Look, this is—"

"I know. I—"

"I mean, we can't do this. I'm—"

"That's fine. I shouldn't—"

Now she looked at him, and he looked back at her, and there was sadness and anger and frustration in their eyes.

"OK."

"Yep. OK. Goodnight, then."

"Goodnight," said Sophie, and unlocked her door quickly and shut it behind her just as quickly and then stood with her back to the door for what seemed like for ever, her eyes stinging with tears as she waited for her breathing to become more regular again.

*

There was only one session on Friday morning: a plenary session, to remind people of all the papers that had been presented during the week, to take stock and draw conclusions. Adam was not there. He hadn't been at breakfast either. Sophie had contemplated missing breakfast too, but in the end that seemed a stupid thing to do: she and Adam were both adults, and there was no reason why there should be any embarrassment or tension between them this morning. No serious boundaries had been crossed the previous night; they had pulled back in plenty of time. So where was he this morning? Why was his place in the lecture theatre empty?

"He took the train back to Paris," François told her during the coffee break. "Apparently there was some emergency at home. He said he was taking an earlier flight back to the States."

Before the morning's session resumed Sophie sent him a simple email—*There was no need to do that! Write to me*—but she received no answer.

Her own flight home on Saturday morning landed in Luton at midday. It was pouring with rain. The sky was slate-grey and heavy with clouds. The train to Birmingham was disrupted due to planned engineering works and buses would be providing a rail replacement service between Kettering and Nuneaton.

"Rail replacement service," "Kettering," "Nuneaton." Were there five more dispiriting words in the English (or any other) language?

As the bus crawled its way through the clogged and stuttering weekend traffic between these Midland towns, Sophie thought—and kept trying not to think—of Thursday night on the Frioul islands. The feel of the water against her skin. The pattern of stars above her in the night sky. The moonlit journey on the boat back to Marseille, sitting on the open-air top deck, Adam's thigh in gentle contact with her own. And then in her head she could hear Naheed's voice, on her wedding night, at the dinner table in the marquee, talking about driving, and how *Every few minutes you come to a different junction, and you have to make a choice. And every choice you make has the potential to alter your life.*

It was four o'clock by the time she had trudged up the hill from New Street Station to Centenary Square, pulling her case behind her, with its cargo of dirty underwear, Marseille fridge magnet and souvenir bottle of pastis. The clouds were thicker, darker, denser than ever, and the unfinished skeleton of Birmingham's new library rose up ahead of her. The lights were already on in the flat. Ian was standing at the window, looking out for her.

15.

At nine o'clock on the evening of Friday, 27 July 2012:

Sophie and Ian were sitting together on the sofa in their flat, watching the Olympic opening ceremony on television.

Colin Trotter was alone at home in Rednal, sitting in his armchair, watching the Olympic opening ceremony on television.

Helena Coleman was alone at home in Kernel Magna, sitting in her armchair, watching the Olympic opening ceremony on television.

Philip and Carol Chase, along with Philip's son Patrick and his wife Mandy, were sitting in the living room of their house in King's Heath, a Chinese takeaway on their laps, watching the Olympic opening ceremony on television.

Sohan Aditya was alone in his flat in Clapham, lying on the sofa, watching the Olympic opening ceremony on television and texting his friends about it.

Christopher and Lois Potter, in the midst of their subdued walking holiday in the Lake District, were watching the Olympic opening ceremony on the television of their rented cottage.

Doug Anderton, his daughter Coriander and his son Ranulph were all sitting in separate rooms of their house in Chelsea, watching the Olympic opening ceremony on different televisions.

Benjamin was alone in the mill house, sitting at the desk in his study, making cuts and revisions to his novel, while listening to a string quartet by Arthur Honegger.

*

Sophie had no great hopes for this particular spectacle. Just as Ian was instinctively drawn towards anything to do with sport, so she was instinctively repelled by it. It had never meant much to her that London was hosting the 2012 Olympics, and now that she didn't live there, it meant even less. Pointedly, she had a book open on her lap (*The Count of Monte Cristo*, in fact, which she was now rereading) when the broadcast started: a none-too-subtle way of signalling that she was prepared to keep Ian company while he was watching it, but she wasn't going to pay any attention. She assumed it was just going to be a whole lot of men in singlets and shorts walking around a race track for three hours while military music played and the Queen waved at people.

"Even Danny Boyle can't make that interesting," she said.

But she was wrong. The ceremony began with a two-minute film: a speeded-up journey along the Thames, from its very source to the heart of London. As the camera raced along the surface of the water to a soundtrack of fast, pulsing electronic music, passing three characters from *The Wind in the Willows* along the way, the soundtrack morphing to include snippets from the Sex Pistols' "God Save the Queen" and the theme tune from *EastEnders*, Sophie's academic interest was piqued. She realized that something clever had been put together here: there were going to be a lot of intertextual references to look out for.

"Why is there a pink pig flying over Battersea Power Station?" she asked Ian.

"Search me," he replied.

*

"You know what that is, don't you?" said Philip in delight, pointing at the screen with a chopstick. "That's a Pink Floyd reference. *Animals*. The album they made in 1977."

"Only you would know that," said Carol.

"Me and a few million others," he said, spearing a prawn ball. Sometimes his wife's musical ignorance alarmed him.

*

Helena found the opening sequence far too confusing and frenetic. She hoped it wasn't all going to be like this. But she relaxed somewhat when the next section featured four different choirs, from all four countries in the United Kingdom, each one singing a different anthem. The young boy singing a solo version of "Jerusalem" in the stadium had the most beautiful voice, and the scenes of rural life being acted out in the arena were very restful and charming. Then a number of stagecoaches entered, bringing actors dressed as Victorian industrialists, and her hackles started to rise again. Several of the businessmen were played by black actors. Why did they have to *do* that? Why? Did people have no respect for history any more?

*

"Wow . . ."

Sohan had noticed that the section of the ceremony featuring the industrialists was called "Pandemonium." He fired off an immediate text message to Sophie.

Did you see that? Pandemonium! They're channelling Humphrey Jennings!

*

Sophie replied:

Amazing. And totally not what I was expecting.

"Who are you texting?" Ian asked.

"Sohan," she said.

"What about? Can't you concentrate on this?"

"That's what I'm texting about. He's just pointed out this whole section is based on a really obscure book called *Pandaemonium*, by Humphrey Jennings." Ian looked at her blankly. "He was a documentary film-maker in the forties."

"Ah. OK." Ian paused, reflecting. "You two have so much in common." He kissed her. "Good job he's gay."

*

Like Sophie, Doug had approached the opening ceremony in a mood of scepticism. Like her, he watched it with a mounting sense of admiration that was soon bordering on awe. The scale of the spectacle, the originality of it—the *weirdness*, at points— the majestic sight of the industrial chimneys rising out of the fake Glastonbury Tor, the hypnotic, accumulating power of the Underworld music . . . This eccentric hymn to Britain's industrial heritage was the last thing he had been expecting, but there was something hugely affecting and persuasive about it . . . Something fundamentally *truthful*, in fact. And what he felt while watching it were the stirrings of an emotion he hadn't experienced for years— had never really experienced at all, perhaps, having grown up in a household where all expressions of patriotism had been considered suspect: national pride. Yes, why not come straight out and admit it, at this moment he felt proud, proud to be British, proud to be part of a nation which had not only achieved such great things but could now celebrate them with such confidence and irony and lack of self-importance.

He could feel a column about this coming on. Definitely.

*

Colin enjoyed the celebration of British history as well. He liked the poem that Kenneth Branagh recited. The only thing that annoyed him was that they had to include a reference to the arrival of HMS *Windrush*, and Britain's first Jamaican immigrants.

"Oh, here we go," he muttered into his lager, as soon as he saw the actors. "The bloody political correctness brigade are at it again . . ."

*

So far, incredibly, Sophie seemed to be more focused on the cer- emony than Ian was. After a few minutes he became restless, got up to get more beers from the fridge, emptied some crisps into a bowl. "Aren't you enjoying this?" she asked. "Sure," he said. "We get the message. Britain's done lots of stuff." He looked even more unimpressed when the next sequence—a short pre-filmed item called "Happy and Glorious"—began with aerial shots of Buckingham Palace. But then he saw a figure walking in through the palace doors, wearing a white dinner jacket, his shoulders swinging in a gesture of suave, gentlemanly confidence, and realized who it was—James Bond: or at any rate Daniel Craig, Bond's latest screen incarnation. Ian sat back down next to Sophie, leaning forward on the sofa, his attention seized. Bond walked through the palace reception rooms until he was facing an actor playing the Queen, seated at her desk with her back towards him. Only then she turned and it wasn't an actor. It really was the Queen. "Good evening, Mr. Bond," she said, stiffly, and it was obvious that she wasn't going to give the most natural performance in the world, even though she was playing herself, but still—they had got the Queen, the Queen of fucking England, to take part in a film for the Olympic opening ceremony, and in fact it was even better than that, because the next thing that happened was that she was following Bond out of the palace and they were getting into a helicopter together, and then the helicopter took off and it was filmed rising high above Buckingham Palace and high above London, and soon afterwards it was approaching the Olympic stadium and then you had the greatest joke of all, the greatest stroke of genius, because they made it look as though the Queen and James Bond were jumping out of the helicopter together and parachuting into the stadium, and as the James Bond music played his parachute opened up and it turned out to be an enormous Union Jack, in a homage to that amazing opening sequence of *The Spy Who Loved Me*, and the effect of these elements—the Queen! James Bond! the Union Jack!—was to induce in Ian an almost orgasmic surge of patriotic excitement, so that he leaped to his feet and shouted "Yes! Yes! Yes!"—and then threw himself down next to Sophie, enfolding her in a tight hug and kissing her again and again.

*

When the music to the next section started, Philip could hardly believe it. He recognized it at once, that unmistakeable hypnotic phrase with its curious time signature, music he had listened to hundreds of times, thousands of times, music which he loved with all his heart although for almost four decades peer pressure had obliged him to keep that love a kind of secret, had made him feel that to love this music was to declare yourself somehow laughable, or at the very least permanently out of step with fashion. But here it was. Being broadcast to the whole world, presented as an example of the very best in British culture. Vindication! Vindication at last!

"Mike Oldfield!" he shouted, spilling rice all over the carpet. "That's Mike Oldfield there! This is *Tubular Bells*!"

He took out his phone and hurried over to a quieter corner of the room and called Benjamin. When the phone was answered Philip could hear music in the background but it was different music, something anguished and discordant. A string quartet by the sound of it.

"Aren't you watching it?" he said.

"Watching what?" said Benjamin.

"The Olympic opening ceremony."

"Is that tonight?"

"Oh, for God's sake. Turn the telly on."

"No, I don't fancy it. I'm working tonight."

"Don't argue. Turn it on *now*."

Benjamin paused, impressed by the urgency in Philip's voice. "Well, all right, then."

Philip could hear the string quartet being turned off and the television being turned on. A few seconds later Benjamin said:

"Blimey, is that Mike Oldfield?"

"Exactly. Mike Oldfield. Mike Oldfield!"

"What's he doing there?"

"He's playing *Tubular Bells*, what does it sound like?"

"But why?"

"Because finally—*finally*—someone has realized what a genius he is. A great British composer! We were right all along!" Benjamin could hear the triumphant smile in his friend's voice. "OK, I'm going now. Keep watching the rest of the ceremony—it's amazing."

Putting his phone down on the arm of the sofa, Benjamin sat in front of the TV and glanced briefly at the strange scene that was unfolding there. A whole lot of people in nurses' uniforms and children in pyjamas were bouncing up and down on giant beds as if they were trampolines while *Tubular Bells* continued to play in the background. Most viewers of the ceremony could have told him that this section was meant to be a celebration of the NHS; and in fact Benjamin could probably have worked that out for himself if he had been concentrating, but he wasn't. He was thinking back to the mid-1970s, a couple of years after Mike Oldfield's album had been released, how he and his friends used to listen to it in the common room at King William's School and have endless nerdy discussions about it. Doug, who at this time was listening mainly to Motown, would not attempt to hide his disdain. To the rest of them, however, it was a sacred musical text. He remembered one lunchtime—yes, it was amazing how these images came back to you sometimes, with razor-sharp clarity, something almost Proustian about it, no doubt it was the music on TV that was providing the trigger—anyway, he and Harding were listening to *Tubular Bells*, this very section in fact, these opening minutes—and they got involved in some stupid argument about the time signature: Benjamin could remember it now, Harding insisting there was nothing strange about it, it was just in normal common time, and Benjamin insisting, No, you're not listening carefully enough, it's in 15/8, and then Philip chipping in and saying, Actually, no, it isn't as complicated as that, there's just a beat missing from the second bar in every four-bar phrase, so it goes 4/4—3/4—4/4—4/4, and Yes, that did mean it was in patterns of fifteen beats, but that didn't mean it was in 15/8, that wasn't the same thing, but then Harding said they were both idiots, they didn't know what they were talking about—he was always, Benjamin realized now, just trying to stir things up, just trying to cause trouble—so in the end they took the record to the head of music, Mr. Sill, and he listened to it and gave a different answer altogether, something even more complicated, and then he'd taken out some more records and got them to identify the time signatures, starting with "Mars, the Bringer of War" by Holst

(5/4) and then moving on to *The Rite of Spring*, and they'd spent the whole of the rest of the lunch break like that . . .

Good times, Benjamin thought. Happy times.

Back in London, the NHS section of the ceremony came to an end but Benjamin failed to notice, as his television flickered quietly in the background and he stared out towards the river, a beatific, reminiscent smile on his face.

*

"That's Simon Rattle, isn't it?" said Christopher, as the eminent conductor strode into the centre of the Olympic stadium.

"Uh-huh," said Lois, looking up briefly from the tapestry she only ever did when she was on holiday, which had never been finished and never would be finished. She didn't look up again until she heard her husband laughing. "What's so funny?"

"Look—Mr. Bean."

Simon Rattle was conducting an orchestra as it played the theme tune from *Chariots of Fire* (another victory for Philip's teenage tastes, as he had also been a Vangelis fan back in the seventies) while Rowan Atkinson, saddled with the task of playing a single note over and over on an electric keyboard, was acting out a diverting mime of boredom and frustration.

"I wonder why they decided to have him?"

"Quite a clever idea, actually," said Christopher. "The whole world loves Mr. Bean."

"Really?" said Lois, going back to her tapestry.

"Don't you remember, that time we were in Arezzo, and we walked past the theatre, and they had a Mr. Bean impersonator on?"

"No."

"And I said—look, that's how popular he is, over here. They even have people impersonating him."

"I don't remember that at all."

"It was in Arezzo. Three years ago."

"Sorry," said Lois, holding the tapestry away from her and regarding it critically. Something was not quite right with the last colour she'd chosen. "I've got no recollection of that conversation."

Christopher sighed, "Of course not. You never remember anything that I say."

He leaned across and kissed her on the cheek, out of habit, out of resignation. Lois smiled thinly but she didn't return the kiss.

*

Coriander had grown restless during the Mr. Bean section and had wandered downstairs to see what her father was doing. She found him on the sofa in the main sitting room with a can of lager in his hand and, to her amazement, faint traces of a tear running down one cheek. She had never seen anything like this before.

"Dad?" she sat down beside him. "Are you all right?"

"I'm sorry," he said, wiping his eyes. "This is so embarrassing. But I'm loving this. I'm loving every minute of it. Go and fetch your mother. She should be watching it too."

Coriander stared at him. "What do you mean? Of course she's watching it. She's *there*."

"She is?"

"She's in the VIP section. I saw her earlier, sitting next to Bryan Ferry."

Doug was briefly surprised by this information, although it made perfect sense when he thought about it.

"How are you two still together?" his daughter asked. "I've never known people so bad at communicating with each other."

"True. If we lived in a smaller house," said Doug, "I'm sure we'd have got divorced by now."

"Well, I wish you would," said Coriander. "It's so lame, having parents who've been together as long as you two."

Doug wasn't sure if she was joking or not. He was pleased, anyway, when she settled down on the sofa next to him.

The ceremony had now moved on to a section called "Frankie and June say . . . thanks, Tim!," which seemed to be a strange, near-incomprehensible mash-up of British musical and film references.

("*A Matter of Life and Death*!," Sophie texted to Sohan. "*The Wicker Man*!" he texted back.) Threading it together was some kind of love story about two teenagers meeting each other and communicating via social media while they travelled on the London Underground. It was all very confusing, but exhilarating too, and the best part of it was just trying to identify all the songs. Doug was amazed by how many of these his daughter seemed to know. She recognized The Jam, The Who, The Rolling Stones, David Bowie and Frankie Goes To Hollywood, as well as the ones he would have expected her to know like Amy Winehouse and Dizzee Rascal. She didn't understand the TV clip of two women kissing and he explained it was from a soap opera called *Brookside*, and it had been one of the first kisses between two women to be shown on mainstream national TV and it was amazing that Britain was now using it to proudly show the whole world how enlightened and progressive it was. "This is being watched in Saudi Arabia, you know," he said, and Coriander had to admit that was incredibly cool and felt a little tingle of excitement as she realized it.

"But who's he?" she said, as the roof was lifted off the set of a gigantic house in the middle of the stadium, to reveal an ordinary, boring-looking, middle-aged man sitting at a desk tapping away at a computer keyboard, while the phrase *THIS IS FOR EVERYONE* flashed up on screens and monitors all around him.

"That's Tim Berners-Lee."

"Who?"

"He invented the internet."

"What? The *British* invented the internet?"

"In a way, yes. At least, he did."

"That's amazing," said Coriander. She took out her BlackBerry and took a picture of the image on the screen, then wrote *I come from an awesome country* and tweeted it to all 379 of her followers.

*

The creative part of the ceremony was over. Now it was time for all the competing athletes to parade through the stadium, and that threatened to go on for ninety minutes at least. The viewers dispersed.

Sophie and Ian went to bed. They hadn't made love for almost a week. They made up for it tonight. Ian fantasized that he was James Bond making love to the beautiful dancing teenager from the "Frankie and June" section.

Colin fell asleep on the sofa, then woke up at 3 a.m., confused, and dragged himself up the stairs to bed.

Helena sat up until 1 a.m., writing a letter to the *Telegraph* complaining about the ceremony's left-wing bias, but it was five hundred words long so unsurprisingly it never got published.

The Chases were on such a high after the ceremony that Philip went online and immediately bought four of the few remaining tickets for one of the athletic events, followed by four return train tickets to London, which turned out to be phenomenally expensive.

Sohan did some research online about Humphrey Jennings and Michael Powell before changing his clothes, having a shave and going out to a club at twelve thirty. The night was still young and full of possibilities.

Christopher made two mugs of hot chocolate, and took his up to bed. Lois joined him ninety minutes later, by which time she judged he would be safely asleep.

Doug started writing his column. He showed Coriander the first two paragraphs and asked her what she thought. She said: "They're shit." After that, she sat down at the desk beside him and they wrote the rest of the column together.

As it was a warm night, Benjamin went out to sit on his terrace, taking a glass of cold white wine with him. He was feeling happy. Work on the pared-down version of his novel was finished. The text—a lightly fictionalized account of his relationship with Cicely, entitled *A Rose Without a Thorn*—was ready to be sent off to publishers now. To celebrate, Benjamin turned on his portable speakers and scrolled his iPod wheel to the piece of music that had inspired it and given him the title: a brooding, passionate duet between the jazz pianist Stan Tracey and the saxophonist Tony Coe, recorded in 1983. He turned it up loud. He could listen to music as loud as he wanted here, and as late as he wanted. But when it was over he felt a kind of relief, and realized that he much preferred the silence. The silence of England sinking into a deep, satisfied sleep, the kind of sleep you enjoy after throwing a successful party, when all the guests have gone home and you know that there is no need to get up early in the morning. England felt like a calm and settled place tonight: a country at ease with itself. The thought that so many millions of disparate people had been united, drawn together by a television broadcast, made him think of his childhood again, and made him smile. All was well. And the river seemed to agree with him: the river that was the only thing still to disturb the silence, proceeding on its timeless course, bubbling and rippling tonight, merrily, merrily, merrily, merrily.

DEEP ENGLAND

✳

To the privileged, equality feels like a step down. Understand
this and you understand a lot of populist politics today.

İyad el-Baghdadi, Twitter, 1:36 p.m., 25 July 2016

16.

"Well," said Sohan. "Congratulations."

"Thanks," said Sophie.

They clinked glasses and drank the champagne, which wasn't anything special. Sohan—who was paying—reflected momentarily on the price, which was very special indeed.

"What are we celebrating, anyway?" Sophie asked.

"You."

"Me? What about me?"

"Everything about you. Your glorious rise to fame."

Sophie smiled. "A slight exaggeration, I think."

Glasses in hand, they moved away from the bar and began to stroll slowly around the observation deck. Beneath them lay London, languid and supine in the early-summer evening heat. The Thames stretched and wound like a vast filthy ribbon, dwindling eventually into a pinpoint of light glimmering through the smog on the eastern horizon.

"Your town," said Sophie, coming up close beside him and putting her arm through his, as they both peered down through the floor-to-ceiling glass of the Shard's viewing platform at the buildings more than two hundred metres below: the tower blocks, the former council flats, the new-builds, the occasional relic of Hawksmoor's London peeping through the grey modern jumble.

"Mine? Not really. London doesn't belong to Londoners any more."

"Then who does it belong to?"

"Foreigners, mainly. Real foreigners." Sophie gave him a sceptical look, so he added: "This building where we're standing. London's latest star attraction. You think it's British? Ninety-five per cent of it is owned by the state of Qatar. The same goes for half those glittery new office blocks you can see from here. Those towers full of luxury riverside apartments. To say nothing of Harrods, that most wonderful old English institution. We've been selling ourselves off for years. Walk anywhere in central London these days and the chances are you're treading on foreign soil."

With a small but vocal band of young Spanish tourists pressing in on them, taking excited pictures and videos of the cityscape with their phones, Sophie and Sohan moved on, walking around the perimeter of the platform to get a different view of the capital. St. Paul's Cathedral looked tiny and vulnerable from here, struggling to assert any kind of identity in the face of the modernist, Brutalist and post-modernist creations which had so recently sprung up around it.

"And is that the Olympic stadium?" Sophie asked, pointing towards a distant circle of white, like a giant polo mint dropped unceremoniously into the middle of the old East End.

"It is." Sohan took another sip from his champagne flute, and said: "God, doesn't it seem like a long time ago, all that? Remember how sceptical we all were at first, and then how excited we all got for about five minutes? I mean, I actually bought tickets for one of the events after that ceremony. A *sporting* event. Me! Watching sport!"

"What was it?"

"Women's football." Sophie laughed, and he explained, defensively: "It was the only thing that wasn't sold out. I know, it was a completely stupid idea. I don't like football and I don't even like women all that much. Present company excepted. I had this foolish notion that I could turn it into a kind of date. I took this guy called Jeremy with me. That was the kiss of death for *that* relationship, anyway . . ."

"What were you thinking? Hardly a candlelit dinner for two, was it?" She put a consoling arm around his shoulder. "I hope there've been some others since then."

"Sure. Plenty. But no one I really liked and . . . well, no one at all for a couple of months." He took a longer than usual sip of the champagne. "Of course, I'm grateful to Mr. Cameron that we can get married now. In fact it's the only thing I'm grateful to him for. But I'm beginning to think there's probably no one out there for me. Getting pretty sure of it, actually."

"Well," said Sophie. "I never thought you were the type to settle down anyway."

"I never thought so either. But now that you and Ian have set such an amazing example of married bliss . . ."

She was pleased to see the glint return to his eye, and to hear the ironic undertone return to his voice; and yet, at the same time, there was something about this jibe that annoyed her.

"As a matter of fact," she said, "we're very happy."

"I don't doubt it for a moment."

And it was more or less true. After the first few, slightly wobbly months their marriage had settled into a routine, a pattern of habits. On Mondays and Fridays Sophie would work either at home or in the recently opened Library of Birmingham. If she was home, Ian would come back between morning and afternoon classes and they would have lunch together. The other days of the week, she went in to the university. On Saturdays he would go to the Villa match with Simon or watch sport at home, and on Sundays they would visit his mother. It was comfortable, it was pleasant, and Sophie was determined to be satisfied with it. And if ever she felt that married life was falling ever so slightly short of expectations (as she sometimes—very occasionally—did, in the still, dark hours of a winter morning, when she had woken early and Ian was still asleep, breathing evenly beside her, her thoughts starting to wander in hazardous, unpredictable directions), she had the consolation of knowing that her career was progressing nicely, one small step at a time. Her thesis had been published. The chapter on Powell's portrait of Dumas, which had also appeared separately in an issue of the *Oxford Art Journal*, had caught the attention of a Radio Four producer, who had invited her on to an early-evening discussion show. She'd handled the programme well and further invitations had followed: some of them from academia, some from the more highbrow end of the media (broadsheet arts pages, mainly, clinging on to their precarious existence for dear life).

And more recently, she had received the most unexpected invitation of all: a request to appear as guest lecturer on a ten-day cruise of the Baltic, setting sail from Dover the day after tomorrow.

And then there was her new job: a permanent lectureship at one of the principal London universities. It would start in October, and Sophie was hugely excited about it. Ian, of course, was ambivalent. Yes, it meant they would have more money: this would certainly be useful—especially if they were going to start a family, as he was anxious to do—but he had also applied for a new job himself (a promotion, in fact, to regional manager) and he was pretty confident of success, and the rise that would go with it. Wouldn't that be enough, for the time being? Behind this question lay his great, voiceless anxiety: his wife would from now on be spending three days a week in London—sleeping on Sohan's couch, probably, until a more satisfactory arrangement could be worked out—and there was something about this idea that disturbed him profoundly. Something more than the prospect of their intermittent separation, and of having to spend two or three nights a week in the flat by himself. Something about her drifting back towards a city, a way of life and a set of friends that had nothing to do with him, that pre-dated him, and for this reason posed a threat to their marital status quo. Ever since the decision had been made, an unspoken but palpable uneasiness had arisen between them.

"Good," was all that Sophie said, in response to Sohan's comment. And she added: "Because it's true." Which immediately made it sound as though it wasn't.

"He's going with you, I suppose? Aboard the good ship *Decrepitude*."

"Don't be so rude all the time."

"Come on, they're all going to be ancient. Don't you have to be at least seventy to go on a Legend cruise?"

"Fifty."

"Well, most of them are going to be way older than that. HMS *Senility*." He laughed, as he had a habit of doing, at his own jokes. Ever since Sophie had told him the news, the very idea of her being stranded for ten days on board a cruise ship with four hundred elderly

British passengers for company had been causing him endless amusement. She suspected an element of professional jealousy.

"Yes, he's coming," she said. "They've been very good about it. He's missing the first three days, but they're flying him out and he's joining the ship in Stockholm."

"That's so romantic," said Sohan. "I'm just picturing the two of you together in your cabin, steaming across the Baltic. Like Kate Winslet and Leonardo DiCaprio. In fact I can see the resemblance, in both cases." He drained the last of the champagne from his glass. "Let's hope there are no icebergs."

"There won't be," said Sophie, and shielded her eyes against the low-lying sun, trying in vain to find the Greenwich Observatory amidst the concrete chaos of the city she would soon be calling home again.

17.

The *Legend Topaz IV* set sail from Dover shortly after 14:00 hours on Wednesday afternoon. It was a fine day and the water was calm. Sophie watched from her tiny private balcony as the white cliffs receded and the ship crested onwards into open seas, sunlight sparkling upon the gentle, unthreatening waves of the English Channel. When the land had disappeared from view completely and she was tired of looking at the water, she went back into her cabin and sank contentedly into its little armchair.

She looked around, with a great feeling of comfort and satisfaction. The cabin was inexpressibly cosy. There were two compact single beds, and a desk upon which she had already arranged her books and the papers for her lecture. Within a small teak cabinet was a minibar stocked with every kind of alcoholic drink, and on top of it a television and a DVD player: having been forewarned about this, Sophie had brought half a dozen of her favourite films with her, although there were many more to be borrowed from the ship's library. On the table between the two beds had been placed a Gideon Bible and, rather more surprisingly, a paperback copy of the Booker-prizewinning *The Twilight of Otters* by Lionel Hampshire.

Sophie could not at first conceive of the explanation for this, although she was to chance upon it a few minutes later. Among the papers waiting for her in her bulging welcome folder was a four-page newsletter entitled *On Board*. This was issue one of what was clearly going to be a daily publication, and it was full of useful information: times of sunrise and sunset, a brief weather forecast, a cruise itinerary and a specification of today's dress code, which Sophie was relieved to see was "Casual." ("Ladies may wish to wear a casual dress or trousers, while gentlemen can enjoy the freedom of an open-neck shirt and smart casual trousers.") It also gave details of the guest artistes and lecturers who would be entertaining and instructing the passengers during the course of the trip. They seemed to be a motley crew—jugglers, magicians, a ventriloquist, an Elvis impersonator and more than a dozen others—and near the bottom of the list was her own name, which she was weirdly proud to see in this context. Next to it, most unexpectedly, was the name of the great writer himself: "We are pleased to inform you," ran the notice, "that the eminent, prizewinning novelist Mr. LIONEL HAMPSHIRE will be on board for the duration of the voyage, to read extracts of his works and to offer writing workshops and discussion groups."

These last five words, in fact, were the very first thing she heard when she arrived at the door of the cruise director's cabin at five o'clock that afternoon to receive instructions about her lecture. An altercation seemed to be taking place inside. She paused in the open doorway and saw the distinguished writer with his back towards her, complaining to some unseen figure in tones of high indignation.

"'Writing workshops and discussion groups'! It says nothing about that in my contract. Nothing at all."

"I know it doesn't," the unseen figure replied. "But I had to put something. We've never had a writer on here before. What else am I supposed to do with you?"

"I shall give one reading," Hampshire insisted, "lasting for thirty-five minutes. Nothing more, nothing less."

"Fine. You can do it on Tuesday evening, in the cabaret theatre. I'll put you on before Molly Parton."

"Dolly Parton's on this ship?"

"Molly Parton. She's a tribute act. You'll be her support. Will that be all?"

Hampshire turned on his heel and said, before departing: "This is outrageous. I shall be writing to my publishers about this."

"Ask them why they put a copy of your book inside every cabin. I've already had complaints."

"*Complaints?*"

Red in the face by now, Hampshire pushed past Sophie without acknowledging her and disappeared down the corridor. A tall, fine-featured, dark-haired man appeared in the doorway and stared after him for a moment, then retreated into his office, muttering—either to himself or to Sophie—"A writer! They're asking me to have writers on the bloody ship now!" He seemed more amused than annoyed by the situation, though, and when Sophie coughed to remind him of her presence, she saw that he was smiling. It was an intelligent, mischievous smile. She warmed to it.

"Hello, I'm Sophie," she said, advancing into the room and holding out her hand. "Sophie Coleman-Potter."

"Robin Walker," he said. "Cruise director." Her name didn't seem to mean anything to him at first, but after a moment his face lit up with realization: "Wait—are you the bird impressions?"

She shook her head. "Sadly not."

"No, you don't look like a bird impressionist. You look like a dancer." Before she could decide whether she was flattered or insulted by this, he clapped his hands: "You're the tap dancer! The one who finishes her act by doing the splits over the live lobster."

"I'm afraid I—"

"OK, I give up."

"I'm an art historian. I'm here to give the lecture on 'Treasures of the Hermitage'."

"Ah! Very good. Art history. Excellent. We need a bit of that. Brainy bunch, some of our passengers. They like a bit of culture. I've got you down for Sunday afternoon, three till four. How does that sound?"

"Sounds fine. What do I do the rest of the time?"

"The rest of the time, my dear, is your own."

"Really? But I'm on board for ten days."

"Relax and enjoy it. Did they give you a good cabin? What number?"

"101."

"Excellent. One of the nicest. And best of all, you get Henry."

"Henry?"

"Your butler."

"I have a butler?"

"Of course. Didn't you read the bumf?"

"Well, I—"

"I'm sorry, my love—duty calls." Four middle-aged men had turned up in his doorway. *Sotto voce*, he muttered to Sophie: "Strippers. New departure for us, but pretty tame stuff from what I've heard." Then, out loud: "Come in, gentlemen." He ushered Sophie into the corridor, and before she left she heard him saying to the new arrivals: "Now, lads, tell me what it is you do. But I hope it doesn't involve full-frontal nudity."

"Not at all," one of the men answered pleasantly. "We're the string quartet."

Sophie spent a relaxed hour in her cabin after that. A plate of canapés had been laid out for her, presumably by her butler, and she nibbled on them while finishing off two gin and tonics and trying on all three of the dresses she had brought, in front of the bathroom's full-length mirror. When she felt that she had achieved the casual look that today's protocol demanded, she made her way to the dining hall for her first evening meal of the voyage.

Here she learned something slightly alarming: the seating plan was fixed, not just for tonight's dinner but for every breakfast, lunch and dinner during the next ten days. She and Ian (when he joined the ship on Saturday) would be sitting with the same eight passengers every day: a Mr. and Mrs. Wilcox, from Ramsbottom, Lancashire; a Mr. and Mrs. Joyce, from Teignmouth, Devon; a Mr. and Mrs. Murphy, from Woking, Surrey; plus two other ladies, Miss Thomsett and Mrs. O'Sullivan, from Bristol, who appeared to be travelling together. Mr. and Mrs. Murphy seemed to be well into their eighties, on top of which one of them (the husband) looked decidedly unwell. He sat throughout this first meal staring wistfully into space, his face white, his lips blueish, barely touching his food, while his wife concentrated on eating as much as possible while giving the occasional antagonistic glance in his direction. Mr. and Mrs. Joyce were perhaps a few years younger, and seemed rather more devoted. The two single ladies were probably a few years younger still, and sounded full of enthusiasm for the destinations and attractions ahead. One of them, it emerged, was recently widowed, and the other had never married. They were both vegetarian. Mr. and Mrs. Wilcox, finally, were at the youngest end of the Legend spectrum, and were much the most voluble of Sophie's dining companions. He made his living—a very comfortable living, they were all given to understand—by selling and hiring out forklift trucks. Coming on this cruise had not been his idea: his wife was the "culture vulture," and it had always been her ambition to visit St. Petersburg. Frankly, he would rather be cruising around the Med, but what was a marriage, after all, without a little bit of give-and-take? Mrs. Wilcox smiled briefly, inscrutably, when he said this. She also caught Sophie's eye, and looked quickly away.

Dinner consisted of five courses. Sophie excused herself after the fourth, forgoing the cheese board and the *digestifs*, and staggered back to her cabin, feeling bloated. She watched about half of Claire Denis's *Beau Travail* on DVD before realizing that she was nodding off, then stepped out on to the balcony to get some fresh air before going to bed. The cold night air, the flecks of sea spray, the sway of the ship, the churning of the waves, the sense of a broad expanse of water surrounding her were all deliciously unfamiliar and invigorating. When she got into bed, she left the door to her balcony slightly ajar, so that she could continue to enjoy them.

She quickly fell into a shallow, uneasy sleep. At one point she dreamed that she could hear noises coming from outside: strange, high-pitched, inhuman cries. She walked out through the door, leaned over the rail and saw that a dolphin was swimming alongside the boat. She reached out, took hold of its flippers and pulled it aboard. She kissed it passionately on the mouth. It was Adam, but it was also a dolphin. She beckoned him inside and they lay down on the bed where she stroked his skin which was as smooth and wet as a dolphin's. He was part-Adam, part-dolphin, but there came a point in the dream where the confusion stopped and he became all-Adam. They made love and she came in her sleep, crying out in the darkness. Afterwards she lay awake for a few minutes, feeling guilty but also inexplicably happy. Then she slept for another nine hours, waking so late that she missed her first breakfast.

*

Hungry now, Sophie decided that this was the moment to experiment with the butler service. She dialled a three-digit number on her bedside telephone. A weightless, musical voice answered, speaking perfect English with a strong but unplaceable foreign accent. Sophie ordered coffee, scrambled eggs, smoked salmon, fresh fruit and orange juice, then took a bath. By the time she emerged from the bathroom, the breakfast had been laid out on her table and a man she assumed to be Henry was carefully putting her dress (which she had left in a crumpled ball on the unused bed) on to a coat hanger and replacing it in the wardrobe.

"Ah—good morning, madam," Henry said, smiling at her and bowing slightly. "I hope you slept well." He was a slender, unobtrusive figure, not much taller than Sophie herself, his brown eyes forever darting around the cabin, looking for items to tidy and adjust with his delicate fingers.

"Thank you," she said. "Please—you don't have to do that. And do call me Sophie."

Henry smiled and bowed again but didn't answer. She had the impression that he was disturbed by the suggestion. She also realized that she had no idea how to behave towards this person. He was a servant. She had never had a servant before. She felt utterly bewildered and tongue-tied.

"Your newspaper is here as well, madam," he said.

"Thank you."

She had no recollection of having ordered a newspaper, and hoped that she wasn't going to be presented with a copy of the *Telegraph* or *Mail* every day. But the four-page tabloid that Henry now handed to her on a silver platter turned out to be the ship's own, entitled *The World Today*. Not for the first time. Sophie was impressed by how many extras seemed to be on offer aboard the *Topaz IV*, and how well organized everything seemed to be. The phrase "We run a tight ship here" occurred to her, in its most literal sense.

"Thank you," she said, for the third time, and turned around to look for her handbag, having some vague idea that she should give

Henry a tip. But by the time she located it, he had silently removed himself from the room, leaving her more frustrated with herself than ever.

She read the newspaper while eating breakfast in front of the balcony door which she had once again left open. Its production values were basic, but otherwise she found that it provided a very useful service, reducing yesterday's world news to four digestible pages, and she wondered why no one published anything similar back home. In a few minutes she had learned that "Yes Scotland" had now secured one million signatories to its campaign for an independent Scotland ahead of the referendum in September; that the number of British people needing emergency supplies from food banks had already risen by one-fifth this year; and that the BBC was being accused of a cover-up over its role in the recent police raid on Sir Cliff Richard's home following sexual assault allegations.

At dinner that night, it was the latter story that supplied most of the fuel for conversation. Mrs. Joyce thought that Sir Cliff had been treated disgracefully; for decades he had brought nothing but pleasure to the nation, and now he was owed a public apology. Mr. Joyce thought the BBC should get its own house in order before targeting other people: ever since the Jimmy Savile scandal it was clear that it was nothing more than a nest of paedophiles, and the director general should be arrested immediately. Miss Thomsett offered a gentle rebuke to this, arguing that there were always a few rotten apples in any organization, and that people should bear in mind all those wonderful period dramas the BBC made, as well as those superb wildlife documentaries with David Attenborough. Mr. Wilcox, who (Sophie could not help noticing) rather liked the sound of his own voice, delivered himself as follows: the BBC was not without its good points, but it was obsessed with political correctness, and had still not recovered from the episode, more than five years earlier, when a popular comedian and a popular radio presenter, live on air, had left a lewd message on the answering machine of the much-loved, elderly actor Andrew Sachs. Ever since then, after coming under heavy fire from the newspapers over the incident, the corporation had been on the defensive, knowing that it was perceived (quite rightly, in Mr. Wilcox's view) as elitist, arrogant, metropolitan and out of touch.

"How's it out of touch?" Sophie asked, in a friendly but combative tone, pouring herself another glass of wine before passing the bottle his way.

"It doesn't speak for ordinary people," he answered. "Not any more."

"I feel that it speaks for me, most of the time. And I'm ordinary."

"No you're not."

She bristled. "Excuse me?"

"I'm talking about people who live in the real world."

"I live in the real world. At least I think I do. Are you telling me I'm hallucinating it all?"

"Of course not. I'm just saying there's a difference between what you do and what people like me do."

"What, and that makes your life more 'real' than mine, somehow?"

"People need forklift trucks."

"I'm not sure I do."

"Of course you do. You just don't think about it."

"Well, maybe you need paintings just as much. Only *you* don't think about *that*."

Mrs. Wilcox laughed at the comeback and clinked her glass with Sophie's.

"There you are, Geoffrey—*touché*."

Mr. Wilcox smiled and joined in the toast. "Don't worry, I'll be there at your lecture all right. I'm not a complete bloody philistine, after all. Am I, Mary?"

Eight more of these dinners to go, Sophie thought, as she walked back to her cabin. Not that they were unbearable, exactly, but it did suddenly seem rather a lot. Perhaps it would be easier if the older couples were to join in the conversation a bit more. But Mr. Joyce seemed to have difficulty hearing anything, and Mr. Murphy had not spoken a word yet, to anybody—not even his wife—or eaten a morsel of food, so far as Sophie could see.

*

The next day would be their third at sea, and the last one before arriving in Stockholm, where Ian would be joining the ship. Sophie had not been very much in contact with him so far. Use of the internet was dependent on the ship's satellite connection: she had only got around to sending him one email, and had received four in return, from which she had learned, among other things, that there was still no news of his possible promotion, although he was still expecting it to be confirmed any day now.

Her last day alone—a Friday—was gloriously bright, and at eleven o'clock she climbed to the upper deck to have a coffee and read her book in the sunshine. Sitting at the next table, sipping a latte and jotting down the occasional reflection in his Moleskine notebook, was Lionel Hampshire. Sophie nodded and smiled at him. He nodded and smiled back, but gave no sign of recognizing her from their encounter in the cruise director's cabin doorway two days earlier.

After a few minutes, a white-haired, strong-jawed woman approached him, clutching a copy of *The Twilight of Otters*.

"Are you the author of this?" she asked, without preamble.

"Ah!" He pushed the notebook aside and took the novel from her, pen at the ready. "My pleasure, of course. Would you like a simple signature, or some sort of dedication . . .?"

"I don't want it signed," she said. "I want to know if I'm expected to read it."

The question took Lionel by surprise. He didn't seem to know how to answer it.

"There was a copy in my cabin when I arrived," she continued. "We've all got them. Only I've brought my own books, so I don't want to read it just now. I was wondering if it was compulsory."

"Compulsory? Not at all . . ." he answered, flustered. "Simply a gesture of largesse on my publishers' part."

"Good. I'm quite relieved because it says on the back that the main character is 'psychologically complex'."

"Indeed."

"Well," she said. "I don't like people who are psychological."

With that, she left him. Lionel sipped his coffee again, chastened. He was clearly aware that Sophie had overheard the conversation, so after a moment or two, in order to relieve him of his embarrassment, she said, boldly:

"That put you in your place."

His smile was prim but on the whole grateful.

"The writer's life is full of such small humiliations."

"I've already read your book. A few years ago. It was very good."

"How very kind. Thank you."

"It's a nice idea—having a writer-in-residence on the ship."

"In principle, yes. In practice, I'm not sure they know quite what to do with me. It's a pilot scheme. My publishers talked me into it."

"Well, as long as they don't work you too hard. I'm feeling quite guilty—I'm only doing one lecture, and I'm getting ten days' holiday out of it."

"Ah, so you're one of the speakers?" He turned and looked at her properly for the first time, and then—apparently liking what he saw—edged a little closer. "Well, look, don't feel *guilty*, for heaven's sake. I'm here for the full two weeks, and I intend to make the most of it. Maximum reward for minimum input. You should treat it the same. We're in it for ourselves. I mean, the punters are hardly going to appreciate us, are they? Talk about pearls before swine . . ."

"I was told that Legend usually pulls in a pretty smart crowd. You know, a cut above the usual cruisers."

Lionel looked at her disbelievingly. "Has that been your impression so far?"

"It's a bit early to say," said Sophie, equivocating.

"What's your subject, by the way?"

"Art history. The Russians, in this instance."

"And are you all by yourself?"

"My husband will be here tomorrow. You?"

"I'm alone until Helsinki. Then my assistant arrives."

"You have an assistant?"

"It sounds very grand, but she's just a young student from Goldsmiths. She helps with my emails, takes a bit of a dictation, that sort of thing."

"Doesn't your wife do all that?" Sophie realized that the question sounded abrupt, so she added: "A few years ago, I heard you give a talk, and you spoke very warmly about your wife, and all the help she gives you."

"Ah, yes. Where was that?"

"In London? You were with a French writer, Philippe Aldebert."

"Hmm . . . I don't recall. Anyway, June can't manage boats, I'm afraid. Terrible seasickness. Look—shall we have dinner together this evening? Would you like that?"

"How would that work? Don't we have to sit with the same people every night?"

"I meant in my cabin. Surely you haven't been eating with the passengers?"

Sophie politely declined the invitation, and was glad to have done so, because when she arrived for dinner at seven o'clock, there had been an unexpected development. Besides Ian's, there were two other empty places at the table. Mr. and Mrs. Joyce were absent.

"Evening, love," said Mr. Wilcox, as he passed her the bread basket. There was a grim twinkle in his eye, and an undertone of satisfaction in his voice as he said: "Well, it's started."

"What's started?" said Sophie. She looked around at the others, and noticed the glaze of shock on their faces. "What do you mean?"

"George has snuffed it. Heart attack. Middle of the night."

"He's . . . He's *dead*?"

"Don't look so upset," he urged her. "You've only known him a day or two. And he was hardly the life and soul of the party, was he?"

18.

"Apparently," said Sophie, "it's quite common on cruises. I mean, they're all getting on a bit, so you have to expect it."

"Bit morbid," said Ian. He peered at himself in the mirror, trying to adjust his bow tie, which insisted on sitting at a slight angle. Meanwhile Henry unobtrusively brushed down his shoulders with delicate strokes of a clothes brush. Tonight's dress code was "Formal," which according to the notice in *On Board* meant that "Ladies may choose to wear a formal evening or cocktail dress, while men may wear a dinner jacket or tuxedo. If preferred, a dark lounge suit may be worn."

"Has one of the passengers ever died while you were looking after them?" Sophie asked Henry, now. She was constantly trying to strike up a conversation with their butler—from whom, this morning, she had finally extracted the information that he came from the Philippines, and had been employed by Legend for just over three years.

"No, madam, this has never happened to me," he answered gravely. "Very upsetting if it were to happen. It happened to a colleague of mine. Very long cruise, to South America. Sometimes at sea for more than one week. It means there is a problem with the body—you know, the corpse? They have to put it in the freezers, down at the bottom of the ship." He picked a final hair from Ian's shoulders and put the brush away in his pocket, where he seemed to keep an extraordinary variety of instruments. "That reminds me—your menu for this evening is here. I put it on the desk."

He made his usual slight bow and then he was gone, leaving

Sophie, as always, with mingled feelings of unease and guilty pleasure at the luxury of being waited on so assiduously. Ian picked up the menu and glanced over it.

"Scandinavian dinner tonight," he said. "The appetizer's from Norway: breaded sweetbread with honey and plum sauce. Soup from Sweden: green pea with vegetables, rice and crayfish. Main course from Denmark: slow-cooked calf's shank with tomato and pearl onion sauce, duchess swede and potatoes. Then a salad: marinated radish and smoked trout . . . Have you been eating this much every night?"

"That's just the start. And that's why I can hardly get into this dress. Zip me up, will you?"

Ian zipped her cocktail dress, tracing the curve of her back that he loved so much, but before reaching the very top he leaned in and kissed the base of her neck, blowing on it softly. Sophie tingled as warm goosepimples spread all over her body. She turned, put her arms around his neck, and they nuzzled against each other. She groaned softly as she felt the weight of his lean, familiar body pressing against hers, the pressure of his erection against her belly. It seemed wrong— indeed, inexplicable—that she could have had an erotic dream about any other man.

"Early night tonight?" she breathed.

"Definitely."

But it was not quite as early as she'd hoped. She had not counted on the warmth of Ian's and Geoffrey Wilcox's immediate liking for each other. From the moment they were introduced at dinner, it was apparent how much they had in common: the same sense of humour, the same devotion to their wives (expressed through gentle teasing and mockery), the same scepticism about the purpose and value of this cruise, the same opinions on almost every subject, political or otherwise, that came up during the course of a two-and-a-half-hour meal. And that wasn't the end of it. When the last crumb of cheese had been eaten and the dregs of the port drunk down, Mr. Wilcox proposed a visit to the bar. He invited everybody at the table to come, but nobody was surprised when Mr. and Mrs. Murphy declined. And after a few minutes' sitting at a corner table for six, listening to the languid strains of Wesley Pritchard at the piano ("Our 'King of the Keys' will serenade you into the night with his personal selection of show tunes and nostalgic wartime favourites"), it also became apparent that Miss Thomsett and Mrs. O'Sullivan were going to be no-shows.

"Doesn't look like the lezzers will be joining us either, then," said Mr. Wilcox.

"The *who*?" Sophie asked.

"Sorry, Sophie, not very PC of me, I know. The two good ladies of alternative sexual orientation, then. Is that better for you?"

"It wasn't the word I was querying," said Sophie. "It was your casual assumption that that's what they are."

"Seems a perfectly fair assumption to me. Two women sharing a cabin together. *Vegetarians*," he added darkly.

"Oh, come on. Women who've lost their husbands, or never had husbands, often travel together. Why shouldn't they? It's nicer than travelling by yourself."

"You may be right," said Mr. Wilcox, holding up his hand in mock-surrender. "Forget I said it."

"Geoffrey considers himself an expert on every aspect of human nature," said Mrs. Wilcox, attempting to ease the tension with an icy joke.

Mr. Wilcox muttered into his whisky, "I know one when I see one, that's all," but everyone pretended not to have heard him.

*

The days continued to slip by. Sophie's lecture on the "Treasures of the Hermitage" was a great success. Demand for places was so high that it had to be moved to a larger room. Robin Walker took great pleasure in telling her, the next day, that she had scored an audience satisfaction rating of 9.3, which was almost unheard-of. The other passengers began treating her as if she were a minor celebrity, and three times that afternoon she was asked to autograph a copy of the day's newsletter, next to the notice announcing her talk. Before coming on board, Ian had suggested that they print up some business cards for her; she had scoffed at the idea, but he'd done it anyway, and now (as was often, gallingly, the case) he had been proved right, and she found herself distributing them freely to the many women who started inviting her to address their local WI meetings or book groups. "You're a hit!" he kept telling her, and the pride in his face could not have been any plainer.

They had a wonderful day in Helsinki together, joining the coach party which drove out to Sibelius's house close to Lake Tuusula, culminating in a performance of *Finlandia* at the local music academy. And that evening, they set sail for St. Petersburg.

The ship docked early, and because of its size was allowed to berth almost in the city centre, on the eastern bank of the Neva. That morning, they were due to join another coach party. Ian went to check his emails quickly in the ship's library; Sophie went to the disembarkation point to wait for him. But she waited and waited, and he didn't appear. The coach was ready to leave, and still he didn't appear. And finally, when the last two stragglers hurried down the gangplank, Ian was not with them. It was Mr. and Mrs. Wilcox, alone.

"He's not coming," Mr. Wilcox told her.

"What?"

"He's too upset. We saw him in the library. He heard about that promotion."

"What? He didn't get it?"

"Apparently not."

"Shit." Her stomach hollowed and she felt suddenly sick. "But he was so sure about it."

"Well . . . These things are never really in the bag, are they?"

Sophie knew what she had to do. "I'll go and talk to him," she said. "Tell everyone to carry on without me."

"You can't do that," Mr. Wilcox insisted. "He doesn't want you to. He said he'll be fine. He just wants a quiet day by himself."

"Come on," said Mrs. Wilcox, taking her by the arm. "We shall all be so disappointed if you aren't with us at the Hermitage."

"Well . . ." Sophie was doubtful. "I suppose it's what I'm here for. But poor Ian . . ."

"He'll be fine," said Mr. Wilcox. "He's just having a bit of a sulk, that's all."

They had a long day's sightseeing. The Hermitage itself was impossibly busy, and they spent more than three hours there shuffling through the crowds, during which time Sophie faced a constant barrage of questions from all sides. She enjoyed the visit, and was pleased to be of such help to so many different people, but it was exhausting work. The party was late getting back to the coach and by the time they returned to *Topaz IV*, dinner had already been in progress for fifteen minutes. The only two people who had taken their places at the table, at this point, were Ian and Mrs. Murphy (who had also not come on the excursion today, for some reason). Ian seemed, quite understandably, relieved to see the new arrivals, and he rose to his feet as Sophie gave him a big, consoling hug.

"I'm so sorry," she said, clasping him tighter. "This is such a bummer. You really deserved that job."

Amidst the hubbub of everyone sitting down, unfolding their napkins, passing around the bread basket and the wine bottles, Ian said: "It's OK. These things happen. I've had the day to think about it. I'm fine. And I'm happy for Naheed."

"Naheed? She . . . They gave the job to her?"

"Yes. I've already sent an email to congratulate her."

"Did you even know she was applying?"

"Yes. Apparently it came down to just the two of us in the end."

Sophie was still digesting this information when, from the other side of the table, Mrs. Murphy spoke. This in itself was a rare enough occurrence. It was rarer still that she should speak in such a loud, attention-commanding voice. What she said, however, was the most surprising thing of all.

"My husband passed away last night."

Silence fell upon the table, immediate and profound.

"He had a stroke. It would have been quite painless. I didn't find out until this morning. I knew something was wrong when he didn't get up to make me a cup of tea."

The others murmured, "I'm so sorry," along with other vague, sympathetic phrases.

"When do you fly home with him, my dear?" Miss Thomsett asked.

"I'm not flying home," said Mrs. Murphy. "I paid for this cruise, and I'm here to enjoy it."

She bit off a portion of bread, and chewed it defiantly. The others glanced at each other, not sure how to respond; and then they, too, resumed their preliminary eating and drinking. No one commented any further, apart from Mr. Wilcox, who picked up his wine glass and, before taking a sip, muttered: "And then there were seven."

*

The following evening, when Sophie and Ian arrived at the cabaret theatre for Lionel Hampshire's reading, they found a notice pinned to the door: "We regret to inform you that Mr. Lionel Hampshire is indisposed, and tonight's advertised reading will no longer take place. Molly Parton will be on stage at 10 p.m."

To Sophie's eyes, when she saw Lionel on the upper deck the following morning, he did not look indisposed at all. In fact he appeared in the rudest of health. He was in his usual spot, sipping a latte as before, but this time he was accompanied by a blonde-haired woman about ten years younger than Sophie, who he introduced as Maxine, his assistant.

"Not going ashore today, then?" Sophie asked. The ship had docked at Tallinn at around six thirty that morning.

"I've been before," said Lionel. "There's not really a lot to see. We thought we might take a stroll round the Old Town this afternoon."

"We had the same idea."

Ian joined them now, and so, a few minutes later, did Mr. and Mrs. Wilcox. This created a rather difficult situation, as Lionel seemed prepared to admit Sophie into the orbit of his conversation, but not the others.

"I'm glad you've recovered, anyway," she said.

"Recovered?"

"I thought you were ill last night."

"Oh, that. Just a dicky tummy. Probably the seafood we had at lunch."

"Has it been rescheduled? Your reading, I mean."

"Not as far as I'm aware."

"Oh dear. But that means you've come all this way for nothing."

"Well." Lionel smiled. "What can you do?"

He didn't seem in the least perturbed. It was at this point, too, that Sophie noticed how extraordinarily beautiful Maxine was, and in what extraordinary proximity her legs and Lionel's had managed to arrange themselves beneath the table. Sophie met her eyes for a brief, complicit moment, but no more was said about it. Maxine leaned in towards her employer and whispered something to him, something evidently not intended to be overheard, and Sophie found herself listening, instead, to the conversation her husband was having with Mr. Wilcox. The subject, unsurprisingly, was Ian's failed bid for promotion.

"So they gave it to your colleague?" Mr. Wilcox was saying.

"Yep."

"And what did you say her name was?"

"Naheed. I've known her for ages. We've worked together for about five years. She's great."

"Hmm. Naheed—so I'm guessing this is . . . an Asian lady, am I right?"

"That's right."

"Well—there you are, then."

He tipped a sachet of sweetener into his coffee, and stirred it two or three times, focusing on the task, and clearly thinking that nothing more needed to be said. Sophie waited for her husband to challenge him, but Ian was silent. When it became obvious that he was going to stay that way, she turned to Mr. Wilcox and said:

"What do you mean?"

He looked up from his stirring. "Sorry, love?"

"What does that mean—'There you are, then'?"

He looked back at her brazenly. "We don't have to spell it out, do we?"

"I think we do. Since I have literally no idea what you're talking about."

"Look," he said, "I don't want to cause trouble. But your husband here is feeling bad about not getting the job, and all I'm saying is, he shouldn't blame himself."

"Go on," said Sophie.

All at once it seemed as though everyone was listening to their conversation—even Lionel and Maxine. Sophie was acutely aware of the stillness of the morning: a cloudless blue sky above them, seagulls whirling but not crying, the growing speck of another, bigger cruise ship advancing towards the harbour from the far horizon.

"We all know what it's like nowadays," said Mr. Wilcox.

"'What it's like'?"

"This country. We all know the score. How it works. People like Ian don't get a fair crack of the whip any more."

Sophie turned to look at Ian. Now, surely, he would intervene, protest, say something? But he didn't. And so, once again, she was the one who had to pursue the point.

"When you say 'people like Ian', I suppose you mean white people?"

Mr. Wilcox, looking slightly embarrassed for the first time, glanced around at the other listeners, seeking support in their faces. He didn't really find it, but he pressed on regardless.

"We don't look after our own any more, do we?" he said. "If you're from a minority—fine. Go to the front of the queue. Blacks, Asians, Muslims, gays: we can't do enough for them. But take a talented bloke like Ian here and it's another story."

"Or maybe," said Sophie, "they just gave the job to the better candidate."

She regretted saying it immediately. Ian was still silent, but she could tell he was smarting; and Mr. Wilcox had pounced upon her misstep in no time.

"I think you'd better decide," he said, "which is more important to you: supporting your husband, or being politically correct."

With that he picked up his novel (the title of which Sophie could not make out, although she could see that it was not *The Twilight of Otters*) and, before resuming his place in it, muttered two words to the table in general—and to Ian in particular: "This country . . ." Words which he invested with a potent mixture of sadness and contempt.

The ensuing silence was broken only when Mrs. Wilcox glanced up at the other cruise ship, now almost parallel to their own, and said: "What a big boat."

*

That afternoon, sitting outside a café in the Old Town, drinking Estonian beer in the shade of a tall, half-timbered building, Sophie said to Ian:

"You didn't buy any of that stuff Geoffrey was saying, did you?"

"No, of course not," he said.

"Good. And I'm sorry if I didn't sound very supportive but—"

"Just drop it, Soph, all right? Like you said, the better candidate won."

He went back to reading his guidebook, but after a few seconds, sensing that Sophie was not satisfied by this assurance, he added: "That's the only explanation, isn't it? I mean, either his theory is right, or your theory is right. So that's it. End of story."

It was clear that he didn't want to discuss the matter any further, so Sophie was really talking to herself when she said: "I've had about as much as I can take of that guy, anyway. Eight nights in a row I've had to sit next to him now. I think tonight we should get there early, and make sure we're sitting next to Joan and Heather." She waited for a reaction from Ian; got none. "Don't you think?"

He grunted. It was the most she was going to get out of him that afternoon. And in any case, Sophie's plan had a flaw. An unforesee-able flaw. Miss Thomsett and Mrs. O'Sullivan did not appear at the dinner table that night. And so once again they sat together, the four of them, on one side of the table, with Mrs. Murphy sitting alone on the other side (still determined to enjoy her cruise, even though she never seemed to come on any of the excursions), while Mr. Wilcox amused himself by speculating—half in jest, half in earnest—as to which of the two elderly companions had passed away this time.

*

The next day, a Friday, was spent at sea en route to Copenhagen. The dress code was "Informal." ("Ladies may wear a less formal dress or separates. Men choose from a lounge suit, sports jacket or blazer with or without a tie; or a smart, closed-neck shirt with a tie.") The daily newsletter announced that there would be a Hair Loss Seminar at ten thirty, a Sit and Be Fit Class at eleven o'clock ("Join David for a gentle exercise class from the comfort of your seat, an ideal warm-up") and a screening of the film *Zulu* in the Cinema Theatre at two thirty. As always, the newsletter was prefaced by a short humorous item under the heading "Robin's Giggle," which on this occasion read:

> Here is today's genuine classified advert: *"Mixing bowl set for sale, designed to please a cook with round bottom for efficient beating."*

Late in the morning Sophie went to the library to check her emails and found the following message:

From: Joan Thomsett
Sent: Friday, August 29, 2014 8:54 AM

To: Sophie Coleman-Potter
Subject: Our absence

Dear Sophie

I am writing to the address printed on your business card and I hope this message finds you. You must be wondering by now why we have left the cruise. Don't worry, we are alive and well, and are not the latest victims of the mysterious curse of Table 19! However, we did have a nasty accident yesterday in Tallinn. Heather slipped and fell down some steps as we were exploring the city walls. She took a nasty tumble and once we got her to the hospital she found that she had broken her leg. Fortunately it was not a severe fracture but once they had put the plaster cast on, it was suggested that she fly back to England for further treatment. Legend were very efficient and found an evening flight for us and now we are already back in Bristol!

Unlike Mrs. Murphy, who I suppose is still persisting with her holiday even in her widowed state, I could not imagine continuing the cruise without my beloved Heather. We have done everything together for more than thirty years now and in all that time I don't believe we have even spent one night apart! Yes, I'm afraid we told a few white lies to the other passengers about our relationship, but I'm sure that you quickly guessed its real nature. After many years' travelling and cruising in particular we have realized that, sadly, even today we cannot rely on the understanding of fellow passengers when we tell them that we are life-partners, although I will observe—in a slightly more optimistic mode—that people do seem to be getting rather more tolerant. (But that itself I have always found a peculiar word in this context: what is there, exactly, in our loyal and loving and supportive relationship that requires people to draw upon their reserves of "tolerance"?) In any case, we both found you and your charming husband to be extremely simpatico, and have no qualms whatsoever in telling you the truth!

I know that you and Ian only have a short time left on board, but I do hope that you enjoy yourselves and make the most of it. Your lecture on Sunday and your informative comments as we toured the Hermitage were a great inspiration to so many of us. Clearly you have a great career ahead of you and I look forward to following it—at a distance, perhaps, but with great interest I am sure.

Affectionately
Joan Thomsett.

*

On Saturday morning, with the ship moored in Copenhagen, Sophie and Ian prepared to leave the cruise and fly home. *Topaz IV* would not return to Dover for four more days yet—there would be further stops in Northern Germany and the Netherlands—but when agreeing to this engagement Sophie had decided that ten days at sea would be enough (a decision she now rather regretted). Now, with their cases packed, she was saying her last goodbyes to Henry. As always, it was a friendly exchange, but she could not find the right tone to strike with him. As always, he was reserved, enigmatic and impeccably polite.

"Well, Henry," she said. "We can't thank you enough for all your help."

"Not at all, madam. All part of the service."

"You went above and beyond the call of duty. Even ironing my husband's underpants. Amazing."

He laughed, and repeated: "All part of the service."

"Here's my card," she said, "in case you . . . I don't know, in case you wanted to keep in touch."

He took the card, still smiling, and put it away in his pocket without looking at it.

"I hope you've enjoyed . . ." She was about to say "looking after us," but that sounded ridiculous. Why should he enjoy looking after them more than anyone else? ". . . this trip," she concluded, lamely. "I mean, I know it's just a job for you and . . . you don't have a cabin like this . . ." His cabin, which he shared with two other crew members, was in the very bowels of the ship, windowless: she knew that much. "Anyway . . ." This was sounding more and more stupid. "Anyway . . . Here's a little . . . token, from Ian and me."

She handed him a white envelope, which contained a small greetings card and some banknotes. They—or rather she—had agonized over how much they should give, and in what currency. Eventually they had settled for fifty euros.

"Thank you, madam," said Henry, putting the envelope away in the same pocket and shaking her by the hand. "You are very kind. It's been very nice meeting you."

"Good. And for us too. Any time you're in London, or Birmingham . . ."

Henry, almost out of the door by now, repeated: "Thank you, madam."

"Well—goodbye. Or *Paalam*, as you would say . . ."

Henry was gone. Ian burst out laughing.

"What's so funny?"

"You. Riddled with liberal angst and desperate to make him your new bestie."

"Just trying to be civil, that's all," said Sophie, spotting a stray lipstick on her bedside shelf and popping it into her bag. That was everything, it seemed. She stood looking at the room, hands on hips, feeling a sudden melancholy steal over her.

"I'm going to miss this cabin," she said. "I've really enjoyed the last ten days."

"I know you have," said Ian, putting his arm around her. "Especially before I arrived, I bet."

She looked at him sharply. "Why do you say that?"

"You like being alone. Don't think I haven't noticed." Before she could deny it (if she was going to) he said: "So—you've said goodbye to the Wilcoxes?"

"Yep."

"And to Lionel?"

"He was still in bed. I knocked and said goodbye through the door."

"Maxine?"

"She wasn't in her room."

"Hm. That figures."

They walked out on to the balcony for a final look at the sea. The harbour itself was anonymous and cheerless. Three other cruise ships, all much larger than *Topaz IV*, were docked there this morning.

"D'you think you'll keep in touch with any of them?" Ian asked.

"Not sure," said Sophie. "Probably not. Heather and Joan, maybe. I rather liked them, I must say."

"The lezzers." Ian smiled. "Funny how Geoffrey was right about them after all."

Sophie said nothing. She looked up towards the sun, wanting to feel the sea breeze on her face for the last time. Ian leaned over the balustrade and gazed into the depths of the water. Neither of them spoke for a few minutes.

"What are you thinking?" Sophie asked, finally.

"Oh, nothing," he said, standing up straight and walking back into the cabin. Although he had been thinking, in fact, that if Mr. Wilcox had been right about those two, why shouldn't he be right about other things as well?

19

Benjamin was standing in the bookshop at Woodlands Garden Centre. He was not looking at any of the gardening books, or any of the books on local history, or any of the books commemorating various aspects of the Second World War. He was not flicking through the cookery books in search of inspiration for tonight's dinner, or browsing in the humour section in a desperate bid to find something that would bring a smile to his face. His attention was fixed, rather, on one of the remotest and least visited areas of the shop, where on a bottom shelf of the furthest bookcase was to be found a section entitled "Miscellaneous." This section consisted of some fifteen or twenty titles. One of them—represented here by two copies—was his own novel, *A Rose Without a Thorn*.

Reaching down to the bottom shelf, he picked up both copies, and turned them over in his hands lovingly. Chase Historical might be a low-budget publisher, but they had done a beautiful production job, he had to credit them with that. The front cover showed a high-definition image of a white rose against a black background. The title and the author's name were in the same discreet white font, all in lower case. It looked incredibly classy. But still, it was a shame, a great shame, that Philip's production values were not matched by his reach as a distributor. The novel had been published more than four weeks earlier and Benjamin had visited almost every bookshop within a fifty-mile radius without locating more than half a dozen copies—and most of those were in garden centres, even though he knew Philip had been hoping that branching out into fiction would gain him an entrée into more respectable outlets. (This had, in fact, been his main reason for publishing Benjamin at all, apart from the bonds of friendship.) Benjamin had not dared, yet, to enquire about sales figures; and as for the book's critical reception, it was non-existent. No reviews in either the national or local papers, of course, nothing on the various readers' websites and no reader reviews on Amazon—where it had a sales ranking of 743,926 (or, if he wanted to cheer himself up, 493 in Bestsellers>Fiction>Literary Fiction>Autobiographical Fiction>Romance>Obsession).

And yes, he should have expected this. He should have known that Philip alone, with no marketing or publicity budget to draw on, could do little more than produce printed copies of his book and hope for the best. But what choice had Benjamin been offered? Every publisher in London, and every independent literary house in the rest of the country, had turned the novel down—or, more often, declined to read it in the first place. No literary agent had bothered to send him anything more than a form letter in response to his submission, usually offering some oleaginous brush-off such as, "We found many qualities to admire in your MS, but feel it is not one for our list at the moment." Some letters had gone into more detail, not about the qualities of the book itself, but about current market conditions and the problems of launching the careers of new writers at this difficult moment. Most publishers and agents had taken more than two months to respond, and even while making multiple submissions, Benjamin had had to endure almost a year of these rejections, arriving through his letterbox daily, just in time to ruin his breakfast, before he had bitten the bullet and called Philip. After that, it had all been very quick and straightforward. The manuscript had been edited, copy-edited and proofed in a matter of weeks. And now here it was, his life's work (or at least a truncated version of it) finally on sale. If only the bookshop had chosen to display it more prominently . . .

With this in mind, and making sure that the sales assistant was not watching, Benjamin took both copies of his novel to the centre of the shop and placed them on the main display table, on top of a pile of books about bonsai trees. The effect was almost immediate.

Withdrawing to the sidelines, and pretending to immerse himself in a biography of Winston Churchill, he only had to wait a few minutes to see three customers in succession wander over to the display table and pick up his book, read the blurb and flick through its pages. None of them went on to buy it, admittedly, but it was clear that he'd given a significant boost to its chances. Satisfied, he went to find his father in the restaurant.

He'd brought him to the garden centre several times in the last couple of months. It had been an act of desperation, at first—they had long since run out of places to go in the vicinity of Rednal itself— but Colin seemed to enjoy the excursion, so it had quickly started to become a habit. Benjamin could hardly be said to relish these visits, even so. Every minute in his father's company was difficult, these days: he was slower on his feet than ever, more gloomy about every- thing, more cynical about everything. He was anything but scintil- lating company, in other words: so Benjamin was more than a little surprised when he made his way to the restaurant and saw his father sitting, not alone, hunched over a plate of steak-and-kidney pie, but enjoying a relatively animated conversation—even sharing a joke— with a figure he didn't recognize at first: a portly figure dressed in gentleman's tweeds of the 1930s, with a gold fob watch in his pocket and a red ping-pong ball on the table next to him, resting inside an upturned, garish, multicoloured mortar board. He had a goatee beard and a reddish, cheerfully welcoming face, and when Benjamin appeared he sprang to his feet and grasped him by the hand and pumped it vigorously and said:

"Ben! It's so good to see you, mate."

Benjamin could only stare back in puzzlement.

"Don't tell me that you don't remember me? Come on, Ben, don't break my heart."

"Sure. You're—" he hesitated, and then came out with the only thing he could be sure of "—Baron Brainbox? The kids' entertainer?"

"And? And?"

Benjamin didn't have a clue. His father looked at him with a mixture of delight and superiority. It wasn't often that he was a step ahead of his son.

"I knew who it was right away. Don't you recognize him? It's Charlie! Charlie Chappell!"

Slowly, realization dawned on Benjamin's face. All the same, he felt that he could be forgiven for not recognizing Charlie Chappell, someone he hadn't seen (or thought about much) for more than forty years. Charlie had once been his next-door neighbour. He had been one of his best friends. They had sat next to each other on their very first day at primary school, aged five. They had played together in the school playground, visited each other's houses constantly, shared sweets, swapped chocolate bars, read their first (and, in Benjamin's case, only) porn magazines side by side. And then, at the age of eleven—for reasons which were not clear to him, even now—Benjamin's parents had made him sit the entrance exam to King William's School, and he had passed. Charlie had carried on through the state system to the local comprehensive, and a gulf had opened up between them. Not an educational or academic gulf, primarily, but a social one. Benjamin had moved to a school where the teachers wore university gowns in class; where the teachers were not, in fact, called "teachers" at all but "masters"; where there not only existed such a thing as "the school song" but it was sung in Latin; where there was only one black boy—Steve Richards—in his entire year, and the other boys called him "Rastus." Benjamin and Charlie had not so much drifted apart as immediately been swept apart by rapid, powerful, diverging currents. They stopped visiting each other's houses. Conversation between them became forced and uncomfortable. And a year or two later, in any case, to make the separation irrevocable, the Chappells had moved to a new house in Northfield, ten minutes' drive away. And that was that. Benjamin and Charlie never saw or spoke to each other again.

But that was all long, long in the past. There was nothing but delight on Charlie's face upon encountering his old friend.

"I'm sure I spotted you here a few years ago," he said. "I was in the middle of one of my shows. I tried to catch your eye."

"Yes, that was me," said Benjamin. "Have you been doing one today?"

"Just come off," said Charlie. "Tough crowd in there, as well."

"So how did you . . .?" Benjamin didn't know how to finish the sentence.

". . . end up doing this for a living?" said Charlie. "Long story. Let's just say that the phone call from the RSC never came through. What about you? Your dad was saying that you've retired already."

"I'm not retired," said Benjamin, indignant. "I look after you—" (staring at his father) "—for a start. I volunteer three mornings a week in the hospital in Shrewsbury, working in the charity shop. And I've been writing. I've just had my first novel published, in fact."

"Why am I not surprised?" said Charlie. "Always the intellectual of the family. Always the creative genius. Where can I get a copy?"

"Right here. They've got a couple in the bookshop."

"Brilliant. You've just made a sale."

Charlie was in no hurry to leave. He had a children's party at four o'clock that afternoon but nothing until then, and in the meantime was happy to enjoy a slow lunch with Benjamin and Colin. Afterwards Colin announced that he wanted to visit the pet department: he liked looking at the koi carp and the tropical fish—would stare at them, sometimes, for minutes at a time, mesmerized by their drooping mouths and melancholy eyes, as if he were trying to understand their dreams and fathom their memories. He said that he would see Benjamin back at the car. So Benjamin and Charlie headed off to the bookshop, passing by the entrance to the children's theatre on the way.

"Look who's on," said Charlie, darkly, nodding towards the open doorway.

Benjamin glanced inside and saw that the figure entertaining the circle of children was wearing a white medical coat, wellington boots, a false moustache and a World War Two pilot's leather helmet. He remembered him from last time; remembered his sullen demeanour off stage, and the crude hostility he had expressed towards Charlie. What was the story between those two? He watched now as Charlie caught Doctor Daredevil's eye and snarled at him; the other clown had seen him immediately and glowered back, without breaking character. In that instant the air was charged with a quivering hatred and malevolence, even though Charlie brightened again so quickly as they walked on, recovering his former cheerfulness as though nothing had happened, that Benjamin didn't feel he could mention the subject or ask what was going on.

In the bookshop Charlie picked up the two copies of *A Rose Without a Thorn* from the central pile, read the cover blurb, complimented Benjamin on the design and said: "Right. I'm having both of these."

Benjamin went over with him to the till, so that he could revel in this moment of triumph. The assistant, perhaps less impressed than he had been expecting, rang up the sale with mechanical indifference.

"This is the author, you know," Charlie said. "You should be making a fuss of him. He's a local celebrity."

"We get a lot of authors in here," she answered.

"Oh well." Charlie glanced at Benjamin and grimaced. "Can you sign these for me, Ben, now that they're paid for?"

"Of course."

Benjamin laid the books on the counter and took out his pen. "Are they both for you?"

"First one's for me. Second one's for 'Aneeqa', please."

"Any special message?"

"Not really." He considered. "In hers you could write 'Good luck with your studies.'"

"'Good luck with your studies,'" Benjamin repeated, as he inscribed the words, and handed the copies to Charlie proudly. They were the first ones he had signed, apart from one for Phil, one for Lois, one for Sophie and one for his father. Turning to the assistant, he said: "You'll have to order a few more of these now."

"It's all right," she said. "We've got about forty out the back."

"Oh. Would you like me to sign those as well?"

"I'd rather you didn't. We have enough trouble selling them as it is. If you sign them, we can't return them. They're considered damaged stock."

Benjamin wasn't sure how much more discouragement he could take from this woman.

"Haven't you sold *any* copies so far?" he asked.

"We did sell a couple," the assistant said, "but the customers brought them back."

"Brought them back? Why?"

"I expect it's the title. They thought it was going to be about growing roses. That's the sort of thing most people come in here for, you see. We don't sell much fiction."

It was time to go and meet Colin at the car. Benjamin could not keep himself from ruminating on the fragile commercial prospects of his book as they weaved their way through the garden furniture, but finally he snapped out of it and remembered to ask Charlie:

"So who's Aneeqa, then?"

"Like everything else in my life, that's a long story," he answered. "Can we have lunch again soon? I'd really like to catch up properly."

"Absolutely. Let's do it."

"Anyway," said Charlie, as they left Woodlands' sprawling interior and began to walk through its equally gigantic car park, "to give you the short version—I'm sort of her stepfather. Her mother's divorced—it's just the two of them at home—and—I mean, I'm not married to her mother or anything, but I spend a lot of time at their house, and I've kind of become the father-figure, I suppose. At least, that's what I'd *like* to be . . . It's complicated. It's a bit of a mess, to be honest, Ben. I could do with talking to you about it some time. I don't know that many people who understand . . . the human heart, and all its mysteries."

Benjamin was touched by the compliment; and also quite surprised to hear Charlie using this sort of phrase, which seemed to hint at unsuspected reserves of sensitivity and tenderness.

"I don't know about that," he said, building up to share a confidence with him. "When you read my book you'll understand that, emotionally, there's been a lot of difficulty in my life, and—"

"Oh, FUCK YOU!" Charlie shouted now. "Fuck you, you cunting CUNT of an arsehole!"

Benjamin stopped and stared in bewilderment. They had reached Charlie's car, an ancient but well-polished and shiny Nissan Micra, and he was looking in fury and anguish at the paintwork on the driver's side. A long, deep scratch had been scored with a coin or other implement, running from headlight to tail light.

"*He* did this," he said, hissing the words out. "*He* did this, the bastard. I'll kill him, I swear. I'll crack his head open and slash his face with a fucking Stanley knife."

He turned and was about to march off back into the garden centre. Benjamin put a restraining hand on his arm.

"Charlie, don't do anything silly," he said. "I've no idea what's going on between you two, but . . . violence isn't the answer. It's never the answer." And then, more to distract him than anything else, he added: "Anyway, when shall we have that lunch?"

Charlie hesitated for a moment, breathing heavily, his anger still almost getting the better of him. Then he said, "Yeah, you're right," took out his phone to look at the calendar, and the moment of crisis passed.

20.

APRIL 2015

On 14 April 2015, the Conservative Party launched its manifesto for the forthcoming general election. Doug read through the first paragraph of David Cameron's introduction while waiting for Nigel to arrive at their usual meeting point, the café at Temple tube station.

"Five years ago," he read "Britain was on the brink . . ."

> Since then, we have turned things around. Britain is now one of the fastest growing major economies in the world. We are getting our national finances back under control. We have halved our deficit as a share of our economy. More people are in work than ever before. Britain is back on its feet, strong and growing stronger every day. This has not happened by accident. It is the result of difficult decisions and of patiently working through our long-term economic plan. Above all, it is the product of a supreme national effort, in which everyone has made sacrifices and everyone has played their part . . . Our friends and competitors overseas look at Britain, and they see a country that is putting its own house in order, a country on the rise. They see a country that believes in itself.

"Did you write any of this rubbish?" Doug asked, as Downing Street's perennially youthful deputy assistant director of communications arrived and sat down opposite him.

Nigel smiled a frosty smile, but seemed neither surprised nor especially put out by this opening gambit.

"Ah, Douglas," he said. "Always on the attack. Always trying to score the first point. If I thought that you meant any of it, I'd be offended. But I've come to know you better than that, after all these years."

"How's morale at Number Ten?" Doug asked, passing Nigel the cappuccino he had already ordered for him. "The panic is off the scale, I should think."

"The *confidence*, Douglas, the *enthusiasm*—that's what's off the scale. Dave's ready for this fight, and do you know why? Because he knows he's going to win."

"He hasn't been reading the opinion polls, then?"

"We never take any notice of opinion polls. They're always wrong."

"The television debate didn't go too well. Ed Miliband put up a pretty good show."

"Ed's a nice guy, but we're not worried about him. The people of this country will never vote for a Marxist as prime minister."

"Where did you read that he was a Marxist?" said Doug. "The *Daily Mail*? Ed Miliband isn't a Marxist."

"His father was. According to the *Daily Mail*."

"Oh, come on, Nigel, don't be silly. Having a father who was a Marxist doesn't make you a Marxist. Your father's a proctologist. What does that make you?"

"You keep bringing up my father's profession, Douglas. Are those piles still giving you trouble?"

Doug sighed. He had been meeting Nigel two or three times a year, now, for five years, and was still no closer, as far as he could tell, to breaking through his façade of cheerful obfuscation.

"I should have known better," he said, "than to think you'd do anything other than pretend everything was hunky-dory. That is your job, after all."

"I wouldn't say everything was hunky-dory, Doug. It's a bit complacent of you to think that, if I may say so. We still face a lot of challenges. Austerity's still biting, and mostly hurting the people who are least able to deal with it. Dave's aware of all this. He's not a monster, however you may like to think of him. But we're pretty good at reading the mood of the country, and it's obvious that when things are so difficult, and the future's so uncertain, people would be mad to vote for change. Continuity, stability—that's what they need to get them through this sticky patch."

Doug scratched his head. "But that literally makes no sense. Under the current administration, the country's in a mess, so the only solution is to vote for the current administration?"

"In a nutshell, yes. That's the very clear message we're going to be putting across to the electorate in the next few weeks."

"Well, good luck with that."

"The choice is between strong and stable government under David, or weak and chaotic leadership under Ed—who would probably have to go into coalition with the Scottish Nationalists. Just think of that!"

"You may have to stay in coalition with the Lib Dems."

"Wouldn't be a problem, but it's not going to happen. We're going to win an overall majority. We're quite confident of that. That's what the opinion polls are telling us."

"But you just said you don't trust opinion polls."

"We don't trust most people's opinion polls. But we do commission our own. Which we trust."

Doug sighed again.

"OK. Let's get down to brass tacks."

"The nitty-gritty," Nigel agreed.

"Exactly. The nitty-gritty. Page seventy-two of the manifesto: 'Real change in our relationship with the European Union'."

Nigel beamed happily. "That's right. A crucial part of the manifesto. Almost its unique selling point, you might say."

"Well, whoever wrote this, I must give them credit—it's pretty clear. 'Only the Conservative Party will deliver real change and real choice on Europe, with an in–out referendum by the end of 2017.'"

"That's right."

"Is that really such a good idea?"

"It's Dave's idea. Of course it's good."

"But supposing there's a referendum and we vote to leave?"

"Then we leave. The people will have spoken."

Impressed as he was by this unqualified commitment to direct democracy, Doug couldn't help objecting: "But people don't really care about the European Union. Whenever the public are asked to list their main political concerns they say things like education or housing, and the EU doesn't even come in the top ten."

Nigel had been looking puzzled, but his face now cleared: "Ah, you're talking about the *public*. Sorry, that's not what I meant by 'people'."

"What did you mean by 'people'?"

"I meant people in the Conservative Party who keep banging on about how much they hate the EU and won't shut up until we do something about it."

"Ah, *those* people."

"Those people."

"So that's why Cameron is promising this referendum. To silence *those* people."

"Don't be silly, Douglas. Holding a referendum on such an important issue just to silence a few annoying people in his own party? That would be a highly irresponsible thing to do."

"But that's just what you said he was doing."

"No I didn't. I said nothing of the sort. Have you not *read* the manifesto?"

"Of course I have."

"Well, it says here why we're promising the referendum." He picked up Doug's copy from the table, where it was still folded at the relevant page. "Listen: 'It will be a fundamental principle of a future Conservative Government that membership of the European Union depends on the consent of the British people. That's why, after the election, we will negotiate a new settlement for Britain in Europe, and then ask the British people whether they want to stay in the EU on this reformed basis or leave. We will hold that in–out referendum before the end of 2017 and respect the outcome.' Now, what could be more simple than that?"

"Hold on a second," said Doug. "You left a bit out."

"I did?"

"Yes—give me that. You missed a bit."

"I don't think so."

"That sentence about the consent of the British people . . ."

"Yes?"

"Just after that. Here . . ." He took the pamphlet back from Nigel and rapidly scanned the page. "Yes, here we are: 'Membership of the European Union depends on the consent of the British people—*and in recent years that consent has worn wafer-thin.*'"

"That's right. It has."

"So what Cameron's doing is extremely risky, in other words?"

"Why do you say that?"

"Because he's proposing to hold an in–out referendum and he knows in advance that the majority is going to be wafer-thin."

Nigel shook his head and tutted. "Honestly, Douglas, you writers! With your ridiculously creative interpretations of things. You take a perfectly clear, perfectly innocent phrase and you twist it, you distort it . . ."

"I suppose you could always make the result dependent on a supermajority—sixty per cent or something like that."

"That idea was suggested, but there's no real need."

"Why not?"

"Because the referendum will be purely advisory."

"Really? But that's not what it says here. It says, 'We will hold that in–out referendum before the end of 2017 *and respect the outcome.*' That doesn't sound like an advisory referendum to me."

"Of course it does. It means the British people will give us their advice, and we'll take it." Doug did not look particularly convinced by this argument, so he added: "In any case, would it be so bad if we left the European Union? As a socialist, you must have a lot of problems with it. Look at the way they've been treating the poor Greeks, for instance."

Finishing his cappuccino, Doug rose to his feet and put the manifesto pamphlet away in his coat pocket. "That's true," he said. "But I assume that Cameron wants to stay in."

"Of course."

"In which case I think he will be taking an enormous gamble if he offers a fifty–fifty vote on something where he already thinks public opinion is closely divided."

"It is a gamble," Nigel agreed. "A huge gamble. The country's future decided on the roll of a dice. The fact that Dave's prepared to take it is what makes him such a strong, decisive leader."

Impressed as always by Nigel's logical contortions, Doug shook his hand and asked one final question:

"So Cameron isn't at all worried about promising this referendum?"

"Well, he would be," Nigel answered, buttoning up his coat. "But the bottom line is, it's not going to happen."

"Why not?" asked Doug.

"Because there's no way he's going to win an overall majority. All the opinion polls say so. Don't you ever look at them, Douglas? You really should."

As a parting shot, that would have been baffling enough to keep Doug occupied all the way home. But Nigel had an even better one up his sleeve.

"And by the way," he said, leaving an expectant pause which he timed to perfection. "Give my regards to Gail, won't you? Dave does regard her as an absolutely crucial member of the team. I hope she realizes that."

21.

Doug never did discover how Nigel had managed to find out. He had only been seeing Gail Ransome for a few weeks, at this point, and they had both tried to be discreet about it. He supposed that, in the cramped, hothouse atmosphere of the Westminster village, it was impossible to keep a new relationship secret for long, particularly when it involved a left-wing journalist and a Conservative MP. That was a gift for the gossip-mongers, certainly. But whatever the explanation, it made Doug feel distinctly uneasy that David Cameron's deputy assistant director of communications was privy to the information when his own daughter wasn't.

But who was to blame for that? He and Coriander barely spoke to each other these days. In fact, he would not have believed it possible for a father and daughter to share such a confined living space and live in such profound ignorance of each other's lives.

Since the night of the Olympic opening ceremony, there had been major upheavals in the Gifford-Anderton household. Doug and Francesca had separated, without too much heartbreak on either side. He had moved into a boxy two-bedroom flat in Lower Holloway, not far from the Caledonian Road. Francesca, he learned (from the *Evening Standard* Londoner's Diary) wasted little time before starting to date a recently divorced reality TV producer rumoured to be one of the hundred richest men in the country. Coriander, whose long-standing disdain for her mother's values and way of life were triumphantly confirmed by this development, waited until the day of her sixteenth birthday and then exercised her legal right to leave the comforts of

Chelsea behind and move in with her father. She also quit her West London private school and entered the sixth form of a state school in Camden which was achingly fashionable with the daughters of North London's liberal intelligentsia.

Doug quickly found that he did not really miss the trappings of the super-wealthy: the shrinking of his living space was more than offset, in his opinion, by the fact that he no longer had to sit through dinner parties in the company of oligarchs or make polite conversation with hedge fund managers at Speech Day. And he welcomed the arrival of Coriander, envisaging a new relationship based on cosy chats over the breakfast table and late-night sessions working on homework together. But he had not been paying attention. His daughter might have rejected her mother's values, but she was no more enamoured of Doug's. In fact she was far to the left of her father these days: her views on racism, inequality and identity politics were utterly uncompromising, and she made no effort at all to hide the fact that she considered him at best a deluded, out-of-touch, middle-of-the-road social democrat, at worst a feeble sell-out whose political compromises actually formed a far greater barrier to social justice than anything the Tory Party could come up with. The current Labour Party, led by Ed Miliband (portrayed by the Conservative media as a Marxist, or at least the son of a Marxist, which amounted to the same thing), she considered a pale, bloodless descendant of Tony Blair's New Labour, irredeemably tainted by the criminal folly of the Iraq War, with no convincing or radical vision to offer in response to the Tories' austerity programme. "But at least they're the lesser of two evils," her father would say, and in return she scoffed. As for those breakfast chats, on school days she left the house at seven thirty and had breakfast with her friends in local coffee shops. With these same friends she would roam the streets of London in the evenings and weekends, touring pubs, clubs, gigs and parties whose precise nature Doug could only guess at (although he preferred not to think about it at all). On a good day, Coriander and her father, if their paths happened to cross in the kitchen or on the way to the bathroom, would conduct themselves with cool civility. But it was not uncommon for them to cohabit for weeks at a time without speaking a word to each other.

On 7 May 2015, however—the night of the general election—
things between them were to get substantially worse.

*

As the BBC's late-night coverage unfolded, Doug watched the
results come in with astonishment. Like everybody else, he had
assumed that this election was going to be close, and would probably
result in a hung parliament. The ten o'clock exit poll was enough to
show that this was not going to happen. After that, it became a question of waiting for the key constituencies to declare. When Nuneaton
showed a big swing to the Conservatives, at one fifty in the morning,
the presenters affirmed that the election was won and all the poll-
sters' expectations had been overturned. Incredible, but true.

He'd agreed to write 1,200 words by 6 a.m. Not for the print
edition, just for the website (at a fraction of the print edition fee). He
went into the kitchen to fix himself a coffee before getting started,
then sat down in front of the television again, opened a new docu-
ment on his laptop and began to type:

Can a bacon sandwich defeat socialism?

Solid opening sentence. Bit predictable, perhaps. But he would
press on.

After all, how else do we explain the inexplicable? This should
surely have been Ed Miliband's moment. The coalition government has really done nothing in the last five years to make itself
popular with voters. Nothing has been done to address the under-
lying causes of the 2008 financial crisis, apart from conceiving
and adhering to a cruel austerity programme whose effects have
been felt by everyone in the country except the super-rich. For
the young middle class, wages have stagnated and living standards have failed to rise. For the poorest, the impact has been
much worse, with an exponential rise in dependence upon food
banks which should be the shame of any civilized country.

At two thirty the front door was unlocked and Coriander came in, looking dishevelled and sleep-deprived. She threw off her coat and flopped down on the sofa beside him.

"Have you heard?" he asked.

"Yep. Stupid cunts."

He gave her a questioning glance, since it wasn't entirely clear who she was referring to.

"Voters," she elaborated.

"Ah."

"The idiots who just voted for their lives to get even worse."

Doug said: "Well, what choice did they have? Since, in your opinion, the Labour Party's just as bad."

"True."

"Which way would you have voted?"

Coriander, who would be eighteen in August, had been spared that particular decision. She shrugged.

"I could do with a coffee," she said, getting up.

"Make me another one too, will you?"

While she was out of the room, two further results were announced on the television: Brecon and Radnorshire, and Yeovil. Both had gone to the Tories, with massive swings against the Liberal Democrats. The Tory campaign had ruthlessly targeted their coalition partners and now it was paying off, apparently. But still Doug was struggling to understand why.

> As for the prime minister himself, he has never been especially well liked by traditional Tories, who regard him as altogether too metropolitan and socially liberal. He may count the introduction of gay marriage as one of his proudest achievements, but it won't have won him many extra voters in Middle England.

At four o'clock in the morning, Twickenham fell to the Tories and Doug put his laptop aside, his mind reeling. Twickenham! Vince Cable's seat! Cable had been the secretary of state for business, president of the Board of Trade and the second-most prominent Lib Dem figure in the government. Now his majority of more than 12,000 had been wiped out. The Tories were massacring their former partners, annihilating them. Even after all that "bantz" between Nick and Dave at the cabinet table . . . And yet still the result that Doug was most anxiously awaiting had not come through. When were they going to announce Coventry South West? He sent a quick text to Gail—

How long now?

—and she texted back:

Don't know. Agony here. Xxx.

Dawn was coming now. Doug considered drawing back the curtains to admit the first of the sunlight, but he didn't want to disturb Coriander, who was recumbent on the sofa beside him, drifting in and out of sleep.

So where did Miliband go wrong? At times his campaign was painful to watch. He never looked at ease with the media, and like many Labour leaders before him struggled to get his message across in a hostile environment where sections of the press were ready to pounce on his every mistake. We should not underestimate the effectiveness of the *Mail*'s campaign to portray his academic father Ralph as a Marxist who "hated Britain," and to imply that the son was guilty by genetic association.

And then, of course, there was the bacon sandwich episode. Incredibly, it happened almost a year ago now, but that one photograph of poor Ed in a café in New Covent Garden, trying to eat a bacon sandwich and getting into a bit of a mess as it fell apart in his hands, continues to resonate. Two days ago the *Sun* splashed it all over its front page and wrote: "This is the pig's ear Ed made of a helpless sarnie. In 48 hours, he could be doing the same to Britain." Is this what we've come to? A genuinely progressive, reforming and inclusive manifesto on one side of the scales, and on the other, a party leader (a Jewish party leader, remember) who struggles to look at ease while eating a pork product and must therefore be portrayed as socially awkward and out of touch with the common people?

He was still working on that paragraph, which was too verbose and complicated for his liking, when he glanced up at the TV and saw that the cameras had gone over to Coventry South West at last. There was Gail, looking tired but upbeat in her best navy-blue suit. She was flanked by the other candidates: her Labour opponent just next to her, on her left-hand side, and the usual bizarre crowd occupying the rest of the platform, including the traditional representative of the Monster Raving Loony Party, sporting a top hat and an enormous fake daffodil in his buttonhole. It crossed Doug's mind, fleetingly, that England was, and always had been, a very strange country.

Then the results were being declared, and suddenly Gail was smiling and thrusting her hand into the air in triumph. Her majority was reduced, but she had won, and the banner at the bottom of the screen announced "Con Hold."

"Yes!" Doug shouted, involuntarily. "She did it."

The shout woke Coriander, who struggled into an upright position and squinted at the TV screen. It took a few seconds for the information she read there to reach her sleepy brain and then she turned to him and said, in a puzzled tone: "Did you just cheer a Tory win?"

He couldn't see any way of denying it.

"Why?" she asked. "Who is that woman, anyway?"

"She's . . ." He paused. He was in his mid-fifties. Words had to be chosen carefully. What was the most appropriate way of putting it? "She's someone I've been seeing."

Coriander greeted this information with a long, long silence. She finally broke it, not by speaking, but by rising to her feet from the creaking sofa and shuffling away in the direction of her bedroom.

As she disappeared, Doug called after her, in desperation: "She's very much on the left of the party!" But he had the strong sense, before the words were even out of his mouth, that they were not going to cut much ice.

*

In the wake of David Cameron's unforeseen victory, events began to move fast. By mid-morning no fewer than three of the main party leaders had resigned: Ed Miliband from Labour, Nick Clegg from the Liberal Democrats and Nigel Farage from UKIP. The political landscape with which Doug had grown familiar over the last few years had been laid waste in a couple of hours. That afternoon, the nation was treated to the strangely comic spectacle of the three main party leaders, two of them now ex-party leaders, standing together in solemn finery while attending the VE Day seventieth-anniversary commemoration at the Cenotaph. And then, at around five o'clock, when Doug would normally have expected his daughter to return (fleetingly) from school, he received a text message from Francesca:

Corrie has just appeared. Says she hates you and wants to move back in here for a while. What have you done?

Doug, who was in the middle of a phone interview with BBC Radio London, texted back:

Shagged a Tory.

Which was perhaps not the most diplomatic way of phrasing it, but was at least concise and accurate. There was no reply.

The rest of the weekend was taken up with intense speculation as to who would succeed to the leadership of Labour and the Lib Dems, with Doug either banging out more think pieces from his desk at home or dashing from TV studio to TV studio. By the time he filed his last article in the early hours of Monday morning—a hefty 2,500 words for the *New Statesman*—his feelings about the result had changed, and he had a new theory. Yes, the Tories had brilliantly and ferociously targeted every marginal Lib Dem seat in the country, but the real deciding factor in their victory had been Scotland. A strident, relentless message had been beamed out to the effect that Ed Miliband would make a weak leader; that Labour could not win an overall majority and so would end up going into coalition with the Scottish National Party; and that it would therefore be the SNP—those pesky, unfriendly Scots—who would end up calling the shots at Westminster. In the words of Gordon Brown (whose own defeat, after that disastrous gaffe about the "bigoted woman," seemed five lifetimes, not five years, earlier): "Instead of playing the British unity card, the Conservatives decided to play the English nationalism card.

All this was designed to give the idea that there was a Scottish menace, a Scottish danger, a Scottish risk."

. . . an undeniably effective strategy, as it turned out [Doug wrote]. But, as our former prime minister observes, one which holds risks for the future: if David Cameron has "turned on the tap of English nationalism," will he be able to turn it off again, or will it continue to flow, with increasing and unstoppable force, during the EU referendum campaign to which he is now committed?

*

By midweek, the frenzy of comment was starting to abate. Doug and his colleagues in the media began (with some difficulty) to regain their sense of proportion. It was easy to forget that the general public, once they had cast their votes, would not spend the next five years obsessing over the consequences as the Westminster commentariat were inclined to do. Yes, there had been a political earthquake, but it was a small one, a local one, seen from a global perspective or *sub specie aeternitatis*. Meanwhile, an English summer beckoned, and the country continued to go about its business. Nothing seismic was to take place in the national life for the next few weeks. The next truly astonishing event would have to wait until 29 July 2015.

That was the day when it was announced that Benjamin Trotter's novel, *A Rose Without a Thorn*, had been longlisted for the Man Booker Prize.

22.

Doug did not see his daughter again for two months. He had to hand it to her: when it came to holding grudges, she was at the top of the premier league. Even then, she had not been planning to see him: the encounter was brokered by Francesca, who asked Doug to meet her for a coffee at the Saatchi Gallery on Duke of York Square one morning in mid-July, and brought Coriander along without forewarning either of them.

"Come on, you two," she said. "This is ridiculous. So your father's got a new girlfriend. What's wrong with that? It happens all the time."

"He's such a hypocrite," Coriander said, scowling into the depths of her latte.

"Listen, Corrie," said Doug. "And forgive me if I sound like an old fart: but when you get a bit older—you know, just a *bit* older than eighteen, which I know feels to you like the pinnacle of wisdom—but when you get a bit older, you realize that not everyone who disagrees with you politically—"

Coriander had no interest in listening to this. "Tories are scum," she said.

Doug turned to Francesca, thinking that she would share his outrage at this statement. Instead she was smiling.

"Oh, that's nice," he said. "That's charming, that is. That's a lovely word to use about the woman your dad's—" He was about to say "in love with," but checked himself just in time, partly because he didn't want to say it in front of his ex-wife and his daughter, but also because he had no idea if it was true. Instead he said, "going out with," which merely prompted Coriander to cringe.

"Will both of you stop using these words?" she complained. "You don't 'go out' with someone at your age. You can't have a 'girlfriend'. You're fifty-five. She's forty-six. It sounds creepy."

So, Doug thought, she knows how old Gail is. Interesting. Someone's been doing some googling.

"Well, don't use the word 'scum' about someone whose opinions don't line up with your own," he said. "Gail is a . . . terrific person. She has very strong principles."

"Ah . . ." said Francesca, "so *that's* why you slept with her."

Coriander was having none of it. "Really? Wasn't her husband's construction company fined for building dodgy social housing?"

(More googling, then.)

"There were some problems—" Doug began, but she cut him off.

"Typical Jewish property developer."

"Hey." He raised his finger in warning. "Less of that." He'd noticed this before: how easily her passionate support for the Palestinian cause could shade into knee-jerk anti-Semitism. "Anyway, she's divorced from her husband. Has been for some time. Why don't the three of us have dinner or something, later this week?"

"I'm busy this week."

"How are you busy? School's over, isn't it?"

"I've got to get ready for Bogotá. In fact—" she got up and swung her bag over her shoulder "—I should be doing some shopping now."

"Bogota? Since when are you going to Bogotá?" He turned again to Francesca. "Did you know about this?"

"I found out yesterday. She's going with Tommy. Apparently they've been planning it for ages."

"Who's Tommy?"

"Current boyfriend, I believe," said Francesca. An explanation which caused Coriander to give her the kind of pitying look a religious elder might give to a novice still living in a dark state of ignorance, and to offer the scornful response:

"Boyfriend/friend. Friend/boyfriend. He's just a guy I share a bed with occasionally. Why does your generation have to be so bloody *binary* about everything?"

And with that, she swept out of the café.

Doug, weighed down by gloom, watched her receding figure and said: "That went well."

"What have we spawned?" Francesca asked, musing aloud. Then she sipped her frappuccino and tried to strike a more cheerful note: "At least we've got a daughter who *cares* about the world. That's something, I suppose."

"Does she, though? Sometimes I think she's just addicted to getting outraged on other people's behalf."

"Possibly. Maybe university will calm her down."

Doug gave a sceptical laugh. "Do we know where she's going?"

"She wants to stay in London. Though not living with either of us, obviously."

"Obviously."

There was a quiet moment while they both continued to reflect on their daughter's errant ways. Then Francesca asked: "Is it serious with this woman? Gail?"

"Pretty serious, yes. You can't really mess around with one-night stands at our age, can you?"

She smiled sadly. "I suppose not. How did you meet?"

"Party at the House of Commons. Just a drinks thing. We hit it off, I don't know why." He stroked his ex-wife's hand briefly, ineffectually. "What about you?"

"Oh, not too bad," she said, with forced brightness. "Jogging along, you know." At which point she remembered something she had been meaning to tell him. "I had a meeting with an old school friend of yours the other day, as it happens. Ronald Culpepper."

"*Culpepper?* Jesus. What were you seeing him for?"

"He wanted me to organize a fundraiser for his charity. The Imperium Foundation."

Doug burst into angry, incredulous laughter. "Christ, he's got a nerve. Three things you should know about Culpepper. One, he's in no need of charitable donations from anyone: he's already worth millions. Two, the Imperium Foundation is not a charity in any normal sense of the word: it's a far-right think tank, pushing free trade and helping big American corporations get an entry into British markets. Especially health care and the welfare system."

Francesca thought about this and said. "That's only two things. What's the third?"

"He's a nasty piece of shit."

*

Doug extracted a promise from Coriander—via Francesca—that she would send him messages from Colombia to reassure him that she was safe. The first one did not arrive, however, until the evening of Benjamin's celebration dinner in the first week of August. Doug was driving in heavy traffic when the phone buzzed. Gail had to read the message to him.

"It says, *Everything good here.*"

"Yes? And . . . ?"

"That's it."

"*Everything good here?* Really? That's all she has to say to her father after ten days' travelling?"

"Better than nothing, I suppose," said Gail. "Why are you never this worried about hearing from your son?"

"Because he's down in London, which is safer than Bogotá."

"That's not it. It's because daughters can wrap their fathers around their little fingers."

Gail had a son, Edward—who would be leaving for university soon—and a daughter, Sarah, who was quite a few years younger. Doug was spending a lot of time with them at the moment, and felt frustrated that Gail had still not met either of his children.

"When Corrie comes back, I'll make sure the two of you get together," he promised.

"There's no hurry," she said. "I've got a feeling that's going to be our first big challenge. Not sure I'm ready for it yet. Let me deal with meeting all your old friends first."

Rather than take the train, they had decided to drive from Gail's house (an impressive three-storey terrace in Earlsdon, one of Coventry's more prosperous districts) to Benjamin's dinner in central Birmingham. The route took them along the A45, a crowded dual carriageway at the edges of which traces of Shakespeare's Forest of Arden could still be glimpsed behind the hotels and the light industrial buildings and the busy sprawl of Birmingham airport. While Doug was driving, Gail was racing through the last pages of Benjamin's novel, which she was determined to finish before meeting him.

"Well," she said, putting it to one side as they neared the city centre, "that was depressing. Beautifully written, but depressing."

"Melancholy," said Doug, "is very much Benjamin's thing. English melancholy in particular. With a side order of morbid nostalgia."

"Sounds like we're in for a fun evening."

"Don't worry. He saves it for the written word."

"Remind me who else is going to be there?"

"There'll be Philip Chase, who we were at school with, and his wife Carol. Second wife. Probably Ben's sister, Lois, and her husband—although she doesn't like coming into the centre of town very much."

"Why not?"

"It makes her jumpy. She was there on the night of the pub bombings. Not just there, but—right in the middle of it. Where it happened. She saw her boyfriend get killed."

"Blimey. Poor woman."

"She's still not over it."

"I shouldn't think you ever get over something like that. Does Benjamin have a partner, or is English melancholy not quite the babe magnet it used to be?"

Doug smiled. "He was single the last time I heard. Of course, he was married for years, but that's going back a bit now."

"Kids?"

"Not with his wife. He has a daughter—Malvina—who lives in the States, but we don't talk about her."

"How complicated. Anything else we don't talk about?"

"No, I think you're safe. Ben's niece might be there. Sophie. Lois's daughter. And maybe Steve Richards, another old friend of ours."

But Steve was not there, in fact: he and his wife were away on holiday. And when Doug asked whether Sophie was coming, her mother told him:

"She would have loved to, but she's in Amsterdam. They're interviewing her for a documentary on Vermeer." She was trying hard to make it sound as though she didn't think this was a big deal.

"Oh, television now, is it?" said Doug, impressed.

"Well—only Sky Arts . . ."

They were sitting in the bar of the restaurant, having a preliminary bottle of champagne. Doug introduced Gail to everyone, presenting her as "the acceptable face of the Tory Party." Philip made a point of finding her a glass and filling it with champagne and inviting her to sit beside him.

"So come on," said Doug, "tell us how this happened. This sounds like the weirdest choice of prizewinner since the EU won the Nobel Peace Prize in 2012."

"I haven't won anything yet," Benjamin pointed out. "I'm not even on the shortlist—only the longlist." But the smile still wouldn't leave his face. Lois, sitting next to him, reflected on what a lovely smile it was and how little she had seen of it, over the years.

"Well, of course, I entered it for the prize," said Philip, "because why wouldn't you? Even though I didn't think it had a hope in hell—I mean, I'm sorry, Benjamin, I didn't mean that to sound . . ."

"That's fine," Benjamin said. "I know what you mean."

"So then I forgot all about it, until last Wednesday I get this phone call, out of the blue. From the prize administrators in London."

"Amazing. Catapulted straight into the first division. Come on, Ben, that's got to be an amazing feeling. I mean, even Lionel Hampshire didn't make it this year."

This was true. When the longlist had been announced, the few newspapers who had bothered to report it had led with the news that the distinguished man of letters had this year been—in the parlance traditionally adopted for such stories—"snubbed" by the judges, who had apparently not been impressed by his slender, whimsical sixth novel, *A Curious Alignment of Artichokes*.

"No wonder," said Lois. "I've read that book and it's rubbish. Not a patch on yours."

"And have Ladbroke's announced the odds yet?" Doug asked. "What are they offering for you?"

"At the moment, a hundred to one."

"I see. Big vote of confidence, then. Still, that has to be worth a punt."

"I won't win," said Benjamin. "I won't even make the shortlist."

"So what?" said Philip. "Me and Carol have been working flat out. Every Waterstones in the country wanted half a dozen copies. Sales have gone up by about three thousand per cent. The phone's been ringing off the hook. Ben's a *story* now, you see. The best story there is: plucky outsider up against the big guns. The English love an underdog. I've been on local radio talking about him, I did an interview down the line for Radio Four. And Ben's got two papers coming to interview him next week."

"Nationals?"

"Nationals."

Doug raised his glass. "Well done, mate. It's been a long time coming. Nobody deserves this more than you." He looked around to make sure that everyone was poised for a toast. "To Benjamin."

"*To Benjamin*," they echoed.

Benjamin was overcome. Looking around at the smiling faces— the faces of his oldest and closest friends, the face of his beloved sister, even the face of Gail (who he'd only just met, but was already warming to)—he felt as though he were drowning in the sweetest possible mortification. Shy at the best of times (and this was certainly the best of times), never very good with words unless he could ponder them at length before committing them to paper, he was enjoying, at that moment, a happiness that was as complete as it was impossible to express. All he could do—as usual—was resort to understatement and self-deprecation.

"Thanks, everybody," he said. "But let's not get carried away. It's a lottery, that's all, and I've just been very, very lucky."

"So *enjoy* it, for God's sake," said Philip, clapping him on the back. "Most people don't get even fifteen minutes of fame."

"I wouldn't describe it as fame . . ."

"Oh, Ben!" Lois chided.

"You've got journalists coming to talk to you, haven't you?" said Doug. "Your picture'll be in the paper. Beautiful women are going to fall at your feet. You're going to be recognized in public places."

Benjamin, still demurring, became aware that someone was now hovering at his elbow. He turned and saw a young blonde woman—who could, without too much exaggeration, have been described as beautiful—standing next to him, looking at him deferentially, waiting to attract his attention.

"Excuse me," she said, with a charming hesitancy in her voice that could easily have been attributed to reverence. "But are you . . . are you Benjamin Trotter?"

The others fell silent. It felt as though they were bearing witness, collectively, to the beginning of Benjamin's new life.

"Yes?" he said, with a rising inflection. And then repeated, in a prouder, more confident tone: "Yes. Yes, I am."

"Great," said the woman. "Your table's ready."

23.

The 2012 Olympic opening ceremony had had a profound and specific effect upon Sohan. It had diverted the course of his research, which after that event became centred upon literary, filmic and musical representations of Englishness. In particular, after working on this subject for a few months, he became fascinated by the concept of "Deep England," a phrase which he began to encounter more and more often in newspaper articles and academic journals. What was it, exactly? Was it a psychogeographical phenomenon, to do with village greens, the thatched roof of the local pub, the red telephone box and the subtle thwack of cricket ball against willow? Or to understand it fully, did you have to immerse yourself in the writings of Chesterton and Priestley, H. E. Bates and L. T. C. Rolt? Did it help to watch Michael Powell's *A Canterbury Tale*, or Cavalcanti's *Went the Day Well?* Was its musical distillation to be found in the work of Elgar, Vaughan Williams or George Butterworth? The paintings of Constable? Or had it been most powerfully expressed, in fact, in allegorical form by J. R. R. Tolkien when he created the Shire and populated its pastoral idyll with doughty, insular hobbits, prone to somnolence and complacence when left to their own devices but fierce when roused, and quite the best—if the seemingly unlikeliest—people to call upon in a crisis? Perhaps there was also a connection, even an essential kinship, with the French ideal of *La France profonde* . . . Sohan would often talk about this with Sophie, late into the Tuesday and Wednesday nights on which she would sleep at his Clapham flat, but they never succeeded in defining their terms, nor in resolving the central questions of what exactly Deep England was, or where you would find it. But on the morning of Sunday, 9 August 2015, Sophie came as close, she felt, as she would ever come to solving the mystery. If Deep England existed, she decided, it was here: here on the fifth hole of the Golf and Country Club at Kernel Magna.

She watched, partly in bafflement, partly in grudging admiration, as Ian sized up the lie of his ball at the edge of the fairway and quickly, decisively, pulled a club out of his bag.

"Seven iron," he explained—as if that was going to mean anything.

"Good choice."

She said it in a way which made it obvious—she thought—that she had no idea what he was talking about; but Ian was positioning himself by the ball and gauging the distance to the green, and was too busy to notice.

The moment before he struck the ball was a moment of almost perfect stillness. There was a chirrup of birdsong, yes, but that only emphasized the otherwise profound silence. Here there was no traffic noise, not even a faint murmur from the nearby M40: perhaps it was the trees that muted it, the elegant line of oaks and larches that bordered the eastern side of the fairway, keeping patient, dutiful watch over this manicured landscape. The sun beat down from a cloudless sky, a sky of rich, flawless cerulean blue. The morning was, indeed, a symphony of blue and green: above Sophie, the sky; to her right in the distance, the shimmering blue of a water hazard, a small artificial lake; around her, all the variegated greens placed there by both man and nature, infinitely calming and pleasing to the eye. The passing of time seemed to have been suspended. A feeling of immense restfulness was stealing over her. Nothing mattered here; there was nothing more important, in this precious cloistered space, than the simple, straightforward task of getting a small ball into a small hole in as few strokes as possible.

Ian continued to shift slightly from side to side, adjusting his centre of gravity; he positioned the club carefully against the ball one more time; then swung the club back, and swung it forward again in a powerful, graceful movement. The ball rose into the air, describing a shapely arc, disappeared from view momentarily, then plopped down on to the green and bounced to a halt about six feet from the hole.

"Lovely," said Mrs. Bishop, standing just behind him.

"Very good indeed," said Mr. Bishop, from the other side of the fairway, where his ball was lodged in the rough.

Mr. Hu, the final member of the four, said nothing. He was standing in the centre of the fairway, and began to walk ahead, pulling his trolley behind him, towards his ball, which had landed just short of a bunker.

"You're good at this," said Sophie, as Ian slid the club back into his bag.

He smiled. "Some days are better than others."

They walked onwards in the sunshine. She put her arm through his.

It had been a source of tension between them, for several months, this new habit of playing golf every Sunday morning. Ian had always enjoyed the game, but now these weekly sessions had become sacrosanct: three hours out on the course, usually with Simon Bishop and his parents, followed by lunch with his mother either at home or in the clubhouse. That, combined with football matches on Saturdays, meant that their weekends were pretty much consumed by sport, and Sophie seemed to spend a good part of each Saturday and Sunday sitting by herself in the flat.

"The thing is," she had said, drunkenly, gazing into what was left of the *schnapps* in her glass and wondering just how strong it was, "that I can't tell if we're *growing* apart or if we've *always* been this far apart and I've only just started to notice it."

Sigrid, the director of the Sky Arts documentary on Vermeer, had leaned forward and touched Sophie on the arm. It was getting on for two o'clock in the morning and they were among the last customers left in a cavernous, dimly lit bar on the Gravenstraat.

"Having lots of things in common with your partner," she said, "doesn't mean anything. Pieter and I had the same interests, the same politics, the same opinions . . . . Where did that get me?"

She had already told Sophie, at some length, the story of her disastrous marriage, which had begun as a union of souls and ended in domestic violence.

"Pieter turned out to be a shit," she said. "A lying shit. A cheating shit. A violent shit. Do you think your husband is a shit?"

"No," said Sophie. "Definitely not."

"Do you love him?"

Sophie paused. It seemed to her an impossible question. "I guess . . ."

"Do you *like* him?"

"Yes." Without hesitation.

"Do you trust him?"

"Yes."

"Would you trust him with your life?"

"Yes, I would."

"Then for fuck's sake hang on to him. So what if he voted Conservative in the last election, and you voted Labour? That's not what life is about. My ex-husband was a socialist and he kicked me in the face one night because I stayed out late with one of my girlfriends."

"Yes," Sophie had said. "Of course. You're absolutely right."

"If you think you're growing apart, try getting closer to him. Make the effort. Then he might notice what you're doing and try getting closer to you."

Sophie had nodded doubtfully and repeated, "Get closer to him . . ."

"I don't know . . . Go and join him on one of those stupid golf matches. Show willing. How bad can it be? At least you'll get some exercise and some fresh air."

And so here she was, a few days later. Spending Sunday morning at the Golf and Country Club at Kernel Magna—somewhere, five years earlier, she would never have imagined even setting foot. And thinking, as she walked arm in arm with her husband in the sunshine, that she had found Deep England at last, and that it wasn't so bad after all.

"What do you think he makes of this?" she asked Ian, nodding in the direction of Mr. Hu.

"I expect they do have golf courses in China," he said.

"Yes, of course, but . . . *this*." She gestured around her. "It's all so stereotypically English. I wonder if it seems exotic to him."

"I'm sure he loves it."

Mr. Hu Dawei was visiting the UK for a few days in order to cement his business relationship with Andrew Bishop, Simon's father. Andrew had spent his working life in dairy farming, and during that time had transformed what was once a small family farm into an expanding international agribusiness. He was approaching his mid-sixties but showed no sign of retiring or running out of ideas: only recently he had discovered a profitable new export market in China, where British milk enjoyed a good reputation and UHT milk, in particular, was in strong demand. Mr. Hu had been staying at the Bishops' handsome eighteenth-century farmhouse since Thursday, had enjoyed thorough tours of the milking sheds and the processing plant, had spent Saturday afternoon in Stratford-upon-Avon with Mrs. Bishop, culminating in a trip to the RSC to see *Coriolanus*, and this morning was seizing the chance to demonstrate his golfing prowess, which was impressive. (It turned out that he played off a handicap of three.) He was partnering Andrew against Ian and Mrs. Bishop—Simon being at work all weekend—and after four holes they were already two up.

"Come on, Mary," said Ian, standing next to his partner as she sized up her next stroke. "We can do this. We can pull one back."

Mary's ball was lying in the centre of the fairway but had fallen almost fifty yards short of the green. If she pitched the ball within putting distance of the hole this time she could still finish this one in par. But she sliced the ball badly: the length was well judged but it landed just off the edge of the green.

"Botheration," she said.

"No problem," said Ian. "All is not lost."

Despite this reassurance, Mary shook her head as she walked on, chiding herself for letting the side down. Then: "I gather you've been in Amsterdam," she said to Sophie, as they approached the green. "Lovely city, isn't it? I went there with the WI once, many years ago. Did you have a nice time? It's so important to take a break now and again, isn't it?"

"Well," said Sophie, "it wasn't a break as such. Although I did—"

"Andrew and I make a point of getting away every couple of months," said Mary, who did not appear to be one of nature's listeners. "Just this year, we've been to . . . let me see . . . Budapest—Seville, that was heavenly—Bari—extraordinary seafood—Tallinn . . ."

"Ah yes," said Sophie. "We've been to Tallinn. Very briefly. It was one of the places Ian and I stopped off on our—"

"And all with direct flights from Birmingham airport," Mary continued. "Isn't that amazing? It's become quite the international hub in the last few years. We've been to corners of Europe we would never have thought of visiting otherwise."

"That's great," said Sophie, for want of anything better.

"Who needs to go anywhere near Heathrow or Gatwick, nowadays? We've got the whole of Europe at our fingertips here."

*

It was not until the seventh hole that Sophie found herself in conversation with Mr. Hu. With his ball lying about thirty yards from the green, he pulled out an eight iron and chose a risky shot, straight over a large bunker, but he cleared it without overshooting the green, and the ball landed within comfortable putting distance.

"I'm no expert," Sophie said, "but I'd say you were pretty good at this game."

"Back home," he said, "I play two, three times a week. But this is different. This is special."

"How do you mean?"

"This is where golf should be played," he said, gesturing around him. "In England. England's 'green and pleasant land'." They walked on. "You teach at university, right? So you know about William Blake?"

"A bit. More as an artist than a writer, to be honest."

"This poem, 'Jerusalem'—it's very beautiful. But it puzzles me."

"Why's that?"

"'And was Jerusalem builded here'. That's what he says, right? But there's no such word as 'builded'. It's not the right word."

"I suppose not. But 'builded' fits the line better."

Mr. Hu considered this, and smiled admiringly. "You see, this is what I like about the English. Everyone thinks you are very safe, conservative people. But you will always break the rules. If it gets you what you want, you are happy to break the rules." He laughed in delight. "Even William Blake!"

*

It was not until the tenth hole that Sophie found herself in conversation with Andrew Bishop.

"I'm afraid this must be a rather dull way for you to spend your Sunday morning," he said. Once again he had lost his ball in the rough, and she was helping him to look for it.

"Not at all," she said. "I've learned masses of things already."

"Really? Such as?"

"I've learned what par means. I've learned the difference between a wedge and a driver. I've learned that a birdie is one below par and an eagle is two below, and an albatross is three below par but hardly anyone ever gets one of those."

"Very good. Though I don't know how useful all this information is going to be in your line of work."

"You never know. Everything is grist to the academic mill."

"I suppose so. Ah, here it is! . . . Oh dear."

His ball was not just deep in long grass, but was lying so close to the trunk of a yew sapling that it was clearly impossible to play. Andrew had to pick it up and drop it behind his back, forfeiting a stroke as he did so.

"I've also learned," said Sophie, as he took out a five iron, "that Britain exports milk to China. Which I would never have guessed before today."

"Damn." He made a mess of the shot: the ball stuttered forward only a few yards, still in the rough. He walked over towards it, carrying the same club. "Yes, it's remarkable, isn't it? I don't think I would have guessed it a few years ago. And I certainly wouldn't have guessed that I'd be one of the ones doing the exporting. It seemed very daunting at first. But my son was a great help in getting everything off the ground. Not Simon—I mean Charles, Simon's brother. He's based in Hong Kong, working for HSBC. So he has some knowledge of that part of the world. And do you know what? Once we got down to it, even allowing for the language problems, the paperwork was simpler than what I have to go through with the EU."

"Really? That's amazing."

"Not really. Those people in Brussels are a nightmare, you know. The red tape." He swung at the ball, which soared cleanly through the air and landed just as cleanly in the centre of a bunker about thirty yards away. Andrew grimaced. "An absolute bloody nightmare."

*

"Enjoying yourself?" Ian asked, as they walked together down the fairway of the fourteenth hole. It was a par three and he was in with the chance of a birdie, having made it all the way to the edge of the green with his first shot.

"I don't think I'll be making it a regular thing," said Sophie. "But it's been nice."

"Well, at least you know what I get up to every Sunday, and it's not that I'm having an affair."

They walked on. It was so quiet that Sophie could hear the noise of Ian's trolley wheels turning, and the fall of her own footsteps on the spongy grass.

"It's very peaceful here," she said. "I can see why you like it."

"Yes," he said. "Wouldn't it be great to be somewhere like this all the time? Somewhere this peaceful."

"You mean living somewhere like this?"

"Yes."

"Isn't that the sort of thing you plan for your retirement?"

"I was thinking more that it was the kind of thing people do when they're ready to have kids."

Sophie stiffened, and quickened her pace.

"We can't have this conversation now," she said. "I'm not ready. You know that."

Ian stopped still. He stood watching her, hands on hips, as she walked on.

*

For lunch, they were to be joined by Ian's mother. Sophie had assumed she would be arriving in her own car but in fact, as she and Ian crossed the tarmac outside the clubhouse, she saw an unfamiliar vehicle approaching, with Helena in the passenger seat. The driver appeared to be Grete. Once they were parked, Helena climbed slowly out of her seat with Ian's help, and then leaned heavily on him as he walked her towards the main door of the clubhouse. Sophie went around to the driver's side to speak to Grete.

"Thank you," she said. "This is very kind."

"I'm always happy to help," said Grete. "I know she doesn't like to drive so much any more."

"Won't you come and join us for a drink?"

"It's all right, thank you. Really I wanted to have a talk with Mrs. Coleman, and this gave me the chance. I'm feeling guilty, to tell you the truth: because I handed in my notice."

"Oh no," said Sophie. "But you've become such good friends."

"Yes, I like to think so," said Grete. "I've been coming to her house a long time now. Four years. Still, I'm leaving for a nice reason. My husband and I are going to have a baby."

In the light of her conversation with Ian on the fourteenth hole, this news struck Sophie with special poignancy. Grete was at least five years younger than she was. But she managed to say, with some sincerity: "That's wonderful news. Congratulations. When's it due?"

"In five months."

"Fantastic." She struggled to remember anything about Grete's husband, apart from his name. "Is Lukas still working at the . . . ?"

"The restaurant, yes."

"The restaurant in . . . ?"

"Stratford. They promoted him to manager."

"Fantastic," she said again. "I'm really happy that everything's going so well."

"Thank you," said Grete. As she drove away, Sophie could see that she was smiling a private, inwardly directed smile that she could not help envying.

The clubhouse dining room was not quite as stuffy as she had feared—dress was "smart casual," it seemed, which meant at least that the men did not have to wear ties—but she still felt out of place. For one thing, she was acutely conscious that she and Ian were the youngest people there: she hadn't seen so much grey and white hair on display since their Legend cruise. The food was on the stodgy side: you had to go up to a counter and stand in a queue, where you would be served slices of well-done beef or pork from the carvery, with heaps of roast potatoes and green vegetables, which Mr. Hu, after watching the diner ahead of him for guidance, duly smothered in pools of rich brown gravy, his face betraying a certain puzzlement as he did so.

No background music issued from the speakers during the meal. There was only the quiet, well-bred chatter of about forty elderly men and women who had either just played, or were about to play, three and a half hours of golf.

"Did your mother tell you Grete's news?" Sophie asked, taking her place next to her husband.

"She did," he said.

"How did she take it?"

Ian glanced at her, mildly surprised. "Fine. The agency'll find her someone else, soon enough."

"She might miss her company."

"She might."

"Perhaps they'll keep in touch."

"Maybe."

"Her husband manages a restaurant in Stratford, apparently. We could take her there one day."

"Good idea." After taking his first mouthful of food, he noticed that Sophie had not yet started to eat, but seemed to be staring ahead of her in a kind of daze. "Everything OK?"

"Sorry," she said. "I suppose I'm a bit tired. That was one of the longest walks I've done in years. And I wasn't really expecting it to bring me out where it has."

"How do you mean?"

"Here," she said. "In the 1950s."

Ian smiled indulgently at the joke but made no further comment at first. He busied himself making sure that his mother had enough wine in her glass, and passed her the salt and pepper.

In the end he said: "You may think it's the 1950s, but for some people this is a perfectly normal part of Britain in 2015. Don't knock it just because it's not what you're used to."

"2015? Really?" said Sophie, and pointed up at the picture which hung on the wall opposite their table. "With that thing looking down at us?"

The picture showed a dozen or so red-coated, top-hatted riders cantering through fields and leaping over hedges in pursuit of a recalcitrant fox, which could be seen running for its life in the corner of the frame, throwing a terrified glance back over its shoulder.

"Now this," said Mr. Hu, "is something I would really like to see. A traditional British hunt. Perhaps for my next visit, Mr. Bishop, you could arrange it? Purely as a spectator, of course. I can swing a golf club but I cannot ride a horse."

Andrew smiled. "I'm afraid it's not quite as simple as that."

"Really?"

There was a brief silence while everyone wondered who was going to break the news to him. Finally Mary stepped up to the mark.

"I'm afraid that fox-hunting is now regarded as a criminal activity in this country," she explained. "It's been banned for quite a number of years."

"Banned? How strange. I didn't realize." He cut himself a thick mouthful of beef and said, while chewing it slowly: "Of course, the British are famous for their love of animals."

"It was a law passed by the last Labour government," said Andrew, "and it had very little to do with animal welfare, and everything to do with class resentment."

"Perhaps you can get the law reversed," said Mr. Hu.

Mary and Helena both gave short, dismissive laughs.

"After all, *you* at least"—this was said in a tone of circumspection— "live in a free and democratic country."

"I'm afraid you're mistaken," said Helena. "England today is not a free country. We live under a tyranny."

"A tyranny?" Feelingly, Mr. Hu said: "Please, madam, choose your words with care."

"I use the term very carefully, I assure you."

"Your Mr. Cameron does not strike me as a tyrant."

"That's not what I mean. A tyrant does not have to be an individual. It can be an idea."

"You live under the tyranny of an idea?"

"Precisely."

"And its name is . . . ?"

"Political correctness, of course," Helena answered. "I'm sure you've heard the phrase."

"Certainly. But not in relation to tyranny."

Helena put down her knife and fork. "Mr. Hu, I have never visited China, and I have no wish to make light of the difficult conditions in which you must live there. But here in Great Britain, we face similar problems. In fact I would almost say that our situation is worse. You have overt censorship; ours is covert. It all happens under a mask of freedom of speech so the tyrants can claim that everything is all right. But we do not have freedom, of speech or of anything else. The people who once kept a great British tradition alive by riding to hounds are not free to do so any more. And if any of us try to complain about it, we are shouted down. Our views are not allowed to be expressed on television or in the newspapers. Our state broadcaster ignores us, or treats us with contempt. Voting becomes a waste of time when all the politicians subscribe to the same fashionable opinions. Of course I voted for Mr. Cameron, but not with any enthusiasm. His values are not our values. He actually knows as little of our way of life as his political opponents do. They're all on the same side, really—and it's not *our* side. Now, since you do not look convinced, I shall give you another example. A quite specific example. One year ago, my son applied for a job—Ian, don't interrupt, let me finish—he applied for a promotion, and if there was any fairness or justice in this country at the moment, he would have got it. But instead they gave it to a rival candidate, because of her ethnic background, and her skin colour. They did this because—Sophie, you can look at me that way as much as you like, but *this needs saying*, somebody has to say it, and I will tell you another thing—my son's life has been damaged, seriously damaged, by this absurd political correctness, and if *you*, Sophie, keep kowtowing to it and not standing up for your own people and your own values it's going to happen to *you too*, you are going to be the next one. And I'm an old woman now and I can say these things and I'm saying them because it breaks my heart to see you two, a beautiful young couple like you, struggling to make do, having to keep two jobs, working in different cities, not seeing each other all week, no time to be together and start a family, and this would not have happened, you would *not be in this situation*, if Ian had got that job. And he *should* have done. He deserved it. He'd worked hard for it, and he deserved it."

Sophie would be angry with herself, for days afterwards, for not protesting against this outburst. Like everyone else around the table, she looked down at her plate and said nothing; although it did occur to her that the others remained silent because they were broadly in agreement. Mr. Hu's reaction was difficult to gauge, beyond the fact that he was taken aback. And in any case, Helena had not quite finished.

"The people of Middle England," she said, addressing the Chinese guest directly, "voted for Mr. Cameron because they had no real choice. The alternative was unthinkable. But if the time ever comes when we are given the opportunity to let him know what we really think of him, then believe me—we will take it."

24.

"Aren't you going to record this?" asked Benjamin.

The journalist, whose name was Hermione Dawes, smiled and shook her head. She had a writing pad open on her lap, and a biro poised over it. Her hair tumbled over her shoulders in blonde curls and her lipstick was bright red.

"I'm a very old-fashioned girl," she said. "Shall we get started?"

"Sure," said Benjamin.

He sat back on the sofa and tried to relax. The view of the Severn streaming past his window normally calmed him, but not this morning. He could not shake the feeling that Hermione (whose pieces, Philip had warned him, could sometimes be "a bit sharp") was coolly surveying the contents of his house and judging every object, every design choice, every item of furniture.

"So—you started writing when you were very young, is that right?"

"Yes. About ten or eleven. I remember—"

"And were your parents writers?"

"No, not at all. My father worked at the British Leyland factory in Longbridge, and my mother stayed at home. She was a housewife."

"And you went to a local school?"

"I went to King William's, which is near the centre of Birmingham. It was my parents' choice."

"Do you think it was the right one?"

"I suppose. I mean . . . Just recently, I got back in touch with one of my oldest friends from primary school, who I hadn't spoken to for more than forty years, and it did make me realize how the British education system can, you know . . . divide people."

"What does he do now?" Hermione asked, scribbling away.

"He's a clown."

She looked up. "A clown?"

"A children's entertainer."

"Well, that's lovely that you're back in touch with him, anyway. Was it at school that you became serious about writing?"

"Now—I'm glad you asked me that," said Benjamin. "Because, looking back, I can pinpoint the moment almost exactly. It was November 1974, and a friend of mine—his name was Malcolm, he was my sister's boyfriend actually—took me to a concert at a club in town called Barbarella's. And one of the bands playing was called Hatfield and the North. Nowadays we'd call what they played 'prog rock', but that term didn't really exist then, as you probably remember . . ."

Hermione, sensing that he was waiting for her to offer some sort of confirmation, merely said: "I was born in 1989."

"Oh. Right. OK. Well, what blew me away about Hatfield and the North that night, you see, was that there was this combination of freshness—originality—complete rethinking of form—while the music was very easy to listen to, it really invited the listener in. And I thought, 'This is what I should be doing as a writer.' For instance, on their first album there's a piece called 'Aigrette', which was written by the guitarist, and if you listen carefully, not only is the time signature changing every few bars, but it goes through these extraordinary modulations, these key changes, and yet the tune is really catchy, really attractive to the ear. And that made me think that yes, if what you're doing is *thematically* easy to follow, if there's a strong throughline for the reader, either in terms of story or ideas or characters or whatever, then . . ."

He became aware that Hermione had stopped writing any of this down some time before.

"Anyway," he concluded. "That was a seminal moment for me. Hatfield and the North. Barbarella's. November 1974."

"Right." She jotted down a few more words, or at least pretended to. "And it was round about now that you fell in love with this girl, and she became the inspiration for your novel?"

"Yes, more or less."

"In the book you call her Lilian. What was her real name?"

"I'm afraid I can't tell you that."

"But she was a real person, yes? And she's still alive?"

"Yes."

"So your book isn't really a novel at all—it's basically a memoir, with the names changed?"

"No, that's too simplistic. I see it as being on the cusp of fiction and memoir. I like to explore these . . . liminal spaces, you see."

"Liminal"—that was a good word. For the first time in the interview, Benjamin was quite pleased with something he had said. But Hermione didn't seem to have written this down either.

"So then you became romantically involved with her in your last year at school, but it fell apart, and she went to America to live with another woman."

"Yes."

"Your novel opens a few years after that. You're listening to a piece of music by an obscure British jazz musician—"

"Quite a famous one actually."

"—and something about this music brings back a vivid memory of the affair, and suddenly—suddenly life seems intolerable. You're studying at Oxford, and you decide to give it all up, to quit?"

"Yes."

"So when did this happen?"

"It was the autumn of 1983. I was just starting the second year of my D.Phil at Balliol. The thing I remember about it—apart from that moment, obviously—was that Boris Johnson arrived that term. He actually had a room on the same corridor as me."

For the first time during the interview, Hermione seemed animated. "Really? So you know Boris?"

"Well, no—I didn't get to know him at all. You know how it is—Etonians don't speak to grammar-school boys. But I do remember thinking, you know, who was this very striking figure, with the posh voice and this extraordinary hair. He certainly made an impression."

Sighing audibly, Hermione wrote a few more words down; then asked (with an air of duty more than enthusiasm): "So then you came back to live in Birmingham, and became . . . an accountant? Why on earth was that?"

"Well, I'd worked in a bank during my year off, and it turned out I was pretty good with figures. And I was in a state of denial. If I couldn't have Cicely—"

"Lilian," Hermione corrected, writing the name down as she did so.

"Yes—if I couldn't have Lilian, then it felt as though nothing I wanted was going to be possible. I couldn't be a writer, I couldn't be a musician . . ."

"Which had been your other ambition."

"Yes. Also, I was going through this religious phase."

"I see. So this religious phase, and this state of denial—how long did they last?"

"About seventeen years."

"Wow. That's . . . quite a phase. And you got married in that time? And worked as an accountant all the way through? Nothing else? I'm just trying to make the story sound more interesting."

"Well, I was working on the book, constantly. I was writing it for more than two decades, on and off."

"Hmm . . ." She sucked on her biro. "Nothing else that you can think of, that you got up to during that time?"

"I did some book reviews. I'd known Doug Anderton at school, and he commissioned me to do a few, while he was literary editor at the—"

"Ah! You know Doug Anderton? That's interesting." She wrote down the name, put the biro back in her mouth, and rattled it between her teeth. "Let's just get the last bit of the story straight, and then I'd like to ask you a few more general questions."

"OK."

"So eventually . . . 'Lilian' came back to find you, and you actually lived together for a few years. She was very ill, and you looked after her. You became her carer, really."

"That's right."

"And this was in London."

"Yes."

"And then she abandoned you again. History repeating itself."

"Yes. So I sold our flat and bought this place. Best move I ever made."

"The scene in the book where you put her on the plane to South America is very moving. You've no idea it's going to be the last time you see her."

"Yes, that was just how it happened. Almost nothing in the book is invented. Except it wasn't South America."

"And are you still in touch?"

"No."

"Not at all?"

"Not at all."

"Hmm . . ."

Hermione wrote a few last words on her pad, and then sucked for a long time on the end of her pen. Benjamin began to feel uneasy. To break the silence, he said:

"Would you like a coffee?"

"Oh, that would be lovely. How kind."

He went into the kitchen and to his alarm she followed him. She sat down at the table while he busied himself with the mugs and the coffee machine. Benjamin wasn't sure, at this point, whether the interview was still in progress. Hermione had her writing pad open on the table in front of her, and the pen lay next to it, temporarily unused, but her tone was still brisk and interrogatory.

"It's very peaceful here," she said. "I can see why that makes it a good place for a writer to live, but don't you also feel that you might be too isolated, in a place like this, to write convincingly about contemporary Britain?"

"I travel about quite a lot. Backwards and forwards to Birmingham, mainly, where my dad lives."

"This part of the country also seems very monocultural. I saw mainly white faces on my way here."

"Well, multiculturalism is largely an urban phenomenon, I suppose." He had to raise his voice above the steaming and bubbling of the machine. "I enjoyed my time living in London but in the end the things that got to me were the crowds, the noise, the pace of life, the stress, the expense. I came here to get away from all that."

"Do you think publishers were less inclined to consider your book because you were sending it from an address in the provinces?"

"Who knows? I expect they get sent a lot of books."

"You must feel an incredible sense of vindication."

"Well, I'm just . . . happy to be finding some readers at last."

He placed a mug in front of her. She thanked him and took a cautious sip.

"Several established authors—such as Lionel Hampshire—didn't find themselves on the longlist this year."

"Well, I haven't read his new one. Though I am a fan." This reminded him of something else that might interest her. "Actually my niece knows him a little. They were on a cruise together last year."

Hermione reached for her pen at once. "Your niece went on a *cruise* with Lionel Hampshire?" she said, starting to write.

"No no no—I mean, they were both guest *speakers* on the cruise. There was nothing . . . I mean, they weren't *together*. She's very happily married, and he . . . he had some other woman with him, his secretary or something . . ."

Hermione couldn't write this down fast enough. Benjamin had to restrain himself from leaning over and physically stopping her.

"This is just what she told me . . . Strictly off the record. You're not going to put any of this in, are you?"

Hermione gave one of her brittle smiles. "It's not really news. Most people know exactly what Lionel's like." She scribbled a few more words, then thought for a moment, looked up and said: "Do you feel, though, that there is a sort of sea-change happening on the British literary scene? Looking at this longlist, it's far more diverse than it would have been even ten years ago. It's not just that there are Americans on the list now: there are also more women writers, more BAME writers. Is the day of the great white middle-aged British writer finally over?"

"I don't know—it's hard to generalize . . ."

"It's almost as if, this year, you're the last one standing."

"I don't really feel I can comment on general literary trends. I'm a real outsider, as far as all that's concerned."

Hermione closed her pad. "That's a nice note to end on," she said, but she said it without much enthusiasm. Benjamin could tell that he had turned out, in her eyes, to be a disappointing interviewee: his answers had been diffident, qualified, lacking in emphasis or conviction. The impression was confirmed when, a few minutes later, he went to the toilet and came back to find that she was out on the terrace, talking to someone—a friend? Her commissioning editor?—on the phone, and although he couldn't make out all of what she said, he was pretty sure that he heard, *Bit of a wasted journey, if you ask me* and—more worryingly—*I'm going to have to get creative . . .*

He offered to drive her into Shrewsbury but she said there was no need, and she phoned for a taxi instead. It took about twenty minutes to arrive, during which time they chatted, and talked with much more ease and openness on both sides than they had managed during the interview. Benjamin drew her out on the subject of her career, her ambitions, the plight of the freelance writer in today's unforgiving economy. He was struck, when he asked if she preferred to be politically aligned with the publications she wrote for, by the phrase she used in response: no, she was prepared to be quite "ideologically flexible" on that front. He concluded, privately, that she would go far. But he liked her, on the whole, and felt that what she was showing was probably not cynicism but pragmatism borne out of difficult circumstances, and when they shook hands at the end he clasped her hand warmly—perhaps for a bit longer than was necessary—and when she was gone and he was washing up the coffee mugs he was reminded that hardly anybody came to visit him any more, and the house felt suddenly empty without her.

*

The interview was published four days later. Philip and Benjamin decided to meet for a coffee at Woodlands Garden Centre to assess the damage.

"Well, it could have been worse," said Philip.

The newspaper lay on the table between them. Benjamin said nothing.

"She could really have laid into you," Philip added.

Benjamin still didn't answer. He picked up the paper and looked yet again at the headline. Even though he must have read it forty or fifty times, the feeling of disbelief never abated:

OUTSIDER ON THE INSIDE

"It's just so unfair," he said. "The way she's written it. So unfair."

Philip took the paper from him and read the standfirst—which he also, by now, knew almost by heart: *Benjamin Trotter likes to think of himself as the plucky underdog in this year's Booker race—but, as* **Hermione Dawes** *finds out, there's more to the well-connected writer than meets the eye.*

"'Well-connected' is putting it a bit strongly," he conceded.

"A bit strongly? It's a lie—an outright lie." Benjamin snatched the paper back. "It says here that I knew Boris Johnson at university. I never said a bloody word to him! We lived on the same corridor for about three weeks, and he used to cut me dead on the way to the toilet. 'For years he has been rubbing shoulders with influential media figures such as Doug Anderton'—that's such bollocks. We were at school together. Forty years ago. As for this bit: 'While claiming to have no access to literary London's inner circle, he is happy to trade salacious gossip about fellow author Lionel Hampshire, who turns out to be a family friend.'"

"She's good," Philip admitted, "I'll give her that. Talk about turning base metal into gold."

"Whose side are you on? She also makes out that I'm a snob—ditching my old primary-school friends when I got into King William's."

"Ah, nobody will care about that," said Philip. Then added, less reassuringly: "I'd be more worried that you come off as a bit of a racist, to be honest."

Benjamin stared at him.

"I mean, is this really what you said?" Philip again took the newspaper from his friend's quivering hands: "'From the comfort of his riverside retreat in the heart of the English countryside, Trotter declares that "Multiculturalism is an urban phenomenon. I left London to get away from all that.'"

Benjamin spluttered with outrage. "I said *something* like that, yes. But there was all sorts of stuff in between, about how I wanted to get away from the noise and the crowds and the stress."

"Selective quotation is a beautiful thing. 'I point out that BAME writers are more strongly represented on this year's list than ever before, and hint that this is something we should be cheering on, to which Trotter's only response is: "I'm the real outsider.'"

Again, Benjamin was incoherent with rage. "'A' real outsider. 'A'. Indefinite article, not definite. And I was talking about publishing. I was talking about the fact that I got dozens of rejections so I ended up being published by you."

Philip laid the newspaper down and shook his head. "Well, sales are still holding up, so no harm done."

"But she seemed so nice. By the end, we were getting on really well. I was giving her career advice and everything, and she said, 'We'll be in touch,' or something like that . . ."

"Pretty, was she?"

Benjamin didn't see any point in dissembling. "I suppose she was pretty, yes."

"Oh, Ben . . . Just put it down to experience. It was your first interview, after all."

"True. When's the other one, by the way?"

"The other one?"

"Wasn't there supposed to be another one?"

"Oh, they never followed up on that. I called them back a couple of times but . . . I think that's gone cold."

"Great." Benjamin hunched over his cappuccino and stared gloomily ahead of him.

"On the other hand—" Philip reached into his pocket and pulled out a handwritten envelope "—you do have a fan letter. At least I assume it's a fan letter."

He passed it over to Benjamin, who submitted it to wary inspection, examining the front and the back, the handwriting and the postcode, until Philip said: "Just open the thing, for Christ's sake."

Benjamin tore the envelope open with his forefinger, read the first couple of sentences and then flipped the letter over to look at the signature.

"Jesus," he said. "You'll never guess who this is from."

Philip wasn't even going to try.

"It's from Jennifer Hawkins."

"Who?"

"You remember Jennifer Hawkins. She was at the Girls' School. I went out with her for a while."

"Her? You mean . . . *that* Jennifer Hawkins? The one in the wardrobe?"

"Exactly. The wardrobe."

Many years earlier, when he was still a schoolboy, Benjamin had attended a party thrown by Doug while his parents were away on holiday. He had blacked out at some point during the evening after drinking three-quarters of a bottle of port, and had woken up just before dawn inside a wardrobe, entwined with the body of a half-naked girl who subsequently turned out to be the aforementioned Jennifer Hawkins. Gallantly, having interpreted their drunken teen-age gropings as some sort of betrothal ceremony, Benjamin had asked her out on a date, and for a few weeks after that they had actually considered themselves boyfriend and girlfriend—although the relationship had fizzled out soon enough.

"Well!" Phil was grinning broadly. "Now *there's* a blast from the past. What does she say?"

Benjamin scanned the letter with quick eye movements. "She saw my name in the paper when the longlist was announced," he said. "It brought back a lot of memories. She bought the book and she really liked it."

"Does she say where she bought it?" Philip asked.

"Yes. In a garden centre just outside Kidderminster. Now she works for an estate agent. Manages one of the local branches. She's—" he turned the page, saw what the next word was and pronounced it with great emphasis "—*divorced* . . ." (There was a pause while his eyes met with Philip's, and they digested the implications of this.) ". . . and she wonders whether I'd like to meet up for dinner, to catch up and talk about the quote good old days unquote. Love, Jennifer. Kiss kiss."

He looked up at Philip, whose smile had grown broader still.

"There you are, then—Doug was right. Women are throwing themselves at you now! They can't resist a successful writer."

"Very funny. There's just one problem. Going out with Jennifer was one of the worst decisions I've ever made."

"And you've made a few shockers, let's face it."

Benjamin took this blow on the chin. "Fair enough. So I'm not about to repeat that one. No way in hell am I meeting Jennifer Hawkins for dinner."

He took a big, angry sip of cappuccino to drive the point home, and scalded his tongue.

25.

Two weeks later, he met Jennifer Hawkins for dinner. She lived in Hagley, these days, about thirty miles from Benjamin's house, so they compromised by meeting in a pub in Bridgnorth which was rumoured to serve good food.

As with Charlie Chappell, Benjamin was not convinced that he would have recognized Jennifer if they had met by chance. She was elegant, well-dressed, attractive—definitely looking good (better than he was) for someone in her mid-fifties—but at first he could see no connection between the woman he was talking to and the teenage girl with whom he'd once been so intimate, with whom he'd shared so many awkward summer evenings drinking in The Grapevine, and who had dragged him out to see *Star Wars* (a film he'd hated ever since) at the cinema on her birthday. He could never have picked the middle-aged Jennifer out in a crowd, and for the first few minutes he had the weird sensation of being in conversation with a complete stranger. The feeling persisted until she said, "Do you remember how I used to call you 'Tiger'?," and he recalled, with a jolt, that this had indeed been her ironic nickname for him, and he was at once both embarrassed and pleased by the reminder, and he began to settle into a reminiscent mode, which made him think that this reunion was not going to be so painful after all.

"It was good of you to put up with me at all, now that I look back on it," he said. "You must have thought I was such a fool."

"Not a fool," she said. "You were never a fool, Benjamin. A bit immature, maybe. But boys don't grow up as quickly as girls, everybody knows that."

She drank some red wine from a large glass that was already half-empty. She had come to the pub by taxi. Benjamin had come in his own car, so he was having to be more careful with the wine.

"Do you remember the last time we met?" she asked. "Do you remember what I said to you?"

"Not really," said Benjamin. "I expect it was in The Grapevine, was it?"

"Of course," said Jennifer. She had a strong Birmingham accent—how had he never noticed that before? "It was late August 1978."

"That's very precise."

"I was keeping a diary at the time. It was just after our A-level results came out."

"That's right."

"You got four As."

"That's right. How did you do?"

Jennifer laughed and said: "Well, it's very nice of you to ask, Benjamin, thirty-seven years after the event, because you didn't ask me at the time. I got two Bs and a C, if you're still interested."

"Congratulations," he found himself saying, absurdly.

"Thank you. You'd invited me out for a drink in order to dump me, as you may recall."

"Really?" said Benjamin, shifting more and more uncomfortably in his seat.

"Don't worry—I was quite ready and willing to be dumped. I was surprised that it hadn't happened already, in fact. Of course, the fact that you were throwing me over for Cicely Boyd was just the icing on the cake. Don't you remember how I reacted when you told me?"

"Well, if you'd poured a glass of beer over my head I would probably have remembered, but I expect it was something along those lines."

"Not really. Don't you remember? I was horrified. I *warned* you, Benjamin. I warned you what she was like. She chews people up and spits them out, I said. And you didn't listen, did you? That little crush buggered up your life for . . . what, the next three decades?"

"Pretty much."

"Well, you got a book out of it, I suppose. Was it worth it?"

Benjamin couldn't think of any simple way to answer that question. As it happened he had thought long and hard, over the years, about the relationship between human suffering and the art it might inspire, but he didn't suppose that Jennifer was really looking for a disquisition on that subject right now.

"Your poor wife, though," Jennifer said. "How on earth did she put up with it?"

"She couldn't, in the end. I suppose I wore her down." More brightly, he added: "You know her, actually—Emily? Emily Sandys? You were in the same year."

"You married *Emily*? Bloody hell, Benjamin, if you were going to marry one of the most boring girls in the school you could at least have chosen me."

"So who did you marry, after I'd disappointed you?"

"Ah, yes—Barry. The lovely Barry. Met him at a works' do in the late eighties. Got married, settled down until he did the classic midlife crisis thing five years ago. Ran off with the checkout girl from the local Decathlon. I did wonder why he was going down there every weekend when he hadn't taken any exercise since about 1995."

"I'm so sorry. Did you have kids?"

"Two. Both at uni now. What about you and Emily?"

"No, that never . . . worked out."

"Ah well. Maybe for the best, eh?"

Benjamin surprised himself, now, by deciding to trust Jennifer with a secret he shared with very few people. "Cicely and I had a daughter," he said.

"You did?"

"Right after school. She never told me, but she was pregnant when she went to America. She had the baby while she was out there. Her name is Malvina. I didn't find out for years." Benjamin swallowed hard. It was a struggle to finish telling this story: these were events he didn't like even to think about, let alone to recount to another person. "Then Malvina came back to England, and met my brother Paul, and he . . . took advantage of her."

Jennifer's eyes widened, aghast.

"That's why I don't speak to him any more."

"And her? Do you speak to her?"

"Sometimes. She's back in the States now. Birthdays, Christmas, that kind of thing. It's difficult. More than difficult—impossible."

Jennifer reached across the table and gave his hand a squeeze. He smiled back. The gesture was commonplace—and the moment passed quickly enough—but he liked it, very much.

*

"What amazes me about getting old," said Jennifer, "is that you start thinking in these . . . new units of time. You don't remember things in years any more. It's *decades*."

"I know," said Benjamin.

"You start doing these sums in your head. Like, a few weeks ago I watched *Jaws* with Grace, my daughter. She's eighteen, and that film's *forty years old* now. Forty years! If I'd watched a forty-year-old film when I was eighteen, it would have been made in the 1930s."

"I suppose a lot of things happened in the world between the thirties and the seventies. A lot changed. Maybe not so much since."

"You think? Is that the reason it all seems so recent, still? Or are we just . . ."

She tailed off. It was half past ten, the meal was over, and she'd had a lot to drink.

"You know how Philip Larkin used to look at it?" Benjamin asked.

"No. Tell me—how did Philip Larkin use to look at it?"

"Well, if you live until you're seventy, each decade is like a day of the week."

"Right."

"So life starts on Monday morning."

"OK."

"So now that we're in our mid-fifties, do you know where we are in the week? It's late on Saturday afternoon."

Jennifer stared at him in horror.

"Saturday afternoon? Bloody hell, Benjamin."

"Basically we've only got Sunday left."

"And Sundays are shit. I hate Sundays. There's never anything on the telly, for a start."

"There you go. That's what we've got to look forward to. 'The hospital years', as I once heard somebody calling them."

"Fuck. You've really depressed me now."

"I know. I'm sorry. Most people live into their eighties these days, I suppose."

"Well, that's something. Still . . ." She drained what was left in her glass, and said: "Well, Benjamin, at least you haven't lost your ability to show a girl a good time. You certainly know how to end an evening on a high note." She looked at her watch. "We should get the bill, and I should call a taxi."

"I'll pay," said Benjamin. "That prize is worth fifty thousand pounds, you know. And it's practically in the bag."

"That's a very handsome gesture. I accept."

"And don't worry about a taxi, either. I can easily drive you home."

*

They both knew that it wasn't an innocent offer. Even if neither of them could be sure what would happen next, they both knew that a decision had been taken—a mutual decision, based on the feeling that whatever process had been set in motion over dinner, it had not yet run its course. And yet this knowledge, which should have drawn them closer together, should have made them thrillingly complicit, seemed only to create a terrible distance between them. As soon as they got into Benjamin's car and began the twenty-minute drive to Jennifer's house, a heavy, frozen silence imposed itself. Benjamin, who by his normal standards had been positively chatty in the pub, now became a perfect mute. It was not difficult to understand why: the prospect—or even the possibility—of physical intimacy with another person, after so many years' enforced abstinence, was enough to render him speechless with both excitement and fear. And his speechlessness communicated itself to Jennifer, who was rendered speechless in turn. Benjamin's mind floundered for anything to say which might be even slightly appropriate in the circumstances, and the more it floundered, the more remote became its chances of coming up with a single phrase or word. He actually felt that his tongue had swollen to twice its normal size and would never be capable of pronouncing a syllable again. He glanced at Jennifer, her face pale beneath the glow of amber streetlamps, and was sure that she was staring at him in disbelief. As he braked to a halt at a set of traffic lights, he was determined to have one last go. There must be something he could say. Here they were, potentially about to embark on the most beautiful journey that two people could undertake together, and there was no reason on earth why he should be lost for words. He was a writer, for God's sake. Silently he exhorted: Come on, Benjamin, you can do this. You can rise to this sweet, hopeful, terrifying occasion.

"So," he said, turning to Jennifer at last.

"So," she repeated, and looked at him questioningly, full of tremulous anticipation.

He took a deep breath. "So . . . If David Cameron *does* hold an in–out referendum on EU membership, which way do you think it will go?"

She gave a loud, despairing sigh. "Bloody hell, Benjamin—is that really what's on your mind right now?"

He shook his head. "No. No, it isn't. Not at all."

"Thank God for that. Because then I really *would* be worried. Here—it's the next left."

He swung into a side street, and said: "I'm sorry. I'm just a bit . . . Well, it's been a nice evening, and I don't want it to . . ."

"Me neither. Here, this is it. Number 42."

He steered the car into her front drive. It seemed incredibly quiet when the engine was switched off.

"You'll come in for a coffee, won't you?"

"Yes, sure."

"Good. Come on, then."

In the kitchen, just as she was putting the kettle on, Benjamin said: "Actually I can't have a coffee. Caffeine keeps me awake. I never drink it after lunchtime."

"I've got decaf."

"It has the same effect."

"Well, then, I've got a suggestion." She took a bottle of Sauvignon Blanc out of the fridge and stood directly in front of him, holding it up. "Why don't you have a nice big glass of wine instead, and stay the night in one of my three spare bedrooms?"

"Where are Grace and David?"

"On holiday with their dad. I've even got a spare toothbrush."

For once, Benjamin didn't hesitate. "OK," he said.

"Good," said Jennifer, and gave him a gentle, lingering kiss on the lips by way of reward.

*

Neither of them was prepared to get naked in front of the other. When they went up to Jennifer's bedroom some time later, the curtains were drawn and the lights were turned off and they undressed in the semi-dark, much to Benjamin's relief. There were full-length mirrors in his bathroom at home, but he had become adept at avoiding looking into them whenever he got in or out of the shower or the bath. He had no wish to see his pale, sagging, fifty-five-year-old body reflected back at him. He assumed that Jennifer felt the same way; but when he climbed into bed beside her and ran his first tentative, exploratory hand along the curve of her hip and beyond, he felt nothing but firmness and smoothness. He felt that a compliment was in order.

"You're in excellent shape," he said.

She turned around to face him. "Excellent shape?" she repeated with a laugh. "What are you, my fitness instructor?"

"Sorry," he said. "I can never think what to say when—"

"Then don't say anything," she advised, putting a finger to his lips. In response, he bit her finger gently; or at least intended to. Going by her sudden yelp of pain he seemed to have misjudged it rather badly.

"Ow! Bloody hell, Benjamin, what are you playing at?"

"Sorry, did that hurt?"

"Yes it fucking did. Jesus . . ."

She sucked on her finger for a few seconds. Benjamin, tense already, grew tenser still.

"Is it bleeding?" he asked.

"No it's not," she said, her voice softening. "Just relax, Tiger. Neither of us has done this for ages. It's going to be fine."

He liked hearing the nickname again. Jennifer put her arms around him and they kissed for a while, in the near-silent almost-dark. He stroked her hair, then slid his hand downwards, on to her breast. It was nearly forty years, he thought, since he had touched this same breast, cupped it, almost unknowingly, in his drunken stupor at Doug's teenage party. Jennifer was right. At this age you found yourself thinking in long units of time. Decades, not years . . .

Jennifer, meanwhile, had reached down between his legs and was beginning to stimulate him with her hand, gently at first, then vigorously. Neither approach seemed to be producing any result.

"What's going on down there, then?" she asked.

"Very little, it would seem."

"What's the matter, would you rather be in bed with a sexy journalist in her twenties than a woman your own age?"

"No, not at all." He kissed her again. "You're beautiful. Keep going."

"I'm going to get repetitive strain injury if I do this much longer," she said, increasing both the speed of her movements and the tightness of her grip.

After a minute or two he laid a hand on her wrist and told her to stop.

"I'm sorry," he said.

"Don't worry. Let's give it some time. It's my turn anyway."

She took his hand, which was still resting on her breast, and drew it slowly across the yielding flatness of her stomach until he had reached the soft mesh of her pubic hair. She encouraged him to explore further, until beneath his fingers he could feel a warm, tender nub, which under her patient guidance he began to rub and caress. Soon Jennifer was murmuring with pleasure, and languidly stretching her legs further apart.

"Lovely," she said, and reached around to kiss him fiercely, her tongue darting into his mouth. "Don't move your finger . . . from that precise spot."

"I was reading the other day . . ." Benjamin said, between kisses.

Breathing more and more heavily now, Jennifer still managed to say, "Books books books. Don't you ever stop thinking about books?"

"No—really," he said, "this is interesting. I was reading the other day about Evangelicals in the U.S. They wrote a pamphlet telling girls why they shouldn't masturbate, and the name they invented for it . . ."

"For what?"

". . . for what I'm touching . . ."

"Oh, Benjamin, shut *up* for once!"

". . . is the Devil's Doorbell."

"*The . . . Devil's . . . Doorbell?*" Jennifer repeated. The words were hard to get out: by now her breathing was even faster and even more excited, and it was breaking up into cries of pleasure, or laughter—it was hard to tell which—a mixture of the two, perhaps—until all at once she screamed out, "*Ring a ding ding!*" at the top of her voice in a moment of exquisite release, and she collapsed on top of Benjamin and gave him the tightest hug and the longest kiss and he had the satisfaction, at least, of knowing that he had performed his modest duty with some distinction.

A few minutes later, as she lay with her head against his chest, Jennifer said: "Now I'm feeling guilty. I got off and you didn't."

"It doesn't matter."

She reached down to check the situation in his crotch area. Still nothing.

"It happens to men your age sometimes. A bit of Viagra would put it right."

"I don't suppose you've got any?"

"Funnily enough I don't keep it around the house. I've got some paracetamol, and some antihistamines, but I don't suppose that would help."

She tweaked the flaccid organ playfully. Benjamin was burning up with frustration. In fact he was extremely aroused, but his body, for some reason, didn't seem to be getting the message.

"Perhaps if I talked dirty to you," said Jennifer. "You know, 'Come on, big boy, give it to me hard'—that sort of thing."

Benjamin was dubious about this. And besides, he had had another idea. "Or *perhaps* . . ." he began.

"Yes?" Jennifer's eyes were gleaming at him.

"Do you remember where we were when we first did it?"

"At Doug Anderton's house."

"More specifically . . ."

"In his parents' wardrobe. Not something you forget in a hurry."

"Exactly. Now, correct me if I'm wrong, but that looks like a pretty big wardrobe you've got over there."

Jennifer raised herself on to one arm. "Are you serious?"

"I don't know . . . it might be worth a try. I think if I can somehow recapture that moment—you know, think my way back into it . . ."

After a few seconds' hesitation, she swung her legs out of bed. "Now I've heard everything," she said. "Come on, then, Tiger."

It was a fitted wardrobe, and extremely capacious. Still, they were not the lithe, flexible teenagers they had once been, and it was with some difficulty that they squeezed their middle-aged bodies into the available space. Once they were inside, however, it was rather cosy.

"This is fun," said Jennifer. "Like a filthy game of sardines."

Shifting his knee into a more comfortable position—and nearly dislocating her chin in the process—Benjamin slid the door closed. Now it was pitch-dark. He reached out, found Jennifer's shoulders and upper arms, stroked them, then brushed her cheek with his fingers, and traced the line of her jaw. Already he could feel a delicious heightening of his sense of touch.

"I think this might work, you know."

"Well," she said, "even if it doesn't give you a hard-on, I suppose we might at least come out in Narnia. Now let's see what's going on down there."

She reached between his legs again, and felt an instantaneous, solid response.

"Blimey," she said. "You're right. We seem to be in business." Clasping the shaft in her right hand, she began slowly, regularly stroking its full length. "How does that feel?"

"Good," said Benjamin—with a slight lack of conviction in his voice.

"Mmm, *goood*," Jennifer repeated, breathing the word out, and stretching the vowel. "That feels good, doesn't it? Does that feel good, big boy?"

"So good," said Benjamin. "So, so good." He didn't like to tell her, but in truth he couldn't feel a thing. Which was even more alarming, in a way, than his earlier problem.

"You're a big boy now, aren't you?" Jennifer said, stroking faster and harder. "You're a much bigger boy than I remember. God, that feels good. I love the feel of you in my hand."

Benjamin shifted his weight against the door, which rattled in complaint. He started to moan, which Jennifer took as her cue to strengthen her hold on the shaft and quicken her movements along it, twisting her hand mercilessly whenever she got to the tip.

"Ooh, you like *that*, don't you? You like it when I do that."

Benjamin moaned some more, and then started to cry out.

"You want me to keep doing that, don't you? You want me to do that over and over again."

"Oh God," Benjamin stammered. "*Oh God!*"

"How does that feel?"

"Fuck! Fuck!"

"Feels *goood*, doesn't it?"

"No! Stop!"

"I'm not going to stop until I've finished, big boy."

"No, stop! Cramp! I've got terrible cramp! I'm in bloody agony here!"

By now the pain in his calves was matched only by the total lack of sensation anywhere else in his body. Benjamin grabbed hold of the door, pushed it open and the two of them tumbled out of the wardrobe together, landing on the bedroom carpet in an unceremonious tangle of limbs. Benjamin continued to clutch his calves and cry out in pain, while Jennifer sat up, took one look at the object she was holding in her hands, and burst out laughing.

"What's the matter?" Benjamin asked, panting with distress.

Jennifer could hardly speak. "Look at this!"

Squinting at it in the gloom, Benjamin said: "What the hell's that?"

"It's the scented candle Aunt Julie gave me for Christmas. I wondered where it had got to. I've been looking for that for months."

As spasms of pain continued to tear through his legs, Benjamin said: "*That* . . . That's what you've been stroking?"

Tears of laughter were beginning to streak down Jennifer's face. "Yes."

"No wonder I couldn't feel anything."

That was about as much as she could take. She collapsed on to her back and lay there on the carpet, naked and helpless with laughter, with the yellow, shrink-wrapped candle still clutched in her hand. With as much dignity as he could muster, Benjamin staggered to his feet and climbed into bed, pulling the duvet over him and rubbing away at his twitching, aching calves. Jennifer was still laughing when she slipped into bed beside him. There was no stopping her, it seemed: not until she had finally laid her head to rest against Benjamin's shoulder, and they had fallen asleep in each other's arms.

26.

NOVEMBER 2015
Hey.

One word; just one syllable; a mere three letters. But as soon as it appeared on the screen, Sophie's heart started racing.

She leaned back in her chair and craned her neck to see what Ian was doing in the kitchen. He was preoccupied, trying to get the cork out of a bottle of wine.

She looked at the screen again.

Hey.

How to reply? It was more than three years since she had seen Adam in Marseille. Three years since she had heard a word from him. Three years since that fumbled goodnight kiss in the corridor outside her room. Since then she had emailed him more than once—each time with a slight sense of shame and embarrassment. In the last email she had given him her Skype contact details. And now here he was, messaging her. What was she supposed to say? What could she possibly say that would express the whole range of her complex, ambiguous feelings?

After thinking for a moment, she typed:

Hey.

Ian was coming up behind her, carrying a glass full of red wine. Quickly she clicked an icon on the taskbar at the bottom of her screen. The Skype window disappeared and was replaced by the PowerPoint file she was getting ready to upload to Moodle.

He put the glass down on the desk beside her.

"Hey," she said.

"Hey," he answered.

She took a sip of the wine.

"Thanks for this," she said, and kissed him.

"I'll start getting dinner ready," he said.

"Have you read the email yet?" she asked him. "I printed it out."

"No. I thought there was no hurry. You said it probably wasn't important."

"It probably isn't."

"Good," he said, and was about to leave.

"But it is annoying," she said.

He stopped; turned. "OK, I'll read it now."

"There's no hurry," she said. "It probably isn't important."

"I'll read it now," said Ian, and went back into the kitchen.

As soon as he was gone she clicked on the Skype icon again. There was a new message.

Just wanted to say, thanks for reaching out and letting me know about the conference.

Her most recent excuse for writing to him had been to flag up a forthcoming conference on film music taking place in London next year. Not by any means sure why she was doing it, and half-hoping that his answer would be no, she wrote:

Will you be coming?

Sadly no.

The sense of disappointment was acute, and immediate. Yes, there was an element of relief as well, but the disappointment was uppermost.

Better things to do?

Kind of. As a matter of fact I'm quitting my job. I've had it with academia.

Ian came back in, carrying a bowlful of crisps, which he put down next to the wine glass on her desk. Just in time, she clicked the PowerPoint icon.

"What are you doing?" he asked, looking at the screen.

"Just admin."

He kissed the top of her head. "Never seems to end, does it?"

"Feels that way sometimes."

"I'm just going to pop the fish in the oven, and then I'll read the email."

"OK."

He left. She typed:

Quitting? How come?

She waited for the answer to come through. It took a few minutes.

"Perhaps you should put the rice on first!" she called through to the kitchen.

"OK."

There are always a ton of different reasons—frustration with the job, hating the internal politics, I guess you know them all—but it always comes down to money in the end. Couldn't carry on as adjunct faculty with no prospect of tenure, making <$20,000 a year. Luckily something else came up.

Something else . . .?

"This is crazy," Ian called, from the kitchen.

"What's crazy?"

"This email."

"I told you it was."

She was still waiting for the next message. Nothing so far.

"Did you put the rice on?"

"Oops—I forgot. I'll do it now."

Yeah, composing, in fact. For video games. A friend of mine started a production company and he wants me on board.

Brilliant! Sounds much more creative than compiling admissions stats or filling out strategic impact forms.

Don't tell me you've gone all cynical since Marseille.

There it was. And he was the one who mentioned it. He was the first one to bring it up.

Maybe I was always cynical. That week I just wasn't letting it show.

"Should I wrap the fish in foil before putting them in, do you think?"

"Yes. And maybe put in some dill or something, if we've got any."

"I'll have a look."

Sound of the fridge being opened, and a search of the vegetable drawer being carried out.

"It says use by the end of September."

"I'm sure it'll be all right."

Sorry not to have been in touch since then. Found it all a bit intense in the end.

No worries. Probably for the best!

How've things been for you, anyway?

That was a complicated question if ever there was one. She hesitated for a minute or more and then wrote:

Up and down. I don't know if you've been getting my emails, but I think I mentioned in one of them that –

Ian was behind her again, with the wine bottle. She switched quickly back to PowerPoint.

"Ready for a top-up?"

"Yes please."

He filled the glass, and said: "It's not serious, though, is it?"

"Serious? What? What's serious? Who said anything about it being serious?"

"The email, I mean."

"Oh. Yes . . . No, I don't think it's serious. It can't be serious. The whole thing's just silly."

"What did you say in this seminar, exactly?"

From the kitchen came a loud hissing: the sound of rice boiling over.

"Shit," said Ian, and ran off to deal with it.

Sophie carried on typing:

I've got a new job, down in London. That's been great, but it does mean I now spend two or three nights away from home, which ~~causes~~ sometimes causes problems. But Ian missed out on a promotion last year, and we definitely need both salaries.

It always comes down to money! I read a piece this week which said that if the Democratic candidate (whoever s/he may be) fails to win the election next year, it will be because most middle Americans can no longer afford to replace their car every couple of years.

We haven't replaced ours for five!

There you go.

Listen to us with our first-world problems.

Ian came back. She switched screens again.

"So—what did you say?"

"When?"

"In the seminar."

"Oh—well, the only thing I can think of . . ." Sophie took a breath. "OK. So I do have this student—Emily—who's a trans woman."

"Meaning . . .?"

"Meaning that she's biologically male, but she identifies as female."

"So she's having a sex change?"

"At some point, yes, but it's a long process. You have to live for two years as a woman before you have the operation."

"So right now we should really be saying *he*, not *she*?"

"No, she wants to use the feminine pronoun. And that's fine."

Ian frowned. "OK. But the woman who's complaining isn't called Emily."

"I know—that's the stupid thing about it."

"Who is she—a friend of hers, or something?"

The phone started ringing.

"I'd better get that," said Ian. "It'll be Mum."

"Can you take it in the kitchen?"

"Sure."

He left. Sophie waited until she could hear him talking to his mother—she could recognize the tone, it was always more deferential than when he spoke to anyone else—and then read Adam's latest message.

Well, look, I've got a class in a few minutes. Better do some prep.

OK. Can't keep 'em waiting.

But it's great to be in touch again. And sorry again that I left it so long.

Like I said, no problem. Sorry for stalking you.

I'm glad you did.

Run along, then.

I'll let you know my new email. The academic one won't work after December.

Great. Let's stay in touch!

OK. Bye.

Bye x.

When the chat was over, she sat back in her chair and breathed deeply, calming herself. She took a few rapid sips of wine. Then she logged off Skype and went into the kitchen to see if there was anything she could do to help.

*

They ate their fish. It was a bit dry. The print-out of the email lay on the table next to Ian. By now it was splattered with tiny grease marks.

The email was from Martin, Sophie's head of department. It said that a complaint had been received from a first-year undergraduate student about transphobic remarks made by Sophie during a seminar one week earlier. It invited her to come and see him in his office at 4 p.m. tomorrow, to give her side of the story before the matter was taken any further.

"But you'd never say anything transphobic," said Ian. The word sounded slightly odd, to Sophie's ears, coming from him.

"Of course not," she said. "It's just a misunderstanding."

She cast her mind back to last week's seminar. Emily Shamma was one of her quieter students, and Sophie could only remember two moments of direct interaction with her this time. Early in the session, she had lobbed her a fairly simple question, in the hope of drawing her out: she'd shown Emily two versions of Munch's *The Scream* and asked her to say which one she thought was painted earlier. The answer (to Sophie's mind) was pretty obvious, but Emily had been unable to come to a definite conclusion. Sophie had not in any way belittled her for this, but had explained the answer patiently, and moved on. Later, as everyone was leaving, they'd had a brief—and once again inconclusive—discussion about whether their forthcoming one-to-one tutorial should take place on Wednesday or Thursday in the penultimate week of term.

"And that was it?" said Ian.

"I think so," said Sophie. "I can't remember anything else."

"Well, then, just tell Martin that, and it'll all be fine."

"Of course it will," said Sophie. She took a mouthful of rice, and thought no more of it: her mind wandered back, instead, to the exchange of messages with Adam and, beyond that, to those few sun-drunk days in Marseille, the boat trip to the Frioul islands, their moonlit bathe on the Calanque de Morgiret, so that she was hardly listening when Ian—more worried by the email than she was, apparently—glanced through the print-out one more time, gave a forced laugh and said:

"Everything about this is ridiculous. Even the name of the student who's complained. I mean, who calls their daughter Coriander, for God's sake?"

27.

The next morning, as usual, Sophie took the seven-forty train from Birmingham New Street to London Euston. Just as the train was passing Milton Keynes, and she was in the middle of sending a text to Sohan confirming their venue for dinner that night (she was supposed to be meeting his new boyfriend for the first time), Ian called.

"Hi," she said. "What's up?"

"Well . . ." he began. He sounded distinctly nervous. "I know you aren't on Twitter, but I've just taken a quick look, and today you're all over it."

Sophie felt a sudden, awful hollowing sensation in her stomach.

"All over it?" she said. "What do you mean?"

"There are a lot of tweets about you. Not that you're trending exactly but . . . well, near enough."

"Tweets? Who from?"

"Students, mainly. It looks like this Coriander woman has been busy spreading the word."

"Oh shit. Are they bad? What do they say?"

"Look, *don't read them,* whatever you do. I know you never listen, but I've told you before what these Social Justice Warrior types are like. There's nothing quite as nasty as a pack of lefties once they're on a moral crusade and they've got a victim in their sights. I was in two minds whether to tell you about this, to be honest, but I thought it was probably best if you knew what was going on before you went into that meeting this afternoon."

"Jesus, how has this happened? I don't even know what I'm supposed to have said yet."

"Nothing, probably. Which is why I'm sure it'll blow over. But at the moment it looks a bit bigger than we thought."

"OK, thanks. Forewarned is forearmed, and all that, I suppose."

"Exactly. Love you."

"Love you too."

She hung up and stared out of the window for a few minutes. But the hollowness in her stomach was just getting worse, and she was fighting off a growing temptation to look at those tweets. To distract herself, she decided to do some work: a few last-minute preparations for her two seminars later that morning.

She needn't have bothered, however. None of her students showed up, for either seminar.

*

"Am I being boycotted?" Sophie asked.

"It would appear so," said Martin.

"But that's ridiculous. That's *fucking ridiculous.*"

"Sophie, please don't get emotional about this. That won't help anyone."

Sophie's head of department, Martin Lomas, was a fifty-two-year-old professor of European history, specializing in the role played by flax in Britain's trade deals with the Baltic in the early seventeenth century, a subject on which he had so far written four books. Looking around his office, with its immaculate shelves of books arranged not by author or subject but by size and spine colour, Sophie could understand why emotion might terrify him.

"This is all, I'm sure, a silly misunderstanding," he continued. "But the university insists that we follow the proper procedures. Let's just follow the proper procedures, and everything will be all right."

"Well, you can start by telling me what I'm supposed to have said."

Martin looked at his meeting notes. "You addressed a transgender student in such a way as to imply that her gender dysphoria was the result of character weakness."

Sophie was speechless for a few seconds. Then managed to say: "Bullshit."

"Sophie, please . . ."

"OK, then, rubbish. Total rubbish. Is that better?"

"Let me just lay out the facts, as reported."

"Reported by whom?"

"First of all, by the student you addressed. Emily Shamma. She reported it to her friend, Corrie Anderton, and Ms. Anderton reported it to the equal ops officer of the Student Union. The remark was overheard by three other students who confirmed the report."

Sophie fell silent. This did not sound so good.

"Apparently you said to Emily: 'You have a lot of difficulty making your mind up about things, don't you?'"

Sophie waited.

"And?"

"That's it."

She looked at him for a moment, then breathed a long sigh of relief. "OK. Well, thank God for that."

"What do you mean?"

"I mean, we don't have anything to worry about. She misunderstood me, that's all."

Martin waited for clarification, looking unconvinced.

"I wasn't talking about her gender choices. It was just a comment about the fact she couldn't decide whether to come to a tutorial on a Wednesday or Thursday."

"I see." He made some notes on the pad in front of him. "But, then, why did you say it?"

"Because she was being indecisive."

"Yes, but this was just one moment of indecision. And yet you generalized from it."

"Oh. No, no . . . I was referring back, in a jokey way, to something we'd talked about earlier in the seminar. I'd shown her these two pictures and asked her which one she thought was painted first and she couldn't decide."

Martin wrote all of this down.

"Well, that gives it some context, I suppose," he said, doubtfully.

"No, it doesn't give it some *context*," Sophie insisted. "It explains it. It explains why I said it, and what I meant."

"Still, it wasn't a very tactful thing to say, to a student who, as I understand it, is considering gender reassignment."

"Tact? Is this about tact, all of a sudden? No, of course it wasn't tactful. In fact it was a stupid thing to say. I can see why it was misconstrued. So I'll go and apologize to her, and then we're done."

"Mm." Once again, Martin looked far from persuaded that things were as simple as Sophie believed. "Let's hope so. You see . . ."

Martin stared through his office window, distracted as always by the banality of the view it offered: the brick wall of the humanities department's North Wing, with its rows of anonymous office windows. He felt an overwhelming ennui steal over him. The previous week he had discovered a new fact about flax and the role it had played in Britain's trade deals with the Baltic in the early seventeenth century, and all he really wanted to do was expand it into an article. Or even a book. Yes, perhaps there might be another book to be written here . . .

Reluctantly, he ditched this train of thought and tried to return his attention to the latest departmental crisis.

"You see, what Ms. Anderton is really saying is that by making this remark, you could be in breach of equal opportunities legislation. That's the crux of it. And of course, that would be a very serious matter."

"But . . ."

"And in the past this could all have been dealt with internally. Not hushed up, exactly, but . . . well, the whole matter could have been settled within this department. But now we have social media to contend with. Have you seen any of the tweets or replies?"

"No, I haven't. Bad?"

"Opinions are being vigorously expressed within the student community."

"Anyone taking my side?"

"Perhaps best if you look at them yourself. You can find them quickly enough by searching the hashtag '#sackColemanPotter'."

"Right," Sophie said. "I can see where that one's going." She felt sick again. Still, she could see no reason, however bad things looked at the moment, why this scandal couldn't be stopped in its tracks. "I'll have a word with Emily, and get this sorted, shall I?"

"It may not be that simple. The person who made the complaint was Ms. Anderton, when the remark was reported to her. I'm not sure what Ms. Shamma's position on the matter is. That might even be beside the point. It sounds to me as if she's rather a passive . . ." He checked himself, just in time. Even in a private conversation like this, it was unwise to make sweeping character judgements about members of vulnerable minority groups.

"Can I see the text of the complaint?"

"It will be released to you, in the fullness of time."

"Can you tell me *exactly* what it said?"

"I'm not sure I have it to hand," said Martin, leafing through the first couple of items in the pile of papers on his desk. "It used the expression 'microaggression', I think."

"'Microaggression'?"

"You're familiar with the term?"

"Yes."

"Well, that's what you were guilty of, in this student's opinion. A 'huge microaggression'."

Sophie frowned. "How can you have a huge microaggression? That would just be . . . an aggression."

Martin smiled wanly, then rose to his feet and extended his hand.

"Let's just follow the proper procedures," he said. "If you do that, in my experience, you can't go wrong."

*

Sohan and Sophie both turned up at the restaurant on time, but Mike had texted that he was going to be half an hour late. They sat reading their menus while waiting for him to arrive. Sophie was looking at the prices in dismay. There was no way this was going to come out at less than £150 a head and Ian would be furious if he learned that she'd paid that much for a meal.

"Doesn't this look incredible?" Sohan was saying. "I can see why this place gets amazing reviews."

"I can see why it's half-empty. Fifteen pounds for a starter?"

"People will pay that on a special night out."

"And what the fuck are 'fermented sardine croquettes'? How do you ferment a sardine and why would you put it in a croquette once you'd fermented it?"

"The hummus sounds good."

"Hummus? You can get that for one pound twenty in Tesco. Throw in a 'pickled Shimeji mushroom'—whatever that is—and they think they can charge twelve quid for it."

"You've changed since you moved to Birmingham," said Sohan, still scouring the menu eagerly. "I know they still serve chicken in a basket and lemon meringue pie up there, but the rest of the country's moved on."

"Hilarious," said Sophie. "Seriously, though, I can't pay these kinds of prices."

"Oh, don't worry about that. Mike will pay for everything."

"No, he won't. I have to pay my own way."

"Darling, he earns ten times as much as you and me. Did you hear that? *Ten times*. I make him pay for everything. We couldn't afford to do anything together otherwise."

"And he's OK with that?"

"It's just common sense. I'm telling you, my lifestyle has improved beyond recognition since I met this guy. He's just a couple of years older than us and he's a bloody *millionaire*!"

Sophie shook her head with reluctant admiration. "How come? Family money?"

"Not at all. He's a genuine prole, believe it or not. His father was a steelworker in one of those Godforsaken northern towns—Harrogate or Halifax or somewhere."

"I don't think either of those ever had much to do with steel."

"Well, something beginning with H."

"Hartlepool?"

"Hartlepool, that's it. But Mike's maths teacher at school reckoned he was a genius. He got into Imperial—first man in his family to go to university—stayed on to do a PhD in Pure Maths and then straight into the City."

"They're still recruiting people like that? I thought that was a pre-crash thing."

"Apparently not." Turning to the menu again, his face lit up. "Wow. Wagyu tenderloin, with fava beans *and* shaved broccoli. For thirty-six pounds!"

Sophie looked at him to see if he was joking. He wasn't.

"Putting your spectacular love life to one side," she said, "do you want to hear the other unbelievable thing about today's fiasco?" She had already given him the full details of her meeting with Martin. "This student who's complained about me—turns out I practically know her. She's the daughter of one of my uncle's best friends."

"Uncle Benjamin the Booker-longlisted novelist?"

"Exactly."

"Well, that's good news, isn't it? He can call his friend and have a civilized chat and get him to tell his daughter to shut the fuck up."

"Possibly." Sophie could see how this might look like a sensible option, but it did not alleviate the sense of impending disaster that had come over her that day. Late in the afternoon her resolve had cracked and she had looked at some of the students' tweets. After two minutes' reading, the sheer number and hostility of the messages had had a physical effect and she'd had to run down the corridor to dry-retch in the ladies' toilet. Perhaps this was another reason why she could not get excited by the items on tonight's menu.

"Anyway, maybe the Left have turned on you but you could end up being a heroine to the Right," said Sohan. "If we can spin it so it looks like you're attacking political correctness, maybe the free-speech libertarians will come riding to your rescue. They'll put you on the front cover of the *Spectator* and the *Daily Mail* will write leaders about you."

Sophie was annoyed that he was making a joke of it. She smiled dutifully but was grateful when they were interrupted, a few seconds later, by the arrival at their table of a tall, blond-haired, confident-looking man in a dark business suit. The man ruffled Sohan's hair and squeezed his shoulders, and Sohan said, "Hey, you," and kissed him on the cheek as he sat down beside him. "Sophie, this is Mike," he said. "Mike, Sophie."

They shook hands across the table.

"We meet at last," said Mike. "Sorry I'm late."

Sophie hadn't been so immediately impressed by a man's good looks since the day she had met Ian for the first time. She glanced across at Sohan and he looked triumphantly back at her, his eyes twinkling like a cat that has just been presented with a rich and generous serving of cream in a saucer made of unalloyed gold.

*

The bill for dinner came to £435. As Sohan had predicted, Mike insisted on paying, although he did it so discreetly that Sophie didn't even realize it had happened until a waitress came back to their table with the receipt.

"No, that's not fair," she protested, as Mike pocketed the receipt after asking whether she could make use of it for tax purposes.

"It's completely fair," said Sohan. "This man gets paid obscene amounts of money for devising bizarre financial instruments which only help the rich to get richer. Meanwhile I'm engaged on important research—*vital* research, you might almost say—into the very nature of what it means to be English, and I'm paid peanuts. A pittance."

"Is this true?" Sophie asked, smiling at Mike. "Not about his research, obviously, but what your job involves?"

"More or less," he said.

"I thought derivatives were considered a bit dangerous after the crash."

"I arrived in the City in 2007," he said. "So I was only just getting settled in when it happened. Bit of a baptism of fire. Sure, everyone was a bit shaky for a while, but then things calmed down again. Nobody's really changed their behaviour, as far as I can see. The sums of money involved are too great. You get hooked on making it. It's like any other kind of addiction—drugs, sex—you can't stop it just by regulating it. Especially when the regulation's half-arsed anyway."

"Doesn't it worry you? The risk? I mean . . . supposing there's another crash?"

"There will be," said Mike. "But with any luck I'll have left the crime scene by then. I only want to do this another couple of years and then I'm getting out."

"To do what?"

"Something completely different. Setting up a charity, maybe? I want to give something back."

"You see what he's like?" said Sohan. "Totally idealistic. An altruist. He wants to save the world, just like the rest of us."

"Do you go back home much?" Sophie asked, ignoring him.

"Not very often. Sadly, the last fifteen years have put quite a distance between me and my parents. I used to go back. I used to give them money, as well, but they didn't like it, so I stopped. I think it embarrassed them."

"Do they know you're gay?"

"I've no idea. I've never come out to them."

"Anyway," said Sohan, "Comrade Corbyn will put a stop to your nasty little financial games when he becomes prime minister. Your days of making money out of nothing are numbered."

"Maybe," said Mike. "But most Labour governments end up making friends with the City after a while. The tax revenues are very useful. Perhaps the next one will be different, we'll see."

Jeremy Corbyn had become leader of the Labour Party in September. The surprising—even astonishing—election of this obscure but long-serving, rebellious backbencher had been seen by many, including Sophie, as a welcome sign that the party was planning to return to the principles it had abandoned under Tony Blair. Less welcome was the fact that, as far as she and Ian were concerned, it placed their own political differences under a harsher light than ever. He saw Corbyn as a Trotskyist; she saw him as a wise, avuncular socialist. He warned her that Corbyn would transform Britain into a repressive dystopia reminiscent of the old Eastern bloc, that people like her were the enemy as far as his followers were concerned, and if she voted for him she would be acting like a turkey who voted for Christmas. This was one reason why she did not intend to share with

Ian the information that, according to the Facebook page she had visited that afternoon, among the many political societies of which Corrie Anderton was an enthusiastic member was a newly formed group called Students for Corbyn.

In the last few hours Sophie had almost forgotten about all this; forgotten about her nemesis and the havoc she had already managed to cause within the department and on social media. Now it all came back to her. Despite his semi-drunken state and the air of beaming smugness he could not help radiating in Mike's company, Sohan noticed her change of mood and knew what had provoked it.

"Come on," he said, taking her hand. "Time for bed."

The three of them took a taxi back to Sohan's flat in Clapham. Sophie made up the sofa bed with which she was now so familiar, and lay there, unblinking and wakeful for more than an hour, listening to the sounds of Mike and Sohan making love in the room next door. She was still awake when Mike emerged from the bedroom, naked except for a towel, and padded past her bed on his way to the kitchen to get some water. On the way back, he noticed her eyes shining in the dark.

"Sorry," he said. "Were we being a bit noisy?"

"That's all right," said Sophie. "It's nice to know that people are enjoying themselves."

He paused in the kitchen doorway, and said: "Don't worry. I'm sure everything will be all right."

"Of course it will."

She turned over and snuggled down beneath the duvet, facing towards him.

"Well, goodnight," he said.

"Goodnight."

She felt oddly comforted by his reassurance, and touched by the note of sympathy in his voice, but even so, he was wrong: the next morning she received an email from Martin announcing that she had been suspended from all teaching until further notice.

28

Benjamin was driving from Shrewsbury to Rednal again, following the course of the River Severn, through the towns of Cressage, Much Wenlock, Bridgnorth, Enville, Stourbridge and Hagley. He didn't even dare to calculate, any more, how many times he had driven this route. The only difference these days (and it was an important difference) was that the journey took him close to where Jennifer lived, and sometimes in the late mornings he would call in at the estate agents' office where she worked, and take her out to lunch, or in the early evenings he would call at her house as he drove home, and they would go out to dinner, and afterwards make love. They had settled, much to his surprise, into a low-key but perfectly satisfactory relationship. They saw each other about once a fortnight, sometimes more, sometimes less. Their sex life had recovered from that initial fiasco with the wardrobe. They found that they enjoyed each other's company, although Benjamin was plagued—much as he had been forty years earlier—by the suspicion that in essence they had little in common. But then he had at least developed enough self-awareness, in his mid-fifties (better late than never), to admit that there were very few people who had anything in common with him. He was a quiet, introverted writer, as much preoccupied with his inner imaginative universe as with the world around him. And Jennifer seemed happy with that, for the moment. It would have been nice if he had won the Man Booker Prize, or even got as far as the shortlist, but there had been tangible benefits from his evanescent period of fame. A London publisher had offered him a small advance for his second, as yet untitled, as yet unwritten (and indeed yet to be conceived) novel. He had been invited to speak at one or two literary festivals, and to be one of the tutors on a week-long residential writing course later in the year. Sales of *A Rose Without a Thorn* had been modest, and nobody had snapped up the film rights, but for Benjamin it was enough. He felt vindicated. He felt lucky.

Would his mother, he sometimes still wondered, have been proud of his achievement? His father rarely mentioned it. Colin had become ever more taciturn and ever more morose; his face, his occasional words, his very posture and body language ever more expressive of a generalized sense of existential doom. On top of which, Benjamin was pretty sure that his memory was starting to fail now. During the 1970s, Colin had worked as a foreman in what had then been the British Leyland car plant in Longbridge; in the early 1980s, he had been promoted to a desk job, from which he'd retired in 1995. Everything that had taken place before that year, the year of his retirement, still seemed to be vivid to him; everything subsequent to that date either seemed to be a blur, or to be forgotten altogether. He knew who Benjamin and Lois were, certainly—and Christopher and Sophie, and to a lesser extent Ian—but he couldn't keep track of what was happening in their lives, or at any rate had no interest in doing so. He still had the *Daily Telegraph* delivered every day, but Benjamin was not convinced that he read it, although he did know the name of the current prime minister, and the current leader of the opposition (who he detested). There was no doubt that Colin remembered the Tory and Labour administrations of the 1970s, though, and had excellent recall of the confrontational politics of the Longbridge factory itself during that decade, when production was often halted by the calling of strikes and (in his version of events, anyway) barely a day went by without thousands of workers gathering for meetings in Cofton Park and being provoked into a state of obdurate militancy by some troublesome shop steward such as Derek Robinson or Bill Anderton. He had been bitter about it at the time, and—it sometimes seemed to Benjamin—was still bitter about it now, four decades later.

Colin rarely left the house these days, and when he did it was always with either Lois or Benjamin, who both invariably drove him out into the countryside, towards the west, away from the urban sprawl of Birmingham. He was too slow and too frail to go for a serious walk, but he could still be manhandled—sometimes with difficulty—in the direction of a garden centre or the lounge bar of a village pub. But he had not been near the site of the old Longbridge plant for years, even though it lay little more than a mile from his house. Today, then, Benjamin was surprised when, fifteen minutes after his arrival, when they had already run out of things to say to each other, his father announced: "I want you to take me to Longbridge this afternoon."

"Longbridge?" said Benjamin. "Why?"

"I want to see the new shop."

"What shop?"

"There's a big new shop opened there. Right in the middle of the factory. It was on the telly last night. I want to see what it's like. And you never know, I might run into some of the old crew while I'm there."

"But Dad—"

Benjamin decided to hold his tongue. From the way his father was talking, it sounded as if he had no idea what had become of the old factory buildings. They had, almost without exception, been demolished, wiped from the face of the earth. Apart from a tiny remnant up by the old Q Gate, where a rump of small-volume manufacturing was clinging on, providing fragile employment for a few hundred people, it was all long gone. The West, North and South Works had been the first to go, and then for a long time the site had stood empty, providing a desolate reminder of the decline in British industry; but now most of it had been filled again, with housing, retail units and a new technical college. Did Colin know any of this? Benjamin was not sure; and he was not sure, either, how his father would respond when confronted for the first time by such a complete transformation, such a radical rewriting of all the history that had once been familiar to him.

"Are you *sure* that's what you want to do?" he asked. "I thought we could go to Woodlands again."

"I'm sick of that place," Colin snapped. "Why does no one believe me when I say that I want to do something?"

*

Benjamin took a long way round to the old factory, approaching it from the west, driving along the A38, past the cinema complex and the bowling alley and Morrisons and McDonald's. At two o'clock on a winter's afternoon the light already seemed to be fading. As he swung right at the roundabout on to the Bristol Road, his father craned his neck in the other direction and said:

"Where are we?"

"You know where we are. This is the Bristol Road."

"No it isn't. The conveyor bridge goes over the Bristol Road. Where's the conveyor bridge?"

The conveyor bridge was a local landmark—or at least it had been, for thirty-five years. A narrow stretch of the Longbridge assembly track, carried over the busy dual carriageway on a covered bridge in order to provide an efficient link between the West and South Works, it had been built in 1971—Benjamin could pinpoint the date exactly because that had been his first year at King William's, and he'd had to travel beneath the bridge on his bus twice a day while it was still a work-in-progress. But those had been busier, more optimistic times for British manufacturing and the bridge, having long out-lived its usefulness, had been torn down in 2006—almost ten years earlier. Had Colin really never noticed, or had he forgotten?

"It's gone, Dad. They demolished it ages ago."

"So how do they get the cars from one side of the plant to the other?"

Benjamin didn't answer. He took the first left turn, into a wide lane between rows of identical, newly built houses, and drove another few hundred yards until they reached a spacious car park surrounded by shops: not just a gigantic branch of Marks & Spencer but also Poundland, Boots and a few others.

"Where are we now?" Colin said, bewildered and exasperated.

"We're where you wanted to come," said Benjamin. He pointed at the massive department store. "This is the big shop that was on the news."

"I didn't mean this one," Colin insisted. "I wanted you to take me to Longbridge."

"This is Longbridge."

"No it isn't."

Grumbling, he got out of the car and started shuffling towards the enormous shop, while Benjamin locked the door and put on his coat and hurried to catch up with him.

Once inside, Colin looked all around, left and right, confused by what he saw and staggered by the scale of everything. He took a few more steps into the ladieswear department and found himself confronted by row after row of stockings, bras and lacy pants, as far as the eye could see. If he had been expecting to find the overwhelming noise, smell and testosterone-fuelled atmosphere of the old Longbridge assembly track, his confusion was understandable.

"What's going on here?" he said, turning to Benjamin.

"It's a shop, Dad. It's a Marks & Spencer. They don't make cars here any more."

"Where do they make the cars, then?"

That was a good question. They wandered a little further until they reached the ground-floor Prosecco bar, which was empty apart from a young, well-dressed couple enjoying what looked to Benjamin like an adulterous date.

"This is never the new canteen, is it?" Colin said.

As they walked on into the Food Hall, and drifted up and down the seemingly endless aisles of pre-packaged salads, cooked meats and imported wines, Benjamin tried to explain.

"Look, Dad, don't you remember that protest rally we all went to in Cannon Hill Park? The Rally for Rover?"

"No, when was that?"

"It was about fifteen years ago. Anyway, it did no good. Four local guys ended up taking over the company but instead of saving it they ran it into the ground and then sold it off in 2005. There's been hardly anything made here since then. Everyone buys their cars from Germany and France and Japan now. They flattened all the factory buildings, and for years there was nothing but empty space here. Come on, Dad, you *must* remember some of this. You and I went to have a look at it once, when they were in the middle of demolishing the South Works."

"The South Works is all gone?"

"We're standing in it now. Where it used to be."

"CAB 1 and CAB 2?"

"Both gone."

"What about the East Works? Down by Groveley Lane?"

"I don't know. I don't know what's happened down there."

"Take me there."

"Really?"

"Take me there now."

They walked back to the car park. The drive to the site of the old East Works only took three minutes, but in that time the sky seemed to get even darker.

"Looks like rain," Benjamin said.

All they found, when they reached the site, was a vast expanse of wasteland, hemmed in by tall metal fencing. Signs posted at regular intervals along the fence warned prospective visitors to keep out. There was also a large billboard announcing the imminent construction of yet more two-, three- and four-bedroom homes.

"Well, there you are," said Benjamin. "What do you want to do now?"

"Park the car," his father said.

Benjamin parked by the side of the road. To his surprise, Colin unfastened his seat belt and got out. Slowly, effortfully, he began to walk towards a set of double gates emblazoned with the logo of the construction company. Benjamin followed him.

Colin stopped when he got to the gates. There was a gap between them which was wide enough to see through. He stood there for several minutes, squinting through the gap. Benjamin stayed beside him, standing on tiptoe and peering over the gates at the same view. There was nothing to see. Hundreds of acres of mud, deserted and featureless in the failing light, stretching right up the hill towards the street where a row of interwar houses could dimly be made out. There was thin moisture in the air—more like mist than drizzle—and the afternoon had turned wincingly cold.

"Come on, Dad," Benjamin said. "There's nothing to see here."

"I don't get it," said Colin.

Benjamin had turned back towards the car. Now he turned again, to face his father.

"What? What don't you get?"

"I don't get how they can just knock all that down. Something that was here for so long, something that . . ."

He stared again through the gap between the gates. But his eyes were glazed and unseeing; and his voice, forcing out more words than he had perhaps spoken in the last twelve months, was as flat and toneless as the landscape.

"I mean, a building isn't just a place, is it?" he said. "It's the people. The people who were inside it.

"I'm not saying . . . I mean, I know we made crap cars. I know the Germans and the Japanese make better cars than we ever did. I'm not daft. I understand all that. I understand why people want to buy a car from Japan that's not going to break down after a couple of years like ours used to do. What I don't understand is . . .

"What I don't understand is, where it's going to end? How we can keep going like this. We don't *make* anything any more. If we don't make anything then we've got nothing to sell, so how . . . how are we going to survive?

"That's what worries me. I mean, *this* doesn't worry me. This big empty space here, that's just . . . nothing. When you knock down a factory, and all those jobs go, that's what you expect to see. Nothing.

"But that shop—that bloody great shop? And all those houses? Hundreds and hundreds of houses? What's that about? How can you replace a factory with shops? If there's no factory, how are people supposed to make the money to spend in the shops? How are people supposed to make the money to buy the houses? It doesn't make sense.

"I think that's what made me . . . come over a bit funny, back there in the shop. I just couldn't take it in, how everything's turned out. And my memory does get a bit fuzzy sometimes. I've noticed it happening. I don't know what it means. It's a bit scary. Everything's a bit scary, when you get to my age, because you know what's waiting for you, just around the corner. But I do still remember a lot of things. Like I said, I'm not daft. Not yet. Of course I remember them knocking the buildings down. I knew they'd done that. I didn't know . . . didn't realize it was all of them, though. And there are things, older things than that, much older, that I remember even more clearly.

"Like this place. This place back then. The East Works. I can see it now, clear as day. People would start pouring in here from about seven thirty. They all came by car. Every road around here would be lined with parked cars for miles. And during the day the noise of the track, the people, the comings and goings would be incredible. That's how I remember it. Nan worked here too, you know. My mum. She used to tell me stories about the war. Where we're standing now, right underneath our feet, there are tunnels. Dozens of them. Huge tunnels. During the war, there were hundreds of people working down there. Nan was one of them. She showed me a photograph, once, of everyone working in the tunnels. We've got it somewhere. Making armaments, they were, munitions, aeroplane parts. Can you imagine! Can you imagine what it was like, hundreds of people, working together like that, for the war effort? What a spirit, eh? What a country we were back then!

"Whatever happened to all that? It was bad enough when I was working here. Every man for himself, survival of the fittest, I'm all right, Jack. That's what was starting to take over. But now it's even worse, it's just . . . fancy clothes and Prosecco bars and bloody . . . packets of salad. We've gone soft, that's the problem. No wonder the rest of the world's laughing at us."

Colin turned away from the gates. It was almost completely dark now, and he was starting to shiver.

"Are they, though, Dad?" Benjamin said. "Who's laughing at us?"

"Of course they are. They think we're a joke. They think we're daft."

Benjamin had no idea what his father meant, or even who he was talking about. He took his arm as they walked back towards the car, opened the passenger door for him and helped him flop down into the seat. Then he got into the driver's seat, but didn't turn the engine on for a while. For a few moments neither of them spoke. They listened to the incipient patter of winter rain against the windscreen.

"I think you're wrong," said Benjamin at last. "I don't think anybody's laughing at us."

"Just take me home," said Colin, miserably.

29.

"Exciting times, Douglas," Nigel said. "Incredibly exciting times. Who was it who said, 'May you live in exciting times'?"

"It was Confucius," said Doug. "And it was 'interesting times'."

"I'm sure what he really meant was 'exciting'," said Nigel. "Perhaps it got lost in translation."

"He said 'interesting'," said Doug. "And it was meant to be a curse. He didn't mean that it was a good thing."

"How can it not be a good thing to live in exciting times?" said Nigel. "You writers and intellectuals—you're so negative about everything."

"That's us," said Doug, tipping two generous spoonfuls of sugar into his cappuccino. "Always looking on the dark side."

"People have had enough of intellectuals," said Nigel. A sudden gleam appeared in his eye, as he was struck by the brilliance of this phrase. "Wait a minute, let me write that down."

"Don't let your pearls of wisdom go to waste," said Doug, smiling as he watched him scribble in a notebook.

"With a bit of tweaking, that could become quite a soundbite," said Nigel.

They were meeting, as usual, at the café next to Temple underground station. A few weeks earlier, David Cameron had visited Brussels to negotiate a new deal with the European Union, hoping to extract concessions which would give Britain exceptional status— even more exceptional that it had already—and pacify the country's seemingly ever more vocal army of Eurosceptics. Immediately after-wards, he announced the date of the promised referendum on Brit-ain's EU membership: 23 June—the second day of the Glastonbury Festival, as it happened.

"Well, then, that's a hundred thousand young people who won't be bothering to vote, isn't it?" Doug said.

"Postal votes will be available, for young and old alike," Nigel said. "Dave has foreseen every eventuality."

"Including the one where he loses and we have to leave the EU?"

"Every *probable* eventuality, I should say."

"What happens if he does lose? Will he resign?"

"Dave? Never. He's not a quitter."

"What if the result's too close to call?"

"Why do journalists love hypothetical questions so much? Every-thing is hypothetical with you. 'What happens if you lose?' 'What hap-pens if we leave the EU?' 'What happens if Donald Trump becomes U.S. president?' You live in a fantasy world, you people. Why don't you ask me some practical questions? Like, 'What will be the three main planks of Dave's campaign strategy?'"

"OK, then—what will be the three main planks of Dave's cam-paign strategy?"

"I'm not at liberty to disclose that."

Frustrated, Doug tried a different tack. "Look, supposing the people vote for Brexit and we—"

"Excuse me," Nigel said. "I have to interrupt you there. Suppos-ing the people vote for *what*?"

"Brexit."

Nigel looked at him in astonishment. "How on earth did you come up with that word?"

"Isn't that what people are calling it?"

"I thought it was called Brixit."

"What? Brixit?"

"That's what we've been calling it."

"Who?"

"Dave and the whole team."

"Everybody else is calling it Brexit. Where did you get Brixit from?"

"I don't know. We thought that's what it was called." He wrote in his notebook again. "Brexit? Are you sure?"

"Quite sure. It's a portmanteau word. British exit."

"British exit . . . But surely that would be Brixit?"

"Well, the Greeks called it Grexit."

"The Greeks? But they haven't left the European Union."

"No, but they were thinking about it."

"But we're not Greeks. We should have our own word for it."

"We do. Brexit."

"But we've been calling it Brixit." Nigel shook his head and made even more extensive notes. "This is going to be an absolute bombshell in the next cabinet meeting. I hope I'm not the one who has to break it to them."

"Well," said Doug, "since you're convinced it's not going to happen, you don't really need a word for it, do you?"

Nigel smiled happily when he heard this. "Of course—you're absolutely right. It's not going to happen, so we don't need a word for it."

"There you are, then."

"After all, in a year's time, all this silly business will be forgotten."

"Exactly."

"Nobody will even remember that some people wanted to Brixit."

"Quite. Although, you know, some of those people . . ." He wondered how to put this. "Well, they're serious players, aren't they? Boris Johnson, for instance. He's a real heavyweight."

"I don't think you should be rude about his personal appearance," Nigel said. "Even though Dave is *very* angry with him."

"He wasn't expecting him to declare for Leave?"

"Not at all."

"There's a rumour going around," said Doug, "that the night before the *Telegraph* went to press, Boris had *two* articles ready for them. One where he made the case for Leave, and the other where he argued for Remain."

"I don't believe that for a moment," said Nigel. "Boris would have had three articles ready—one for Leave, one for Remain, and one for not being able to make up his mind. He likes to cover all the bases."

"And then Michael Gove. Another big hitter coming out for Leave."

"I know. Dave is *very* angry with Michael. Luckily, there are still a lot of loyal, sensible Conservatives who appreciate the benefits of EU membership. I believe you're sleeping with one of them. But imagine how Dave feels about Michael and some of the others. I mean, he went all the way to Brussels and got us this wonderful deal, and these people still aren't happy."

"A lot of people just don't like the EU," said Doug. "They think it's undemocratic."

"Yes, but leaving it would be bad for the economy."

"They think that Germany pushes the other countries around."

"Yes, but leaving it would be bad for the economy."

"They think too many immigrants have come in from Poland and Romania, and are pushing wages down."

"Yes, but leaving it would be bad for the economy."

"OK," said Doug, "I think I've just found out what the three main planks of Dave's campaign strategy are going to be." Now it was his turn to make some notes. "And what about Jeremy Corbyn?"

Nigel drew in his breath with a long hissing sound, and seemed to visibly recoil. "Jeremy Corbyn?"

"Yes. Where does he fit into this?"

"We don't talk about Jeremy."

"Why not?"

"Why not? Because he's a Marxist. A Marxist, a Leninist, a Trotskyist and a Communist. A Maoist, a Bolshevik, an anarchist and a Leftist. A radical socialist, an anti-capitalist, an anti-royalist and a pro-terrorist."

"But he's also a Remainer."

"Really?"

"Apparently."

"Then of course, we're thrilled to have him on board. But I don't think Dave would be prepared to share a platform with him."

"He won't have to. Jeremy refuses to share a platform with *him*."

"Good. Well, there you are—it's good to see that political opponents can put aside their differences in the service of a common cause, and agree on something for once."

"Namely, refusing to share a platform with each other."

"Precisely."

"And what about Nigel Farage?"

Nigel drew in his breath with a hiss again. "We don't talk about Nigel Farage."

"There seem to be a lot of things you don't talk about. Why don't you talk about Nigel Farage?"

"Dave came up with a very memorable phrase about UKIP and its supporters. I've forgotten it for the moment, but it was very memorable."

"He called them 'fruitcakes, loonies and closet racists'."

"Really? That was nasty of him. Anyway, we don't take Nigel Farage seriously. Or UKIP. They only have one MP, after all."

"But that's because of first-past-the-post. Actually they have twelve per cent support—which makes them the third-most popular party."

"That's the beauty of our parliamentary system. It keeps the— what was Dave's phrase again?"

"Fruitcakes, loonies and closet racists."

"It keeps the fruitcakes, loonies and closet racists from having any real influence. I mean, think of all the fruitcakes, loonies and closet racists up and down the country, and imagine what would happen if they were given an equal say with everyone else on matters of national importance."

"But that's exactly what this referendum *is* going to give them."

Nigel sighed. "Negative thinking, Douglas. Always with the negative thinking. Negativity, negativity, negativity. We're about to embark on an *amazing* exercise in direct democracy. Now come on—you live and breathe politics, don't you? It's been your lifelong passion. Don't you want to see that passion shared with your fellow citizens? What Dave's doing here is starting a *conversation*. For the next three months, the country is going to be consumed, riveted, by a national conversation about Britain's place in Europe and its place in the world. Just think of that! Just think of Mrs. Jones . . ."

"Who?"

"I'm just giving you an example, a hypothetical example. Just think of Mrs. Jones going into the butcher's shop on a Saturday morning. 'Good morning, Mrs. Jones,' the butcher might say. 'A dozen rashers of finest back bacon for you and your family, as per usual?' And while he's putting them on the counter and trimming them and wrapping them up, he might say: 'So, what about the impact of these pesky non-tariff barriers, eh? Blow me if they wouldn't have a significant effect on the UK service sector, which makes up eighty per cent of the economy.' And Mrs. Jones might say, 'Ah, but under WTO rules—'"

"Nigel," Doug interrupted, "you're completely crazy if you think people are going to be having that kind of conversation. There can't be more than about twelve people in the country who understand how the EU works, never mind how its regulations dovetail into the global economic system. *You* don't understand that and I certainly don't understand it and if you think people are going to be any better informed in three months' time you're living in cloud cuckoo land. People are going to vote how they always vote—with their gut. This campaign's going to be won on slogans and soundbites, and instincts and emotions. Not to mention prejudices—which Farage and his fruitcakes are pretty good at appealing to, incidentally."

Nigel sat back with his arms folded. His face was suffused with an expression of the purest pity. He drummed his fingers on his upper arms, and said: "Douglas, Douglas, Douglas. Do you know how long it is, how many years, since we started meeting at this café? Almost six years. In that time, we've had so many interesting conversations. And I like to think that in many ways, despite the differences between us, in politics, age, physical health—you know what I'm talking about here, I won't embarrass you by bringing it up again, although I will leave you my father's card, for future reference—I like to think that we've formed a genuine friendship. So many things have happened to you in that time. Many of the newspapers you used to work for have closed down. Commentators like you no longer wield the influence you used to. And every time we meet, and we talk about this government I'm so privileged to serve, and this prime minister I'm so lucky to work with—and, yes, also to count as a friend, of sorts—every time, you act like a prophet of doom. Always foreseeing disaster and failure. But David's a *winner*, Douglas. He's a *fighter*. He intends to fight this campaign and win it. Just like he won the election last year—in the face of all the nay-sayers. In the face of all those ridiculous opinion polls which told us he was going to lose. I mean—" he gave an incredulous laugh "—do you remember how badly they got it wrong? Who would listen to a pundit ever again, after that? Who would put the slightest faith in the opinion polls?"

"Which this time," Doug pointed out, "say that Remain is going to win in June."

"And they're right!" said Nigel triumphantly. "Dave *is* going to win! He *has* to win. He has to win because he has four more years in office and he has so much work to do, and he owes it to the British people to carry on."

"Great," said Doug. "Four more years of austerity, cuts to social services, cuts to welfare, creeping privatization of the NHS . . ."

"Exactly. You see? There's so much to do! Talking of which . . ." Nigel looked at his watch and jumped to his feet. "I have to be on my way. Can you take care of these coffees? It'll be my turn next time."

He was gone. Doug paid the bill and walked slowly along the Embankment towards Waterloo Bridge, shaking his head and thinking, as always, that he could never predict the direction that these conversations were going to take. Ten minutes later, his phone vibrated as he received a text. It was from Nigel.

What do you know—it turns out that people "are" *calling it Brexit. Thanks for the tip!*

30.

"I do sometimes wonder," said Benjamin, "what my life would have been like if I hadn't gone to that school."

Charlie shook his head and said: "Don't go there, mate. The 'what if' question. It's not allowed. That way madness lies."

"No, but—"

"Everything works out for the best. You have to believe that. When I met Yasmin, for instance, that wasn't *chance*. It was fate, destiny, Kismet."

"Kismet?" Benjamin repeated, sceptically. He took a sip from his Guinness. Charlie had already finished his pint and was waiting for him to catch up. Benjamin was a slow drinker.

"Yes. You have these moments—you have these moments when everything in your life suddenly comes together. It doesn't have to happen in Shangri-La, or wherever . . . For me it happened in *Toys'R'Us* just outside Dudley. Beggars can't always be choosers, you know."

"I suppose not," said Benjamin.

"But think about all the things that followed from that: if I hadn't been working there when she came in with Aneeqa, and if they hadn't asked me to fetch down that table tennis set from the top shelf, then I never would've started talking to them. I never would've started seeing her, I never would've started taking Aneeqa to school and I never would've known there was another girl there called Krystal who hated her and was jealous of her. And I never would've known Krystal had a father called Duncan who was also a children's entertainer and who started hating me just because I was looking after a girl his daughter happened to hate."

Charlie had already told Benjamin this story, at one of their first lunches together: the story of Duncan Field, also known as Doctor Daredevil, who worked the same area as Charlie and for the last five years had been trying to make his working life difficult in every way possible. He would turn up at Charlie's Woodlands Theatre shows and sabotage them by standing in the wings and heckling, or even coming on stage uninvited. He would find out which children's parties Charlie was booked for (Charlie was never able to work out how) and arrive at the same house himself twenty minutes early, claiming that he was the replacement booking and taking over the whole show. The styles of the two entertainers were diametrically opposed: Baron Brainbox was gentle, whimsical, educative; Doctor Daredevil was raucous and rude, and placed an emphasis on chemically dangerous magic tricks which were frequently in breach of Health and Safety regulations and more than once had caused the fire brigade to be called out. The two men were divided by intense professional rivalry and maintained a deep personal loathing for one another.

At the root of their enmity was the hatred between Krystal and Aneeqa at school. She was not Charlie's stepdaughter, exactly, although he sometimes referred to her as such. He had been in a relationship with Yasmin, Aneeqa's mother, for more than six years, but Benjamin had already formed the strong impression—just from hearing Charlie's version of things—that the affection was mainly on one side. He spent some nights at Yasmin's house but she would not allow him to move in there, so he was also obliged to keep a flat of his own. She was a difficult woman, by the sound of it: bad-tempered and fiery, still bitter about her divorce, untrusting of other men. She had no job and depended on Charlie for financial support; this in itself being a bone of contention, because he had left his job in retail to pursue his new ambition of being a full-time children's entertainer, and ever since, they had been living hand-to-mouth. Aneeqa, it seemed, was a promising student, now in her A-level year, with a particular talent for languages. Krystal had bullied her from the moment they met, on the very first day of Year Seven, and in all that time her father had never offered a word of criticism, or troubled to conceal his outrage that the daughter of a Muslim family might be considered brighter or more impressive than his own daughter.

Taking all this into account, and having noticed over the last few months that his old friend, despite his façade of cheerfulness, bore a permanent and more deep-seated air of anxiety and frustration, Benjamin could not quite share in Charlie's conviction that that chance encounter in a Black Country toyshop had transformed his life for the better. But perhaps tonight would change his mind, since, for the first time, he'd been invited to come back to Yasmin's house and have dinner with the family.

"I've just got to get a bit of shopping done first," Charlie said now. "Pop down to Sainsbury's or something."

"OK," said Benjamin, beginning to drink up. "I'll come with you."

"No, no need to do that. You stay here and have another drink."

"Honestly, I'd rather come with you."

"Don't be silly. You wait here. I'll be twenty minutes or so."

Charlie was so insistent—to the point of physically restraining him when he tried to rise from his seat—that Benjamin gave up and bought himself another half of Guinness that he didn't really want. While waiting for Charlie to come back, he played a few games of Sudoku on his smartphone and half-watched the silent TV screen in the corner of the pub. A man in a suit was talking to camera while at the bottom of the screen a banner headline declared: "Brexit to cost families £4,300 a year, Treasury claims." "How do they know that?" a man at the bar was saying. "Rubbish, isn't it?" his friend agreed. Benjamin went back to his puzzle. This whole referendum campaign was a big, silly waste of time as far as he could see. The result was a foregone conclusion and the sooner everything went back to normal the better.

Charlie returned with his shopping bags. They went out into the car park together and, as they loaded the bags into the car, Benjamin noticed there was a sleeping bag in the boot. But, as usual, he thought nothing of it.

It was a short drive to Yasmin's house in Moseley: a modest mid-terrace on a side road leading off the high street, which was still busy in the sunshine of this mid-April evening. As they stood on the door-step waiting for someone to let them in, clutching the bags of shopping, Charlie (who didn't seem to have his own key) closed his eyes against the low sun and said: "We could have drinks in the garden, I reckon. It's warm enough. What do you think?"

"Sounds nice," said Benjamin.

Yasmin opened the door and gave them a friendly, welcoming smile.

"Charlie's told me everything about you," she said, leading them through the narrow hallway. "He never stops talking about his super-star friend. Neeqs!" she called. "Neeqs, where are you? Charlie and his friend are here."

"I'm doing something," called a voice from the room next door.

"Never mind that. Come and be polite."

"My hands are covered in paint."

Yasmin turned to the two visitors. "You see what I have to put up with? She won't do anything I ask her to. She answers back all the time."

Charlie led Benjamin through the doorway and they both peeped into a small, dark dining room, looking out over a patio garden and dominated by a drop-leaf table which was currently covered with small paint pots and a sheet of artist's paper. Bent over the paper was Aneeqa: a diminutive figure doing her best to focus on her work, despite the long trail of thick black hair falling over her face and obscuring most of it apart from her frown of concentration.

"Hi love," said Charlie. "This is Benjamin."

"Hi," Aneeqa said, not looking up. She was working on a line drawing of a woman breastfeeding; above it she had painted the word "Beloved" in elaborate multicoloured lettering. The drawing itself was strong, simple and confident, but it was the calligraphy that really drew the eye, being executed with amazing flair and attention to detail.

"I gave you his book, remember? He signed it for you."

Aneeqa looked up. She had warm brown eyes and a full, expres-sive mouth.

"Oh yeah. That Benjamin. Hello."

"Hello."

"I started your book. I haven't finished it yet."

"Is this part of your coursework?" Charlie asked.

"Mm-hm," she said, returning to her work, which involved adding some sort of ochre colouring to the bottom of the letter "V."

"Looks great."

"It's meant to be a book cover."

"Well, there you go," said Charlie. "You should design his next one." Then, when it became clear that no more conversation was forthcoming, he said: "We'll leave you to it, then."

"OK. Nearly done anyway."

"Come and have a drink with us out in the garden."

"In a minute."

They took the shopping bags into the kitchen and put them down on the table. Yasmin was washing glasses at the sink.

"I thought we'd have drinks in the garden maybe," said Charlie.

She turned around. "The garden? Why the garden?"

"Because it's such a nice evening."

"I just cleaned up the front room. Took me almost half an hour. The patio furniture is filthy. It hasn't been used since last year."

"Then give me a cloth and I'll wipe it down. Simples."

He took a cloth from one of the kitchen drawers and walked out into the garden, whistling a cheery tune as he did so. Benjamin could see him at work through the window, repositioning the plastic furniture. The garden was only a few yards square and was entirely paved over. Left alone with Yasmin, who was also looking out of the window, Benjamin was still trying to think of something to say to her when she clicked her tongue with annoyance and threw down her dishcloth.

"That's not how you do it," she said. "He doesn't have a clue."

She marched outside and soon Benjamin could hear the sounds of an argument. Then he heard someone come into the kitchen and he turned. It was Aneeqa.

"Don't worry," she said, referring to the quarrelsome voices outside. "This is just normality. Our normality."

She rinsed her paint-covered hands in the washing-up water, dried them with paper towel, then wandered over to the bags of food on the kitchen table.

"I suppose someone had better put this lot away."

"I'll unpack," Benjamin suggested. "You shelve."

"Why not."

As he removed the tins and packets and handed them to Aneeqa, he noticed something strange. Charlie had said that he would be shopping at Sainsbury's but this food was from many different shops. There were tins of Tesco soup, Sainsbury's tomatoes, beans and canned meat from Morrisons and Lidl. Aneeqa could see that he was puzzled but she said nothing at first: not until she had put a few more items away in the cupboards.

"I suppose he told you he was going to the supermarket, did he?" she said finally.

"Yes. Why, where *did* he go?"

Again, Aneeqa said nothing. Slowly, the truth dawned on him.

"You don't use a food bank?"

She opened a pack of rice and began to pour the contents into a jar. "Mum won't go. She finds it too embarrassing. So Charlie normally does it for her." In response to the look on Benjamin's face, she added: "Don't look so shocked. We've been using it for a couple of years, on and off. You get used to it."

"But . . ."

"I don't enquire much into the family finances but they're pretty terrible. Mum isn't very good at holding down jobs and, let's face it, no one ever got rich by juggling Rubik's cubes at children's parties." The argument out in the garden was still in full swing. "Hence the fact that they're always at each other's throats these days. When money gets tight, tempers fray."

"But Charlie still manages to pay for another flat," Benjamin said, and then remembered the sleeping bag in the boot of the car and wondered if everything his friend had told him was true.

"I wouldn't know about that. All I know is that when Mum met him he had a steady job. Then Baron Brainbox came into our lives and Mum may have tolerated him at first, but there's no love lost between her and the Baron at the moment. Sadly—" she took a can of pears from Benjamin's hand "—that's how she operates. Charlie's a lovely man. I think he really loves her, however badly she treats him, but what she's always wanted is a Sugar Daddy. It's kind of heart-breaking to see."

"That's sad," said Benjamin. "Really sad. There's much more to life than money."

"Says the man who's never had to use a food bank." She stood on tiptoe to put the can of fruit on to a top shelf; then turned and looked at him. "You're not actually *rich*, are you?"

Benjamin wavered. "These things are relative."

"Well, just watch out for her, that's all. She'll take aim at you and it won't be subtle. Right under Charlie's nose she'll be all, 'Ooh, I've always wanted to meet an author, why don't we go out for a drink some time?'"

Benjamin, who had already been wondering what "drinks" in the garden were going to consist of, said: "You do drink, then?"

"Me? Alcohol?" It seemed a bizarrely personal question, until Aneeqa understood that Benjamin was making a general cultural enquiry.

"Oh, you mean my . . . *people*." Her eyes shone at him with gentle mockery. "Sorry, I didn't realize."

"I didn't mean to—"

"Some do, some don't." She smiled brightly. "I know—complicated, isn't it? Life must have been much more simple in this country before the brown people arrived."

Annoyed with himself, Benjamin thought that a swift change of subject was called for. "I liked your illustration. Is it for the Toni Morrison book?"

"Yes. I don't know how appropriate the image is. I suppose I should read the book some time."

"Maybe. You're very talented. And good at languages, as well, Charlie told me. French and Spanish."

"Yes. That's what I want to do at uni. Which, hopefully, is where I'll be in about five months' time . . ."

Later, as they were drinking beer in the garden while Yasmin and her daughter started to prepare dinner, Benjamin repeated this last part of the conversation to Charlie. And Charlie (who was forever surprising him by revealing hitherto unsuspected depths of feeling) stared into the distance (or as far into the distance as the three brick walls surrounding them would allow) and said: "I'd do anything, you know, to make that girl's dreams happen. Absolutely anything."

Benjamin glanced across at him and saw that his eyes had misted over. He was about to answer when his phone rang.

"Better take this," he said. "Sophie, my niece. She's over at Dad's tonight."

Sophie was calling to tell Benjamin to come over to Rednal as quickly as possible. His father appeared to have had a stroke, and an ambulance was on its way.

31

The last five months had been quiet for Sophie. She had received no official word from her department saying whether or not the complaint against her had been upheld, but in the meantime they seemed to be operating a policy of guilty until proven innocent. She had been taken off departmental mailing lists and put on indefinite "gardening leave." A tribunal hearing had been promised, but so far had been cancelled twice: once because of a strike on the London Underground, once because Sophie's union rep had fallen ill.

She did her best to keep busy, but it wasn't easy. She was working on a book—an adaptation of her thesis—and tried to spend a few hours every day at her desk (the kitchen table) at home. She was also writing a new series of lectures, although she did not know if she would ever get to deliver them. But the time weighed heavily upon her and, simply as a means of filling it, she was not unwilling to help her mother and uncle by visiting Colin as often as possible. The previous evening she had offered to come round at six o'clock and cook his dinner. After ten or fifteen minutes' effortful conversation, she had gone into the kitchen to peel the potatoes and put the meat in the oven. When she returned and asked Colin whether he wanted a sherry, she couldn't understand his answer. "Sorry, Grandpa?" she said, coming a little closer, and then she noticed that his face appeared to have fallen on one side, and then he attempted to speak to her again, and this time what issued from his mouth was a stream of arbitrary sounds, unrecognizable as any form of meaningful expression except that he seemed to be speaking in a tone of panic and anguish. She called 999 and had to wait twenty minutes for an ambulance and in that time she also called Benjamin, who drove straight over from his friend's house in Moseley. Benjamin and the ambulance arrived within a few seconds of each other.

Colin was taken to a specialist stroke unit and was diagnosed with a transient ischaemic attack or mini-stroke. He stayed in overnight. In the morning, Benjamin telephoned Sophie to announce, in a tone of great, if temporary, relief, that his father's symptoms were gone and he already seemed to be on the way to making a recovery.

"I'm so glad," said Helena, later that evening, as they sat at a table for three, waiting for their first course to arrive. "I do worry about your grandfather sometimes, you know. Of course one always wants to live in one's own home for as long as possible, but I wonder if it's getting to the point now where your mother should consider moving him to . . ."

"She knows that something needs to change," said Sophie. "She and Benjamin are going to talk about it."

"Very traumatic for you, as well, of course. I hope you've had a chance to rest today."

A waiter arrived, bearing two glasses of champagne on a silver tray. He offered a glass to Helena first, and she was about to take it, but then said:

"Oh—but we asked for red wine. At least I did."

"These are on the house," said the waiter. "Compliments of the manager."

"Goodness!" Flustered, as she always was when something unexpected happened, Helena took a glass and turned to her son for an explanation: "Did you have anything to do with this?"

"I told you," said Ian. "This is the place Lukas manages."

"Lukas?"

"Grete's husband. The woman who used to clean for you? I told him it was your birthday when I made the booking."

"Well . . . How very kind of him."

"Happy birthday, Helena," said Sophie, raising her glass. "Seventy-six years young today. Unbelievable."

She and Helena took sips of their champagne. Ian drank from his water glass. He'd already told them that his day had been dreadful, and he looked very much like a man who needed a drink, but he never touched alcohol when driving.

"Do they still live in the village?" Sophie asked.

"Who, dear?"

"Grete and Lukas."

"Oh. Well . . . yes, I think they do. I saw them outside the shop just a week or two ago. She was carrying her baby in one of those . . . things. A papoose, or whatever it's called. They looked very happy." She hesitated, very briefly, and Sophie knew what was coming next. Sure enough: "I don't suppose you two have . . . had any further thoughts, on that subject . . . ?"

Sophie shook her head. "Not lately."

"The great irony is," said Ian, "that now would actually have been the perfect time for us to have one. With Sophie being off work for so long."

"Oh, great," she said, her voice loaded with sarcasm. "Who needs maternity leave, when you can get suspended on full pay, totally unexpectedly and for absolutely no reason?"

"I just meant—"

"Is that really what you think? That now would have been a good time to slip a baby in, while the university makes up its mind whether I'll ever be allowed to teach again?"

She glared at him until he was obliged to look away. Just before taking a sip of water, he said: "Something good might as well come out of this fiasco."

There was a long silence, until Helena said, gently:

"Maybe you won't."

Sophie looked up.

"Maybe I won't what?"

"Ever be allowed to teach again." In response to Sophie's disbelieving look, Helena added: "Well, it *has* been almost six months. What makes you think that—"

"Things are moving slowly, that's all. That's how it is, in the academic world."

"Have you considered . . .?" Helena began.

Sophie looked at her enquiringly.

"We wondered if you had considered trying something else. Another line of work."

"*We?*"

"Ian and I were talking about it earlier."

Sophie fell silent. She was too angry to speak.

"You might as well drop it, Mum," Ian said. "I've tried all this before."

It was a timely moment for the starters to arrive. They were placed wordlessly in front of them. The waiter, who was used to such things, could sense the chill between the three diners immediately.

After taking a mouthful of salmon mousse, Sophie turned to Ian and said: "I can't believe you want me to give up."

"I can't believe you'd want to carry on in that environment. You haven't had a scrap of support from those people."

Helena said: "I thought you were going to ask your uncle to contact his friend?"

"He did. He just said he had no control over anything his daughter did. Apparently they hardly speak to each other."

"You should have told them what to do with their job by now," Ian said.

"What, and throw everything away? It's taken me eight years to get where I am."

"I appreciate that. I appreciate all the work you put into it. But it's toxic, Soph, the environment you work in."

"Toxic? What's toxic about it?"

"The atmosphere there, the way people think . . . it's crazy. They've lost the plot."

"There's been a misunderstanding, that's all. It's just one of those things. And anyway, I don't see what's crazy about having respect for minorities."

Ian threw his fork down on the table in frustration.

"Will you *stop* being so bloody . . . PC about all of this!"

Sophie sat back and smiled. "There we are. I wondered how long it would take before those two little letters were introduced into the conversation."

"Meaning?"

"Do you have any idea, Ian, how often you accuse me and everyone else of being too 'PC' for your liking these days? It's become your obsession. And I don't even think you know what it means."

"I know exactly what it means. What you call respect for minorities basically means two fingers to the rest of us. OK, so protect your precious . . . transgender students from the horrible things people say about them. Swaddle them in cotton wool. What happens if you're white, and male, and straight, and middle class, hmm? People can say whatever the fuck they like about you then."

His mother winced at the swear word. Sophie thought for a moment and then asked: "You were meeting with Naheed today, weren't you? The quarterly assessment."

"Yep."

"How did it go?"

"Oh, it was fantastic. If you like being patronized and talked down to by someone who used to be your colleague, and who's sitting behind the desk you should be sitting behind, it was just great."

"And that's why you're in such a nasty mood? Isn't it about time you got over that blow to your male ego, and moved on?"

"My *male* ego? There you go. Why not just my ego? No, you have to make it about me being a man. You'll be talking about my white privilege next. Go on, tell me how fucking privileged I am. Tell me that people like me haven't become victims in our own country."

Sophie glanced across at Helena, who was staring at them, horrified, most of the food uneaten on her plate. She felt suddenly ashamed.

"Now you're being stupid," she said. "And we shouldn't be talking like this on your mother's birthday. I'm sorry, Helena."

"No, you shouldn't." Helena put down her knife and fork. "Would you excuse me for a moment? I'm going to find the Ladies."

She pushed back her chair and made her way slowly to the back of the restaurant. Ian and Sophie ate in silence for a while.

"Don't you think you could dial it down a bit?" Sophie asked eventually. "For her sake—tonight at least?"

"She agrees with me, you know. She's on my side."

"When did it become about sides?"

Ian looked directly at her and said, bitterly: "You have no idea, do you?"

"No idea about what?"

"About how angry it makes us feel, this air of moral superiority you lot project all the time—"

Sophie interrupted him. "I'm sorry, but who *are* these people? Who's 'us'? Who's 'you lot'?"

Instead of answering this question, Ian posed another one: "Which way do you think the referendum's going to go?"

"Don't change the subject."

"I'm not. Which way do you think it's going to go?"

Sophie could see that he meant to persist with this line of enquiry. She blew out her cheeks and said: "I don't know . . . Remain, probably."

Ian gave a satisfied smile and shook his head. "Wrong," he said. "Leave is going to win. Do you know why?"

Sophie shook her head.

"People like you," he said, with a note of quiet triumph. And then he repeated, with a jab of his finger: "People like *you*."

*

Helena came back from the Ladies, and they managed to fill the next hour and a half with safe, uncontentious smalltalk. At the end of the meal, Lukas himself appeared, bearing two glasses of port—also on the house—and a small sponge cake baked by Grete for Helena's birthday. They thanked him effusively, but they were all too full to eat any of the cake, so Helena took it home with her. Then Ian and Sophie drove back to Birmingham.

They didn't talk much in the car. Sophie could only guess at what Ian was thinking. For her part, she was looking back over all the hours she had spent, over the last few years, in the company of Ian and his mother: going with them to places where she didn't feel at home, eating food that wasn't to her taste, listening to opinions she didn't agree with, having conversations she didn't enjoy, meeting people she had nothing in common with, and all the while driving backwards and forwards, backwards and forwards along these roads, these monotonous roads which connected Birmingham with Kernel Magna, backwards and forwards through the heart of Middle England, the heart that beat on through everything with its regular, determined beat, quiet and implacable. She thought of all the hours she might have spent in other places, with other people, having other conversations. She thought about how different her life might have been if she had not been caught speeding on the way to Solihull station that day; how different her life might be now if she had not made that clumsy joke to Emily Shamma at the end of a seminar. These weary, over-familiar thoughts depressed her and gave her a headache. So perhaps she should have been grateful when Ian tried to lighten the mood by suddenly pointing at a passing car and saying, "Look at that."

Sophie raised her head and opened her half-closed eyes. "Mm?"

"FYI," he said. "For Your Information."

Ah, yes. The number-plate game. It seemed years since they had played it. Perhaps it was. She tried to summon a smile but couldn't manage it. When it occurred to her, instead, that the letters also stood for Fuck You Ian, she felt sad and ashamed.

32.

WEDNESDAY, 20 APRIL 2016

When Benjamin answered the telephone, the first thing Lois said was: "Have you heard about Victoria Wood?"

It took him a moment or two to remember who she was talking about. Comedian. On television a lot. Very funny. Wrote nice songs. That was her.

"No, what about her? Is she going on tour?"

"She *died*, Benjamin. Victoria Wood died."

"Really? How old was she?"

Lois's voice was shaking. "She was sixty-two. Only a few years older than me. I *loved* her, Benjamin. She was such a part of my life. I feel as though my best friend or my sister has just died."

Not being able to think of anything consoling to say, Benjamin simply mused aloud: "What is it about 2016? Everyone's dying. David Bowie, Alan Rickman . . ."

But this was not, as it turned out, the news that Lois had been calling to give him. She was calling to say that she had given in her notice at the library in York, and was moving back to Birmingham.

"I have to," she said. "You can't have all the responsibility of looking after Dad any more. It's not fair. I've given a month's notice. I can look for a new job once I'm down there. I know it sounds dramatic but I don't have a good feeling about him. I think things are going to get worse. We've got to come together at a time like this, you and me. These could be the end days."

*

THURSDAY, 21 APRIL 2016

When Benjamin answered the telephone, the first thing Philip said was: "Have you heard about Prince?"

"No, what about him? Has he got a new album out?"

"He's dead, Benjamin. Prince is dead."

Benjamin had never been a great fan of Prince. Nevertheless, he was staggered to learn that 2016 was bringing news of yet another celebrity death.

"Prince? Dead? You're kidding me. How old was he?"

"He was fifty-seven. Our age, pretty much."

"That's terrible. What's going on this year? David Bowie . . ."

"Alan Rickman . . ."

"Victoria Wood . . ."

"It's like they're all getting out while they still can."

"It's as if they know something that we don't."

But this was not, as it turned out, the news that Phil had been calling to give him. He was calling to say that a major publishing house in Paris wanted to buy the French rights to *A Rose Without a Thorn*.

"That's fantastic," said Benjamin. "Can you put them in touch with my agent? She handles all that kind of stuff now."

*

FRIDAY, 22 APRIL 2016

Part of being friends is to be honest, and to let you know what I think. And speaking honestly, the outcome of that decision is a matter of deep interest to the United States, because it affects our prospects as well. The United States wants a strong United Kingdom as a partner. And the United Kingdom is at its best when it's helping to lead a strong Europe . . . The Single Market brings extraordinary economic benefits to the United Kingdom . . . All of us cherish our sovereignty. My country's pretty vocal about that. But the U.S. also recognizes that we strengthen our security through our membership of NATO. We strengthen our prosperity through organizations like the G7 and the G20. And I believe the UK strengthens both our collective security and prosperity through the EU . . . I think it's fair to say that maybe at some point down the line there might be a UK–U.S. trade agreement but it's not going to happen any time soon, because our focus is in negotiating with a big bloc—the European Union—to get a trade agreement done. And the UK is going to be in the back of the queue. Not because we don't have a special relationship, but because, given the heavy lift on any trade agreement, us having access to a big market, with a lot of countries, rather than trying to do piecemeal trade agreements, is hugely more efficient.

President Obama made his comments at a morning press conference in London, standing next to David Cameron. Gail Ransome was due to give a speech to the Coventry and Warwickshire Chamber of Commerce that evening, and when the latest draft came through from her researcher Damon late that afternoon, she saw that he had quoted the U.S. president extensively.

She couldn't get hold of Damon at first. By the time they managed to talk on the telephone, Doug was home, watching *Channel 4 News* in the sitting room. Gail withdrew into the hallway and tried to block out the sound by cupping one hand over her ear.

"The thing is," she was saying to Damon, "I'm not sure it's going to play as well as you think.

"I'm not sure that's true. Yes, I know *we* both love Obama. But not everybody does.

"Well, for the obvious reason, for one thing.

"Don't sound so shocked. It's true, sadly.

"I've just been looking at the reaction online, that's all. A lot of people are very angry about the 'back of the queue' line. They think it was staged, with Dave standing there next to him and the two of them looking all chummy. And they think it sounds like a threat.

"Yes, precisely. All part of 'Project Fear'.

"No, I still want to mention it, but can you tone it down a bit maybe? Don't mention the words 'back of the queue'. And be as quick as you can because I have to leave in—" she checked her watch "—twenty-five minutes."

Just as she was hanging up she heard Doug's voice from the sitting room, shouting out the words "FUCKING HELL!"

She came running in. "What's up?"

"They're doing an item," he said, freeze-framing the picture and rewinding it a few seconds, "on the biggest donors to the Leave campaign. And look at this."

The screen was now frozen on the image of a doorway in what appeared to be a well-to-do district of central London. There were Greek columns on either side of the door and three men in suits were pictured coming down the steps of an impressive Georgian building. One of them had the gaunt, loose-skinned look of someone who used to be fat but has lost a lot of weight. His darting, watchful eyes were encircled by the round frames of an expensive pair of gold-rimmed spectacles, and he was entirely bald.

"I was at school with that tosser," he said. "God, we all used to hate him! Still, he had the last laugh. Apparently he's worth millions now."

"How much has he donated?"

"Two million so far. I wonder what his ulterior motive is. The greedy, devious tosser."

"I've never heard of him," said Gail, squinting at the caption on the screen which announced his name, in capital letters, as "RONALD CULPEPPER (IMPERIUM FOUNDATION)."

*

MONDAY, 9 MAY 2016

There were nine of them around the pub table, squeezed together in what Benjamin considered to be uncomfortable proximity. He rather enjoyed being pressed up against Jennifer but was not so keen on her lanky colleague Daniel, seated to his right. They were there to celebrate the thirtieth birthday of Marina, one of the newest arrivals in Jennifer's branch. He was beginning to regret coming, although Jennifer had been insistent that he did.

The conversation consisted mainly of jokes and office gossip so he wasn't listening too carefully. He had no idea what Daniel was replying to when he said, "Well, apparently, we're all going to die anyway, if we leave the European Union," but the remark caught his attention. "What do you mean?" somebody asked, and Daniel explained that in one of his campaign speeches David Cameron had claimed, according to some of this morning's papers, that leaving the EU might lead to World War Three. Someone else said, "I don't think that's what he really meant. He just meant there's been no war in Europe for a long time and that's partly down to the EU," and Daniel said, "Well, that's not what was reported in the papers," and Benjamin said:

"He was almost certainly misquoted."

His voice was so quiet that it was a miracle anyone heard him at all. But hear him they did, and because these were virtually the first words spoken by this shy, grey-haired stranger all evening, everyone around the table stopped to listen. Seeing that he suddenly had the floor, Benjamin hesitated, then cleared his throat and added:

"It doesn't matter what you say. The papers are only interested in getting a story out of it. And if the story isn't strong enough, they'll make it stronger. Any figure in public life who talks to the media does so at their own peril. I know, because this is what happened to me. I don't have much time for David Cameron normally but I sympathize with him in this case. It's not easy, being in the public eye."

After this speech had been delivered and the conversation had moved on, Jennifer squeezed his arm and when he turned to look at her he saw that she was smiling, and her eyes shone in a way that was teasing but affectionate. "'Being in the public eye'!" she said. "You're so sweet." She kissed him on the mouth. Her lips were moist and tasted of red wine. "Love you, Tiger."

She stood up to go to the toilet, squeezing past the others as best she could. Benjamin pondered her words. "Love you." On the one hand, this could be momentous: she might actually have been declaring her love for him, for the first time. But then surely she would have said "*I love you.*" Wasn't "Love you" something altogether more commonplace, a mere formula, a shorthand way of saying that you were fond of someone? Benjamin didn't understand.

Jennifer had left her phone behind. It buzzed while lying on the table in front of him so he picked it up and saw that she had a text message:

Can make Thursday if that would suit. Robert xx

He didn't really understand that, either. Who was Robert? Afterwards, she told him that he was a former client who had since become a friend. So that was probably all right.

*

WEDNESDAY, 11 MAY 2016

Sohan was sitting on the sofa, wearing only a T-shirt. His legs were spread and Mike's head was resting on his bare thigh. Mike was staring with fondness at Sohan's still-flaccid penis, flicking it occasionally to make it stir. Then he kissed it and took it in his mouth.

Meanwhile, on the television screen, Boris Johnson was down in Cornwall launching the Leave campaign's battle bus. This involved addressing the cameras while standing with a pint of fine Cornish ale in one hand, in front of a big red bus with some statistics painted on it. In this attitude, the Conservative MP for Uxbridge and South Ruislip radiated his trademark air of self-mocking bonhomie which the British public seemed to find so endearing, although today, as always, it set Sohan's teeth on edge.

"Three hundred and fifty million pounds for the NHS?" he said. "Yeah—in your dreams, BoJo."

"Can you turn that thing off?" Mike said. "I'm planning to put a lot of effort into this. Your full attention would be appreciated."

Johnson was now telling his interviewer that the next country to join the EU would be Turkey, with the consequence that millions of Muslim men and women would soon have unrestricted access to the United Kingdom.

Sohan snorted.

"Bollocks!" he said.

"All right," said Mike, and began licking his left testicle. "But you could at least have said please."

*

SUNDAY, 15 MAY 2016

"Are you cold?" Benjamin asked.

"No," said Colin. "I'm not cold."

"I just wondered why you needed the blanket, that's all."

Since coming back from the hospital a month earlier, Colin had not left the house. In fact, he had barely stirred from the living room, or the armchair in front of the television, although Benjamin assumed he left it occasionally, to go to bed or the toilet. Permanently draped over his knees was a stripy multicoloured blanket, the product of a creative phase Sheila had passed through in her sixties, when she had flirted for a while with the art of crochet.

"I like it," said Colin. "It's a nice blanket." Also open on his knees was a copy of the *Sunday Telegraph*, complete with half-page picture of Boris Johnson looking serious and statesmanlike, his eyes narrowed against the light, his mind fixed on distant, Churchillian thoughts. "You were at college with him, weren't you?"

Benjamin sighed. He was getting rather tired of this myth, which seemed to be in ever-wider circulation.

"I didn't know him," he said. "Our paths crossed. Briefly."

"I saw that piece about you in the paper. It said you were friends at college."

Reflecting once again that there seemed to be no pattern, no rhyme or reason, to the things his father remembered and the things he forgot, Benjamin reached across and picked up the newspaper.

"Come on, then," he said, "what's he saying this time?"

Johnson was now drawing an analogy between the European Union and Nazi Germany. Both, he argued, had the design of creating a German-dominated European superstate, using means that were military in the one case, economic in the other. Benjamin, whose interest in politics had grown exponentially in the last few weeks, was aghast. Was this what political debate had become in this country, now? Was it happening because of the referendum campaign, or had it been this way all along, and he hadn't been paying attention? Could a British politician now fling this kind of comparison around and be confident of getting away with it, or was that privilege reserved for Johnson, with his lovably floppy hair and his bumbling Etonian manner and the ironic smirk that always hovered around the edges of his mouth? Benjamin handed the paper back to his father, who said:

"All that money we spent sending you to Oxford. Worked out a lot better for him than it did for you, didn't it?"

"Seriously?"

"He talks sense. He's about the only one who does. It took us six years to stop the Germans in their tracks. Bugger the help we got from anybody else, apart from the Americans at the last minute. And now look at them. Pushing us around. Telling us what to do. Laughing at us behind our backs."

This was depressing stuff. Benjamin no longer knew what to do when his father spoke like this. "Cup of tea, Dad?" he suggested, a bit desperately.

"No thanks. But you can get me a postal vote."

"A what?"

"For the referendum. I may not be able to leave the house but that's not going to stop me having my say."

Benjamin nodded.

"OK. Sure."

"I need a form, and an envelope, and a stamp. See to it, will you?"

"No problem."

He glanced at the clock on the wall. Decency required that he stayed another thirty minutes or so. Things would be better when Lois moved down.

*

MONDAY, 23 MAY 2016

Aneeqa was much too old to need picking up from school now, but every few days Charlie did it anyway and he assumed that she liked it because she had never asked him to stop. The drive back to Yasmin's house always followed the same pattern, which he'd found puzzling at first but which had then started to amuse him and was now something he simply accepted. Replete with experiences from her long day, full of stories which needed to be told and pent-up feelings which needed to be vented, Aneeqa would deluge him with a monologue lasting about fifteen minutes, a manic torrent of words which did not allow space for the smallest interruption. Then it would finish as abruptly as it had begun. Without waiting for Charlie to make any comments in return, she would simply stop, take out her smartphone and stare frowning at the screen for the remainder of the drive, occasionally scrolling and clicking. They would complete the journey in silence. Charlie had come to understand, by now, that he was expected merely to serve as listener, a necessary, passive receptacle for her thoughts and confidences, and he was happy to fulfil that role.

Today she described a run-in with her Spanish teacher in the lesson before break—she was notorious for having favourites (Aneeqa not being among them) and giving them shamelessly preferential treatment—and then:

". . . and then at lunchtime the Debating Society was talking about the referendum—no surprise there—and Krystal was speaking—for Leave of course—and she started going on about how the important thing was immigration—that was really the main problem with the EU—freedom of movement had been a disaster for this country, she said—we were just full up and we can't take any more people—and if that means British people can't go and live in Berlin whenever they want or get a job in Amsterdam, well, so what, it was only posh, wealthy people who could afford to do that anyway—she said it's all a price worth paying to keep out the Poles and the Romanians—and I've heard that from Mum as well, believe it or not—I think she's going to vote Leave because she reckons if we vote to stop people from Europe coming here then we can bring in more people from Pakistan and all her cousins can come over—but the thing is I'm not even sure Krystal believes any of this stuff anyway—I think she just gets it from her dad—I mean, you know what he's like, don't you?—he's an absolute nightmare—no wonder you two can't stand each other . . ."

*

THURSDAY, 26 MAY 2016

Three days later, figures published by the government showed that annual net migration into the United Kingdom had risen to 330,000, an all-time high. And Sophie, at last, travelled down to London for her much-postponed tribunal.

She had not visited the capital for several weeks, and she had not set foot inside the humanities department for almost six months. It was a profoundly disconcerting experience. As she walked down the corridor to her office, some colleagues nodded a brief, embarrassed hello. Others avoided eye contact and hurried by without saying a word. None of them stopped to talk, to ask how she was, to ask what she had been doing since they had last seen her. Everything about her department—the lay-out of the rooms, the location of the pictures and noticeboards on the walls, even the play of sunlight through the windows on to the parquet floor—seemed both strange and familiar at the same time.

It was with a curious sense of relief that she unlocked the door of her own office and pushed it open. She had been half-expecting that someone might have changed the locks. Inside, it felt very quiet and still. A thin coating of dust lay over everything: the books on the shelves, the kettle on the windowsill, her empty desktop. The three pot plants on the shelves had shrivelled and died long ago. She flopped down into the easy chair—the one her students used to sit in when she was allowed to give one-to-one tutorials—but rose to her feet again almost at once. It was too depressing in here. She would go to the café, where she was meant to be meeting her union rep, even though she wasn't due to arrive for another half an hour.

Ninety minutes later Sophie was back in her office, none the wiser about her academic future. The union rep, Angela, had turned out to be a chilly and guarded jobsworth with an attitude towards Sophie's case so studiedly impartial that she didn't seem able to offer any tangible support at all. In the tribunal itself, Angela and Sophie had sat on one side of a long table, opposite four antagonists including Martin Lomas and Corrie Anderton, whom Sophie was decidedly unnerved to meet in person at last. (She was surly and rude, and never once looked Sophie in the eye, but her knowledge of university regulations and equal ops legislation was impressive.) Sophie had put her side of the case as best she could, although it didn't amount to much apart from her repeated insistence that all she had done was to make a light-hearted remark that had been misunderstood. Her opponents made notes and asked questions. All Martin had said to her, at the end of the forty-minute hearing, was, "Thank you, Sophie, we'll be in touch with you shortly." Angela had left the building as quickly as possible, just allowing Sophie time to ask how she thought the hearing had gone, to which she had simply answered: "Always difficult to tell, really."

So that was that, it seemed. More uncertainty, and more waiting.

She hadn't been intending to linger in her office. She merely wanted to retrieve a couple of books and take them back to Birmingham with her. But while she was searching for them, there was a diffident tap on her open door. Sophie turned and saw that Emily Shamma was standing framed in the doorway. Her red hair had grown longer now, reaching almost down to her shoulders, and the paleness of her face was offset by two slashes of blood-red lipstick.

"Hello," she said.

"Hi," said Sophie.

"Is it OK if I come in?"

"Of course. Take a seat."

"It's OK. I won't stay long. Only, I just heard that you'd come back today and . . . I wanted to see you." She had a gentle Welsh accent that gave her words a quiet, lilting musicality. "The thing is, I feel really terrible about what's happened. When I told Corrie what you'd said, it wasn't like I felt devastated by it or anything. I was just like, 'That was a bit off.' I didn't realize she was going to blow it up into this huge thing."

Sophie smiled and murmured, "Ah well . . ." There wasn't much else she could say.

"I'm not even friends with her any more. I mean, I can't stand the way she's so judgemental about everything. I just feel so *guilty* about you, and all the hassle you've been going through."

Sophie stepped forward, intending to give Emily a hug, then thought better of it. Everything could be misinterpreted.

"They are going to take you back, aren't they?"

"I hope so."

"I hate to think you're just sitting around at home."

"Well, I've started a book. Don't know if I'll finish it. And I've got an elderly grandfather who needs a lot of looking after. And some television work has come up."

"Television? That's exciting."

"I did something for Sky last year and got on well with the director and now—just last week in fact—she's asked me to front a series."

"Awesome."

"Well, it's pretty bog-standard stuff. Just going to a lot of famous European galleries and talking about a lot of famous pictures. I don't think I'm going to be able to put much of a personal stamp on it."

"Still . . ."

"Still . . ." Her tone brightened as she said: "What about you?"

"Well . . . Not so good, to be honest. I've been finding this whole process pretty difficult. I was supposed to have my op next month—the point of no return—but I've put it off for now. And I'm going to take a year out. Think things through."

Doing her best to speak carefully, non-committally, Sophie was on the point of saying, "That sounds like the right decision," then changed it to something even safer: "I'm sure you'll do the right thing. Good luck."

Emily smiled a sad, anxious smile. "Thanks."

They remained like that for a few more moments, two figures

who might in another life have been friends, now standing a cautious distance from one another, scared to embrace, scared to show their feelings, numb and motionless in the glow of what little sunshine Sophie's grime-streaked windows were able to admit on this long, warm, languid summer's afternoon. Then Emily said, "I'd better go," and Sophie said, "Thanks for coming to see me, I really appreciate it," and they shook hands fleetingly and Emily was gone.

Sophie took the five-forty train home from Euston and it was still light when she reached the flat. Ian had made pasta and it was very nice and he nodded with sympathy when she told him about the tribunal and the meeting with Emily. But when it became clear that there was nothing he could say that would make the situation any better, and there were no practical steps he could take to help her, he grew frustrated and wanted instead to talk about the immigration figures which were all over the papers and the television news.

"Three hundred and thirty thousand is *way* too high," he kept saying. "We're full up. The country's full up. Something's got to be done about it now—even you must see that."

"I read somewhere," Sophie said, "that it was fewer people leaving, rather than more people arriving." But she was bored with having this conversation and didn't bother to argue the point any further.

33.

The publication of these latest immigration figures had a galvanizing effect on the referendum campaign as it entered its final phase. The debate shifted. There was less discussion of economic forecasts and sovereignty and the political benefits of EU membership: now, everything seemed to hinge upon immigration and border control. The tone changed too. It became more bitter, more personal, more rancorous. One half of the country seemed to have become fiercely hostile towards the other. More and more people began to wish, like Benjamin, that the whole wearying, nasty, divisive business could be finished and forgotten as soon as possible.

Meanwhile, Lois put her house in York on the market and moved down to Birmingham. On the evening of 13 June 2016, ten days after her return, she invited Sophie and Ian round for dinner. She baked a lasagne and they drank plenty of Montepulciano and it was all very jolly but after the meal Lois seemed to disappear from the table while they were still drinking coffee, and a few minutes later Sophie found her in the sitting room all alone, listening to Classic FM and finishing off the last of the wine.

"You all right, Mum?" she asked.

Lois looked up and smiled.

"Yes, I'm fine."

"Didn't you want to stay and talk?"

"Not really."

Sophie sat down beside her. On the coffee table next to the sofa was a pile of newspapers and other odds and ends. Four sheets of

A4 on top of the pile caught Sophie's eye. She picked them up and glanced through them.

"What are these?"

"What do they look like?"

"They look like adverts for houses in France."

"Then that's what they are."

"You're thinking of buying somewhere in France?"

"Your father is."

Sophie looked at the brochures more closely. The properties, all priced at around 300,000 euros, seemed to boast the kinds of idyllic settings and generous proportions that would set the purchaser back twice as much if they were located somewhere in England.

"Well, aren't you keen?" she said. "You've always wanted a place in France. You've been talking about it for ages. And Dad'll be retiring in a couple of years. It could be great—for both of you."

Lois nodded. "Yes, it could." But she didn't sound over-enthusiastic.

Sophie said, nervously: "You are intending to *spend* your retirement with Dad, aren't you?"

"Well, I don't have anyone else to spend it with," said Lois, sipping her wine. "And I don't want to spend it in this bloody city, that's for sure."

Sophie laid a hand on her mother's arm. Lois turned to look at her. Her eyes were brimming.

"It's forty-three years, since that bomb went off," she said. "Forty-one years, six months and twenty-three days. Every night, I still hear it. That bomb going off is the last thing I hear, before I go to sleep. If I go to sleep. I daren't watch the news on television, in case there's something that reminds me. I can't even go to the cinema or watch a DVD in case there's anything in it—anything at all—any blood, any violence, any noise. Anything that reminds me what human beings can do to each other. Politics can make people do terrible things . . ." She looked at Sophie closely now, and her voice became more urgent. "You and Ian are in trouble, aren't you?"

"Not really," said Sophie, after a brief hesitation. "We'll get through it. We'll sort it out."

"Politics can tear people apart," said Lois. "Stupid, isn't it? But true. That's what happened to my Malcolm. That's what killed him. Politics."

There was a noise behind them—the creaking of a floorboard—and both women turned around. It was Ian, standing in the doorway with his coffee mug in his hand.

"Everything OK in here?" he asked.

"Come in," said Lois, moving up to make room for him on the sofa. "Sit down, and tell me what you think of these houses."

*

"Oh, hi, Phil," Benjamin said. "Thanks for calling back."

"Is this a good time? Your voice sounds a bit strange."

"I'm in the car. I'm on my way to the station."

"Oh? Where are you off to?"

"I'm picking someone up. My friend Charlie."

"Oh yes." Phil was yet to meet this mysterious revenant from Benjamin's past. "The kids' party guy."

"He's coming to stay for a day or two. Phoned me up this morning. Bit of a cry for help. I think he's in a bad way."

"Would this be a good time for me to say something about the tears of a clown?"

Benjamin gave a mirthless laugh. "Not really."

"OK. Well, look, I won't keep you. What did you want to talk about?"

"I just wanted your advice about this piece I'm writing."

"Piece?"

"Didn't I tell you? I'm writing something about the referendum." There was a long silence at the other end of the line. "Are you still there?"

"I'm still here, yes. I'm just . . . gobsmacked."

"Gobsmacked? Why?"

"*You're* writing something about the referendum? You mean . . . you're going to take a position on something?"

Benjamin seemed unclear on this point. "Possibly. It's for one of those newspaper features, you know. They're asking lots of writers how they're going to vote."

"So tell them," said Philip. But he was then struck by a sudden suspicion. "You have decided, haven't you?"

"I thought I had. I was pretty sure I was going to vote for Remain."

Philip waited. "But . . . ?" he prompted.

"Well, it's complicated, isn't it? There are a lot of different arguments on both sides."

"True."

"I've been doing some research online. There are so many things to take into account. Sovereignty, immigration, trading partnerships, the Maastricht Agreement, the Lisbon Treaty, the Common Agricultural Policy, the European Court, the Commission—I mean, the Commission has far too much power, doesn't it? There's a real democratic deficit in the European institutions."

"Sounds to me like you're well up to speed on this. What's the problem?"

"I'm not up to speed at all. I'm drowning in information and contradictory opinions. I've been reading about this for three days. I've got forty-seven different tabs open on my computer."

"How much do they want you to write? A thousand words, two thousand?"

"No, it's only fifty words. They've asked dozens of writers, they don't have much space."

"Oh, for Christ's sake, Benjamin—you've spent three days on fifty words? That's crazy. Are they paying you?"

"No, I don't think so. I forgot to ask."

Philip was losing patience. "Just do what everyone else is going to do—vote with your gut. Do you want to be on the same side as Nigel Farage and Boris Johnson?"

"No, of course not."

"Well, then—there you go."

"Yes, but that's not good enough, is it? This whole thing's ridiculous. It's all so complicated. How's anybody supposed to decide?"

Reflecting on the absurdity of it, he lost concentration and jumped a red light and attracted an angry chorus of horns. "Oh, shit. Anyway, I'm nearly at the station now—I'd better go."

"Righto," said Philip. "Glad to have been of help."

*

Charlie looked terrible. He hadn't shaved, hadn't washed his hair, hadn't slept, hadn't cleaned his teeth, and hadn't stopped drinking for about thirty-six hours. It was after eleven when they arrived back at Benjamin's house. Charlie grabbed a bottle of white wine from the kitchen, unscrewed the cap without waiting to ask and took it out on to the terrace. Benjamin followed with a couple of glasses. If there was any kind of moon that night, it was hidden behind banks of thick cloud, and it was too cold—in Benjamin's opinion—to be drinking outside.

"She's kicked me out again," Charlie said, once they were sitting at the table. "And she says it's final this time."

"You can stay here for a while," said Benjamin.

Charlie didn't appear to be listening. "I shall have to find somewhere to live," he said.

"You can stay here," said Benjamin. "There's plenty of room."

"How am I supposed to find somewhere to live? I'm only earning about fifty quid a week at the moment. And they won't give me benefits while I'm earning."

"You can stay here as long as you like," said Benjamin.

"I always wanted us to be a family, you know? I always saw us as a family. The three of us. That's all I ever wanted. But she doesn't see it like that. Never has. She hates the fact that me and Neeqs are so close. She thinks we're in some sort of conspiracy against her or . . . I don't know. Something worse. She's paranoid, she's aggressive, she's incredibly unhappy, and as usual she's taking it out on me."

"Maybe she could get some help?" Benjamin said. "Professional help?"

"There's no way that can happen," said Charlie. "She won't listen to me. She won't even let me back in the house."

"She can't stop you seeing Aneeqa, and helping her, if that's what you want."

"Neeqs'll be at uni before I know it. Glasgow, she's applied to. Glasgow! Fucking miles away."

"Then maybe she doesn't need you any more. Maybe it's time to let it all go."

"Fucking . . . BITCH," said Charlie, and picked up his wine glass but seized it so violently in his unsteady hand that it shattered in his grasp. There was blood everywhere and Benjamin had to run off to find the First Aid box. He persuaded Charlie it was time to go to sleep and when he peeped around his bedroom door half an hour later he saw that he was crashed out on the bed fast asleep, fully clothed and with all the lights on.

Early on the morning of the next day, Wednesday 15 June, it began to rain heavily. Charlie didn't surface until one o'clock in the afternoon. Benjamin made some lunch for him but then couldn't find him. He looked everywhere. Charlie's bag was still in his room, but he was nowhere to be seen. An hour later he texted to say that he'd gone for a walk, and he would be back in time for dinner, and Benjamin was not to worry. The rain continued, unabated. Benjamin sat in the window bay, and watched through the rain-spattered glass as the river began to rise, the water splashing and pushing angrily through the mill's man-made channel like a queue of bad-tempered commuters trying to squeeze through the ticket barrier of a crowded station. The noise of the rain and the noise of the river became a loud, relentless backdrop to his thoughts as he wrote and rewrote his newspaper contribution in his head and worried about Charlie. Towards the end of the afternoon he tried to distract himself by making an elaborate curry.

When Charlie returned, at six o'clock, he was, unsurprisingly, wet through. He went upstairs for a long, hot bath and a change of clothes. Over dinner he was much calmer than he'd been the night before. Benjamin started to feel that he was almost too calm. He was evidently in the midst of a deep depression, and spoke very little. When he did speak, it was about money. "I thought going for that walk would help me think things through," he said, "but it all comes down to money. Without money, I can't see my way out. And it's been like this for years. Fucking years. They keep saying it's going to get easier. That there's light at the end of the tunnel. How long is this fucking tunnel? Where's the fucking light? I've been plugging away at this for six years now. Six years on the party circuit. Fucking Duncan Field earns three times as much as me. Four times. Kids would rather see his stupid smoke bombs and explosions any day of the week. I don't know why I bother." After a long, long pause, he looked pleadingly at Benjamin and said: "Can I have a drink, mate?"

"Don't you think you had enough yesterday?" Benjamin said.

"Oh, come on. Just the one."

Benjamin nodded. "Help yourself."

Charlie poured himself a whisky.

Benjamin went to bed early. Charlie said that he was ready for bed as well, but he wanted to phone Yasmin first. Even from his bathroom, Benjamin could hear that the conversation was going badly, and was quickly deteriorating into a shouting match. When it was over there was a loud bang (Charlie slamming the phone down on a table?) and then the sound of a door opening and closing. Benjamin went into his bedroom, opened the window and looked out. It was another moonless night. Rain continued to sheet down. He could make out Charlie's tall, heavy, shadowy figure as he paced backwards and forwards down below. And then, in a sudden, decisive movement, he climbed up on to the top of the terrace wall. He stood there, in the pouring rain, looking down into the swirling, gushing, furious water as it pounded by beneath him.

Benjamin screamed: "Charlie! What the hell are you doing? Get down from there!"

Charlie didn't move. Oblivious to the rain drenching him from head to foot, he remained standing on the wall, and then stretched out his arms, as if attempting to balance, or perhaps preparing to dive.

"Charlie!"

Twenty or thirty seconds went by.

"Charlie! Get down!"

Slowly, as if he had heard Benjamin's voice for the first time,

Charlie turned his head. He looked up at his friend. His face was pale and haggard. Tears streaked down his cheeks.

They stared at each other like that for a minute or more, Benjamin pleading, Charlie staring with sightless eyes, as if he were a sleepwalker and all this was happening in a dream.

Then, carefully, he turned around, stooped down and jumped back on to the terrace. He stayed there, squatting on his haunches, head in hands, until Benjamin came clanging down the metal steps, put his arm around his shoulder and helped him back inside.

*

The next morning, Charlie was up and dressed by nine o'clock. Benjamin was frying eggs in the kitchen when he appeared in the doorway, with his coat on and his bag already packed.

He said: "Time to leave you in peace, I think."

Benjamin said: "Where will you go?"

"Think I'll go and stay with my mom for a while."

Benjamin nodded.

"Have some breakfast and I'll drive you to the station."

"It's all right, I'll walk to the village. Get a bus. At least the rain's stopped."

"True."

They hugged.

"Thanks for everything, mate."

After he'd gone, Benjamin turned on the television. It was tuned to the BBC News Channel. He kept it on all morning, in the background. There was an item about Nigel Farage, who was unveiling the new poster for the Leave.EU campaign. It showed a long, winding queue of young people, mainly men, mainly dark-skinned. They were meant to be migrants, obviously. Splashed across the image, in big red capitals, were the two words: "BREAKING POINT." In smaller type, it also said: "The EU has failed us all" and "We must break free of the EU and take back control of our borders."

Benjamin actually shuddered at the crude, unapologetic xenophobia of the image. It was the ugliest thing he had seen yet in this ugly campaign. As soon as he saw it, he knew that his mind was made up. Deciding to waste no more time on his public declaration, he forgot all about the nuanced, even-handed words he had been wrestling with for the last few days, typed out a brisk, decisive, fifty-word statement and emailed it to the newspaper.

The telephone rang. It was his father. Although his pronunciation had become unclear since the mini-stroke, there was no mistaking the unaccustomed note of jauntiness in his voice.

"Guess where I've been?" he said.

"What do you mean, where you've been? You didn't leave the house, did you?"

"Yes."

"What for?"

"I voted. I took that form you gave me and filled it in and I posted it."

Benjamin was horrified. "Dad, you shouldn't have walked all the way to the postbox by yourself. Lois or I could have done that for you. The doctors told you to take it easy."

"That was weeks ago."

"How did you vote?" Benjamin asked, although he was already pretty sure of the answer.

"Leave, of course." Defiantly, he added: "You knew that, didn't you?"

"What about Sophie?"

"What about her?"

"You know she wanted you to vote the other way. It's *her* future, you know. She's the one who's going to be around the longest."

"She's a nice girl but she's very naive. I've done her a favour. She'll thank me one day."

"How are you feeling after the walk, anyway?"

"A bit tired. I think I'll have a sit down for a while."

"OK. Lois is coming round about four, all right?"

"Perfect. I'll have my nap and then we can have a cup of tea."

"OK. 'Bye, Dad."

"'Bye, son."

Disheartened by the conversation, Benjamin turned back to the television. Farage was standing in front of the poster now, beaming and joking with the various camera crews. At the bottom of the screen, a selection of the morning's tweets was scrolling by. One of them was from the novelist Robert Harris. It said:

How foul this referendum is. The most depressing, divisive, duplicitous political event of my lifetime. May there never be another.

Amen to that, Benjamin thought.

*

Early that same afternoon—the afternoon of 16 June 2016—Lois was in the kitchen, writing a shopping list. She planned to call at the Longbridge branch of Marks & Spencer on the way to her father's house. She had the radio on, tuned to Radio Two, but she was not paying it much attention. The music was bland, and she had given up listening to the news, being sick of the referendum by now: like everyone else, it seemed.

Shortly after two o'clock, however, there was an item of breaking news which brought her afternoon to a halt. A member of parliament had been attacked in her constituency; attacked in the street as she walked to her local library, where she had been intending to hold a surgery.

Lois had never heard of the MP. Her name was Jo Cox. She was the MP for Batley and Spen, a constituency in Yorkshire. A young woman. The attack sounded horrific. She had been both shot and stabbed by her assailant. As he attacked her he had shouted some wild, seemingly incoherent words which were later reported to have been a cry of "Britain first. This is for Britain." A passer-by had run to give help and had also been stabbed. The attacker had walked off casually but a few minutes later had surrendered himself to the police. Jo Cox herself had been rushed to hospital in a critical condition.

As soon as she heard this news, Lois felt a terrible sickness, dizziness and fatigue come over her. She turned the radio off and went into the sitting room, where she lay down on the sofa. Within a few minutes she had a raging thirst and the beginnings of a headache. She went back into the kitchen and drank a glass of cold water and took two painkillers and turned on the radio again. There was no further news about the wounded MP except that police were due to give a press conference shortly after five o'clock.

Shaking uncontrollably, Lois placed her laptop on the kitchen table, turned it on and googled Jo Cox. A married mother of two. Forty-one years old—forty-two next week. Popular local MP, who had been elected for the first time little more than a year earlier and had increased the Labour majority. Founder of the All Parliamentary Friends of Syria group. Remain supporter. Working on a report called *The Geography of Anti-Muslim Hatred*.

Lois knew that she should not try to imagine the details of the attack, but she couldn't help herself. An ordinary day—insofar as any day was ordinary at this extraordinary time—and a routine task: walking towards a library, along a familiar street, in the company of your manager and your case worker. And then the stabbing, the shooting, the frenzy. Everyday life suddenly obliterated, rendered meaningless, by unpredictable, murderous violence. *That night in November 1974 . . .* Lois stood up quickly—too quickly—then closed her eyes and felt herself swooning, falling . . . Gradually the room came into focus again. She leaned against the kitchen table for support. From the way the attack had been described on the radio, it sounded as though no one could survive it, but surely it was impossible for anyone to be killed in such circumstances. A local MP, going about her daily business on a typical Thursday, at lunchtime—it couldn't happen. Lois clung to this hope—fully aware of how irrational it was—as the minutes dragged by and she waited to hear what the police had to say.

She turned on the television at five o'clock. The press conference began a couple of minutes later. A middle-aged officer, with her thin, gingery hair combed severely forward on to her forehead, talked in a grave monotone above the constant noise of camera flash bulbs.

"Just before one o'clock today," she began, "Jo Cox, MP for Batley and Spenborough, was attacked in Market Street, Birstall. I am now very sad to have to report . . ."

Lois gasped and screwed her eyes tight shut.

". . . that she has died as a result of her injuries."

"No, no, no, no, *NO!*" she wailed, and threw herself down on the sofa. He body was racked with sobs. "No!" she kept saying, again and again. "No, no, *NO!*" Then she stood up and yelled at the TV screen: "You stupid people!" She strode over to the window and looked out at the quiet street and shouted, louder than ever: "*You stupid people— letting this happen!*" She went over to the coffee table and grabbed a newspaper and crumpled it into a ball and threw it at the television and for the next few minutes she was kicking furniture, throwing cushions, pounding the walls with her fists. She smashed a vase and soaked the carpet with water. How long the fit lasted, she couldn't say. Eventually she blacked out.

It was about ten to six when she started clearing up. It was an oddly calming activity, and she had almost finished by the time Christopher came home.

"What's been going on here?" he asked, when he noticed first of all the state of the house, and then the state of Lois herself. He hugged her tightly and she started shaking again when she asked him: "Didn't you hear?"

"About the MP? Yes, I heard."

He kissed the top of her head, taking in the scent of her hair, as he savoured the unusual pleasure of having his wife cling to him. "It's so sad, isn't it? I know how it makes you feel. I know what it brings back."

They embraced for a few minutes, until Lois's composure had more or less returned. She sat down at the kitchen table and he continued to stand over her, stroking her hair.

"How was your father?" he asked at last. "I didn't think you'd be back so soon."

"Dad . . ." said Lois. "Oh shit—I forgot all about him."

"Really? Hasn't he phoned?"

"No. I'd better go over there now."

"I'll come with you. I don't want you driving when you're like this."

"I was going to get some food on the way."

"Let's get there first. I can always pop out and get something."

Lois went to fetch her coat from the cloakroom and said, abstractedly: "I can't believe I forgot about him." She took one last look at the television before turning it off. "That poor woman . . . Those poor children . . ."

"Do you think we should call him?"

"Huh?" She turned. It took a moment for the question to reach her. "No, I'll call him from the car."

But there was no answer. And when they arrived at the house in Rednal, Lois peered through the living-room window and could see that Colin was not sitting in his usual armchair. She unlocked the front door and there he was, stretched out in the hallway, face down, quite still and—she knew at once—quite lifeless.

It was the walk to the postbox that had done for him. He had been lying there, Lois learned afterwards, since about one o'clock. Death had occurred a few hours later. Which meant that she could probably have saved him, if only she had remembered to come at the appointed time.

OLD ENGLAND

✦

What surprises me time and time again as I travel around
the constituency is that we are far more united and have far
more in common with each other than things that divide us.

Jo Cox, maiden speech to the House of Commons,
3 June 2015

OLD ENGLAND

34.

SEPTEMBER 2017

Here at the top of Beacon Hill, when autumn arrived it was not announced by any changes in the colour of the trees. The woods which surrounded the bald summit of the hill, like a monk's tonsure, were made up of firs, pines and other evergreens. Only if you advanced to the path at the very edge of the hill, and looked down across the greens and fairways of the municipal golf club, could you glimpse the tops of sycamores, maples and oaks, now burnished red and gold, signalling the end of summer and the slow passing of the seasons. Here, on a quiet, almost silent Friday afternoon in September, beneath a sky of cloudless blue, Benjamin and Lois stood solemnly, preparing to pay their final respects to their mother and father.

Colin had left very specific instructions for the disposal of his remains. Having kept his wife's ashes in an urn on the mantelpiece at home for more than six years, he had stipulated in his will that they should be mingled with his own and scattered at the top of Beacon Hill, the highest point of the Lickey Hills, little more than a mile from the house in Rednal where they had spent the whole of their married life. He had also requested that the scattering take place on the day of their wedding anniversary, 15 September. He had not, however, specified the year; and as bad luck would have it, on 15 September 2016, Benjamin was holed up in a remote backwater of Scotland, halfway through a gruelling week spent in the company of a dozen would-be poets and novelists who had all parted with good money to imbibe his writerly wisdom. Fortunately, in 2017, that day (along with about thirty others on either side) was blank in his diary.

As for Lois, who had finally taken up a new job as librarian at an Oxford college and was commuting there and back every day, she felt this was an occasion that warranted an afternoon off.

And so there they stood, brother and sister, on a hillside filled with memories, looking out over a view that had changed very little in the last forty-one years, since the time when Benjamin used to bring Lois here for long walks, to get her away from hospital and into the outside world, and would tell her rambling stories of the goings-on at school and try to coax a response out of her, to help her forget, for a few hours at least, the horror of the Birmingham pub bombings. True, the three white aluminium-clad towers of the new Queen Elizabeth Hospital now dominated the far horizon, as they had not done in 1976, and—more dramatically—there was no Longbridge factory any more, parts of it now replaced by houses, shops and college buildings, other parts simply obliterated, leaving large, ugly scars on the landscape. But otherwise, the view was the same, the view towards Waseley Country Park and Frankley Beeches, towards the Clent Hills and Hagley and the Black Country beyond. Its permanence was comforting: a reminder of stillness and continuity in a world which seemed to be changing faster than either of them could understand. However young they might have felt inside, to a passer-by they looked elderly now: Benjamin with his silver hair, Lois with her streaks of grey and incipient stoop. She had turned sixty a few months earlier.

Benjamin took a portable speaker out of his coat pocket, put it down on a wooden bench and placed his iPod Classic in the dock. He had already scrolled to the relevant song in anticipation of this moment, and all he had to do was press Play. The music was turned up loud: he didn't care who heard it this afternoon, or who witnessed this ceremony. Almost at once, the gentle, modal chords rose up, unmistakeably English: Benjamin closed his eyes and for a few seconds lost himself in the music, music which he had heard thousands of times but would never tire of, music which spoke to him in the subtlest, most persuasive way of his roots, his sense of self, his feeling of profound attachment to this landscape, this country. He turned to look at his sister, hoping for a moment of connection, some sign that she was feeling the same way. But Lois had more practical things on her mind.

"I can't get the bloody lid off," she said.

"I'm not surprised," said Benjamin. "I don't suppose it's been opened since they put her in there. Here, let me try."

With a certain amount of effort, he managed to prise the lids from both of the urns. Lois was holding Sheila's, and Benjamin was holding Colin's—although in fact, since they both came from the same funeral director and looked identical, he couldn't be one hundred per cent sure it wasn't the other way around. Well, it didn't seem to matter really.

"OK, then?" he said, holding out his father's remains in readiness.

"We didn't bring anything to read," said Lois.

"Why, are you planning to spend the rest of the afternoon up here?"

"No, I mean to read *now*. A poem or something."

"Oh. Well . . . Just think of something to say yourself. Try to improvise."

"OK," said Lois, uncertainly.

Benjamin clicked his iPod to return it to the beginning of the song. The chords rose again, and the violin began its slow, skyward journey.

"Here goes," said Lois. "Goodbye, Mum. You were a wonderful mother to all of us. You gave us everything we could ever have wanted."

With a strong, sweeping movement, she swung the urn upwards and discharged its contents into the air. Benjamin, after saying a quick "Goodbye, Dad," did the same thing, and then, in a miraculous instance of the synchronicity that rarely blessed the lives of the Trotter family, a gust of wind rose up, caught the ashes and carried them upwards, up into the sky where before Lois's and Benjamin's eyes they danced, whirled and coalesced into one spiralling blur, before being caught by another gust and swept apart, scattering in every direction, settling on the gorse, the heather, the long grass, the pathway, or simply disappearing from view, flying homewards with animal instinct, either in the direction of the house where Sheila had been so happy or the vanished factory where Colin had spent so many productive hours. And all the while the music went on its calm and resolute way, the violin rising, rising like those ashes until it too was just a speck in the blue sky, too small and too distant to be seen any longer by the two figures standing before the bench.

Finally they both sat down and listened to the music for another two minutes or more, not wanting to speak at first.

Then: "This is beautiful," said Lois, dabbing at her eyes with a tissue. "What's it called?"

"'The Lark Ascending'."

"You are clever," said Lois, her voice wobbling, her tears welling, "to remember what their favourite piece of music was."

Benjamin smiled. "No, it's *my* favourite piece of music. Or one of them. Do you remember either of our parents ever saying that they liked a piece of music?"

Lois thought about this, then shook her head. "You're right. Or reading a book. Or going to an art gallery." Then a memory returned. "Dad did like 'The Birdie Song', though."

"Yes, he did."

They both laughed, and through her laughter Lois said: "Oh God, do you remember how he used to put it on at Christmas parties, and strut around the living room flapping his arms like a chicken?"

"How could I forget?" said Benjamin. He had been in his second year at Oxford at the time, and witnessing Colin's impromptu performance, even in the privacy of the family home, had been one of the most mortifying experiences of his life.

"Well, I'm glad you didn't choose to play that this afternoon," said Lois. "Not very appropriate."

"Although . . ." said Benjamin, listening to the swirls and curlicues of the violin as it subtly mirrored the lark's looping progress, "when you think about it, this is 'The Birdie Song' as well. Just a posher version."

They fell into silence, while Benjamin allowed his thoughts to wander along the path suggested by the music. He thought about Vaughan Williams: his conception of music as "the soul of a nation," the way he had uncovered so many old English folk tunes, helping to rescue a whole tradition almost from oblivion, and yet there was no contradiction, no tension even, between this deep cultural patriotism and his other political beliefs, which seemed to have been so liberal and progressive. He thought about how badly this country, this crisis-riven country, stood in need of figures like that at the moment . . .

Meanwhile, Lois was thinking along different lines altogether.

"They had a good marriage, didn't they?" she said. "We can allow them that, at least."

"Mm . . .?"

"Mum and Dad."

"Oh. Yes, I think so. I mean, not . . . passionate exactly, but that probably wasn't in their natures."

"Better than mine, anyway," said Lois.

Benjamin glanced at her sharply. He had never heard her say anything like this before. He was shocked.

"I feel so guilty," she said, "and so sorry for Chris. He's stuck by me, all this time. Knowing full well that he's not the one. I should never have married him. I've never got over Malcolm. Nobody could ever replace him. I shouldn't have pretended . . . He's had a shit life, because of me."

Benjamin tried to form an answer. The words wouldn't come. Lois turned to him and said:

"We always thought you were the one stuck in your romantic obsession. Stuck in the 1970s. But it's been me, always me. You've moved on." Convulsed by a sudden sob, she leaned forward and curled in upon herself. "I have to move on, Ben. *I have to move on.*"

He laid a hand on her back and moved it around feebly.

"Well . . . You've got a new job, haven't you?"

"I don't want to hide away in libraries for the rest of my life. I'm sick of it."

"Yes, but it's a start."

"A start? I'm *sixty.* I shouldn't just be starting."

She stared ahead of her. Perhaps her eyes were searching, Benjamin thought, for the distant outline of Rubery Hill Hospital, where she had once been confined. It had been demolished in the 1990s.

"It *is* getting better," Lois said. "Just in the last year or so. I think with the Jo Cox thing, I kind of peaked. It made me realize I couldn't go on reacting that way. What happened in London this morning . . . I heard about it on the radio. It was all right. I was OK with it."

Benjamin had been wondering about this. A bomb had gone off on a tube train at Parsons Green station that morning. More than twenty people were now being treated for their injuries, mainly burns. It was the kind of incident that normally upset Lois greatly.

"What happened to Malcolm—and me—was more than forty years ago. I won't be . . . kept prisoner by it any more."

"Good," said Benjamin. "Good for you."

"And it's not fair to Chris. I have to let him go as well."

Benjamin absorbed the information, and nodded gravely. It was all a lot to take in.

"Sounds as though you've made up your mind, anyway," he said.

"I have. It's not going to be easy, and it's not going to be quick. And I can't do it alone. I need somebody's help."

Her eyes met Benjamin's. And at that moment, they were nineteen and sixteen again, and they were standing on this same hill, hand in hand, on another autumn day, a day which seemed impossibly far in the past but was also, for both of them, eternally present.

"Yours," said Lois.

35.

From: Emily Shamma
Sent: Monday, October 2, 2017 11:33 AM
To: Sophie Coleman-Potter
Subject: Next week

Dear Sophie

I'm so glad you're back teaching again, and really looking
forward to working with you this term. This is just to let you
know that my (long-delayed) op is scheduled for this Thursday
(the 5th). Since they'll probably keep me in for at least a week
afterwards, it looks like I'll miss the first American modernism
seminar on the 11th. Sorry about that.

Also, re the date for our first one-to-one, I would like to express
a strong, decisive preference for October 24th.

Best wishes
Emily

*

Six days later, on 8 October, Sophie herself took an impulsive
decision.

Sundays were still the strangest days, the days when she came as
close as she ever came to missing Ian and wanting to contact him.

Ironic, really, given how she used to resent those Sunday mornings alone in the flat, while he played golf and had lunch with his mother. Even then, however, there had always been the prospect of his late-afternoon return, and a shared dinner in the evening. Here in Hammersmith, there was nothing to break up the day, and Sundays seemed to drag on for ever, empty and shapeless. Usually she couldn't wait to get out of the tiny terraced house she shared with three other people (and paid a small fortune for). Her room—just big enough to accommodate a single bed, a desk and a chest of drawers, with almost no space to walk between them—saw no sunlight until about two o'clock, so Sophie would go out in the mornings, to walk along the river if it was fine, to sit in a branch of Starbucks or Pret if it wasn't. The British Library reading rooms were closed, so she couldn't find refuge there. Once or twice she'd tried going to the university itself, but the humanities department on Sunday seemed a forlorn place, silent and deserted. Sometimes she would see Sohan and Mike, but they were often busy, and she had started to notice that, for all her love of this city, she didn't have many friends here. Her housemates were nice enough but she had little in common with them, and they were all about ten years younger than her. At thirty-four, Sophie felt that she was too old to be sharing a house with anyone, but it was the only way she could afford to live in London, by herself, on a lecturer's salary.

It weighed on her mind, this Sunday, that Emily Shamma was recuperating from a major operation in a hospital which stood only a few hundred yards from her house. Doubtless she would have no shortage of visitors, but once Sophie had had the idea of paying a visit herself, it took hold and would not go away. She retained a fond memory of their last conversation in her office, more than a year earlier, and had not seen her since. (As Emily had mentioned at the time, she had been finding the transitioning process stressful, and decided to take a year out from her studies.) At two o'clock that afternoon, then, Sophie arrived at Charing Cross Hospital, armed with a box of Belgian chocolates. She made her way to the reception desk, reflecting that the ground floors of British hospitals were beginning to look more and more like shopping malls, and was swiftly directed to Emily's ward.

She was sitting up in bed, with her eyes closed. She looked paler than ever, and her reddish hair lay flat against the pillow, tangled and damp with sweat. She was breathing heavily. Sophie assumed that she was asleep, and was about to leave the chocolates on her bedside table and tiptoe away when Emily opened her eyes. She was startled to see Sophie, and seemed not to recognize her at first. Then she smiled tiredly, and struggled into an upright position, wincing as she did so.

"Hello," she said. "This is an . . . unexpected pleasure."

Sophie laid the chocolates down on the table and said, "I brought you these," as if that had been her main motivation for coming. "Did it all go well? How are you feeling?"

"I feel bloody awful," said Emily. "But thanks for asking." She saw that Sophie was unsure whether to draw up a chair and sit down. "Yes," she said. "Please do."

"Did I wake you?" Sophie asked.

"No, I'm not really sleeping. Not much, anyway." Her smile now was stronger, braver. "It's very nice to see you. I hope you're not here to set me an assignment, or anything like that."

Sophie laughed. "Nothing like that. I was worried about just turning up like this, though. I thought you might have loads of visitors."

"My mum's come up from Cardiff," said Emily. "She should be here in a bit. But the doctors warned me about seeing too many people. They said rest was more important."

"I won't stay long."

"It's nice to see you," Emily repeated.

Sophie reached out and squeezed her hand. It was very cold. This was the moment of closeness, of solidarity, that she had been wanting to share with Emily ever since she had turned up at her office to apologize and offer her support. Sophie held on to her hand for a few seconds and it occurred to her, as she did so, that in reality she knew very little about this appealing, enigmatic student who had unwittingly managed to derail her career.

"Is that where you're from, then?" she asked. "Cardiff?"

Emily nodded. "You're wondering about my name, aren't you? It's Arabic. My dad came over from Iraq in the eighties to study architecture. He met my mum at Cardiff Uni and that was that. They got married and he stayed here. Actually my name is Al Shamma'a." (She pronounced it with a heavy stress on the long final syllable.) "Everybody says it wrong. I don't bother to correct them any more."

"So you're . . . ?"

"Half-Arab and half-Welsh. My first name was Emlyn, before I changed it. Emlyn Al Shamma'a. Bit of a mouthful."

The effort of talking seemed to be tiring her. She reached for a water glass and Sophie filled it up before passing it to her. She took a very small sip and handed it back.

"I daren't drink too much," she said, "in case I need to pee again."

"I suppose it's painful, is it?"

"Not just that—the stuff goes everywhere. I mean, how do you—how do you make it . . . *directional* ?"

Sophie had not expected to be drawn into this kind of discussion quite so quickly. "Practice, I suppose. I dare say you'll get used to it." Tentatively, she asked: "Any more . . ."

". . . vagina-related questions? No, not right now."

Sophie could see that Emily was wincing again. "Must be terribly sore."

"It's because I have two dilators in there, to keep it from closing up."

"Ooh . . ."

"I have to keep them in for twenty minutes, five times a day."

"*Ooh* . . . You poor thing. That would be a bit like—"

"Shall we move on from the subject of my new genitals, maybe?"

"Good idea," said Sophie.

"I saw some of your TV show. It was great. You're very good in front of the camera."

"Thank you."

"I hope the uni was pleased you did it? Raises their profile a bit, I imagine."

"Funny you should mention that," said Sophie. "Did they ever tell you why Coriander's complaint against me was thrown out, in the end?"

"No."

"Me neither. I just got a message saying that the tribunal had found in my favour and all my courses had been reinstated. That was less than a week after I'd emailed them to say I was going to be fronting a TV series. Could be a coincidence."

"Wow," said Emily. "People are shameless."

"You're looking very tired," said Sophie. "Maybe I should go."

"I do feel shattered. You feel as though you're never going to be able to walk or eat or do anything else normally ever again. But it's nice to have company. Hospitals are such lonely places. You're the first person I've spoken to all day, apart from the nurse who came to change my drip."

"You're the first person I've spoken to as well."

It did not sound like a simple statement of fact. It sounded more like the offering of a confidence—and Emily, despite her state of exhaustion, was intuitive enough to notice it.

"Oh?" she said. "I always assumed . . ." She was scared of overstepping the mark. "I don't know . . . that you had a family, or something. Husband, kids. That you had all of that going for you."

"I do have a husband," said Sophie. "He just doesn't live with me at the moment. I suppose we're having a trial separation."

"Ah. I'm sorry. When did that happen?"

"It's been about nine months now. I say that it's only a trial but, to be honest, it's beginning to feel more like a permanent state of affairs."

"Have you tried counselling, and all that stuff?"

"Oh yes. A very specific form of counselling, in fact. Post-Brexit counselling."

Emily gave a quick, disbelieving laugh, and immediately screwed up her face in pain, clutching herself in the groin area.

"Shit," she said, when the spasm was over. "That really hurt. Remind me not to laugh again. I shouldn't have laughed anyway, but—seriously, that's a thing?"

"It is indeed."

"And that's why you split up with your husband?"

"More or less. Crazy, isn't it?"

She was ready to elaborate on this, but at that moment Mrs. Shamma arrived on the ward. She had her daughter's colouring: the red hair and the pale skin. Sophie did wonder why her father wasn't there, whether he was comfortable with this whole situation, whether parental disapproval might have contributed to Emily's stress last year. Her mother seemed bubbly, solicitous and talkative. Sophie introduced herself and lingered for the requisite two or three minutes, then made her excuses and said her goodbyes. Feeling emboldened by her conversation with Emily, she kissed her on the cheek before leaving, and whispered:

"It may not feel like it now, but you're going to look beautiful."

*

Afterwards, in a reflective frame of mind, she strolled down to the river and began to walk eastwards in the direction of Fulham. The Thames was full, its brown-grey waters slapping turgidly against the embankment walls. Seagulls whirled and cried out. Lazy river traffic chugged by. She had no real idea where she was heading, or what she would do when she got there. This aimlessness appeared to be a new but recurrent feature of her life.

Sophie thought back to the moment when her conversation with Emily had been cut off. What she had said was true: from every rational point of view, the trigger for her separation from Ian looked crazy. A couple might decide to separate for all sorts of reasons: adultery, cruelty, domestic abuse, lack of sex. But a difference of opinion over whether Britain should be a member of the European Union or not? It seemed absurd. It was absurd. And yet Sophie knew, deep down, that it had not so much been a reason as a tipping point. Ian had reacted (to her mind) so bizarrely to the referendum result, with such gleeful, infantile triumphalism (he kept using the word "freedom" as if he were the citizen of a tiny African country that had finally won independence from its colonial oppressor) that, for the first time, she genuinely realized that she no longer understood why her husband thought and felt the way that he did. At the same time, she herself had been possessed by the immediate sense, that morning, that a small but important part of her own identity—her modern, layered, multiple identity—had been taken away from her.

During their first session a few weeks later, their relationship counsellor, Lorna, told them that many of the couples she was seeing at the moment had mentioned Brexit as a key factor in their growing estrangement.

"I usually start by asking each of you the same question," she said. "Sophie, why are you so angry that Ian voted Leave? And Ian, why are you so angry that Sophie voted Remain?"

Sophie had thought for a long time before answering:

"I suppose because it made me think that, as a person, he's not as open as I thought he was. That his basic model for relationships comes down to antagonism and competition, not cooperation."

Lorna had nodded, and turned to Ian, who had answered:

"It makes me think that she's very naive, that she lives in a bubble and can't see how other people around her might have a different opinion to hers. And this gives her a certain attitude. An attitude of moral superiority."

To which Lorna had said:

"What's interesting about both of those answers is that neither of you mentioned politics. As if the referendum wasn't about Europe at all. Maybe something much more fundamental and personal was going on. Which is why this might be a difficult problem to resolve."

She had suggested a course of six sessions, but it turned out that she was being optimistic. In fact they attended nine, before admitting defeat, and calling it a day.

36.

24 June 2016 was remembered by Doug as the day when three things had happened:

It was announced that the British people had voted to leave the European Union.

David Cameron had resigned as prime minister.

Nigel Ives had stopped returning his telephone calls.

Sixteen months on, he was still trying to secure another meeting with the government's elusive deputy assistant director of communications. In this he was also assisted by Gail, who would sometimes spot Nigel scuttling down the corridors of the Palace of Westminster or Conservative Party headquarters, although he was always very skilled at avoiding her. All she was ever able to report back to Doug was that he looked "very harassed."

So it was with considerable surprise that he received a text message from Nigel on the morning of 16 October 2017. All it said was:

Meet at the usual place on Thursday? 11 am?

*

Doug felt about the café at Temple tube station very much as Benjamin and Lois felt about the view from Beacon Hill: there was something profoundly reassuring about the way that it hardly seemed to change. As the same chains of coffee shops continued to take over the capital and indeed the whole country, here was a place that still served bacon rolls, salt beef sandwiches and frothy cappuccinos, with not a decaf soya latte in sight. It seemed to preserve a corner of Britain that was left over from the 1970s or even earlier: and this gave it a distinctive charm, as even Doug wouldn't deny.

"Good morning, Douglas."

The greeting was stale and world-weary. Doug looked up from his notebook and saw Nigel taking the seat opposite him. The youthful rosiness was gone from his face. He was sporting several days' worth of stubble. His cheeks were pale and sunken, his tie was badly and hastily knotted, his hair did not look like it had seen a comb for weeks. He sipped gratefully on the coffee Doug had already ordered for him.

"Nigel, good to see you again," Doug said. "At long last."

"Yes, it has been a while, hasn't it? When did we last do this?"

"I think it was just a month or two before the referendum."

"Ah yes . . ." When he heard those three words, "before the referendum," Nigel's eyes took on a wistful, almost spiritual glimmer, and he stared past Doug's shoulder as if into the distant past, towards a better, prelapsarian time, a time of carefree innocence and simple, childlike joy.

"Sixteen months, more or less."

"Really?" said Nigel. "Is it only sixteen months? Somehow it seems . . . longer. Much, much longer." He shook his head sadly.

"So," said Doug, "to what do I owe this rare privilege?"

"Well, I shall be honest with you, Douglas—whatever else you may think of me, I've always tried to be honest. Keep this strictly to yourself, but I'm probably going to be leaving this job. I thought we should have one more chat before I go."

"Really? This means promotion, I hope."

"I'm afraid not. I think it's time for me to leave the world of politics. Pastures new."

"Well," said Doug, "you've had a good run."

"I suppose so," said Nigel, not sounding especially convinced. "But before I do that, I wanted to set the record straight."

"Go on," said Doug.

"OK. Since the referendum," said Nigel, "you've said several things about David Cameron which, in my personal opinion, all things considered, and not to put too fine a point on it, seem rather unfair."

"Surely not."

"Calling him 'the worst British prime minister of my lifetime', for instance."

"Did I say that?"

"Saying he was 'a reckless incompetent cushioned by wealth and privilege'."

"Bit harsh, maybe."

"'The great white hope of modern Conservatism who turned out to be a weak, cowardly, malignant, narcissistic fool.'"

"Yeah, they might have been paying me by the word for that one."

"The point is," said Nigel, "that you're wrong. The Cameron years will come to be looked back on as a halcyon era. I truly believe that."

"You do?"

"He was a radical. A modernizer. A man of vision. A man of great personal and moral courage."

"Was it courageous of him to resign the day after the referendum, and leave other people to clear up the mess he'd made?"

"That showed him to be a man of principle. A man who keeps his promises."

"But he promised not to resign if he lost the vote."

"And a man who's prepared to change his mind when the circumstances require it."

Nigel was speaking with great passion. Doug felt suddenly sorry for him.

"Are the two of you still in touch?"

"I don't like to impose," said Nigel. "I don't feel I should disturb him. Dave has become a very different person since resigning. Very humble. Contemplative. He realized that it was time for him to take some big decisions in his life."

"Such as?"

"Well, buying a shed for instance."

"Ah yes. I read about the shed."

"Buying that shed was such an important step for him. You wouldn't believe how much he's been changed by that shed."

"I'm not surprised. It cost twenty-five thousand pounds. I hope it's a nice shed."

"Douglas," said Nigel, fixing him with solemn eyes, "it's a beautiful shed. And what Dave is doing in there is beautiful."

"Namely . . .?"

"Writing his memoirs. The story of the referendum. The *true* story of the referendum. What a gift to the world that's going to be."

"A gift? You mean he's not going to charge for it?"

Nigel smiled. For a moment it seemed that he was going to rise to Doug's provocations again. But he no longer seemed to have it in him.

"I gather he's been lecturing on this subject in the States already. Charging a hundred and twenty thousand dollars an hour, according to the papers."

"*You*, Douglas, of all people, should know that very few of the stories printed in British newspapers have any truth in them. As someone who's been feeding stories to the papers for years, I do know what I'm talking about."

In the past, Doug thought, Nigel used to say these things as if totally unaware of how self-incriminating they sounded; now he spoke in the tone of someone merely giving voice to a melancholy truth. Perhaps more revelations could be prised out of him while he was in confessional mode. This was the first time they had met since Theresa May had become prime minister in the chaotic wake of the referendum. Few journalists had been able to fathom her in that time; few people had been able to understand how someone so supportive of Britain's EU membership could have performed such a smooth U-turn and assumed the task of steering the country towards Brexit. Could this be a chance to approach the heart of that mystery?

Doug leaned forward. "So, come on, Nigel—one last favour. Tell me what it's like. Tell me what it's *really* like."

Nigel gave him a questioning glance.

"What it's like?"

"Working for Theresa. What's *she* like? She's such an enigma. None of us can work out what she really wants, or really thinks, or really believes."

Nigel's manner changed abruptly in the face of this question. At once he reverted to his old guarded and mysterious self.

"Theresa is . . . very different to Dave," he said.

"Yes . . . ?"

"I would say she was a woman of . . . many contradictions."

"Such as?"

"Well, she's very ambitious, but rather cautious. She knows her own mind, but relies heavily on her advisors. She believes in strong leadership, but also in following the will of the people."

"Ah, 'the will of the people'. I wondered how long it would be before that phrase popped up."

"You hear it a lot at Party HQ these days. A *lot*."

He was starting to look depressed again. Doug took the opportunity to ask:

"How's morale, then? Generally speaking."

"Morale is . . . absolutely tip-top," said Nigel, swallowing hard. "It's a fascinating moment, obviously. Britain is at a turning point, and we're at the very epicentre . . . of . . . the epicentre of the maelstrom which is . . . transfiguring the political reality of what is obviously a very . . . seismic development in which the . . . the tectonic plates of our national history are shifting in a way which is . . . transformational, and being a witness to this . . . ."

Suddenly he stopped talking. A blankness came into his eyes. His shoulders slumped. He stared down at the foamy surface of his coffee for a minute or more. Finally he looked up again, and the next words he spoke were the most heartfelt words Doug had ever heard from his lips.

"We're fucked."

"Excuse me?"

"We're utterly and irredeemably fucked. It's all chaos. Everyone's running around like headless chickens. Nobody has the faintest idea what they're doing. We're so, so fucked."

Doug quickly whipped out his phone and started recording a voice memo.

"Is this on the record?" he said.

"Who cares? We're fucked, so what does it matter?"

"What sort of chaos? Who's running around like a headless chicken?"

"Every sort. Everyone. Nobody was expecting this. Nobody was ready for it. Nobody knows what Brexit is. Nobody knows how you do it. A year and a half ago they were all calling it Brixit. Nobody knows what Brexit means."

"I thought Brexit means Brexit."

"Very funny. And what kind of Brexit would that be?"

"'A red, white and blue Brexit'," Doug quoted, then started to feel sorry for Nigel again, he looked so wretched. "But surely they must have plenty of policy advisors . . . experts . . . ?"

"Experts?" said Nigel bitterly. "We don't believe in experts any more, remember? It's a very simple chain of command. Everyone takes their instructions from Theresa, and she takes her instructions from the *Daily Mail*. Them, and a couple of think tanks who are so bonkers about free trade that you wouldn't allow them—"

"These think tanks . . ." said Doug, his curiosity roused. "I don't suppose one of them would be the Imperium Foundation, would it?"

"Oh God," said Nigel, his head in his hands. "They're all over us, those guys. Always coming in for meetings. Bombarding us with spreadsheets. Forget about the will of the people. These are the kinds of lunatics who've taken over."

"Would Cameron have stood up to them any better, do you think?"

"Cameron?" said Nigel, his face twisting. "What a twat. What a grade-one, first-class, copper-bottomed arsehole. Sitting in his fucking shed writing his memoirs. Look at the mess he's left behind. Everyone at each other's throats. Foreigners being shouted at in the streets. Being attacked on the bus and told to go back where they came from. Anyone who doesn't toe the line being called traitors and enemies of the people. Cameron *broke the country*, Doug. He broke the country and ran away!"

He broke you too, by the looks of it, Doug thought, taking a Kleenex out of his pocket and handing it to Nigel, who dabbed his eyes with it for a few seconds. His hands were trembling as he did so. Not sure if it was the right moment to ask this favour, but fairly certain that another such opportunity would never present itself, Doug now said gently: "I don't suppose you have any paperwork on those people, do you? The Imperium Foundation. Nothing you could show me?"

Nigel's expression gave little away as he said: "Leaking confidential documents? Is that what you're asking me to do?"

Doug looked away, embarrassed, and changed the subject at once. "Anyway," he said, "I can see why you want to get away from all this. I'm sure you'll find the perfect niche somewhere—PR, advertising, maybe? Marketing, media training, something like that?"

A rather disturbing change started to come over Nigel's face. His eyes began to shine again—this time with amusement, if anything. Doug imagined that he could see the hint of a smile hovering around his lips too.

"What's wrong?" he said. "Those are pretty good suggestions, aren't they?"

Nigel shook his head slowly. "I've got a much better one."

Doug said: "Would you like to tell me about it?"

Nigel looked from left to right, then over his shoulder, then leaned very close to Doug's face. "I'm going to travel round the world." And just as Doug was on the point of nodding and saying, "That sounds good," he added, with a note of inexpressible triumph, ". . . *in a hot-air balloon!*"

Seeing that he had reduced his companion to open-mouthed silence, Nigel rose to his feet and started declaiming, first to Doug himself and then to the bemused patrons of the café as a whole: "Oh, yes! That's the life for me! Cresting the superb peaks of the French Pyrenees! Following the course of the Ganges as it rolls majestically towards the Bay of Bengal!" He began wriggling into his coat with some difficulty, struggling to force his arms into the turned-out sleeves. "No more lying to the newspapers! No more spouting out the rubbish that politicians are too embarrassed to say themselves! I'm free! Free, I tell you! Free to soar like a bird through the open skies!"

As the other customers looked on with increasing alarm, Nigel flung open the door of the café and strode out into the fresh air. Doug tried to wave after him, but Nigel no longer seemed to be looking. Doug's last glimpse of his long-time trusted source was of a flapping, agitated figure striding off into the distance, his arms still trapped across his chest as he wrestled with the sleeves of his recalcitrant coat. For some reason—who knows why?—it made him think of a straitjacket.

37.

Ben? . . .

. . . moments in life worth purchasing with worlds, yes, I remember that phrase, it's from a novel by Fielding, *Amelia*, the one that nobody has read, nobody except me, obviously, and of course it's meant ironically, he's sending up the character who says it, because Fielding was the very opposite of a sentimentalist, but still there is something wonderful in the phrase, something very appealing, but what I do start to wonder, as I get older, is whether those moments are gifted only to young people, whether it's the kind of thing you only experience in your teens or early twenties or at least during puberty, which in my case probably went on for much longer than that, in fact I might not even have emerged from it yet, better not speculate about that, best not to go there, but the question has to be asked, am I ever going to experience any of those moments again, anything like the morning after Cicely and I slept together for the first time, for instance, when I sat in The Grapevine and finished my beer all by myself and so many thoughts rushed through my head and, looking back, that may even have been my pinnacle of happiness, certainly my pinnacle of happiness with her because I didn't see her again after that for God knows how many years, but was it also my pinnacle of happiness more generally, have I ever been as happy in my whole life as I was at that moment, did I peak at the age of eighteen, in other words, that's the crucial question, but maybe it's more complicated than that, more nuanced, because there are different kinds of happiness, aren't there, there are kinds of happiness which are maybe not so intense but which go deeper, and last longer, and perhaps that's what I'm feeling now, standing in the Garden Quad at Balliol and looking across the Croquet Lawn at my old staircase and thinking, OK, I'm fifty-seven now, but probably the last few years have been the best in my life, living alone, living in comfort, seeing friends, no longer obsessing over Cicely, and then getting the book published, and then the lucky break, and then hearing from *readers*, real, genuine readers who've written letters to me and emailed me and come up to me at events, the thrill of knowing that some people, even if it's only a handful, have been touched by what I wrote, and then the weirdness of meeting Jennifer again, and the even greater weirdness of going out with her, no, you can't call it that when you're in your fifties, being in a relationship with her, although it's been an odd kind of relationship, I wouldn't say that our feelings for each other have been all that strong, I thought she said she loved me at one point but that was just a misunderstanding, I realize now, and then there is one little inconvenient fact, the fact that she's probably sleeping with someone else, this guy called Robert, but the strange thing is it turns out I'm not really bothered about that, I don't want to spend all my time with her, it's nice just to see her occasionally, and the sex is good, better than good, great even, I mean, Jesus, who would have thought I'd be having the best sex of my life at fifty-seven, wonders will never cease, but even so, what I have with Jennifer is not really the same as what Doug has with Gail, say, now that's amazing, to see the two of them together, after years of him always going for these posh Sloaney women, finally he seems to have found someone who is on his wavelength, it just goes to show you don't have to share someone's politics to fall in love with them, I suppose that's what I thought about Sophie and Ian once as well, and yet they've foundered, haven't they, it doesn't seem to have worked out for them after all, but maybe the differences between them were just too serious, or perhaps there were other things going on that I never knew about, anyway, it's a great shame that they've broken up, I know how much Sophie wanted to make that work, and I do worry about her, now, being lonely, feeling that all her relationships are doomed, but surely it can't be long before someone like her finds somebody else, she's a strong woman, there's no denying that, look how she survived those troubles at work, which would probably have broken some people, but Sophie is made of stronger stuff, she rode it out, and if I have one quarrel with Doug, actually, it's that he never really intervened to help her while that was going on, he should have made more of an effort with Coriander, it's all very well saying she never listens to him but she is his daughter, for God's sake, there must have been some way he could have done it, there must be some channel of communication still left open, I should really have mentioned it the other night, why do I never really confront my friends about the things I think are important?, it's always been like that, I'm a coward, in many ways, a moral coward, but on the other hand when you're in somebody's house, when they've invited you as a guest, when you're sitting around their table and eating the food they've prepared for you, it would seem a bit churlish to start criticizing their parenting skills, especially when Doug and Gail were both being so helpful over dinner, helping me out with my current problem, after all it was a pretty boring topic to bring up, I hadn't really been planning to mention it, it wasn't my plan to make everyone listen to me droning on about the fact that I have a new book to deliver in less than six months and I don't have the faintest idea what it's supposed to be about yet, someone could easily have changed the subject, moved swiftly on, but no, they all took an interest, or pretended to, and it turned into quite an interesting conversation actually, or at least I thought so, a conversation about what a writer should or shouldn't be doing at a time like this, whether writers should attempt to be *engagés*, as I believe the French expression is, or whether it's best for them to be "inner emigrants," retreating inside themselves as an escape from reality, but not just an escape, also a means of responding to it, creating an alternative reality, something solid, something consoling, and when I mentioned this idea Doug laughed and said, Well, of course, that's what you'll be doing, isn't it, Ben?, that describes you perfectly, and I suppose I bridled a little because he's been taking the piss out of me for forty years about the fact that I have no interest in politics, as far as he can see, certainly not to anything like the extent that he has, but then Doug has always been a little bit obsessed on that front, in my opinion, but anyway this time I decided not to take it lying down, so I said that actually I didn't want my next book to be like the last one, completely personal and auto-biographical, I wanted to write something broader, something about the state this country has got itself into in the last few years, and Doug thought about this for a while and said, Fine, why don't you write about the time you met Boris Johnson at Oxford, and at first I thought he was taking the piss again, because this has become a bit of a joke lately, the fact that I shared a corridor with Boris Johnson at Balliol College for about three weeks in the autumn of 1983, and we used to pass each other in the corridor on the way to the toilet and back, so I said, Oh yes, very funny, but Doug insisted that he was being serious and said, No, but think about it, you were actually there at the beginning of something very important, that was the beginning of the time when a whole generation of Conservative students basi-cally took over the Oxford Union, and they all became friends—rivals as well, of course, but friends most of all—and they would play out their little political rivalries in the debating chamber of the Oxford Union and argue about stuff like whether Margaret Thatcher was the greatest British prime minister of all time and whether we should stay in the European Union or not, and of course a lot of them joined the Bullingdon Club as well and when they weren't pretending to run the country in the Oxford Union debating chamber they were busy getting pissed and smashing up restaurants and getting their parents to pick up the bill, and now look at them all, thirty years later, David Cameron, he was at Oxford in the eighties, Michael Gove, he was at Oxford in the eighties, Jeremy Hunt, he was at Oxford in the eighties, George Osborne, he was at Oxford a few years later, these cunts (Doug's word, not mine) all knew each other, and now these self-satisfied, entitled twats (Doug's phrase, not mine) were running the country, and they were still jostling for power and having their sad little arguments but instead of doing it at the Oxford Union they were doing it on the national stage and we were all having our lives shaped and redirected by these people and their stupid infighting whether we'd voted for them or not, and how was *that* as the subject for a novel, and of course Gail looked a bit horrified because he was talking about some of her colleagues but she took it all in good part and even agreed with a lot of it, I wouldn't be surprised, and although I was pretty sceptical at the time I thought it over for a while and the upshot of it is that here I am, a few days later, revisiting Oxford, which is a city I've successfully managed to avoid revisiting more than a handful of times since I was here as a student, even though of course my sister lives here now, she finally left Chris, she's renting a bedsit somewhere on the Cowley Road and I'm meeting her here today, in fact she should be here any moment, and coming back has been a peculiar experience so far, I must say, bittersweet I suppose is how you would describe it, there is something distinctive about this city, something in the way the past and present collide here that I don't remember finding anywhere else, I suppose it's the way these chain shops and chain restaurants and chain coffee shops, the places you see wherever you go in this country now and make every city look and feel exactly the same, it's the way they've been tucked away inside all these lovely old buildings, nestling alongside the college buildings which are so beautiful, so old, so full of history, that's what creates the strange and complicated flavour of this place, and so yes, this is the perfect city to come and surrender to your memories, to let the present be invaded by the past, and that's what I've been doing this afternoon so far, autumn is a good time for it as well, the season when things start to fade and decay, that's how most people see it, but here in Oxford, if you're an academic, it's a time of renewal, the beginning of a new year, a time of hope and possibility, and standing here, here in the Garden Quad, looking across the Croquet Lawn at my old staircase, that's what I'm feeling, the stirrings of it at least, the stirrings of creativity, but I don't think I'll be taking it in the direction Doug suggested, that sort of thing isn't for me, if anyone's going to write a book about how the country's still being run by a bunch of public schoolboys who all cut their teeth at Oxford it should be him, I have to write something more personal than that, "write about what you know," isn't that the first and most obvious piece of advice any new writer gets?, but I don't mean it literally, I'm not going to write a book about an old man, OK not quite old yet, but starting to feel as if he's getting that way, an old man standing in an Oxford quad looking back on his student days and asking *où sont les neiges d'antan?* or anything like that, I need to look not quite so close to home, so I know what I'm going to take a stab at—yes, Charlie!, the story of Charlie Chappell and his bitter rivalry with Duncan Field and how he's managed to end up in prison, of course I will change all the names and so on and so forth but I reckon I'm on to something there, there's a book in that, and if there isn't, well, maybe I don't need to write another book anyway, maybe the story of me and Cicely was the only story I had to tell, and I shall just have to give my advance back and find something else to do, but I really will have to do *something*, not just because I'm finally running out of money but also because I haven't done a real job now, I haven't made what you might call a meaningful contribution, for almost . . .

. . . *Benjamin!*

*

He turned and saw that Lois was standing beside him.

"Didn't you hear me? I've been looking for you for ages."

38.

In the first week of November 2017, Charlie came to the mill house in Shropshire to discuss Benjamin's idea for a book based on his story.

His short prison term had ended in July, and he was now looking thinner and older than Benjamin remembered, but his cheerfulness seemed undiminished. Banned for life from working with children in the UK, he remained unbowed even though his career as a clown was over. Something would turn up, and in a bizarre way he felt better for his three months inside. He'd had time to reflect, and he no longer felt corroded by anger and bitterness, as he had done for so long. Benjamin realized that in Charlie's eyes, life had always been a series of accidents which could not be halted or controlled, so that the only thing you could do was to accept them and capitalize upon them whenever possible. It was a healthy outlook, he thought. One which he had never quite managed to attain himself.

Charlie was positively excited about being immortalized in Benjamin's next work of fiction. He had brought along a folder full of paperwork to help with the research.

"I made a lot of notes," he said, "in the run-up to the trial, and while I was inside. Also, I've been keeping a diary, on and off, for a few years."

"Brilliant," said Benjamin. "That'll be incredibly useful. But of course I shall have to tell the story in my own words."

"Sure," said Charlie. "I understand that. But maybe I could make a few suggestions?"

"Of course."

"You see, if *I* was writing this book," said Charlie, fishing a piece of paper out of the folder, "I would start with *this*. To get the reader's interest up."

Benjamin took the paper from his hand and began reading. It was a clipping from a local newspaper, the *Bromsgrove Advertiser*, dated 7 September 2016.

"A sort of prologue," Charlie added, "to explain what happened, before you rewind to tell some of the backstory."

Benjamin nodded. "Sounds good," he agreed.

The clipping read:

CLASH OF THE CLOWNS

Shocked children were treated to a surprise horror show at a birthday party on Saturday afternoon—a punch-up between two rival entertainers.

Much-loved kids' comic Doctor Daredevil (also known as Duncan Field) was showcasing his trademark buffoonery at Richard Parker's ninth birthday bash in Alvechurch when fellow entertainer Baron Brainbox (also known as Charlie Chappell) turned up at the same venue. Apparently the two clowns had been double-booked.

Witnesses said that they withdrew to the kitchen to settle the argument but within a few minutes they were at each other's throats—literally. Fun gave way to fisticuffs and the police were quickly summoned to the scene.

Richard's mum Susan Parker said: "It was horrific. One minute the kids were having a great time making stink bombs, then suddenly it was mayhem. The kids were screaming and before I knew what was happening two of my kitchen chairs were broken up and some of my best crockery had been smashed."

Afterwards Mr. Field, who sustained a fractured jaw among other injuries, commented: "This was a vicious and unprovoked assault by someone who has always been professionally jealous of me. Rest assured I shall be pressing charges and invoking the full force of the law."

Mr. Chappell said the fight had nothing to do with professional rivalry and arose from "an argument about Brexit." He was remanded in custody.

Or should that be . . . custard-y?

Benjamin winced when he saw the joke. "Ew . . . that last line needs a bit of work."

"Definitely. What do you think of reprinting that clipping, though, as a way of starting things off?"

"I think it's a great idea."

"Then you'd flash back, you see, to the story of how I met Yasmin and Aneeqa and how Duncan and me started hating each other."

"I see, yes. Starting with your meeting in the toyshop."

"That's right."

Benjamin began to write something down in his notebook, then paused, pen between his lips.

"What *was* it about Aneeqa that gave you such a connection with her, do you think? Could you put it into words?"

"Hang on," said Charlie, searching through his folder once again. "I wrote something about this in my diary. This is from—" he took a pair of glasses from his shirt pocket and peered through them at the roughly scrawled manuscript "—2015. Do you mind if I read it out to you?"

"Go ahead," said Benjamin, settling down in his seat.

"OK." Charlie cleared his throat, and read:

"*She turns eighteen tomorrow. Maybe it's because I don't have any children of my own that I've started to think of her as my own daughter. Maybe it's because I've started to think of her as my own daughter that Yasmin feels such jealousy when she sees us together, and can't find any way of hiding it. It's not something we can have a conversation about. If there's one thing I've discovered, over the last few years, it's that, however fine your intentions, there can be no tactful way of telling a woman that she undervalues her own daughter.*

"It's three o'clock on a bright September Sunday afternoon and she is sitting out in the garden. The sun is falling on her, filtered through the branches of the sumac tree, creating shifting and dancing patterns on her hair, taking its blackness and circling it in a halo of light, adding shades of dark and pale brown, dark like the mahogany dressing table in Mum's old bedroom, pale like the sand of a beach at low tide on one of my long-forgotten summer holidays."

"Nice," Benjamin felt moved to say, as Charlie paused for breath.

"She's reading a volume of Lorca poems, in Spanish. Because I love to hear her speaking Spanish, I ask her to read a few lines to me. She reads: 'Por las ramas indecisas, iba una doncella que era la vida. Por las ramas indecisas. Con un espejito reflejaba el día que era un resplandor de su frente limpia.' *Her voice makes a strange kind of music: strange because her normal accent has gone, the accent that ties her to Birmingham, her home, and the accent that replaces it is different, unfamiliar: to me, it sounds exotic and beautiful. I ask her to translate the lines and she frowns for a moment and then, thinking about it carefully, she says:* 'Through the indecisive branches went a girl who was life. Through the indecisive branches. She reflected daylight with a tiny mirror which was the splendour of her unclouded forehead.'

"Afterwards, I can't get these lines out of my head. 'A girl who was life' is exactly how I think of Aneeqa. I think of the woman she will become, when she leaves home, leaves her mother, leaves this city and achieves her dream: her dream of freedom. Freedom to live where she wants, to be where she wants, to speak the languages that she loves. I think of this beautiful Muslim girl, the daughter of Pakistani parents, living in Seville or Granada or Cordoba and speaking her perfect Spanish and I think what a bright future we have in front of us, if this is what we choose to become: people no longer tethered by the narrow, imprisoning bonds of blood or religion or nationhood. To me, she is a symbol of that future. But at the same time, I don't want to diminish her, reduce her to a symbol, because she is something much more important than that: a human being, a think-

ing and feeling and loving person, free to make her own choices and to follow her own path, answerable to nobody. Just like the girl in the poem. A woman 'who reflects daylight with a tiny mirror, which is the splendour of her unclouded forehead'."

Charlie laid the notebook down and took off his glasses. His voice had begun to slow down and falter with emotion as he read the closing words.

"Bloody hell, Charlie," Benjamin said, after a pause. "That's beautiful. I didn't think you could . . . I mean, I never expected . . . Where did you learn to write like that?"

Charlie shrugged. "I've always read a lot of books, I suppose. Ever since I was a kid. Why—do you think it's all right?"

"I think it's terrific. So moving. I wonder what she'd say if she read it?"

"I doubt if she ever will."

"Well, would you mind . . . would you mind if I put it in the book, just like you've written it?"

Charlie smiled. "No, of course not, mate. All this stuff is yours. Do what you like with it."

It was getting on for one o'clock, so they went into the kitchen for some lunch. Lois had been visiting over the weekend: in the wake of her separation from Christopher she had become slightly obsessed with cooking, and since Benjamin's kitchen was so much larger than the one in her Oxford bedsit she had begun visiting whenever she could. His fridge-freezer was currently full of her soups and casseroles. He filled two bowls with spicy lentil and tomato soup and, while sawing off some chunks of granary bread (also baked by his sister) he asked Charlie:

"So how's she getting on at university?"

"Very well, I think. Getting good marks for everything. And she'll be spending next year in Spain."

"Fantastic. What about her art?"

"Yeah, she still does a bit of that. Helped design a mural, or something, for the student union. I think that's what kept her sane, you know, all the time she was living with her mom. If you've got a talent like that, it helps with other issues, doesn't it? Anger and frustration and so on. Gives you somewhere to channel it. That's what I need. Better than thumping people. Not that the bastard didn't deserve it."

"Are you ready to tell me what happened?"

"Let's eat first," said Charlie.

They listened to the news headlines on Radio Four. The leading story was President Trump's tour of Asia, which had now reached South Korea and had so far managed to pass without any major diplomatic incidents, even though, as usual, the president seemed to delight in keeping his global audience on a knife-edge, waiting with bated breath for that calculated provocation or accidental faux pas that would tip the whole world into chaos. After a few seconds Benjamin was about to switch channels to Radio Three, but stopped himself: no, he thought—that was the sort of thing the old Benjamin would do, before the referendum, before the election of Donald Trump. The world was changing now, things were spinning out of control in unpredictable ways, and it was important to stay informed, to have an opinion. He and Charlie listened in attentive silence for a minute or two.

Finally Benjamin said: "I don't like Trump, do you?"

"Nope," Charlie said. "Can't stand the bloke."

Benjamin nodded. With the political discussion out of the way, he followed his original instinct and retuned the radio, to be greeted by the opening bars of Brahms's Clarinet Quintet. It was a calming accompaniment to the rest of their meal.

Back in the sitting room, he and Charlie took their seats opposite each other again and Benjamin said, "So we can't put this question off any longer, really. I have to ask—what got into you that day? Why the violence? What was the final straw?"

"A lot of people inside asked me that," said Charlie, hunting around in his folder again. "They all had the impression that deep down I was quite a gentle, amiable sort of person, so to try and explain it—to them and myself . . ."

". . . you wrote about it, maybe?"

"Funnily enough, yes, I wrote about it."

He had extracted two or three sheets of paper and was taking his glasses out of his pocket again.

"You really seem to have got the writing bug lately."

"To be honest, Ben, it was your book that inspired me," he said. "You should be taking all of the credit."

"Nonsense," said Benjamin. "Come on, then. Let's hear what you've got."

Charlie sat forward, cleared his throat again, and began to read.

"*Seventeenth of September,*" he began, "*2016.*"

"*I was ten minutes early arriving at the house.*

"*Call it my natural pessimism, call it professional intuition, but I had a weird feeling that Daredevil would have got there before me that day. On two or three occasions already, he'd hacked into my email, got one of my bookings cancelled and taken it himself. I'd confronted him about it, of course, but had always met with barefaced denial. But I wasn't going to let him get away with it today. As soon as I saw that poxy little grey Vauxhall parked in the driveway along with all the parents' cars, I knew that this was going to be the day for our long-delayed showdown. I could feel the anger rising inside me but I was determined to be calm and dignified about it—although, as it happened, I'd already put my costume on: and you'd be surprised how many people don't take you seriously when you're wearing an undersized tweed suit, a multicoloured mortar board and a red ping-pong ball on your nose.*

"*I rang the front-door bell and must admit that I didn't linger over the niceties when the birthday boy's mother opened the door. 'Where is he?' I said, pushing past her. I strode into the living room and there was Daredevil, surrounded by a circle of bored-looking children, up to his old tricks—literally, since he hasn't changed his act for about fifteen years. I grabbed him by the lapels of his stupid white coat and said—trying to keep in character for the time being—'Bally heck, old bean, what the deuce do you think you're doing?'*

"*Some of the children started to laugh, since this was undoubtedly the most entertaining thing they would have seen in the last ten minutes and they must have thought they were witnessing the birth of a new double act. But Daredevil wasn't in the mood to play ball. 'Fuck off, Brainbox,'* he said, which even those dopey kids must have realized wasn't part of the script for a children's show, although it did make them laugh again. 'Oy!' I said, pulling him closer towards me. 'Mind your language. There are children present, you evil little twat.'

"'What are you doing here?' he asked.

"'This was my gig, and you know it.'

"'I don't know what you're talking about. Get out. You're making a fool of yourself.'

"'I should be making a fool of myself, you mean. I should be getting paid for making a fool of myself. It's what I do for a living. But every time somebody books me, you seem to keep turning up and getting in the way.'

"'Would you mind leaving now? These young ladies and gentlemen are waiting to be entertained.'

"'They'll be waiting a fuck of a long time if you're all they've got.'

"That seemed to seriously rile him. 'Right!' he said. 'Let's settle this outside.'

"We marched out of the living room but got no further than the kitchen when he turned on me. He took off his World War Two pilot's helmet and I took off the mortar board. He grabbed the ping-pong ball off my nose and threw it to the other side of the room. By some fluke it went straight into an empty jam jar and rattled to a standstill. We both stared at it.

"'Bloody hell,' I said. 'That was clever. I bet you couldn't do that if you tried.'

"Somehow this little incident seemed to defuse the tension. On his side, at least.

"'Look, Charlie,' he said, spreading his arms and trying to sound conciliatory, 'why do we have to fight all the time?'

"'I don't know—because we hate each other?'

"'I don't hate you, Charlie. I don't have a malicious bone in my body. In fact it's just the opposite. I feel sorry for you.'

"My voice sank low. 'Oh yes?'

"'You're a nice guy, underneath. Anyone can see that. You just happen to be one of those people. You know—one of life's losers.'

"I waited for him to continue, breathing heavily.

"'Someone who's always going to be on the losing side, am I right? You want to be as popular with the kids as I am, but you just aren't. I *don't know why—they don't like you as much. It's just one of those things. Perhaps they know you're a loser too. Perhaps they can smell it. I mean, think about it. You don't really have a family. You don't really have a home. You sleep in your car half the time. Your daughter was never as popular as my daughter at school.'*

"'She's not my daughter,' I said.

"'Oh, that's right, I forgot. I keep thinking she must be your daughter, because you're so close. But I suppose there must be something else going on to explain that. Who knows what, eh, Charlie? Perhaps best not to go there . . .'

"My right hand was beginning to twitch by my side. The temptation to bring it into sharp, sudden contact with his face was growing. But something stopped me, even now: the knowledge that if I did that, Duncan would have won.

"'Krystal and Neeqs never got on, really, did they? The thing is, winners and losers don't often get on with each other. Different species, you see. One's strong, the other's weak. Do you know what Krystal's never done, since she was a baby? Cried. Never cries, that one.'

"I was waiting to see where this was going.

"'Did Neeqs get into university, by the way?'

"I nodded.

"'Spanish was her thing, wasn't it?'

"I nodded again.

"'Bit upset by the referendum result, I gather.'

"I didn't answer.

"'Krystal told me she was crying about it the morning after. Crying about it at school! Didn't you know that?'

"I said, 'Doesn't surprise me. Always been very European in her outlook. Always had this idea she might end up working somewhere like Spain. That's all going to be much harder for her now.'

"'Like I said,' Duncan repeated, annoyingly, 'winners and losers.'

"'Except in this case,' I said, 'Krystal lost as well.'

"He frowned. 'How do you mean?'

"'I mean that everything Aneeqa lost because of that vote, Krystal lost too. Same for every young person.'

"At which point Duncan smiled one of the most evil smiles I've ever seen in my life, and said: 'Ah, no—that's my point. Krystal's going to be fine. My dad was Irish, you see.' He smiled some more, goading me. 'Didn't you know that? Oh, yes. We all applied for Irish citizenship right away. Came through last week. Got the passports and everything. We're all sorted. Nothing changes for Krystal. EU citizen till she dies.' He watched me standing there, gaping. 'I wouldn't have voted to take that away from my own daughter, now would I?'

"He put his hands into the pockets of his white doctor's coat and stood back, challenging me to respond. In retrospect, I have to give him credit. Of all the things he could have said to infuriate me, that was pretty much the most deadly. Going straight for my weakest, most vulnerable points. He had managed to display the most perfect, most seamless, most noxious combination of mean-spiritedness, arrogance and hypocrisy; and as I looked at him now, years of hatred began to well up inside me, coming to the boil.

"'Anyway,' he said, 'why the hell have we started talking about Brexit? Of all the stupid things to fall out over. Anyone'd think the whole country had gone mad. Come on, they told me there's some cider in the fridge here. Let's have a drink and forget our diff—'

"I assume he was going to say 'differences'. But Duncan never got the chance to finish the sentence. My first punch went in and caught him on the left cheek, mid-word. I think it must have been the fourth or fifth one that fractured his jaw. And we had already made quite a mess of the kitchen by then. The first thing I really remember, after that, was the sound of the police sirens."

Charlie laid down his manuscript and took off his glasses.

Benjamin said: "And that's exactly what happened—word for word?"

"Word for word. I suppose the short version is . . . I lost control. I inflicted ABH and I took the rap for it. Maybe I'd do it again, who knows?"

He put the sheets of paper back into his folder and tried to pass it over to Benjamin.

"Here you go, anyway. This lot's all yours. If you think there's a book in this, do what you like with it."

Benjamin shook his head and gently pushed the folder back in Charlie's direction.

"Sounds to me like you've already written it."

"What, this? But these are just . . . ramblings. There's no rhyme or reason to them. No shape or anything."

"That's what an editor's for."

"I don't have an editor."

"I'll do it for you."

It took a while for the meaning of these words to sink in. When it did, Charlie's face coloured with gratitude. Too moved to look Benjamin directly in the eye, he said: "You'd do that for me?"

"Of course."

Charlie stood up, and beckoned Benjamin to stand as well. They faced each other, in a moment charged with emotion. What followed was a little crisis of masculinity in microcosm. Charlie held out his hand, and Benjamin went to grasp it, but Charlie was already moving forward, so Benjamin missed the hand and ended up clasping him by the wrist, and then Charlie put his other arm around Benjamin and they attempted a hug, with Charlie murmuring something all the while about how Benjamin was not just his first and oldest friend but also his best friend, the best friend a man could wish for. They stood like that, hugging and patting each other on the back, and then it occurred to them that they didn't really know how to stop and disentangle themselves, so they did it very slowly and stiffly, and then to escape the situation Benjamin made for the kitchen and said that he would make some coffee. As he was leaving the room, Charlie called after him, "But what about *your* next book? What are you going to write next?," and Benjamin reflected that these were good questions, still unresolved, and it was probably at that moment, that precise moment (he realized afterwards), that it became blindingly clear to him that his well of creativity was dry, that in telling the story of his love for Cicely he had told the only story that he'd ever wanted to tell, and he would never write again. But all he said to Charlie was:

"Oh, something will come up. Bound to. It always does."

39.

Britain had voted. It had sent David Cameron packing. It had made its views on the European Union clear. And now, having made this momentous choice, it did not want to think about the matter any more, but preferred to return to its everyday concerns, and leave the problem of implementing its decision to those traditionally charged with such tasks: the governing class. In November 2017 the European Union (Withdrawal) Bill was still passing through its committee stage in the House of Commons. A number of troublesome MPs had tabled more than four hundred amendments and new clauses, each of which had to be debated and voted on. These amendments were designed, primarily, to prevent the government from awarding too many sweeping new powers to itself, but there was also one detail of the Bill to which the rebel MPs particularly objected: the prime minister's decision to impose a deadline (eleven o'clock on the night of 29 March 2019) for Britain's withdrawal from Europe. "It is quite unnecessary," one of them argued, "to actually close down our options as severely as this, when we don't know yet what will happen, when it is perfectly possible that there is a mutually beneficial, European and British, need to keep the negotiations going for a time longer to get them settled." But certain sections of the press, and certain sections of the public, did not buy this argument. They were convinced that these dissenting Tories had another, more sinister objective in mind: to overturn the referendum result altogether.

Gail found it hard to understand how this popular fantasy had taken hold. Even her own Constituency Association was not immune—to the extent that one Friday afternoon in November she was obliged to visit its chairman, Dennis Bryars, in order to offer him reassurance on this point. She found him feeding his pigs.

"What handsome creatures," said Gail, who was not fond of pigs.

"Beauties, aren't they?" said Dennis, who was extremely fond of them. "They'll be even better when they're sliced up on your plate with some mushrooms and scrambled eggs."

It was a grey and cheerless afternoon, with a bone-chilling wind blowing in from the east, and Gail felt that she had come ill-prepared in her lightweight mackintosh. The pigs, however, housed as they were in thirty or forty straw-bedded huts heated with overhead braziers, looked warm enough. Dennis believed in rearing them humanely prior to slaughtering them.

"What are you feeding them?" Gail asked.

"Wheat, barley," he said, scattering the feed on the ground to the grunting approval of the ravenous animals.

"Sounds very healthy."

"Threonine. Metheonine. Lycine HCL."

"Very nutritious, I'm sure," said Gail, less certainly.

"Waste of bloody money if you ask me," said Dennis. "In the old days we just used to give them swill. Cost us next to nothing. Better for the environment than this stuff, as well."

"Ah—yes," said Gail, who knew exactly what was coming next.

"Of course, the EU knew better than us," said Dennis, sure enough, "and soon put a stop to that. But hopefully one of these days we can go back to being a sovereign nation again, and start making our own laws. Not that you lot seem to be in any hurry to get on with it."

"About that . . ." said Gail. "I do hope that the Association understands why I shall be voting against the government on some of the amendments."

"People have their theories," said Dennis, moving on to another hut.

"As you know," said Gail, hurrying to keep up with him, "I voted Remain myself, but I absolutely respect the referendum result."

"So you say."

Gail felt a squelch underfoot and looked down to see, as expected, that she had just stepped in a large puddle of liquid pigshit. She walked on gingerly, rubbing the side of her shoe against the ground. "But I feel I would be failing in my duty as a member of parliament," she continued, "if I didn't make sure that the legislation was fit for purpose."

"It seems to be good enough for most of your colleagues."

"Yes, but this idea—this stupid idea of setting a particular date and then having to stick to it . . ."

"Look, Gail," said Dennis, turning around and laying both of his buckets to rest for the time being. "I don't see eye to eye with you on this. None of us see eye to eye with you on this. You want to defy your own Constituency Association—not to mention the whips—and vote with your conscience, fine. As long as you accept the consequences."

"Consequences? What consequences?"

"Let's wait and see," said Dennis.

Gail was incredulous. "Are you threatening me?" she asked. "And if so, with what?"

"Don't forget that you'll be depending on our support for the nomination, when the next election comes around. Other candidates may be available."

That had been her first intimation of the difficult days ahead. Worse was to come the following Monday evening, when she and her fellow rebels had to sit through a long and stormy meeting in London with the party whips, whose threats of recrimination were even more explicit. And yet neither of these things prepared her for what was to happen later in the week.

*

Gail's duties in Westminster required her to spend four days of each week in London while parliament was sitting. Her son Edward was away at university, but her daughter Sarah was still at school in Coventry, and so Sarah would typically spend those four days at her father's house. This week, however, he happened to be away on business. In these circumstances Doug (as had occasionally happened before) volunteered to move into the house in Earlsdon and assume the role of carer.

It was a role he took on with mixed feelings. Having failed, fairly comprehensively, to build a satisfactory relationship with his own daughter, he had been sceptical at first of his chances with another fourteen-year-old. But over time he had started to grow fond of Sarah, even though it was hard to tell whether she felt the same way. She had none of Coriander's self-assurance or sense of entitlement. She was quiet, obedient, studious and a little bit dowdy. She wore braces on her teeth and horn-rimmed glasses that gave her the look of a tomboy. She had no boyfriend and showed little interest in acquiring one, appearing happy instead to live a life of quiet domestic contentment with her mother (and Doug, if he was around). A few years earlier he might have been concerned by her lack of rebellious spirit; now he was simply relieved to be spending time with someone who gave him so little trouble.

On the morning of Wednesday, 15 November, shortly after seven o'clock, he was busy in the kitchen, preparing Sarah's breakfast and packed lunch. It was still dark outside and Sarah, although she was awake, had not yet managed to drag herself out of bed. Doug was in the middle of mixing some salad and cold pasta together in a tupperware box when his phone rang. It was Gail, calling from London.

"Have you seen it?" she said. Her voice was strained and unsteady.

"No. Seen what?"

"The paper."

"What about it?"

"I'm on the front page."

"Really? What do they—?"

"I should just go out and get one."

The newsagent was only thirty seconds' walk away. After shouting up the stairs to tell Sarah her cereal was on the table, Doug hurried around the corner of the street. He quickly saw what Gail was talking about. Word of her meeting with the whips had leaked out and one of the papers had decided to make a front-page splash of it. Hers was one of sixteen faces pictured under the banner headline: "THE BREXIT MUTINEERS."

The headline was nasty. The publication of each MP's photograph was done with a clear intent to point the finger, to identify. In the fevered, polarized atmosphere that still pervaded the country more than a year after the referendum, it was a dangerous thing to do.

Hugely irresponsible, in fact: that was Doug's first thought, as he walked back to the house with a copy folded under his arm.

Sarah was in the kitchen. She had finished her cereal and was spreading Nutella on a slice of toast. Doug called Gail from the sitting room and spoke in a low voice.

"Well, that's pretty horrible. Any fallout yet?"

"I'll say. My Twitter feed's gone berserk. Emails too."

"Bad?"

"I've forwarded the worst on to the office and they reckon four or five of them should be passed on to the police. Do you want to hear them?"

"Not really. But go on."

"OK, so we've got . . . *Ransom you bitch*—that's Ransome without an 'e', of course—*you will burn in hell for this. Look over ur shoulder when u r walking home tonight. You attack the people the people will attack you.* Oh, and this is a nice one: *Remember Jo Cox it could happen again.*"

"Jesus Christ. Are you OK? Do you . . . I don't know, do you want me to come down?"

Gail sighed. "I don't think so. Life has to go on, doesn't it? I don't suppose anyone'll come round to the house, or anything like that. Just make sure that Sarah's OK."

"Sure." He looked at the headline again, with the newspaper spread out in front of him on the coffee table. "I can't believe they'd do something like that."

"I know," said Gail. "I mean, I never liked its politics, but that used to be a respectable paper. What's going on, do you think?"

"I don't know. This country's gone mad."

"I hope Sarah's all right at school. I hope nobody says anything horrid to her."

"Don't worry," Doug said. "I've got my eye on her."

*

It was tempting to think, at times like this, that some bizarre hysteria had gripped the British people; that the pitch of collective madness to which everyone had risen during the campaign of 2016 had simply not abated yet. But Doug was not entirely satisfied with this explanation. He knew that a headline like that was calculated. He knew that the outrage it was designed to foment was being stoked because it was valuable to someone: not to any one individual, of course, or even to any one clearly identifiable movement or political party, but to a disparate, amorphous coalition of vested interests who were being careful not to declare themselves too openly. The first thing he did, after walking Sarah to school, was to settle down at his desk upstairs and reach for a Manila envelope containing forty or fifty pages of A4 which had arrived in the post, anonymously, three days after his meeting with Nigel Ives.

There had been no note accompanying them: no written farewell message from the eccentric informant with whom he'd shared so many bizarre, circular conversations over the last few years. Doug had simply been presented with the papers, and expected to make what he could of them. Briefing notes; draft press releases; minutes of confidential meetings; reports marked "Classified" and "Not for Publication." Many of them bore the initials "R. C." or the signature "Ronald Culpepper." Most of them were printed on the headed notepaper of the Imperium Foundation.

He had read through these documents many times, and knew exactly where to find the one that seemed most germane to today's events. It was a paper of some two and a half thousand words, jointly authored by an academic and a well-known journalist and commentator. The title was: *Keeping the Fires Burning: Media Strategies for Sustaining and Harnessing the Energies behind the Referendum Result.*

Doug flipped to the first page. The paper began:

The EU referendum result of 23 June 2016 presents a great, and unexpected, opportunity to further the aims that Imperium has always supported.

The narrow victory for the Leave campaign represented a coalition of different groups, all of whom wanted something different from Brexit. Some voted to restore sovereignty and to repatriate laws, some to reduce immigration and to increase border controls, some were hoping to restore Britain's sense of self-worth as an independent nation, while some (a small minority, perhaps, but the group with which Imperium is itself most closely aligned) voted to liberate Britain from the EU's oppressive tax and other regulations and allow it to become a genuine free-trading country with its principal endeavours directed towards Asian and U.S. markets.

Thus we have an opportunity for radical and permanent change. However, the window of opportunity is small. It must not be allowed to close altogether.

A complete, immediate, root-and-branch break from the EU would have been the ideal outcome, but given the smallness of the Leave majority, arguing that a mandate for this exists is problematic. The government has embarked upon a protracted period of negotiations and, while we have had some success in arguing for the imposition of a deadline to leave (currently set at 29-03-2019) this will be followed by a transitional period of two years or more. The grave danger regarding such a gradual and incremental process of departing the EU is that public enthusiasm for Brexit might wane if negative economic effects start to become apparent.

This paper will set out the steps we can take to minimize this danger, with specific emphasis on the role played by the building of friendships and informal alliances with the print and broadcast media, thereby putting the Foundation in a position to influence editorial direction and tone. (A separate paper will be prepared on social media strategy.) Imperium already has excellent and close relationships with a number of broadsheet and tabloid newspaper editors: these contacts must be renewed regularly and exploited to the full.

Our central argument is that the various and disparate forms of discontent which led 51.9% of voters to vote Leave must not be allowed to fade away until the Brexit process is complete. This discontent is the energy which will power our programmes. If Brexit was fuelled, first and foremost, by a sense on the part of many of the British people that the political class had betrayed them, that sense of betrayal must be sustained. Indeed, it can now be focused more accurately since, with the reframing of Leave's narrow majority as the "will of the people," public anger will be turned most effectively on those members of the political and media establishment who can be portrayed as frustrating that will . . .

*

The day passed quietly, for the most part. Doug spoke to Gail three or four times; in all she had received several dozen tweets which could be construed as threatening, as had the other MPs pictured on the front page. The police were investigating, and would probably pay Doug a visit later. He thanked her for the warning. Meeting Sarah at the school gates, he did not ask her directly whether there had been any problems today, but took reassurance from the fact that she didn't mention any. After dinner she went up to her bedroom to do some homework.

At around eight thirty there was a loud knock on the front door. Doug opened it to find two uniformed police officers standing on the step. Invited inside, they explained that this was purely a routine visit; that a number of threatening messages against Gail Ransome had been reported to them that day; that they just wanted to check no one had seen any unusual activity in the vicinity of the house, and that no one had received any unusual phone calls or texts or emails. In the course of this conversation Sarah came down from her room and was now standing at the foot of the stairs, listening. The police officers took her to one side and quizzed her about her day at school. Had any of her friends mentioned the newspaper headline? Had she experienced any bullying as a result?

Their visit lasted about fifteen minutes in all. When it was over, Sarah seemed reluctant to go back upstairs. She was very quiet. She sat on the sofa in the sitting room, her knees apart, looking down at the floor.

"You OK?" Doug asked, from the doorway.

She looked up. "Do you think I could speak to Mum?"

Doug glanced at his watch. "She's probably still in the Chamber. You could try texting her first."

He went into the kitchen while Sarah sent a text message. It seemed to have the required effect, because after a few minutes he could hear her talking on the phone. She carried the phone upstairs with her, still talking to her mother. Doug went back to his laptop at the kitchen table, and the pile of papers from the Imperium Foundation.

A few hours later, shortly after midnight, a taxi pulled up outside the house, and he heard a key turning in the front door. He went into the hallway and saw Gail, overnight bag in hand, looking pale and tired.

"Hello," he said. "What are you doing here?"

She put the bag down and seized him in a hug, then kissed him fiercely, passionately on the mouth. The embrace was hungry, almost feral in its intensity. He had never known her like this before.

"Sarah sounded awful on the phone," she said, as they eased apart. "Is she all right?"

Doug didn't like to admit he'd been so preoccupied that he hadn't checked on her or even said goodnight.

"Did you take a taxi all the way from London?" he asked.

"Had to. The last vote was at ten thirty."

"How much did that cost?"

"A lot. I'll get the train back first thing in the morning. Only I couldn't leave her alone tonight. She's been really shaken up today."

She went directly upstairs to her daughter's bedroom. When Doug looked in on them, a couple of minutes later, Gail was sitting on the edge of Sarah's bed, stroking her hair, murmuring something, the same soothing phrase over and over again.

Then she looked up at Doug and whispered: "Down in a minute."

"OK. Fancy a drink?"

"Yes please."

He poured two glasses of whisky and waited for her to come down. It took longer than expected, so while he was waiting, he carried some rubbish out to the bins at the back of the house. When he came back inside, all was quiet except for a strange noise coming from the sitting room. Doug couldn't identify it at first. It was high-pitched, with a touch of vibrato. It stopped and started, came and went with an irregular pattern. He thought at first that it might be some sort of electronic alarm. Then he realized: it was Gail, and she was crying. In fact "crying" wasn't the right word: there was another word for this, a word that described the sound perfectly: she was keening. He stepped into the sitting room and found that she was sitting forward on the sofa, shaking, one hand supporting her forehead, the other twitching open and closed on the cushion beside her. She looked at him and her face was a mask of grief and anger.

He thrust the whisky glass towards her and she took a long drink. Then she leaned forward and rested her face against him as his arms enfolded her. The keening stopped, but she continued to shake noiselessly for a while. He stroked her hair. Then she pulled away and took another drink.

"I'm sorry," she said. "What must you think of me?"

"What are you talking about?"

"I don't have moments of weakness. 'Woman of steel', someone called me in a profile once. Remember?"

Doug smiled. He had written that profile himself, before they'd met.

"Now look at me."

It was true, Doug had never seen her cry. It was a terrible, heart-breaking sight. She was unrecognizable.

"It's not me," she said, pulling some Kleenex out of a box and rubbing at her tears and mascara. "They can say what they bloody well like to me. But when your kids—when *your own daughter* thinks you're in danger . . ."

She finished cleaning herself up. Doug sat beside her and put his arm around her. She nestled against him, curling her legs beneath her, resting the full weight of her head gratefully against his shoulder.

He put his lips to the top of her head, breathing in the scent of her, pressing a long kiss into her thick, greying hair.

"I love you," he said.

She squeezed him tightly and said, "I love you too," exhaling the words, sighing them into his chest. Within a few minutes she was asleep. He could feel the dampness of her tears on his shirt.

40.

As the train left London, as it sped through flat, featureless Bedford-shire, as it pressed on through the Lincolnshire fens until it reached York, as it passed through the towns of Thirsk and Northallerton and finally entered the wilder, more dramatic reaches of North Yorkshire, Sohan began to look more and more woebegone.

"Look at these dreary houses!" he was saying.

"They're just houses," Sophie countered. "People have to live somewhere."

"It's all so . . . *empty*. All these miles and miles of empty space with nothing but grass."

"They're called 'fields'. Farmers grow things in them."

"You don't understand. I'm going to be surrounded by all this from now on. Can't you see the horror of that?"

"But this is England. You're fascinated by England. It's what you're writing a book about."

"So? Just because I'm writing a book about it doesn't mean I want to live in it, for Christ's sake. Do you think Orwell wanted to live in Airstrip One?"

"He was writing a dystopia. A nightmare."

"Which is what my life's about to become!" He leaned forward and grabbed her by the arm. "My husband—my soon-to-be-hus-band—is dragging me away from everything I love and forcing me to live among a strange, alien people. Miles from civilization. I'm being sent into exile—like Ovid. An outcast from polite society."

"Ovid was sent to Tomis, on the remote shores of the Black Sea. You're going to Hartlepool. Hardly the same thing."

"It's exactly the same thing!"

"You're going to be teaching in the English department of Durham University. Your students will be the same nice, privately educated girls that you've been teaching in London. Even posher, if anything. You're hardly going to be slumming it."

"But Hartlepool? Why is he doing this to me? Why does he hate me so much? Why is he marrying me if he hates me?"

"It can't be that bad."

"Have you been there before?"

"No."

"It's Brexit central. Seventy per cent of them voted Leave."

"Then you can help redress the balance."

"They hang monkeys."

This seemed to surprise Sophie, at least. "They do what?"

"It's a famous story. A monkey got washed ashore once after a shipwreck and they thought it was a Frenchman because they'd never seen one before so they hanged it."

"When was this?"

"I don't know . . . Some time in the 1980s."

She raised an eyebrow.

"OK, so it was the Napoleonic Wars," he admitted. "But they still call them monkey-hangers."

"It'll be good for you," she said. "You'll be out of the London bubble. You'll have your metropolitan assumptions challenged. You might even make some new friends."

Sohan scowled, but she knew that secretly he was beside himself with happiness. Mike had finally proposed to him over dinner at The Ivy on the second anniversary of their first date. Now, six months later, they were returning to County Durham, where Mike had grown up: to get married in a civil ceremony, first of all, but after that, to settle permanently. Mike had quit his job in the City, having amassed a personal fortune that even Sohan (who was not allowed to see his bank statements) could not begin to estimate; and now, he said, he wanted to put something back into the community that had raised him, and which he had seen brought to its knees, over the last forty years, by the ravages of de-industrialization. To this end, he was setting up his own charity: an educational trust which would provide a centre for digital skills training. Premises had been bought, staff had been hired (although the team was by no means complete) and the plan was to have courses up and running by autumn 2019. Fees would be minimal, and training in web development, coding, digital content creation and emerging technologies would be offered from scratch to local people of all ages. Mike was confident that, with the help of good teachers, even men and women in their fifties and sixties, even those who had found little or no employment for decades, could be retrained and given basic competencies in the new skills required by the digital workplace. It was all, he said, a question of attitude.

"This will all have to be gutted and redesigned," he said, later that afternoon, as he took Sophie and Sohan on a tour of the abandoned sports community centre he had bought to house the new academy. "It was closed down three years ago and it's just been crumbling here ever since. But I can see plenty of scope for workrooms here, a digital lab, a café—even a couple of small lecture theatres."

"It's a fabulous space," said Sophie. "I can see the potential."

Sohan said nothing.

"What's the matter?" she whispered to him, as they walked back across the car park to the spot where Mike's Tesla Model S was waiting for them. "Can't you be encouraging?"

"I wasn't listening to a bloody word," he answered. "I'm terrified about tonight."

Sophie and Sohan had very different evenings ahead of them. Hers would consist of going back to Bewes Hall, the country hotel where the ceremony would be taking place the next day, and sitting in her room watching television while availing herself of room service and the minibar. Sohan, meanwhile, would be meeting Mike's parents for the first time.

"They'll love you," she assured him. "You could charm the socks off anybody."

"Are you kidding? They've never come to terms with the fact that he's gay. Never will, either. And they're both probably UKIP voters."

"Probably? Has Mike told you that?"

"No. But everyone up here votes for them, don't they?"

Sophie gave him what she hoped was a reproachful stare. "For God's sake . . ."

"Well, never mind any of that. The fact is, I know they're going to hate me on sight."

*

The next morning, at breakfast, she asked him how it had gone and was pleasantly surprised when he answered: "It was fine. They were very friendly, very welcoming. Incredibly nervous, of course, but then so was I. We got over it, after a few beers. And the food was great. I was kind of hoping we'd have fish and chips and mushy peas but instead Mike's Mum made a *malu mirisata*, which is a proper Sri Lankan dish, a red chilli fish curry."

Sophie was impressed. "Was it up to scratch?"

"I don't know," said Sohan, shrugging. "I never eat Sri Lankan food. Haven't done since I was a kid. But it tasted good to me."

Sophie poured more coffee for both of them, and spread some marmalade on a slice of the pale, lifeless hotel toast.

"So they're OK with the whole gay thing?"

Sohan shook his head. "Not at all. But there's not much they can do, I suppose. He's their only son, and they don't want to lose him."

During the ceremony that afternoon, Sophie could not stop herself from looking at Mike's parents—particularly his father—and trying to read their emotions. He was a big, solid man in his early sixties, barrel-chested, his hair shaved down almost to nothing. His mother was taller and leaner: she had Mike's build, and her height was accentuated by her sleeveless, full-length dress in navy blue. Neither of them seemed to display much feeling as the vows were exchanged. Mr. Newland stared straight ahead, through the picture windows of the hotel's meeting room and across the golf course out-side, but he did not appear to be taking in the view: rather, his eyes were glazed over and it looked as though he were trying to imag-ine himself somewhere—anywhere—else. Meanwhile his wife's eyes were darting around the room, glancing nervously at the other guests; but there was the hint of a smile as Sohan slid a wedding ring on to her son's finger, at which point she tried to catch her husband's eye, without success. When the ceremony was over they both joined in the applause, uncertainly and a few seconds after it had started.

There were sixty or seventy guests, but Sophie didn't know many of them: just a few of Sohan's academic colleagues. Dinner, and the disco afterwards, were something of an ordeal. She found that she was thinking about Ian a lot, although she told herself that this did not mean, for certain, that she was missing him specifically, more that on this sociable, happy occasion she was missing the more general feeling of being partnered. By eleven o'clock that night, in any case, after dancing a couple of times with both Sohan and Mike, and then being dragged around the floor by an over-enthusiastic but flat-footed specialist in eco-criticism from Sohan's department, she decided that she'd had enough. It also occurred to her that she had been drinking fairly solidly for the last twelve hours or so, and was probably about to pass out. She fetched herself a glass of water from the bar and was standing there drinking it when Mike and his parents passed by on their way to the exit.

"You've met my mum and dad, haven't you, Sophie?"

"Yes, we spoke earlier. Calling it a day?" she asked.

Mr. Newland nodded. "Past our bedtime."

"I hope you've had a good time," said Sophie.

"It's been great," said his wife.

"They're putting a brave face on it," said Mike, patting his moth-er's arm. "It's not quite what they envisaged for their son's wedding."

"Got to move with the times, haven't you?" said his father, who seemed altogether jollier than he had a few hours ago.

"I think I'll go to bed as well," said Sophie. "I'm starting to feel a bit woozy."

"Don't move, then," said Mike. "So and I have had enough too.

Stay where you are for a couple of minutes and we'll help you up the stairs."

*

Sophie was much drunker than she had thought. She remembered leaving the hotel ballroom, and climbing the stairs with the grooms supporting her on either side. But she did not remember going into their room, kicking off her shoes, crashing down on their double bed and falling asleep fully clothed. But presumably, that's what had happened: a few hours later she woke up, with an agonizing headache and a terrible craving for a glass of water, to find that Sohan and Mike were asleep on either side of her.

"What the hell's going on?" she said in a cracked voice.

Mike rolled over and opened his eyes. "Oh, hello," he said. "You're still alive, then."

"What am I doing here?"

"Well, you passed out, and we couldn't be bothered to move you."

"But this is your wedding night. I can't sleep in your bed on your wedding night."

"Don't worry. You didn't stop us from doing anything."

"You mean—while I was here . . . ?"

"No. I mean that So and I are sort of past that stage. You may have noticed that neither of us was wearing white."

"Even so . . ."

"This time tomorrow we'll be in Verona. I'm sure we'll make up for it then."

"I need a glass of water."

Sophie got up, went into the bathroom and ran a glass of cold water. She drank three of them, in fact. Then she got back into bed, but on the edge this time, with Mike lying in the middle. He had already gone back to sleep, and his left arm was flung across his husband's chest. In the half-light Sophie looked at the two of them, their eyes closed, their breathing regular, the ghost of a snore emanating from Sohan's half-open mouth. They looked utterly content, at peace and at ease with each other. A stab of envy ran through her. This wasn't supposed to happen. How had Sohan ended up happily married when she was on her own?

It was four in the morning. She dozed fitfully for a couple of hours but by six o'clock she was wide awake. The grooms were going to be driving to Newcastle airport later that morning. Her own train back to London left just after ten. What could she do in the meantime?

She certainly didn't relish the prospect of a hotel breakfast with the other wedding guests. Stealthily she slid out from beneath the bedclothes, put her shoes on and staggered back to her room. Then she packed, went downstairs, checked out and called a cab.

The driver took her to Hartlepool station but there was no café open: indeed, no sign of life anywhere. It was a warm morning, with shafts of sunlight attempting to break through the wispy banks of grey, shapeshifting cloud. The only place serving coffee appeared to be McDonald's. The young woman who served it seemed friendly enough, so Sophie asked her if there was a beach nearby, somewhere she could sit and look at the sea. As soon as she asked it, she felt ashamed that the question made her sound like a stupid Southerner, but she needn't have worried: the woman was East European, and told her that the easiest thing was probably to take a number seven bus to Headland. Sophie thanked her and walked to the bus stop, pulling her case with one hand and carrying her coffee in the other.

The bus took her along an empty dual carriageway, past an Asda superstore and a retail park which reminded her of the one on the site of the old Longbridge factory. When the bus reached Headland, she found that what must once have been an elegant parade of shops, complete with handsome wrought-iron canopies, had fallen into decay, with many of the units vacant and abandoned. A row of old terraced houses which faced directly on to the high wall surrounding the docks was punctuated at regular intervals by boarded-up windows. The docks themselves stood ghostly and inactive. It was not long after eight o'clock on a Sunday morning—a time, it's true, when not many urban spaces are throbbing with life—but even so it felt preternaturally quiet here.

There was one place open—a One-Stop shop where Sophie bought herself an egg-and-cress sandwich before walking to the old town wall. On her way she saw not a soul. Not a single car passed by. In her fatigued, hungover state, a feeling of unreality began to steal over her. She suddenly had the powerful feeling that she did not understand this place, that she had no sense of the life it contained. Surely this was wrong: her childhood home was less than a hundred miles from here, and in any case, this was England after all—her country—but she felt wholly estranged from this corner of it. For the last ten years, despite the time she had spent in the Midlands, her heart had always been in London. She considered herself a Londoner, now, and from London she could not only travel by train to Paris or Brussels more quickly than she could come here, but she would probably feel far more at home on the Boulevard Saint-Michel or Grand-Place than she did sitting on this bench, looking out across the charcoal waters of the North Sea towards the cranes, tankers and wind turbines that rose on the horizon.

She thought again of Sohan and Mike wrapped together in their sleepy marital bed and felt the piercing sting of loneliness. She thought, briefly, of Ian. And then she thought of somebody else: and before she had time to consider how doomed the enterprise was, she had already shut herself off from contemplation of the hushed, austere seascape all around her. She had taken out her phone, and was checking the prices of flights to Chicago.

41.

Dear Adam

Wow, it's been a long time since we were in touch! *(Though I'm sure it doesn't feel that way to him.)* Just been looking through old emails and realized that it was April 2016 when I last heard from you. I sent you a couple of emails since then but maybe they went into Spam. *(No they didn't, he just didn't feel like answering.)* It's hard work keeping a virtual correspondence going *(especially when one of you isn't really interested)*, but hopefully there might be the opportunity to meet up in person soon. More of that in a moment . . . *(The suspense will be killing him.)*

Well, there has been one major development in my life since I last wrote, which is that Ian and I have separated.

A lot of things came to a head in the summer of 2016 and after we'd tried relationship counselling for a few weeks I decided to move out. In a way I suppose it's amazing, looking back, that we managed to brush things under the carpet for as long as we did. I'm a big fan of keeping your political differences under wraps—a pretty unfashionable view over here at the moment, where the vogue seems to be for picking fights and shouting your opponents down as loudly as possible—but when you're sharing a living space with someone and rubbing up against them twenty-four hours a day, eventually that no longer becomes practical. We just disagreed about too much.

Meanwhile, I've been thinking of the way you jumped the academic ship a couple of years ago, and wondering how spontaneous a decision that was. Had it been brewing for some time—weeks or months or even years? I'm asking because I've recently become tempted to pack it in myself. As of yesterday, in fact. I spent most of the weekend at a friend's wedding, which involved leaving London and slipping into a slightly gentler pace for a couple of days. Yesterday in particular I had a lot of time and space just to sit around and contemplate life and get some perspective on things. It would be crazy to take a life-changing decision on the basis of twenty-four hours' thinking, though, wouldn't it? And yet the more I turn it over in my mind, the more it seems to make sense. The job's not what it was, or at least not what I once thought it was going to be. Everything has become transactional. Students (or their parents) pay vast sums up front and expect value for money in return. Younger lecturers work themselves to the bone while the older generation sit around waiting for their retirement packages to kick in and meanwhile will do anything to preserve a quiet life: my head of department being a prime example . . .

What a self-indulgent ramble this has become. (*And that, my dear, is the first and only honest sentence you've written in this whole fucking email.*) Let me come straight to the point. (*OK, how big a lie is this going to be? Might as well make it a whopper.*) A friend of mine moved to Chicago earlier this year, and has been badgering me to come and visit her. So I've booked my flight (*no I haven't, not yet*) and will be coming out for a long weekend, starting on Friday 20. Do you think you'll have an hour or two *(a night or two, is what I'm really saying)* to spare that weekend? It would be great to meet up again after all this time. A lot has happened since Marseille! I long to hear tales of how you're coping with Trump's America. *(Yeah, that's definitely what I long for. Better send this before I write something even more stupid.)*

With love,
Sophie xx

*

From: Adam Turner
Sent: Wednesday, April 11, 2018 07:22 AM

To: Sophie Coleman-Potter
Subject: Re: Chicago bound

Dear Sophie

It's always great to hear from you, and even more exciting to hear that you'll be coming to my neck of the woods. And I can only apologize for my abject failure to keep our correspondence going. Put it down to the pressures of fatherhood, if you will. *(What? WHAT???)*

Yes, this is <u>my</u> great news since we were last in contact. Pat and I got married the summer before last *(Pat? Who the FUCK is Pat?)* and our daughter was born—with somewhat indecent haste, I'm ashamed to say—a few months later. We called her Alice—a neat coming-together of homages, if you will, mine being to Alice Coltrane, Pat's to Alice Walker. Now, at 16 months, I won't bore you with a father's doting recital of the many ways in which I think she's adorable—but I am attaching a picture. You'll allow me that, at least? (*What choice do I have?*)

(*And, oh shit, I think I need another cup of coffee before I can read any more of this.*)

(*OK, let's hear the rest.*)

I'm sorry to hear things have been so difficult for you, personally and professionally. I remember when we met in Marseille and you were so recently married and seemed so happy and excited about it. Well, I suppose shit happens . . . Not very profound, I know, but what else can I say? (*True, that just about sums it up.*) And at least on the professional thing I can sound a little more encouraging: getting out of the academy was definitely one of the best decisions I ever made. Of course, I got lucky: the gaming company I joined has been doing well and they like my work and now I've got some shares in the company, and that's all great: but the important thing is that I'm living off my creativity. I love the work that I do and it pays the bills and if it's not quite the kind of music-making I grew up with there are other ways of doing that. I've formed a trio with a couple of friends and we've been doing some gigging on the side—in fact we're playing here on the 21st, so if you and your friend have no plans that evening, you can come and hear us, which would be amazing! No charge—straight on to the guest list.

So, everything is going well on that front but with reference to the last sentence of your mail I can't say that I'm too happy with the bigger picture. Like every other fool in America, Pat and I were not expecting Trump to become president. Alice was born about ten days before the election and it was the weirdest feeling, because it meant we had about ten days of pure joy and excitement and then that damned result came

through and we were like, What the f*** has just happened?
It was like a cloud descended on the house that day, and to
be honest with you it hasn't lifted yet, and it won't lift until
our president has been replaced by somebody else—however
that happens, and however long it takes. Not that Hillary was
perfect by any means but there was a sort of basic competence
and temperamental stability there which is just something you
expect from your Head of State. The morning of November 9
I was mainly just angry and disbelieving but I guess it was even
worse for Pat. It was incredible how quickly and dramatically
the emotional temperature changed. The day before we had
been looking at Alice and taking nothing but delight in her
freshness and innocence and vulnerability and now we looked
at her and couldn't believe how insecure her future felt, how
our country and the world had come to feel so much more
unstable and malign and dangerous overnight.

Anyway, we can talk about all this when I see you—which is in
just over a week, right? You and your friend can come to the
show Saturday and maybe on Sunday you could come over to
our place for lunch, if you're not too busy. I know Pat would
love to meet you and of course I can't wait to show off the
lovely Alice. :)

So let me know your plans and call me the minute you hit
town.

À bientôt (one of the few useful French phrases I still
remember).

Adam

42.

After reading the email, Sophie lay down on the narrow bed in the tiny room and curled up tight for about fifteen minutes. It was almost six years since she had met Adam in Marseille but ever since then a fantasy, a foolish, unworkable fantasy, had lodged in her mind and this morning she was furious with herself not just for clinging to it but now, even more foolishly, for acting upon it and exposing it to him so starkly and eliciting this gracious, tactful, mortifying response.

How could she write back?

Three days later she sent off another email—it was the eighth or ninth draft—explaining that her friend's mother had died suddenly and she was going to be flying home that weekend and Sophie needed to be here for her. Sending it was perhaps the most embarrassing thing she had ever done but she couldn't think of an alternative. As for Adam's reply, she could only bring herself to skim it and then send it quickly down to the foot of her computer screen at the bottom of her flagged email list. At least she had saved herself the price of a flight to Chicago, something she could ill afford at the moment.

So it was that, on Friday, 20 April 2018, she found herself taking a train to Birmingham Moor Street rather than a plane to Chicago O'Hare. A weekend with her father, rather than a weekend with Adam. On Friday evening, an Indian takeaway, a four-pack of lager, and the exchanging of family news. Sophie felt so depressed and drained of hope that she could barely speak.

Her father, on the other hand, was uncharacteristically voluble.

"I'm putting this place on the market," Christopher said. "You don't mind, do you?"

Sophie shook her head.

"I always got the impression you didn't like it much anyway."

"I didn't," she admitted. "Where will you move to?"

"Well . . ." He took a breath. "That's the other thing. I've been seeing somebody."

"Somebody?"

"Another woman. You don't mind, do you?"

"Someone you're going to move in with?"

"Yes."

Sophie was both impressed and deflated. Even her father's love life was healthier than her own. "That was quick," she said.

"I know. You don't mind, do you?"

"Will you stop asking me if I mind? Why should I mind? I just want you and Mum to be happy."

"Good. Well, I am. Very happy."

"What's her name?"

"Judith."

"What does she do?"

"She's a divorce lawyer."

"That should come in handy."

Christopher smiled. "What about your mother?"

"What about her?"

"Has she found anybody else?"

"I don't think she's looking for anybody else. She is looking for a house in France, though."

"Oh?" He seemed taken aback by this. "She didn't seem to like that idea when I suggested it."

"Well, she and Benjamin are talking about moving there together now. He's putting the mill house up for sale. They want to buy somewhere big so they can take guests."

"Quite a change for them."

"Change seems to be in the air."

"At least you're staying put," said Christopher. "Providing a bit of continuity in our lives."

"I'm going to quit my job," Sophie announced. "Give my notice."

Christopher almost dropped his onion bhaji. "What? Why?"

"I suppose," she said, "it turned out not to be the job I always dreamed it would be. The things I liked about it slowly got overwhelmed by the things I hated." And then she reached out and touched her father's arm, and added, more brightly: "Don't worry about me, Dad. I've got something else in mind. Everything's going to be all right."

*

Late the following morning, as she took the bus into the centre of Birmingham, she asked herself when she had got into the habit of lying to everybody. She didn't believe for a minute that everything was going to be all right, and she certainly had nothing else in mind. Many years earlier, when she was doing her A-levels, she had talked about becoming a therapist. Right up until the submission of her PhD thesis, that plan had remained at the back of her mind. Lorna, the woman who had provided relationship counselling for her and Ian, had not impressed Sophie much: she was pretty sure she could do a better job than that, even though her own relationships didn't provide much of a blueprint for success. But could she face the task of retraining, at this stage? The years of low-paid (or even, for much of the time, unpaid) work? It wasn't an appealing prospect. Easier to get a job in a museum, a gallery, the National Trust. Not really the kind of thing she had been working towards, all her life, but it would still be public service, of a sort . . .

She left the bus when it reached the city centre, and began to wander at random through the crowded streets, jostled by eager shoppers. After months of indifferent weather, temperatures had climbed freakishly in the last few days, and the sun had drawn people to New Street and Broad Street and Corporation Street in large numbers. Pale, freckly teenage girls, their skin exposed in vest tops and denim shorts, contrasted oddly with the black outlines of women in full niqab. Sophie felt relaxed in the crowd, happy to lose herself in it.

But she had no desire to go shopping and was not exactly sure why she had come here today. She had been preoccupied lately by the thought that she should really contact Ian and discuss getting a formal divorce: this had been on her mind for several months, in fact, but she shied away from the idea, the crushing finality of it. Still, it was cowardly of her (of both of them) to let the situation just drift on like this. She was only about five hundred yards from his flat—from the flat she had shared with him for so long—and it would be easy enough to call him, meet up for a friendly chat in some coffee shop, see where the conversation led. Besides which, it would be nice to see him again, in some ways . . .

Sophie sat down on a bench in Cathedral Square and spread herself out in the sunshine. Here in the very centre of Birmingham, she realized that she was surrounded by memories of him. Just opposite her on Colmore Row was the office building where she'd taken her Speed Awareness Course. Behind her, on Corporation Street, was the sweet shop where Ian had intervened and got himself injured during the summer riots of 2011. Thinking back to that week set a complex chain of reflections in motion . . . Her most vivid memory—even more vivid, oddly, than the moment in hospital when Ian had proposed to her—was of driving to the hospital with Helena and feeling a yawning silence open up between them in the car when she had spoken the unforgiveable words: "He was quite right, you know. 'Rivers of blood.' He was the only one brave enough to say it . . ." It was amazing, Sophie thought, how some people remembered that speech, clung to that speech, delivered to a Birmingham audience by a Birmingham-born politician, how it had impressed them as the expression of an essential but unspeakable truth and had lain hidden in their hearts like a cancer, festered, for . . . Jesus, for fifty years now. Half a century! Only last week the BBC had broadcast it again, delivered by an actor this time, in order to mark its fiftieth anniversary (as if, Sophie thought, this was an anniversary worth marking), and she had caught a few minutes of it on the radio, and the banal dreariness of it had depressed her, while Enoch Powell's nasal voice and eerie cadences (in the actor's excellent impersonation) had chilled her to the bone, but today a more cheering thought rose up: the realization that here, on this sunny day in April, the people of Birmingham—young people, mainly—were going about their lives in happy and peaceful acceptance of precisely that melding of different cultures that Powell's pinched, ungenerous mind had only been able to imagine leading to violence. She remembered Sohan's scornful response, all those years ago, when Lionel Hampshire had described his fellow countrymen as being essentially welcoming and easy-going—the very opposite of Powell's lethally well-spoken, well-bred racism—but she couldn't help hoping that the author had been right, not just about the English but about people the world over. Otherwise, what hope was there?

She began to walk along Waterloo Street, through Victoria Square, past the site of the old Central Library—now gone—and The Grapevine pub—now also gone—until she emerged into Centenary Square, in front of the sleek and monumental new library building. She was only one hundred yards from Ian's flat, at this point, but she carried on walking, through the International Convention Centre and out into Brindley Place, where she stood for a few minutes on the bridge over the canal, watching the passing traffic of shoppers on the towpaths. It was lunchtime and people were starting to look for places to eat. Her hand was clasping the phone in the pocket of her jeans and she was wondering, yet again, whether to give Ian a call when—like an omen—she felt a tap on her arm and she turned to see two people she was not at all expecting to see: two people she recognized, but had not spoken to since before her separation: Mrs. Coleman's one-time cleaner Grete, and her husband Lukas.

They were laden with shopping bags and dressed far too warmly for the summery weather. They were also about to go to Pizza Express for lunch. They invited Sophie to join them.

Over lunch they stuck to inconsequential topics—the weather, the restaurant business, the new shops in the city centre—and avoided mentioning the thing (the person, rather) that had brought them together in the first place. But when the meal was over and coffee arrived, Sophie asked them if they had any news of Ian or Mrs. Coleman. The question seemed to provoke some embarrassment.

"To be honest," said Lukas, "we see Helena in the village sometimes, but we're not on good terms with her. As for Ian . . ."

"I don't think he's been around much lately," said Grete. "Probably not for a couple of months."

"Why do you think that?" Sophie asked. It sounded to her as though there might be a particular reason.

Lukas said: "Something happened, earlier this year. It was very ugly . . . Very upsetting for all concerned."

"We had something to do with it," said his wife. "In fact we were the cause. Which makes me feel terrible, I must say. I think there must have been a rift between Ian and his mother and we were basically the reason for it."

"Don't say that," said Lukas. "Don't blame yourself. Don't blame *us*. We weren't at fault. You were the victim, in case you'd forgotten."

They fell silent. Sophie could see that a difficult subject had been raised, but her curiosity to know more was fierce.

"If you don't want to tell me . . ." she prompted, disingenuously.

"No, of course," said Grete. "You should really know about it. I mean, I'm not sure where things stand at the moment, between you and Ian, but—I think you'd like to know about this."

Sophie nodded, urging Grete on with her eyes. After a moment or two, she continued:

"So—you remember the village shop, of course?"

"Of course."

"Well, this happened in the shop in February. It was a Saturday lunchtime and it was a rather cold day, I remember, so there were not many customers—but as you know, that shop is never busy. Anyway, that doesn't matter. It began like this. There were just four of us in the shop. Two people behind the tills, serving two customers. I was one of the customers. The other was a man, maybe about twenty-five or thirty. I think he must have come from a pub somewhere because we could all see that he had been drinking, and now he was trying to buy more alcohol, some cans of lager. I was just buying a few things, toothpaste and dishcloths and stuff like that. But also, I admit I was being quite rude and doing something which I normally don't do, which was talking on the telephone while I paid. I must say it annoys me when other people do that, but my sister had just called me and I was quite pleased because I hadn't heard from her for a long time and I'd been getting a little bit worried. So I was talking to her all the time I was paying and leaving the shop. In our own language, of course.

"Meanwhile this other man, this young man, was at the other till and he seemed to be having some difficulty paying. He was trying to pay with his card and the machine was not accepting the card. He was having an argument about it with the woman at the till. He had no cash with him—just this card—so finally he had to accept that he could not buy these cans of lager. But he wasn't happy about it. He snatched the card out of the little card reader and he slammed the card reader down on the counter and then, just as he was leaving, he saw me. Or heard me, as I should rather say. He saw me walking towards the door out of the shop, talking to my sister on the phone, talking in another language, and he caught my eye. I didn't like the way he was looking at me so I looked away but it was too late. I left the shop and as I left it I saw Mrs. Coleman coming towards me, approaching the shop from outside, but we didn't say hello because suddenly this man was shouting at me. He shouted, 'Get off your effing phone,' and then just as we were both outside the door he grabbed me by the arm and said, 'Who are you speaking to?' and 'What language were you speaking?' I shouted, 'Let go of me,' but he just repeated, 'What effing language were you speaking?', and then 'We speak English in this country,' and then he called me a Polish bitch. I didn't say anything, I wasn't going to correct him, I'm used to people thinking that I'm Polish anyway, I just wanted to ignore him, but he didn't stop there, now he grabbed my phone and took it off me and threw it on the ground and started stamping on it." Grete's eyes had moistened and her voice was trembling as she described the incident. "He kept saying Polish this and Polish that—I can't repeat the actual words he used—and told me, 'We don't have to put up with you . . . people any more' ('people' wasn't the word he used, either), and then he spat at me. Actually spat. Luckily not in my face, but . . ."

Shaking visibly now, she put her head in her hands. Lukas put his arms around her. Sophie leaned across the table and clasped her hand as well.

For a while it seemed that Grete was not going to be able to finish telling the story. And so it was Lukas who continued:

"Grete was really upset by this episode. Really shaken. It was the first time—I mean, ever since the referendum, we had felt, both of us had felt, this slight change in the way that people—some people—spoke to us, or looked at us when they heard us speaking, even when we were speaking English, but this was the first time anything like this had happened, anything really aggressive or violent. In the end we decided that we should go to the police and report it. The guy had just got into his car and driven off and we didn't know the number or anything but we thought he would be pretty easy to find. But we also thought it would be helpful if we had some witnesses, so we decided to call on Mrs. Coleman, because she had seen the whole thing.

"We visited her house the next morning, which was a Sunday, and when we got there we could see that Ian's car was parked outside."

"To tell the truth, I was quite glad," said Grete, who seemed to have recovered some of her composure now, "because I had always found Ian to be a little easier to talk to and—I hope it's all right for me to say this—a little . . . friendlier, than Mrs. Coleman herself? I mean, I had worked for her for quite some years and spent quite a lot of time in her house and in all that time I had never really . . ."

"I know what you mean," said Sophie.

Grete smiled thankfully and continued: "Well, it was Ian who answered the door to us. He was very pleased to see us, very warm and very kind. He and his mother had been drinking tea in the kitchen. We had our daughter with us, our daughter Justina, and although she is very well behaved we didn't want to put them to any inconvenience, so Lukas took Justina into the front room and played with her there while I talked to Ian and his mother. Ian asked me to sit down and offered me a cup of tea but I said it was all right, I wasn't going to stay for very long. I sat at the kitchen table between them but I had not been speaking for long when Mrs. Coleman started to gather up their tea things and took them to the sink to wash them. It's not that she wasn't listening, I don't think. It was more that she already knew what I was going to say, and wanted to prepare her answer. Briefly I told Ian what had happened—in fact they had already been discussing it, and he was very kind about it, very sympathetic—and then I said that we'd decided to go to the police, and would Mrs. Coleman be prepared to come forward as a witness and just confirm what had happened.

"Helena was still standing by the sink, her hands immersed in the water, looking out through the kitchen window. Ian said to her: 'That would be OK, wouldn't it, Mum? I mean, you did see the whole thing.'

"She did not speak at first but eventually she replied: 'Yes, I did.' "We waited for her to say something else. We waited for quite a long time."

Sophie, too, waited for Grete to continue. Despite the clatter of cutlery all around her, the comings and goings of the busy restaurant, she could hear and picture the scene clearly: the terrible stillness of that too-familiar kitchen; the gentle swishing of the water in the sink as Helena moved her hands; Helena's eyes, the palest of blues, liquid, rheumy, staring out fixedly at the rose garden her husband had planted years earlier: the buds that were yet to open, the flowers that were yet to bloom. She remembered sitting out in that garden herself, the very first day she had met Ian's mother. She remembered the ferocity with which the old woman had gripped her arm, the unnerving strength and steadiness of those eyes.

"Finally," Grete said, "Helena spoke. She spoke very quietly; and there was a sadness in her voice too. A real sadness. That was what made it so hurtful, in a way. She said . . ." Grete took a deep breath. Clearly it pained her to repeat these words. "She said: 'I think, on the whole, it would be better if you and your husband went home.'

"I honestly didn't understand at first. I thought she was just referring to our house at the other end of the village. But that's not what she meant. 'I'm afraid,' she said (and I have to admit, by the way, that it always puzzles me how the English use this phrase, as if it actually frightens them to say something bad, when of course it's the person they are talking to who should be frightened—it's a strange thing, I don't think you find it in any other language), anyway, 'I'm afraid,' she said, 'that what happened yesterday is only going to continue happening, in one form or another. It was always going to happen. It's inevitable.'

"'Inevitable?' I repeated. But she didn't speak again.

"I sat there, trying to take in what she had just said. I was lost for words, actually. Then Ian said something like, 'Mum, all she's asking is that you tell people what happened,' but I rose to my feet and stopped him and said: 'It's all right, Ian. Your mother has made herself very clear. I know exactly what she is trying to tell me. I'm going now.'

"I walked quickly out of the kitchen and into the front room, where Lukas and Justina were playing. I picked my daughter up and said, 'Come on, we're going now,' and took her to the front door. He—" glancing at her husband "—followed me, not really understanding what was going on. Ian was at the front door and he tried to stop me leaving but I brushed past him and took Justina straight out to the car."

"I went out to the car as well," Lukas said, "to try and ask what was the matter. But Grete wouldn't tell me. She was just strapping Justina into the car seat and not really speaking. But the front door was still open and so I went back into the house. I went down the corridor and into the kitchen and when I got there Ian and his mother were having a terrible argument."

"What was he saying?" Sophie asked.

"I don't remember. They were raising their voices—not shouting at each other, exactly, but . . . certainly they were very angry. It was a bad argument. But I don't remember what they were saying."

*

"I realized that what really outraged her," Ian said to Sophie later that night, as they lay in bed together, and he trailed his fingers delicately along the soft ridge of her bare shoulder, "was the simple fact that I wasn't supporting her. That's what she wanted from me. That's what she expected. Unconditional support." He kissed her shoulder, now, then moved his hand across the lovely plateau of her stomach, feeling the subtle indentation of her belly button, until it came to rest on the curve of her hip. "She kept saying to me, 'Whose side are you on? Whose side?' That was how she saw it. I couldn't believe I hadn't noticed it before—that this was basically how she'd been living her whole life. In a state of undeclared war."

Sophie stroked his thigh. It felt nice to be touching him again: his muscle, his skin, the fair, downy hairs on the inside of his thigh and the coarser, thicker hair as her hand moved in closer.

"When did you last speak to her?" she asked.

"That morning. Two months ago." He kissed her.

"You'll have to make it up."

"Eventually. But we'll never –" he kissed her again "– go back to how it was before."

"Neither will we," said Sophie, her heart fluttering as she felt his hand begin to circle her breast.

"But at least you're back," said Ian, kissing her one more time, then brushing his lips gently along the line of her jaw. "Aren't you?"

"We'll see," said Sophie.

*

"What will you do now?" Sophie had asked, as she left the restaurant with Lukas and Grete and stepped out into the sunshine.

"Now?" Lukas looked at his watch. "I suppose a bit more shopping, and then back—"

"I didn't mean this afternoon," said Sophie. "I meant . . . Will you be staying in the village?"

"Actually," said Grete, "we are taking Mrs. Coleman's advice."

"No! You can't leave, because of this."

"It's not because of this," said Lukas. "We just feel . . ."

"It's not that we've fallen out of love with England . . ." said Grete.

"Just that . . . We feel there are other countries now where life might be easier for us."

"What other countries?"

"We're not sure. We have plenty of time to decide. We gave notice on our house but we don't have to leave until the end of August."

Sophie looked at them standing hand in hand beside the canal, and knew that she was looking at two people who had made up their minds.

"That's terribly sad," she said.

"Not really," said Lukas. "It's always good to move on."

"And what about you?" Grete asked.

They had both urged her, in the strongest possible terms, to call Ian as soon as possible. But Sophie had decided to take an even more direct course of action. And so, after they had said goodbye outside the entrance to the Birmingham Rep, and she had watched their dwindling figures as they walked past the Hall of Memory in the direction of Paradise Place, she turned her steps towards the back of the theatre, and made her way slowly, but with no flagging of resolve, towards the apartment building where she and Ian had shared their years of married life. She remembered, of course, the four-digit code for the communal entrance. She still had a key to the flat, as well: but she did not use it, on this occasion. Instead she rang the doorbell, and when Ian came to answer it, with the quizzical, slightly aggrieved look of someone who has just been interrupted watching a football match on TV, she merely said: "Hello, stranger."

43.

Coriander had taken her finals and was waiting for the results. Perhaps in an effort to kill time—or even, just possibly, to build bridges with her father—she had finally consented to spend a day or two with Doug and Gail at the house in Earlsdon. It was a stressful but mainly unremarkable visit, characterized by strenuous politeness on all sides. When it was over, on the evening of 17 May 2018, she walked with Doug to Coventry station: she was heading back to London, he was en route to Birmingham to attend (with the mixed feelings that always accompany such occasions) a school reunion. It was a twenty-minute walk in the mellow sunshine of an early-summer evening, and Coriander set a brisk pace.

"Can't you slow down a bit?" said Doug, as she strode onwards, two or three yards ahead of him. "Anyone would think you were ashamed to be seen walking next to me."

"I am."

"Charming."

"What do you expect?" she said. "It's the suit. The penguin suit. You look like a paid-up member of the ruling class. It's embarrassing."

"It's not my fault there's a dress code."

"Oh, please. In days gone by you would just have said fuck 'em and put on a suit and tie. You've become such a cop-out in your old age."

Doug hurried to catch up with her. "My *middle* age, thank you very much. I'm not old."

"Whatever."

He put his arm through hers and was relieved that, for a minute or two at least, she did not try to disentangle herself.

"Will Benjamin be there?" she asked.

"Yep. Why, have you got a message for him?"

"Nope."

"Because if you gave the message to me, I could pass it on to him, and he could pass it on to Sophie." He glanced at his daughter, whose face was a blank. "It could be . . . oh, I don't know—an apology or something?"

"If I'd done anything wrong," Coriander said, "I'd apologize."

"You took a year out of her life."

"During which time she wrote a book and made a TV series. Meanwhile, seventy per cent of trans people in this country consider suicide. I know whose side I'm on. Drop it, Dad. It's not going to happen."

At the station they kissed goodbye and Doug crossed over the footbridge which led to the platform for Birmingham-bound trains. A train arrived almost at once, but then didn't move for several minutes. It meant that Doug, sitting in a window seat, had a clear view of his daughter as she stood waiting for her train on the opposite platform. Her strength of character, her obstinacy, her refusal to compromise were all clearly inscribed in her attitude and posture: the placing of her feet on the platform, the half-scowl on her face as she stared impatiently at the horizon, her aloofness towards the other passengers. Doug hoped that she would overcome, sooner or later, her anger at the world and more specifically at the world that his generation had bequeathed to her. They had spoken of apologies but he realized now that *he* was the one oppressed by the permanent sense of owing an apology: to her, in the first instance, and then to all her friends and contemporaries. Had Doug and his peers really screwed up so badly? Perhaps they had. The country was in a wretched state at the moment: bad-tempered, fractured, groaning under the pressure of an austerity programme that seemed never likely to end. Maybe it was inevitable that Coriander should despise him for his part in all this, however small. Maybe it was time to learn from *her*, to remind himself that there were some principles that should never be abandoned or diluted, and that it was not necessarily a noble thing to gravitate towards the centre ground in pursuit of a quiet life . . .

Instinctively he pulled at the bow tie fastened chokingly around his neck. He was about to unclip it, but checked himself. He did know a futile gesture when he saw one, after all.

*

As Doug was walking down the main drive of King William's School, experiencing Proustian rushes of recollection with every step and every glance to either side (the science labs to his right, the once-forbidden kingdom of the Girls' School to his left), he saw Benjamin a few yards ahead, parking his car and locking the door. Together they walked on until they reached the old dining hall, where a multicoloured banner announced that "King William's School Welcomes The Class Of 1978" and they found Philip Chase and Steve Richards already waiting for them at the end of one of the long bench tables.

"Who the hell *are* all these people?" Steve asked, looking around at the sea of thinning hair, wire-rimmed spectacles, stooped shoulders and evolving paunches. "I don't recognize anybody. They all look the same."

"Some of the teachers are supposed to be coming. Mr. Serkis said he'd be here."

Steve laughed. "I love how you still call him 'Mr'."

"Look!" said Phil. "Isn't that Nick Bond?"

"No, that's not him. That's David Nagle. I'd know him anywhere."

"Shall we go and say hello?"

"I'd rather not. We didn't have much in common forty years ago. We'd have even less now."

"Then what are we doing here? Why did we come? We could've just gone for a quiet Chinese."

"Over there," said Doug, "is the reason why I came."

The others stopped talking and followed his gaze towards the door of the dining hall, where Ronald Culpepper had just made his entrance. He was deep in conversation with the school's current headmaster, who was chatting to him deferentially while escorting him to the centre seat at the top table.

"You came all the way here," said Steve, incredulous, "to listen to that plonker talking about—" he picked up the printed order of ceremonies "—'Global Opportunities in Post-Brexit Britain'?"

"No," said Doug. "I came because I intend to have a private word with him at the end of the evening. As for his crappy talk, I don't know about you lot, but I won't be staying to listen to it."

True to his word, as soon as dessert was over and the chairman of the Imperium Foundation was rising to his feet, Doug led a well-coordinated walk-out at their end of the table. He was followed by Philip, Steve and Benjamin, who made their exit from the dining hall with much orchestrated clanging of cutlery and scraping back of benches, at the very moment when Culpepper was beginning to speak. The other fifty or sixty guests turned to look at them as they pushed their way through towards the door. It was a childish gesture, but deeply satisfying. And it was a relief, after so much stodgy food and cheap red wine, to get out into the fresh air and enjoy the last minutes of evening sunlight.

They followed the path that wound itself around the perimeter of the school buildings—most of them dating from the redbrick inter-war era and all too familiar, some of them much more recent, and oddly unfamiliar: most prominent among these was the new prayer centre, built to accommodate the thirty per cent of King William's boys who now practised the Islamic faith. Soon they reached the grassy bank that led down to the playing fields, where the rugby posts rose up spectral and imposing in the summer twilight, like unexplained monuments from an ancient civilization. They sat down on the grass, just as they had done almost forty years ago, on a hot summer afternoon at the end of their final term, when Doug had brought cans of lager for them to drink but Benjamin had abstained, primly conscious of his responsibilities as a prefect. The memory of that afternoon made him smile now, and sent him off on a reminiscent trail.

"Do you remember," he said, looking north towards the wall that enclosed the outdoor swimming pool, tucked behind the school chapel, "how they used to make us swim with nothing on if we forgot our swimming trunks?"

"Oh yes," said Phil.

"The amazing thing," said Steve, "is how our parents let them get away with it. Nowadays that would be a case for the police and social services. At least you'd hope so."

"True," said Phil. "So much of what we took for normality in the seventies would be defined as abuse today."

"Well, we emerged unscathed, at any rate," said Benjamin, to which Doug merely replied, "Did we, though?" and for a while the question hung in the air, unanswered and unanswerable.

"It's nice to look back sometimes," Benjamin said at last, in a defensive way.

"Nostalgia is the English disease," said Doug. "Obsessed with their bloody past, the English are—and look where that's got us recently. Times change. Deal with it."

"Well, you don't," said Benjamin.

"Excuse me?"

"You don't change much. Still making huge generalizations about the English national character, I see. 'Subtlety is the English disease,' was what you said last time."

"What? When did I ever say that?"

"You said it here, forty years ago, when we were arguing about a headline in the school magazine."

"I said 'subtlety is the English disease'?"

"Yep."

"I remember that," said Phil. "It was when we did that story about Eric Clapton going all Enoch Powell during his gig at the Odeon."

"How can you remember something that happened so long ago?" said Doug. "This is my point exactly—you guys are obsessed with the past. You remember it way too well and you think about it way too much. It's time to move on. We have to focus on the future."

"I agree," said Steve.

"I run a historical publishing company," Phil pointed out. "I have to think about the past."

"And I'm very focused on the future, if you must know," said Benjamin. "I've taken a big decision."

Doug snorted. "Really? You're going to start buying green notebooks from now on, are you, instead of blue ones?"

The others laughed, but Benjamin put a stop to that by announcing: "Lois and I are moving to France." After taking a moment to enjoy their surprise, he continued: "She's left Christopher. She doesn't want to be anywhere near Birmingham. She doesn't want to stay in this country any more. But she doesn't want to be alone. So I said that I'd go with her. We're going to find somewhere in Provence—we've got the money from Dad's house, as well as mine. She wants somewhere big enough to take guests. Paying guests." He glanced in turn at each of their faces. They looked sombre now, rather than shocked. "You're all welcome, any time you want to come," he assured them. "Discount rates will apply."

Darkness was creeping rapidly over the playing fields. From the dining hall, a distant round of applause could be heard. Doug rose to his feet, brushing the grass from the trousers of his dinner suit. He touched Benjamin on the shoulder.

"Sounds like you're doing the right thing there, mate," he said. "But now you'll have to excuse me. The speech seems to be over, and I doubt if Ronnie will be hanging around for long. Time for our little chat, I think. I'll catch you guys later."

As he hurried off in the direction of the fading applause, Steve called after him: "Don't do anything stupid!"

*

Doug's instinct proved correct. Ronald Culpepper, in all his slimmed-down glory, was already waiting outside the dining hall, his summer overcoat slung over the arm of his dinner jacket, lamplight glinting off his bald pate as he spoke on his mobile phone in a murmurous undertone. "Summoning his driver," Doug thought, guessing—again correctly—that so distinguished a guest would not have driven to the school under his own steam, let alone taken an

Uber. There would be a Daimler or some such coming to pick up him up in a few minutes. Doug would have to move swiftly.

Culpepper spotted and recognized him when he was still a few yards away, and duly arranged his features into a look of resigned contempt. There was no handshake as the two old adversaries greeted one another.

"Ronald," said Doug.

"Douglas," he replied.

"Leaving us already? Not staying around to sign autographs?"

"If you're jealous," said Culpepper, "because it was me they asked to address this gathering, rather than yourself, perhaps think about which one of us best reflects the school's values. Alternatively, of course, you could coerce your friends into staging a pathetic act of rebellion. Which impressed nobody, by the way. People were embarrassed by it if anything."

"We left for medical reasons. We didn't think our blood pressure could survive listening to you for twenty minutes."

Culpepper gave a pitying smile. "Still fighting the same old, old battles, eh, Doug? Forty years on and nothing has changed."

"Forty years isn't such a long time in the scheme of things. And it's not that the battle is 'old'. It's the same battle. The battle never changes."

"For you, maybe. Some of us move on."

Culpepper looked at his watch. His driver was taking longer than he would have liked.

"And what have you moved on to, these days?" Doug asked. "Tell me a bit about the Imperium Foundation and what it stands for."

Culpepper's composure wavered momentarily when this name was mentioned; but he recovered it quickly enough. "It's a highly respected think tank," he said. "Information about it is freely available online."

"Who runs it?"

"If you're looking to identify some sinister cartel or conspiracy, you're out of luck," said Culpepper, beginning to walk up the drive towards the school gates. "We're just a group of ordinary British businessmen, trying to do what's best for our country in every way possible. Surely even you could find nothing to object to in that."

"True, I couldn't. If I believed a word of it, that is."

"Your trouble, Anderton," Culpepper said, suddenly stopping in his tracks and turning on him, "is that you've never taken the trouble to understand business, and never taken the trouble to understand patriotism. Neither has the rest of the liberal commentariat, for that matter. If you did, you'd realize that the two things can quite happily go hand-in-hand. I do read your columns, you know. It's always interesting to see what the opposition is thinking. But I'm afraid I've never been very impressed. Your analysis is shallow, and since the referendum everyone's been able to see what some of us have seen for some time: it's you and your fellow anti-establishment poseurs who are the real establishment, and now the people have turned on you and you don't like it."

Doug thought about this for a moment and then shook his head. "Sorry, Ronnie, but I don't buy it."

"Buy what?"

"You see, the thing is, whenever I hear someone like you talking about 'the people', my bullshit detector goes crazy. Seems to me you've spent your adult life trying to put as much distance between you and 'the people' as possible. Do you use public transport, or the NHS, or send your kids to state schools? Of course not. The last thing you want to do is come into contact with the proles. But Brexit has been your wet dream for years, for one reason or another, and now, as soon as 'the people' deliver what you've been praying for, suddenly you're all over them. You're happy to use them just like you use everybody else. It's how someone like you operates. But I hope you realize that this time you're playing with fire."

"Playing with fire? For God's sake, you do love to over-dramatize."

"I'm not over-dramatizing. We all know there's a lot of anger in this country at the moment and to get what you want you've got to keep that anger burning. But people show their anger in different ways. Some of them grumble into their tea and huff and puff over the *Daily Telegraph* and vote for Brexit and that's fine. But some of them go out into the street one morning with a flak jacket full of knives and stab their local MP to death, and that's not so good, is it? And the more the papers stoke up the anger by using words like 'treason' and 'mutiny' and 'enemy of the people', the more likely it gets that something like that will happen again."

They had reached the top of the school drive. Rather desperately, Culpepper looked left and right along the main road, but there was still no sign of his car.

"I fail to see," he said, "what this has got to do with—"

He was cut off mid-sentence as Doug seized his bow tie, and used it to pull him roughly forwards until they were face to face.

"Know who Gail Ransome is, Ronnie? Know who she lives with, these days? I bet you do. Know what it's like to have the woman you love crying in your arms because she's been getting death threats all day? Crying because her daughter's scared shitless?" He pulled the tie further forward, twisting it tight until a purplish hue started to appear in Culpepper's face. "Well? Do you? Do you?"

"Let go of me, you fucking animal."

The words were breathless and strangulated. They stared at each other, eyeball to eyeball, for ten seconds or more, while Culpepper's face grew more and more puce. Finally, Doug relaxed his grip, just as a large black BMW drew up alongside them by the kerb. Without another word, Culpepper yanked the back door open and stepped inside, rubbing at the circle of sore redness around his neck where his collar had dug into it. He glared at Doug as the car pulled away, but neither of them could think of a parting shot. The rank odour of hatred hung in the air even after the car had disappeared from view.

*

Meanwhile, Benjamin too was on a personal mission; but his was an altogether more reflective one. Retracing the path which was imprinted on his memory even though so many decades had passed since he had last followed it, he entered the main school building and climbed the stairs to the upper corridor where, on the left, a small arched doorway led to an altogether steeper and more occult flight of stone-flagged steps. This was the entrance to the Carlton corridor, an area of the school which in his day had been accessible to sixth-formers only, and even then only to a select few. The first room you passed, on the left, used to be the meeting room of the Carlton Club itself, where the privileged minority who had been elected to this elite organization (by a secret committee whose reasonings were never explained) could disport themselves in leather-covered armchairs while reading copies of *The Times*, the *Telegraph*, *Punch*, the *Economist* and any other publications which were considered suitable reading, back in those innocent times, for the future leaders of the country. Nowadays it appeared to serve as a more inclusive sixth-form common room. Benjamin stole past it, in any case, and made his way directly towards a pair of rooms which lay at the very end of the corridor, where the overhead lights had already been turned on by some earlier visitor. Here, on Friday afternoons, he and his friends used to put together a weekly edition of the school newspaper known as *The Bill Board*. Combative editorial arguments would ensue, with Doug constantly trying to push things in a more politically engaged direction, while Benjamin wrestled with the questions of cultural and literary value that would go on to preoccupy him—to little avail—all his life. The first room was dominated by the large, squat, rectangular table around which they all used to sit. Benjamin glanced around this room and then walked over to the window to see if the view would jog any memories. All he could see, at first, was his own middle-aged reflection, so he flicked a light switch—an act which seemed to plunge the whole corridor, unexpectedly, into near-darkness. Moving on into the second room, Benjamin could immediately make out the chair and desk where he used to sit writing his theatre and book reviews. From here you could look out over the rooftops of the school and, beyond them, the two tall oak trees which flanked the South Drive and tonight stood still and vigilant in the windless summer air.

Benjamin sank down into the chair and peered through the window. It was not completely dark outside yet; the muted light was gentle and soothing and within a few seconds he felt the familiar, calming pleasure of being alone steal over him. It had been good to see his friends, of course, but he would always prefer this solitude. Bored as he often was by his own thoughts, he none the less took a kind of comfort in their predictable routes and patterns. It was here, in this very chair, that he had sat alone after all his colleagues had left, one chilly Friday afternoon in January 1977: until, after a few minutes, he had realized that he was not alone at all, and that Cicely Boyd was waiting for him in the next room: sitting—or rather crouching—at the editorial table, with her back to the door and one bare foot tucked beneath her bottom, the famous golden hair swept into a long ponytail which reached almost to the small of her back. The first thing that had alerted him to her presence (her momentous, soon-to-be-life-changing presence) had been the smell of her cigarette smoke. The memory was so powerful still—the image so vivid—that he almost felt he could smell the smoke again. Almost felt that he could see it, floating across the room, drifting in spirals and arabesques towards the desk and in front of his eyes . . .

Benjamin gasped, and wheeled around. A figure was sitting behind him, in a chair with its back against the wall. A shadowy, amorphous figure, its only distinguishing feature a pinprick of orange light glowing at the end of a cigarette. A figure which now spoke one portentous word, quietly but with disconcerting emphasis as another plume of cigarette smoke was exhaled and blown across the room:

"*Ghosts . . .*"

Benjamin recognized the voice, and as the figure leaned forward in his chair, he recognized the speaker too. It was Mr. Serkis.

"Ghosts, eh, Benjamin?" he repeated. "Remembrance of things past."

He scraped his chair forward until the faint light from the window was falling on to his lined, reassuring face.

"What are you doing here?" Benjamin asked.

"The same as you, I expect. Revisiting the old days. Chasing ghosts."

"You gave me a shock."

"Sorry about that. Cigarette?"

"No thanks."

"You're not at school any more. They can't put you in detention."

"I don't smoke. Never did."

"Very wise," said Mr. Serkis. "Very boring, but very wise. Wisdom is often boring, have you noticed that? Better to be an entertaining idiot than a wise old bore. I know which I'm turning into." He stood up and began to pace slowly around the darkened room. "Well, this was where it all started, wasn't it? Ever think you'd find yourself sitting here again with your old English teacher?"

"Nothing that happens surprises me any more," said Benjamin. "And nobody can see into the future."

"True. But I knew you'd all go a long way. I was never in any doubt about that."

"Really? You think we've gone a long way? Doug, maybe . . . I'm not so sure about the rest of us."

"I read that book of yours, eventually," said Mr. Serkis. "Once you'd taken all the rubbish out, that was quite the little gem you wrote there. Small but perfectly formed. You should be proud of yourself."

"It's not much," said Benjamin, sadly. "It's not much of a mark to leave, in the end, is it? One little book that's been read by a few thousand people."

"There'll be other books," said Mr. Serkis.

"I don't think so."

"It may take ten years. Twenty. But you'll write something new, don't worry."

"And in the meantime? What am I supposed to do?"

"What do you want to do?"

"Lois and I are moving to France."

"Perfect."

"Yes, but what am I going to do when I'm there?"

Mr. Serkis took a last drag on his cigarette, then stubbed it out in a teacup on Benjamin's desk.

"Weren't you listening," he said, "the last time we met? In that gloomy pub."

"Of course I was listening."

"I told you then what you should do. It was the last thing I said to you. I said you should take up teaching."

Benjamin laughed. "I thought that was a joke."

"It was. A serious joke." Meeting only with silence, he continued: "You'd be a good teacher. I've always thought so."

"What would I teach in France?"

"Teach people how to write. How to write and edit. You know how to do both those things. And everybody wants to be a writer these days, haven't you noticed? 'Everyone's got a book inside them.' That's the received wisdom. The trouble is, hardly anyone knows how to get it out. That's where you could help."

Benjamin thought about this for a while. It had sounded a crazy idea at first, but maybe it made sense. "'The Benjamin Trotter Writing School,'" he said, thinking aloud.

"I should try to come up with a snappier name than that," said Mr. Serkis. "In fact, it wouldn't be difficult." He touched Benjamin between the shoulder blades: somewhere between a pat on the back and a rub. "Come on, let's go and see your friends. It may be the last time we're all together like this. We should get a selfie, at least."

44.

The Lenchford Inn stands on the western bank of the River Severn, just outside the village of Shrawley in Worcestershire. On a Tuesday evening in June 2018, Benjamin and Jennifer met there for a drink. Their last drink together, as it turned out. It was a fine summer evening, with the sun setting unhurriedly over the river and burnishing its surface with a deep, coppery sheen, as skylarks and sparrows skimmed back and forth across the water. After their drink, Jennifer and Benjamin strolled along the northbound path that followed the river's diffident curve. They did not walk hand in hand, or arm in arm—this was not their style—but their bodies were in close proximity, and it gave them both a feeling of comfort when they occasionally touched, at the hip or the thigh or the shoulder. These gentle collisions were subtle, welcome reminders of their physical intimacy.

Finally, with a sinking heart, Benjamin did what he could no longer put off: he told Jennifer that he was planning to move to France with his sister. She received the news with more equanimity than he had been expecting.

"Well, that's exciting," she said. "I mean, I shall miss you, of course, but . . . Well, congratulations. I'm sure you know what you're doing."

"I hope you'll come and see me."

"Of course I will." She glanced at him. "I'm sorry, were you expecting my reaction to be a bit more dramatic? You've dumped me once before, remember—forty years ago—and I didn't really mind then, either." She could not bear to see him looking so crestfallen, all the same. "Anyway, this isn't exactly a dumping, is it? We've only been seeing each other once a month or so. Less than that, recently."

"There's someone else, isn't there?" Benjamin said.

Jennifer slowed down, and drew in her breath, then looked him earnestly in the eye.

"How long have you known about that?" she asked.

Benjamin walked on. "Quite a while," he said. "His name's Robert, I think?"

"Why didn't you say anything, if you knew?"

"I suppose because . . . because I realized I didn't mind all that much."

This seemed to hurt Jennifer more than anything.

"Well, there you are," she said, catching up with him. "That's my point exactly. If you can't even summon the strength to be jealous about it . . ."

"I thought that what we had . . . I thought it suited both of us."

Jennifer sighed and shook her head.

"You're such an idiot. Really, you are. I was *always* waiting for it to become more. In the end I could see that it never would—that's why I started seeing Robert, I suppose—but for ages I was willing you to make some sort of move. Take some sort of *decision*. Part of me kept clinging on to that hope, as well. That's why I never said yes when Robert asked me to marry him."

"He's asked you to marry him?"

"Of course he has. About twenty times."

"And you said no, because of me?"

"Oh, Benjamin! Don't you understand anything? I would have done anything to get you closer to me. Started reading Flaubert. Rationed myself to films with subtitles. Learned to love the symphonies of Arthur Honecker."

"It's Honegger," said Benjamin, before he could stop himself.

"I told you that I loved you, for God's sake. Surely you remember that?"

"Yes, but I thought . . . I thought that was just one of those things people say."

"Yes, it *is*, Benjamin. That's exactly what it is. It's one of those things people say. Usually when they mean it."

Close to the edge of the water, at this point, they turned and faced each other, and for the first time Jennifer took both his hands in hers. Her eyes were filling up with tears.

"I'm over it, Ben, don't worry," she said. "Or rather, I'm beyond it now. In fact I saw Robert last week and he asked me to marry him again and I didn't say no this time. I told him I'd think about it. It was worth it just to see how happy he looked."

Benjamin tried to smile, but made a poor show of it. So he tried to hug Jennifer instead, and she put her arms around him in return, but she would not relax into the embrace. He could feel her resistance.

"I hurt you," he said. "I'm so sorry."

Wiping her eyes on his shoulder and pulling gently away, Jennifer said: "Don't worry about it, Tiger. Like I said, I'm beyond it now. For a while I kidded myself that we might be soulmates, but . . . Well, you found your soulmate years ago, didn't you, and nobody will ever quite replace her."

Benjamin nodded. "Cicely, you mean."

"No, not *her*," said Jennifer, scornfully. "I mean your sister, of course."

"You mean Lois?"

"Looking back," said Jennifer, "it's obvious really. Even at school, we could all see how much you meant to each other. It's lovely when you see that between a brother and sister. That loyalty. That support. That's why we had a joint nickname for you. Benjamin and Lois Trotter: the Rotters. Bent Rotter, and Lowest Rotter. That was it, wasn't it?"

"Yes, but I never thought—I mean, I never saw it like that before . . ."

"It makes perfect sense for you to go away together. Much more sense than you hanging around Middle England trying to make things work out with me."

Benjamin leaned towards her and kissed her on the mouth. She responded, but again the response was wary, reluctant.

"I'm so sorry," he repeated.

Jennifer turned back towards the pub, walked on and shifted the conversation briskly towards practicalities.

"Is now a good time to be moving to Europe?" she asked. "With Brexit and everything?"

"We've looked into that," said Benjamin. "As long as you move before 29 March next year, nothing changes."

"You've probably chosen a good time to get out."

"I don't know . . . I feel very torn about it. I'm going to miss this country. I'm going to miss my house. I'm going to miss living by the river. This river . . ." He looked wistfully at the friendly, meandering Severn, now turning a deep crimson in the dying sunlight as it wandered past the pub on its slow, endless journey down from his mill house forty miles away. "All my life I'd wanted to live by a river."

"They've got them in France, now," Jennifer said. "I was reading about it in the paper just the other day."

Benjamin was pleased to hear her making a joke again. She smiled at him and took his hand. They walked like this along the path for a few minutes. Then he put his arm around her shoulder, and she rested against him. That was even better. It was enough to give him the courage he needed.

"There was one other thing I wanted to say to you," he began.

She looked up at him questioningly. Her eyes glistened. "Yes?"

"I wanted to say thank you."

"Thank you? What for?"

"For . . . Well, for all the sex."

The questioning look mutated into an expression of disbelief. It seemed that, even now, Benjamin still had the capacity to astonish her.

"I *beg* your pardon?"

"It's just that I never thought . . . At my age, I'd sort of given up hope. I mean, I'm not exactly Colin Firth, and I'm not very good in bed."

Jennifer laughed now, silently but for quite a long time. When she turned to Benjamin again, her lips were still twitching with amusement as she said: "I suppose I could punish you for that, just by agreeing with you. But the fact is—you did have your moments."

"Really?" He pulled her closely towards him, kissed her and whispered in her ear: "Robert's a lucky man. You have the loveliest body. Thank you for sharing it with me."

And there they stood, cheek to cheek, pressed tightly against each other, the embrace lasting for so long that the fisherman sitting a few yards away might easily have mistaken them for a married couple rediscovering their youthful passion, rather than what they really were: a pair of rueful lovers saying goodbye for the last time.

45.

"Well," said Lois, "I got you a river."

Indeed she had. The house stood on the banks of the Sorgue: and even if this particular stretch of water didn't carry, for Benjamin, quite the symbolic weight that he invested in his beloved Severn, or hold the same repository of memories for him, it certainly had charms of its own. Theirs was a mill house, once again. For as long as anyone could remember it had been known simply as "Le Vieux Moulin," and it nestled in a curve of the river not far from its source in Fontaine-de-Vaucluse, clasped so snugly in the water's embrace that it might almost have been planted rather than built there, to grow alongside the willow and magnolia trees that surrounded it. Benjamin and Lois had taken possession in the middle of August, and, while the house was in good condition, the last three weeks had been busy and stressful, with workmen coming and going every day, receiving their often approximate instructions from the new owners in broken French. Things had been easier after the first week, when Grete and Lukas had arrived. Grete spoke good French, and had agreed to take on the role of housekeeper. Lukas intended to look for work in nearby Avignon, and in the meantime was on hand to help Benjamin with the many practicalities that he found so daunting. Together with their little girl, Justina, they would be living in a small, two-bedroomed cottage which lay within the grounds of the house, just a few yards from the main building.

On this hot, breathless afternoon, Lois found her brother leaning up against the rusty iron fence that formed a boundary between their terrace and the idling, grey-green river. He had a beer glass in his hand, and gave every impression of idling himself.

"Were you having a rest?" she asked, with a slight undertone of impatience. It was Friday. Le Vieux Moulin was due to open for guests on Sunday evening.

"Just a quick beer, that's all."

"There's still a lot to do."

"I know. Just give me twenty minutes."

"There's still no electricity in any of the rooms on the top floor."

"It's probably a fuse. I'll sort it."

"Well, I'm going to finish putting sheets on the beds."

"OK. Don't worry. I'm just going to be twenty minutes."

Once his sister had disappeared inside, Benjamin sat down at the old wrought-iron table: the table he had brought all the way from Shropshire, the table which had borne witness to so many conversations with family and friends over the years, and so many solitary hours of writing and contemplation. He could not have left it behind in England. He took a sip from his glass and gave a quiet sigh of satisfaction. Tilting his face, he felt the full heat of the mid-afternoon sun. Wonderful. You didn't get that in the Midlands. He closed his eyes and listened to the river as it continued to drift placidly by. He had just succeeded in losing himself in its gentle music when another, less soothing sound reached his ears, and grew louder and louder: the sound of a car approaching down the long, cool, poplar-lined lane. Soon the car had entered the house's main courtyard, pulled to a halt and a familiar voice could be heard calling from the hallway: "Anyone home?"

It was Sophie. She quickly found her uncle out on the terrace and, after they had kissed, she walked across to the fence and leaned against it, looking over the river, and said: "Well, isn't this lovely?"

"I'll give you the tour in a minute. Have a drink first. You look hot. Good flight? Long drive from Marseille?"

"Not too bad. About an hour and a half. Motorway mainly."

"I'll get you a beer."

Benjamin and Sophie sat in the sunshine for a few minutes,

4413

savouring their drinks and exchanging news. He forgot that his sister was upstairs working.

"So you're all ready for the first students?" she asked.

"Not quite. There's still a few things to be done. Anyway, there's only one."

"Only one?"

"Bookings have been a bit slow, to be honest. I suppose that was bound to happen at the beginning. I'm sure it will pick up. Of course, it would have helped if Lionel Hampshire could have been here for the opening. Thanks for contacting him, by the way."

"He's not coming? When he emailed me he sounded quite keen."

"Oh, he was keen all right. I'll show you the letter he sent us."

Benjamin fetched a sheet of paper from the kitchen and handed it to Sophie. She took off her sunglasses and started to read.

Dear Mr. Trotter,

Mr. Hampshire is in receipt of your kind invitation to be the guest of honour at the opening ceremony of your new writing school, forwarded to him by your niece.

He would like to convey his sincere thanks for the invitation, and in principle would be delighted to attend. As a keen European, who deplores the political direction his country has taken in the last two years, he applauds the gesture of Anglo-French cooperation represented by your school.

Mr. Hampshire would be willing to visit Le Vieux Moulin for three or four days on and around the evening of Sunday 16 September, as specified. He would be prepared to give one reading from his works (duration 45 minutes) and his terms are as follows.

· *First-class travel by train from London to Avignon for himself and his assistant (myself).*
· *Transfer by car from Avignon to Le Vieux Moulin.*
· *Double room with river view, and the same for his assistant.*

- *All meals to be provided, including unlimited visits to local restaurants.*
- *Copies of all of Mr. Hampshire's books to be on sale to students, in French- and English-language editions. He will be happy to sign them.*
- *Excursions to Aix-en-Provence and Manosque to be arranged, at Le Vieux Moulin's expense.*
- *Honorarium of 10,000 euros, to be paid by bank transfer before arrival.*

Assuming these terms are agreeable, Mr. Hampshire looks forward to his visit, and to your prompt reply.

Sincerely
Ella Buchanan

Sophie let out a low whistle and handed the letter back.

"What, and you're telling me the terms weren't agreeable?"

"Sadly not. Lois didn't seem to think it would be a good idea to blow our entire annual budget on one celebrity guest."

"I can see her point. Talking of Mum, I'd better go and say hello. Is she around?"

"She's upstairs. Tell her I'll be up in a few minutes to do the electricity."

"OK."

Sophie was just about to leave on this errand when Grete emerged from the kitchen carrying a mop and a bucket. They greeted each other warmly, like old friends.

"Ah, you're looking well!" Grete said, holding her at arm's length. "Better than I've ever seen you."

"I agree," said Benjamin. And when they both turned to look at him, he added: "You've put on a bit of weight. It suits you."

Sophie chose to ignore this remark, and Grete asked her: "You're not tired after your journey?"

"Not really. And how are you? And Lukas and Justina?"

"Very well, all very well. I think we're going to like it here very much. They've just gone into the town, into Avignon, to buy some things. Paint and so on. He's about to start painting the barn."

With all this activity around him—Grete washing down the terrace, Lukas and Justina on their shopping expedition, Lois fitting the sheets, Sophie unpacking—it was a wonder that Benjamin could get any relaxing done at all. But after pouring himself another beer, and allowing the sun to beat down for a few more minutes on his closed eyelids, he began to sink into an agreeable state of calm. He was on the point of falling asleep, in fact, when he heard the noise of another car approaching down the lane.

Two minutes later, Charlie and Aneeqa appeared on the terrace.

"Ah!" said Benjamin, getting up. "You found it, then."

"Hello, mate." Charlie gave him a hug. "Yeah, no problem. Long drive from Calais, though. Bloody long. What a place, though, eh? This is absolutely gorgeous."

Aneeqa was lingering in the background. Benjamin shook her hand, feeling a sudden shyness. He had only met her once before, more than two years earlier. She looked much more mature now, and had grown very beautiful.

"Well, welcome to Le Vieux Moulin," he said to both of them. "We're happy to have you here. Stay as long as you like."

"She has to be in Segovia on Tuesday," said Charlie. "It'll take us a couple of days from here, I reckon. But we'll stay till Monday, if that's all right."

"Perfectly all right. Come on—let me get you both something to drink."

He poured Charlie some beer and Aneeqa a *citron pressé*. It was a great stroke of good fortune, he thought, that he was able to offer them somewhere to break their long journey: she was on her way to begin a year's course of study in Spain, and Charlie had offered to drive her all the way there—for the sheer pleasure, it seemed, of being in her company for five or six days. They looked tired from their long day's travelling, all the same, so before long Benjamin directed them upstairs to their rooms.

"My sister's up there somewhere," he said. "I'm not sure where she's decided to put you—you'll just have to ask."

He contemplated going down to the cellar to check the fuse box at this point: but really, he hadn't had his twenty minutes' break yet. With those two interruptions, he'd barely been able to rest for five minutes. Oddly, however, his beer glass did seem to be empty, so he poured himself another drink and sat down again at the wrought-iron table. The sun was losing some of its intensity now, and the shade from the biggest willow on the riverbank was starting to steal over the terrace. The temperature was perfect, at this hour of day. If he couldn't get inspiration for a new book in these conditions, it was never going to happen. Thankfully Grete had finished cleaning the terrace and there was nothing to impede his train of thought, or disturb his tranquillity. Not, at least, until he heard another car approaching from the distance down the poplar-lined lane.

A few minutes later, two more people appeared on the terrace. It was Claire Newman, one of his oldest friends from King William's, and her husband Stefano. They had driven all the way from Lucca, via La Spezia, Genoa, Nice, Cannes and Aix.

Claire and Benjamin had not seen each other for about fifteen years. It had been an impulsive decision to invite her here for the opening party. "After all, in European terms, we'll more or less be next-door neighbours from now on," he had emailed, facetiously, not expecting her to be swayed by this argument. But here she was, after all. And just as he remembered her: grey hair cut into a stylish bob which made her look younger—much younger—than he or Lois did, perfect cheekbones, crow's feet and laughter-lines drawing attention to the open and generous shape of her eyes. After kissing her tenderly on the cheek, and releasing himself from Stefano's firm, protracted handshake, Benjamin went to the kitchen to fetch a bottle of Pro-secco in their honour. He called for Lois to come down from the first floor but she didn't seem to hear him. He brought four glasses outside anyway, but the fourth one remained empty, and then, after Claire, Stefano and Benjamin had all clinked glasses and wished each other "*Santé!*," Claire looked at him with that searching gaze that he remembered so well (and which always made him slightly fearful), and said, "Well, Ben, you're looking wonderful, but what we all want to know is—what the *hell* is going on in Britain at the moment? All the Italians think the Brits have gone completely crazy."

*

The next morning, Sophie found Aneeqa sitting on the riverbank opposite the house. She had a sketchpad open on her knees and was just finishing a fine, delicate drawing of the old mill wheel and the attractive jumble of outbuildings that surrounded it, their pale, dry-stone walls patterned with ivy and bougainvillea.

"That's lovely," said Sophie. "They said you were good at this sort of thing."

"I have my moments," said Aneeqa, tilting her head to look at the drawing and privately concluding that it wasn't bad.

"I may have a job for you," said Sophie. "Do you think you could paint a sign for us?"

"What sort of a sign?"

"We need something to replace *that*." Sophie pointed at the archway which led to the house's front drive, and to which someone, many years ago, had nailed a now decaying rectangle of wood with the words "Le Vieux Moulin" painted on it in faded capitals.

"Really? I think it has a certain . . . period charm."

"It's not the sign itself. It's the name."

"What's wrong with the name?"

"'The Old Mill'? What could be more boring than calling an old mill 'The Old Mill'?"

"True. Do you have a better idea?"

"Yes, I think so."

Aneeqa pursed her lips. "Do we have the right sort of paints? The right brushes?"

"Probably not. But I was going to drive back to Marseille today anyway. I'm sure I could find something, if you tell me what you need."

"Or I could come with you. I've been dying to go there. Do you mind?"

"Not at all."

Sophie was, in truth, glad to have the company. Compelled though she felt to revisit the city, to allow herself another, yearning glimpse of the Frioul islands, she was also somewhat dreading it. And so it was a relief, after leaving behind the coolness and quietude of the mill house, enduring a hot and gruelling ninety-minute drive down the busy A55, cooling off with drinks in the Cours Julien, readjusting herself to the urban energies of the city, the noise and the music everywhere, the walls encrusted with graffiti, the kids on skateboards, the rappers and street entertainers, the tangy aroma of North African spices in the air, after reminding herself of all that, and after finding a shop that sold artists' materials fifteen minutes before it closed for the weekend, giving Aneeqa just enough time to scoop up the things she needed, after they had done all of these things, and walked down to the Vieux Port and rushed aboard a *navette* that was on the point of leaving, it was a relief for Sophie to have Aneeqa by her side, so that she could talk to her, and point out landmarks, and tell her something of her personal history with this city, and not be left alone with melancholy thoughts of that week in the summer of 2012 and the missed opportunity that sometimes, even now, she felt it represented.

"I feel like I'm walking on the moon," Aneeqa said, as they trudged across the barren, stony landscape of Ratonneau on their way to the Calanque de Morgiret, where Sophie and Adam had once had their moonlit swim. It was five o'clock in the afternoon, and the heat was almost unbearable. The sun assaulted their eyes from two directions: bearing down on them from a sky of flawless pale blue, and dancing in patterns of fragmented, dazzling light on the surface of the sea.

"You'll feel great once we get in the water," said Sophie, who had insisted that they both bring bathing costumes.

The beach was crowded with swimmers that afternoon. Wading into the water, Sophie struck out, as she had done once before, towards the mouth of the cove, heading for its furthest, deepest point, and then swam strongly backwards and forwards across the bay, from one rocky side to the other. Aneeqa—much as Adam had done—stayed in the shallows, crouching down, simply enjoying the coolness of the water and not really attempting to swim. Afterwards, they walked up the winding path which led to a ridge high above the beach, and Sophie recognized the same wide, flat rock where she and Adam had sat down to talk. Here they both rested: Sophie sitting upright, clutching her knees, Aneeqa stretched out full-length on the rock, shielding her eyes from the sun's fierceness.

"I'm not used to this kind of light," she said. "I could get used to it, all right. Hopefully it'll be the same down in Spain. But if you've grown up in Birmingham, and spent the last two years in Glasgow, it's a bit overwhelming. Imagine living with this light all the time. You'd actually be able to *see* the world, instead of just making it out through a grey fog occasionally."

"I know what you mean," said Sophie. "And yet I'm moving up to the North-east next week. Where the light is as grey as it gets, and not many people go swimming in the North Sea to cool off."

"You don't sound wildly enthusiastic," said Aneeqa, lifting her hand from her eyes temporarily to gauge Sophie's expression. "What's taking you up there?"

"New job," said Sophie. "My best friend's husband's started a charity. He's setting up a new sort of college and he's asked me to be director of studies. Running the timetable, scheduling the courses, coordinating everything. It's a great opportunity, actually. I'm quite fired up about it."

"Well, that's good," said Aneeqa. "And at least you know some people there already. So you won't be alone."

Sophie smiled. "I won't be alone anyway. My husband's coming with me. In fact he's packing up our old flat this weekend. That's why he couldn't come here."

"Very self-sacrificing of him," Aneeqa said. "Must be a nice guy."

"Yes," said Sophie. "He is a nice guy." It was a statement of fact, and not a complicated one, and she knew that her task for the next few years—probably longer, much longer, although she was too scared to use the phrase "the rest of her life"—was to reach an accommodation with this fact, to accept it, to allow it to be enough for her. In the last few months, since her unannounced arrival at the flat that afternoon and the reconciliation that followed, it had proved an easy enough task. Whether it would continue to be so, who could say? But for the moment, she felt that this was where she had to place her trust.

"Does he have a job up there as well?" Aneeqa asked.

"Not yet," said Sophie. "He might start giving driving lessons again. That's his thing—driving."

"Somebody's got to do it."

"And in the meantime, he's going to have plenty to occupy him."

She looked at Aneeqa, and felt a sudden urge to say more, to confide in her. She felt very close, today, to this friendly, reserved, obviously very talented woman who had turned out to be her unexpected companion on this indulgent sentimental journey. How easy it would be, and how liberating, to unburden herself to someone like this, a sympathetic stranger she would probably never see again once the weekend was over.

But Sophie managed to resist the urge, and stuck fast to her original resolve: to share the secret with her mother, for now, and nobody else.

*

Late on Sunday afternoon, there was a momentous arrival at Le Vieux Moulin: Benjamin's first writing student.

His name was Alexandre, and he was a small, earnest young man who had come by train all the way from Strasbourg. He smiled nervously when Lois greeted him and looked around in bewilderment at the signs of frantic last-minute activity: Lukas carrying three planks of wood through the hallway, Sophie and Claire on their knees in the kitchen, painting a skirting board. Lois ushered him away from these tell-tale signs of unpreparedness and offered words of welcome, showing him up to his room and telling him that he was invited to join them all for dinner at nine o'clock that evening.

And so there were ten of them, in all, seated around the long oak table out on the second and larger of the terraces overlooking the river, as the light began to fade. Above the table, grapevines interwoven with lavender and flame-coloured campsis were coiled densely around an ancient pergola. Lois and Grete and Benjamin had prepared huge bowls of *salade Niçoise*, to be followed by steaming pots of *ratatouille* made with fresh Provençal courgettes and aubergines. There seemed also to be an endless supply of red wine. Then there were *calissons* and *tartes Tropéziennes*, and then dessert wines and cheese, and coffee for those who wanted it, and brandy and cognac and even pastis for those who wanted to carry on drinking, all furnished in such abundance that it was long after midnight before the end of the meal was even distantly in sight.

As conversation became more sporadic and subdued, and the candles ranged on the table and on the walls all around them started to burn low, Claire turned to Alexandre and said:

"So, what are you hoping to learn from your week here, I wonder?"

Alexandre, who was not used to being among strangers and had been quieter than anyone all evening, now cleared his throat and said: "I've brought with me a collection of short stories—unpublished, of course—and I'm hoping that Mr. Trotter will be able to read them and tell me how I can make them better. It will be an honour for me to hear the opinion of the author of *A Rose Without a Thorn*. Or *Rose sans épine*, as it's called in France."

"It's a beautiful book, isn't it?" Lois said.

"What for me is most moving about your brother's book," said Alexandre, picking his way through the words carefully, "is that it conveys the desolation of a life which is built entirely upon failure. For me, it's the story of a man who has failed in every area of his life, and so he entrusts all his dreams of happiness to this one woman, this one love affair, and this turns out to be the greatest failure of all. It's a life which lacks any kind of achievement, any kind of self-knowledge and so, in the end, any kind of hope."

A short but fathomless silence descended upon the table at the end of this speech. One or two of the other guests laughed nervously.

"I'm sorry," said Alexandre, "did I say something funny? Is my English not so good?"

"Your English is perfect," said Claire. "It's just that you gave the most brutal assessment of Benjamin's life that he's probably ever heard."

"Oh, but I didn't mean—"

The silence returned, but was broken this time by Benjamin himself:

"Sitting here in this amazing place," he said, "with you guys for company, I find it hard to see my life as a failure. In fact—" he rose unsteadily to his feet "—I think this calls for a speech."

Lois and Claire put their heads in their hands. Benjamin had been drinking for several hours now, and didn't look as though he was capable of talking coherently about anything. However, there didn't seem to be any way of stopping him.

"Six English people," he began, "two Lithuanians, a Frenchman and an Italian all had dinner together one beautiful evening in September. Sadly, this is not the set-up for a joke. I wish it was. Nor is it the opening sentence of my new novel. I wish it was that too. In fact I wish I *had* a new novel for it to be the opening sentence of. But what it is—if anything—what it represents, what it *symbolizes*, I should say . . ."

"We get the message," said Claire, when it seemed likely that he was going to stutter to a halt altogether. "It's a wonderful example of European harmonization."

"*Exactly*," said Benjamin, striking the table for emphasis. "That's exactly what I'm trying to say. What could be more inspiring, what could be a more powerful . . . metaphor . . . for the spirit of cooperation—international cooperation—which prevails, which *has* prevailed—which *ought* to prevail, if . . . if we, as a nation, hadn't made this . . . regrettable, but understandable—in *some* ways understandable . . ."

"Sit down and shut up," said Lois.

"I will not," said Benjamin. "I have something to say."

"Then do you mind saying it a bit more concisely?"

"Concision," said Benjamin, "is the English disease."

"Well, you seem to have been cured, and made a full recovery," said Claire.

"Fine," said Benjamin. "I can say what I want to say in two words." He paused and looked around the table at the circle of expectant faces. Then, in a tone of belligerent triumph, he said, "*Fuck Brexit!*," and sat down to a round of applause.

"Really?" said Stefano, after a moment's reflection. "There are six English people here, and not a single person who voted to leave? Not a very representative selection."

"I almost did," said Charlie, sitting next to him. "I was in such a bad place round about then that I almost did it just to give Cameron a kick in the nuts. Benjamin saw me that week. He knows how low I was. Broke and sleeping in my car. Him and his fucking austerity. But I decided it would be a stupid way of making my point. Not nearly as satisfying as punching him in the face, if I ever got the chance." Stefano was starting to give Charlie a wary look, and to lean away from him slightly in his seat. "Oh, no—don't get me wrong," he said. "I'm not a violent person. I mean, I used to be, but prison knocked that out of me."

Looking less than reassured, Stefano merely said, "Of course. I understand."

"Cameron's only part of the story anyway," Charlie continued. "The way I see it, everything changed in Britain in May 1979. Forty years on, we're still dealing with that. You see—me and Benjamin, we're children of the seventies. We may have been only kids then, but that was the world we grew up in. Welfare state, NHS. Everything that was put in place after the war. Well, all that's been unravelling since '79. It's still being unravelled. That's the real story. I don't know if Brexit's a symptom of that, or just a distraction. But the process is pretty much complete now. It'll all be gone soon."

From the other side of the table, Aneeqa said: "I don't want to go back to the 1970s, thank you very much."

"Fair enough," Charlie agreed. "It would have been a shit decade for someone like you. But try to think of what was good about it. Something's been lost, since then. Something huge."

Claire intervened, at this point, to challenge Charlie's interpretation of history, and to point out that the decade he was seeking to idealize had also seen record inflation, economic instability and industrial unrest. The conversation among the four middle-aged English diners became heated, and then broadened out to include Brexit, Donald Trump, Syria, North Korea, Vladimir Putin, Facebook, immigration, Emmanuel Macron, the 5-Star movement and the contentious result of the Eurovision song contest in 1968. Everybody around the table had something to say (at least that was Benjamin's memory afterwards) but also, one by one, people started to drift away and go to bed. Those who lingered drank more wine and lost track of how late it was until, finally, the only two left were Benjamin and Charlie. And Charlie was almost falling asleep.

"Listen," said Benjamin. "I want to play you a song."

"Uh?" said Charlie, opening his eyes slowly.

"What you were saying before—about the world we lived in when we were kids, and how it's all gone. I've got a song to play you. It sums it all up."

"All right. Bring it on."

"I'll just go and get my iPod."

Finding the iPod in his bedroom was easy; finding the portable speaker more difficult; finding batteries for the portable speaker almost impossible. When he returned to the dining table, about ten minutes later, Charlie was gone.

"Oh," said Benjamin, aloud. He sat down at the table, took a sip of wine, and looked around him. Where was everybody?

All was quiet. The only thing to break the silence was the rippling of the river as it slid past. Benjamin sat and listened to it for a few minutes. It sounded strange, not what he was used to. Alien. This was a French river. He felt a keen pang of homesickness, both for the country he had grown up in and the country he had just left behind, even though these two countries were by no means the same.

He turned the volume on the speaker up loud, and pressed Play, and soon the haunted, resonant voice of Shirley Collins was sounding out through the night, singing the ballad that Benjamin had not dared to listen to since the day of his mother's funeral.

Adieu to old England, adieu
And adieu to some hundreds of pounds
If the world had been ended when I had been young
My sorrows I'd never have known

He took a final sip of wine, but knew that he'd drunk far too much tonight, and that it was time to sober up.

Once I could drink of the best
The very best brandy and rum
Now I am glad of a cup of spring water
That flows from town to town

Hearing this verse, he thought of his mother, sitting upright in bed, staring out at the grey sky through her bedroom window and feebly trying to sing along. Once again he asked himself: had she recognized this music from somewhere? Some buried childhood memory?

Once I could eat of good bread
Good bread that was made of good wheat
Now I am glad with a hard mouldy crust
And glad that I've got it to eat

And then he thought of his father, the awful manner of his death, that strange visit they had paid to the old Longbridge factory in the depth of winter, his father's bitterness, the sourness that corroded him in those last months, and then the day that Benjamin and Lois had scattered their parents' ashes, at the top of the hill. Beacon Hill at the beginning of autumn . . .

Once I could lie on a good bed
A good bed that was made of soft down
Now I am glad of a clot of clean straw
To keep meself from the cold ground

Beacon Hill. The landscape of his own childhood. Tobogganing in the winter. Walks in the woods on Sunday afternoon, holding tightly on to his mother's gloved hand. Then running ahead along the path through the woods to hide and wait for his parents, in that strange, hollowed-out rhododendron bush by the side of the path that was like a hobbit's house. With Lois crouched beside him. Always Lois, never Paul.

> *Once I could ride in me carriage*
> *With servants to drive me along*
> *Now I'm in prison, in prison so strong*
> *Not knowing which way I can turn*

Would he and Lois be enough for each other, here? Would they live here together for the next ten years, twenty? Benjamin had always assumed that he would grow old and die at home; that he was bound to end his life by returning to the country of his childhood. But he was starting to understand, at last, that this place had only ever existed in his imagination.

> *Adieu to old England, adieu*
> *And adieu to some hundreds of pounds*
> *If the world had been ended when I had been young*
> *My sorrows I'd never have known*

As the final verse came to an end, and the music's last echoes drifted away across the slow-moving water, Benjamin heard the sound of a shutter opening. He raised his eyes and saw Grete looking down at him from the first-floor window of her cottage.

"It's a very nice song," she called. "She sings the way I feel."

Benjamin said nothing; just nodded a befuddled mixture of greeting and agreement.

"Now can we have no more music, please? We're trying to get to sleep."

The shutter closed again. Benjamin turned off the iPod, and the portable speaker, and closed his eyes.

Next, he became aware that Lois was standing over him. It was not quite as dark as before. He didn't know how long he had been asleep.

"I know," he said. "I'm going to bed."

"I came to get you up," said Lois. "You've got to say goodbye to Sophie. She's leaving for the airport soon."

He followed her into the kitchen, where she had already brewed up a pot of coffee.

"Have you been up all night?" she asked.

"I suppose so."

"That's a bit silly. You've got to have a tutorial with Alexandre in a few hours."

"I've been thinking about that," said Benjamin, draining a much-needed espresso cup. "I can't read his stories."

"Why not?" said Lois.

"They're in French."

She stared at him. Just then Sophie appeared in the doorway, with her suitcase.

"We'll talk about this later," said Lois, ominously.

*

Quietly Benjamin opened the front door of the house, and the three of them stepped out into the courtyard. The first glimmerings of dawn could be felt now. Tiny fragments of birdsong were beginning to mingle with the murmur of the river. But the loudest noises were their footsteps on the driveway, and the rumble of Sophie's suitcase as Benjamin pulled it along on its wheels. Her car was parked in the little enclosure further down the drive, about twenty yards beyond the arch.

Just before they passed through the archway itself, Sophie stopped them both and said:

"You haven't seen the new sign yet, have you?"

"What new sign?"

"Aneeqa and I made you a little present. And we renamed the house for you. I hope you don't mind."

"Renamed it?" said Lois. "What for? What's wrong with The Old Mill?"

"Nothing," said Sophie. "I just thought of something better."

Sceptical, they walked through the arch and turned around to find out what she meant. There was just enough light to read the lettering, and when she saw it, Lois gasped out loud. Benjamin merely smiled—a long, proud, private smile—and clasped his niece's hand.

"Do you like it?" she asked.

"It's perfect," said Lois.

"Perfect," Benjamin agreed.

Aneeqa had excelled herself. The calligraphy was bold, striking and deceptively simple at first glance. But when you looked more closely, there was extraordinary detail in her handiwork—changes of texture, a hint of three-dimensional perspective and subtle variations of colour in each of the individual letters. Letters which, collectively, spelt out three words:

THE ROTTERS' CLUB

Benjamin and Lois looked at it in silence. Silently, too, Lois reached out her arm and slipped it around her brother's waist. He leaned into her. The birdsong was getting louder. More shafts of sunlight began to peep over the trees.

"Come on," said Sophie, "I don't want to be late."

They walked on towards the car, loaded her suitcase into the boot and kissed her goodbye.

"Take care, precious," said Lois. "And give our love to Ian. Be careful up in the frozen North, both of you. There be dragons up there."

"Don't be silly," said Sophie, hugging her closely.

"Thanks for everything," said Benjamin. "Come and see us again soon. Please. And don't lose any of that weight. It suits you."

As Sophie's car was driving off down the long, poplar-lined lane, Lois turned to her brother and said:

"Are you really that stupid, or is just an act you put on?"

"What do you mean?"

"Sophie isn't putting on weight. She's pregnant."

He gaped at her. "What?"

"Almost three months."

He turned back and stared after the car, still lost for words.

"In fact," said Lois. "Her due date is the end of March. The twenty-ninth."

His heart thumping, his spirits soaring as the news gradually permeated his weary, addled consciousness, Benjamin raised his arm at the receding car and began to wave in quick frantic movements. But his niece was not looking back. Her eyes were fixed on the road ahead as she accelerated down the lane, one hand on the steering wheel, the other resting on her swollen belly: home, for now, to Sophie and Ian's tentative gesture of faith in their equivocal, unknowable future: their beautiful Brexit baby.

Author's Note

This story features a number of characters from my novel *The Rotters' Club*, a book which already has a sequel, called *The Closed Circle*. For many years I had no intention of continuing the series, but in 2016 two things conspired to change my mind.

Firstly, I went to see Richard Cameron's fine dramatization of *The Rotters' Club* at the Birmingham Rep. Richard's take on the book, and the brilliant performances of the young cast, made me see that the original novel had a central feature I'd never noticed before, and had certainly never pursued in *The Closed Circle*: namely, the love between Benjamin Trotter and his sister Lois.

Secondly, the novelist Alice Adams spoke so warmly in an online interview about *The Closed Circle* that I felt compelled to contact her. I'd never considered the novel a particular success so it was intriguing to me that she should count it among her favourites. We corresponded, then met, and her enthusiasm persuaded me that I should revisit these abandoned characters. At the same time I was discussing with my editor at Penguin, Mary Mount, the possibility of a novel based around the Brexit referendum, and I soon began to feel that I could only approach the subject by resurrecting—and adding to—*The Rotters' Club* cast.

All of these people, therefore, played a crucial role in bringing this novel into being. I'd also like to thank Fiona Fylan (for helpful background information on speed-awareness instructors); Ralph Pite, Paul Daintry and Caroline Hennigan (for being encouraging readers of the book when it was only half-written); Charlotte Stretch (for being one of the first and best readers of the finished version, not to mention years of supportive friendship); Andrew Hodgkiss, Robert Coe and Julie Coe (for offering me secluded bolt-holes in which to write); and, for various invaluable forms of help and inspiration, Steve Swannell, Aneeqa Munir, Vanessa Guignery, Michele O'Leary, Michael Singer, Peter Cartwright, Catherine Poust, Andrew Brewerton, Anne Philippe Besson, Julia Jordan, Philippe Auclair and Judith Hawley.

Late in 2016, at an auction for the charity Freedom from Torture, Emily Shamma bid to have a character in the book named after her, and Samuel Morton of Freedom from Torture subsequently sent me a message about the origins of Emily's name. I'm grateful to Emily for making the bid—and for having such an interesting name: I hope she likes what I've done with it.

The characters of Lionel Hampshire and Hermione Dawes first appeared in my story "Canadians Can't Flirt," included in the anthology *Tales from a Master's Notebook* (Jonathan Cape, 2018). My thanks to Philip Horne for commissioning the story, and to the ghost of Henry James for inspiring it.

Many of the details in Chapters 9 and 10 are taken from *Mad Mobs and Englishmen?: Myths and Realities of the 2011 Riots*, by Cliff Stott and Steve Reicher (Robinson, 2011).

Most of the "Merrie England" section was written in Marseille, during a residency funded by the literary organization La Marelle. I'd like to thank Pascal Jourdana for inviting me to that city, and for the friendship that followed; and also Fanny Pomarède for providing me with such a warm and welcoming space in which to write those early chapters.

Last, but not least, my thanks go to Tony Peake: my agent for almost thirty years, my dear friend for just as long, a superb reader and critic, a generous man in every way, without whose unfailing loyalty and support this book—and most of my others—would not even exist.

THE RAIN BEFORE IT FALLS

As a young girl, Rosamond is sent to Shropshire to escape the Blitz. Here, in the countryside, she forms a close bond with her older cousin, Beatrix, a young woman haunted by anger and resentment. Sixty years later, just before her death, Rosamond records her memories on cassettes, addressing them to a distant cousin—a near stranger named Imogen. As Gill, her beloved niece, listens to these tapes, a heart-stopping family saga is revealed. In this masterful portrait of three generations of women, Jonathan Coe exposes the profound reserves of hope and loss within the lives of ordinary women.

Fiction

THE ROTTERS' CLUB

Birmingham, England, circa 1973: industrial strikes, bad pop music, corrosive class warfare, adolescent angst, IRA bombings. Four friends: a class clown who stoops very low for a laugh; a confused artist enthralled by guitar rock; an earnest radical with socialist leanings; and a quiet dreamer obsessed with poetry, God, and the prettiest girl in school. As the world appears to self-destruct around them, they hold together to navigate the choppy waters of a decidedly ambiguous decade.

Fiction

ALSO AVAILABLE
The Closed Circle

ALSO AVAILABLE FROM
VINTAGE BOOKS
Number 11
The Winshaw Legacy